FIND EDSELL!

ELSA BONSTEIN

abbott press
A DIVISION OF WRITERS DIGEST

FIND EDSELL! is a work of fiction. Names, characters, places, and incidents are
a product of the author's imagination or are used fictitiously. Any resemblance
to actual persons, living or dead, events, or locales is entirely coincidental.

Abbott Press books may be ordered through booksellers or by contacting:

Abbott Press
1663 Liberty Drive
Bloomington, IN 47403
www.abbottpress.com
Phone: 1-866-697-5310

Because of the dynamic nature of the Internet, any web addresses or links contained in
this book may have changed since publication and may no longer be valid. The views
expressed in this work are solely those of the author and do not necessarily reflect the
views of the publisher, and the publisher hereby disclaims any responsibility for them.

ISBN: 978-1-4582-1326-6 (sc)
ISBN: 978-1-4582-1325-9 (hc)
ISBN: 978-1-4582-1324-2 (e)

Library of Congress Control Number: 2013922536

Printed in the United States of America.

Abbott Press rev. date: 03/04/2014

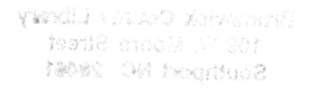

For the persevering and enduring people of the Jersey Shore and the brave men and women of the New Jersey Forest Fire Service who guard our Pinelands.

PROLOGUE

Betits uetween the rumble of Philadelphia and the roar of New York lies a strange, still land—a land where quiet lakes mirror stunted pine trees, where gnarled oaks and tall cedars sink their roots into pure white sand, and where small carnivorous plants digest their prey in black-watered swamps.

These are the New Jersey Pine Barrens, a beautiful, vast, and untouched forest preserve where contradictions and continuities exist side by side. Forest fires regularly devour the tinder-dry pines, yet those same fires nourish the soil with their ashes. Rare species of plants and animals thrive near dusty foot trails and meandering tea-colored streams.

The white, sandy soil of the Barrens is four hundred feet deep, and through it flows one of the largest, purest aquifers in the world. Yet despite the plentiful water beneath its surface, drought is often fierce in the pinewoods.

Two hundred years ago, there were bustling towns all through central New Jersey, but when cheap iron ore was discovered in Pennsylvania, the bog iron smelters closed. Factories and mills shut down, and lumbering ceased. The soil was too poor for farming, and soon all that remained were rotting ghost towns scattered among the pines.

Current maps of central New Jersey are dotted with the curious names of nonexistent towns—Hampton Furnace, Dover Forge,

Bodine's Tavern, Ongs Hat, and Dukes Bridge. A hunter following the footprints of a deer might stumble over scattered stones and fallen chimneys. He'll pause for a moment in the stillness, not listening for the deer anymore, but strangely stirred by the aura of what used to be.

There are legends about the Barrens, legends of a Jersey Devil, of pirates who buried casks of gold, and bank robbers who hid gold bullion under the scraggly pines. In modern times, there are whispers about mob victims who rest in the deep, white sand.

The Pine Barrens are still, calm, and beautiful.

The Pine Barrens are dangerous.

It all depends on who you are and what you have to hide.

CHAPTER 1

I t was long past midnight on the Jersey Shore on June 19, 1988. A blue van rolled quietly along Kearney Avenue in Seaside Heights, its headlights carving weak circles into the moist sea air.

The man behind the wheel was dressed entirely in black. His round, flat face gleamed in the reflected light of the dashboard as he slowly looked left and right, his hooded eyes peering into the dark alleys and shadowy double-deck porches of the old Victorian beach houses that lined the street.

Seaside Heights, a summer town of sand and surf, was asleep. The carousel was still. The pizza joints, bars, and arcades were quiet.

A faint light shone in an upstairs window. The van slowed to a crawl, and the driver's window slid down. A flashlight clicked on, and a narrow ray of light illuminated a rusted number on the side of a white, wooden column.

Smiling, the man parked across the street and then turned off the headlights.

Ten minutes later, a door opened, and a figure came down the stairs. The upstairs light went out.

Two dark eyes from within the van watched as the dark silhouette stumbled down the street. The driver sat and waited and then turned the ignition key.

Under the street lamps, the kid was tall and thin and looked younger than his seventeen years. He was dressed in baggy jeans, a loose, white T-shirt, and a black baseball cap. As the headlights of the van fell upon him, the kid turned and blinked slowly at the harsh white light. He stepped aside, tripping and stumbling against a parked car, and then pulled himself upright and waited for the bulky vehicle to pass on the narrow street.

The van pulled up next to him, and the driver leaned out. "Looks like you're in rough shape, son," he said.

"Yeah. R-rough shape." The kid spoke slowly, struggling with the words. "Basically, I'm wasted." He giggled, shrugging his narrow shoulders.

"Want a ride?"

"Nah." The kid leaned forward and peered at the man. "Wait, I know you. You're that guy from …"

The man smiled. "Yep, that's me. I was just having a late dinner with my sister, back there down the street." He gestured with his thumb. "I'm on my way back to Toms River, and I'd be glad to give you a ride home."

The kid stood unsteadily as the passenger door swung open. The voice was kind, solicitous, soft.

"You know, son, I've got a boy your age, and I wouldn't want him wandering around at this hour of the night, especially over that causeway. You don't know what kind of weirdoes might be out and about. C'mon, get in. I'll get you home safely."

The kid stared and tried to focus on the man's face.

"Trust me. I'll get you home safely," the man repeated and leaned toward the boy.

The kid shook his head as if to clear it, and then he launched his body forward into the van. The driver's thick arm shot forward, his stubby fingers grasping the boy's thin arm, pulling him into the van.

The kid slumped onto the tan vinyl seat with a long sigh as he pulled the door shut. As the van accelerated through the silent town, the windows slid up with a soft whir, and the doors locked with a soft click.

"Thanks, man," the kid mumbled. "Thanks for picking me up. I was gonna walk home."

"No problem. Where do you live?"

"Uh, Toms River, Rambling Brook Road. Near the water tower."

"I know the street. What number?"

"Six. Third house on the left, but you can leave me off at the c-corner."

"No problem." The man's voice sank lower. "Why don't you lean back and relax. I'll wake you up when we get there."

The kid's head fell back slowly, and his eyes closed. As the van gently accelerated, the boy's worn Pittsburgh Steelers cap fell off. The driver laughed softly and fingered the hypodermic needle in his jacket. He hadn't needed it after all. This one was a piece of cake.

Did he know where number 6 Rambling Brook Road is? Yes, indeed he did. He knew everything about Edsell Jones—everything. There was a pint of cheap vodka behind a dictionary on the top shelf of the kid's locker at school. There was a stash of pot under a raggedy, old sweatshirt. In his three years at Toms River South High School, Edsell Jones had been called to the principal's office six times. He'd been suspended twice.

Edsell had a high IQ, a low grade-point average, and few friends.

Best of all, there was no Mr. Jones, no brothers or sisters or bothersome aunts, uncles, and cousins. There was just a booze-loving single mama who worked the night shift at Rosie's Diner.

Nelson glanced at the boy. His eyes were closed; the thin face was relaxed. Sometimes a kid stayed asleep all the way to the Barrens. That always made his job easier.

He fingered the hypodermic again. The doctor had warned him, told him to use the needle only if absolutely necessary, and Wilbur Nelson always followed the doctor's orders. There would be serious problems if security was breached.

Nelson smiled, pressed his foot on the accelerator, and turned onto the causeway to Toms River. Fifteen minutes later, the van was in the darkness of the Pine Barrens.

CHAPTER 2

The gray, still light of early dawn crept slowly across a woodland meadow. At the edge of the woods, Joshua Reed silently stepped behind the dark, twisted trunk of a pitch pine and stood motionless. His eyes narrowed at a movement on the far side of the field. The stirring was slight. An upright twig moved in the absence of wind.

As the minutes went slowly by, Joshua slowly and imperceptibly shifted his weight from one foot to the other. Stalking had taught him patience; bow hunting had taught him silence. That might be Old Mitch out there.

He remembered the first time he had seen the great deer. Last fall on the second day of bow season, he'd stepped over a shallow creek, looked up, and there, on a small rise not a hundred yards away, stood a huge ten-point buck. The deer had looked right at him, smart-alecky and bold, as if he knew the exact range of Joshua's eighty-five-pound compound bow.

Then suddenly, with an echoing snort and a huge leap that showed white tail and a flash of hooves, the deer had vanished. Joshua trailed him through the scrub oaks and small pines on that cold November morning until the tracks led to a wide, slow-moving stream. He followed the creek for over a mile with his eyes trained on the banks for any sign of the buck, but then the sluggish, tea-colored water emptied into a wide bog. Before him, the dark water lay still as glass between clumps of marsh grass and a tiny island of scrub brush.

The deer had outsmarted him.

For the next few days, Joshua had tried to find the great buck. He stood patiently in the early morning, watching and listening, his breath blowing clouds of coffee-scented steam into the cold morning air. In the autumn gold of late afternoons, Joshua searched the edges of bogs, walking the overgrown trails and abandoned railways of the Pine Barrens, but he never saw the deer again. He even named him Old Mitch, after a barrel-chested sergeant he'd known in his army days.

When firearm season started, Joshua hated it more than usual because during those weeks, citified, bumble-footed, gun-toting assholes wearing Dayglow suits filled the Barrens. They lugged two-way radios, portable tree stands, range finders, artificial scents, and electronic calling devices. Christ almighty, soon they'd be bringing in radar and helicopters to make sure they bagged a deer. The clueless idiots crashed through the trees, sometimes stumbling on a deer, more often as not shooting at cows and dogs and each other in a desperate effort to kill something, anything.

If they were lucky enough to find a deer stupid enough to let them shoot it, some of them did the unconscionable: they cut off the head and antlers and left the carcass for the buzzards.

Joshua sighed heavily. Idiots all, with no sense of the forest or the hunt. Deer were part of the intricate pattern of nature. They were to be judiciously harvested; they were to be used; they were to be respected. Their hides were to be tanned and cured, their meat wrapped and labeled and stacked in the freezer. There was nothing finer on a cold winter evening than the pungent smell of venison surrounded by onions, carrots, peppercorns, and bay leaves slow-cooking in his grandma's old cast-iron pot.

Joshua's mouth watered at the thought as he focused on a patch of darkness under the branches of a small red maple. Something was in the shadows that edged the field.

Joshua stood relaxed and motionless, thankful that the slight currents of air blew toward him, not away. As he watched, the darkness moved, and a magnificent buck slowly walked into the meadow, followed by two does.

Old Mitch's mighty rack was covered with the downy moss of summer. It rose above his head like a great, soft crown. With his deep, broad chest and well-muscled neck, he dwarfed the smaller whitetails that grazed on the far side of the meadow.

After a few minutes of browsing, Old Mitch raised his head from the wild oat grass and looked around. He turned and sniffed the air and then looked right at Joshua.

Damn. Joshua cursed his luck. The buck had picked up his scent.

The rounded ears pointed toward the pitch pine where Joshua stood. The large, black eyes with their ring of white lashes were trained right on him.

He stepped toward Joshua and then paused. Again he stepped forward and paused. Again and again this hesitant advance continued until Old Mitch stood a mere ten yards away.

Joshua held his breath, scarcely daring to breathe, knowing that if he even blinked, the spell would be broken. Then Joshua's stomach rumbled.

It was enough. Old Mitch snorted a warning, turned in one graceful motion, and bounded across the field with his smaller companions following. With bobbing white tails, they disappeared into the woods on the far side of the field. Joshua released his breath in one long sigh.

Old Mitch had given him a singular gift—a memory to be treasured and brought out again and again. Someday he'd tell his son about a midsummer morning when the biggest buck in the Barrens walked right up and almost shook his hand. He'd tell him about it, that is, if he ever had a son.

Joshua turned and walked back to his cabin, elated at his morning's adventure and anticipating the bacon and eggs he'd cook before heading out to his job site. A half mile from his cabin, a blue van whizzed by him on the old dirt trail, headed east toward Toms River.

He coughed as the dust cloud enveloped him.

Dumb ass, driving that fast in here. What was his hurry?

CHAPTER 3

Lorraine Jones wiped her sweaty hands on her blue polyester uniform and then inserted the key into the lock. The door of the old tract home creaked as she pushed it open with the flat of her hand. A wall of stale, cigarette-laced air hit her as she stepped inside. *Damn,* she thought, *Edsell forgot to turn on the air conditioner when he got in last night.*

She walked into the tiny living room and flicked the window unit on high. The hell with the electric bill; she needed some pleasure after eight hours of waiting tables at Rosie's.

In the kitchen, Lorraine opened a small orange packet of decaf, poured it into a white mug, added water, and placed it in the microwave. She lit a cigarette and inhaled deeply.

When the microwave beeped, she grabbed the hot mug and sank down into the old plaid couch in the tiny living room. No morning TV shows today; she was too damn tired.

Lorraine sighed and leaned back. She knew the old, yellow hamper overflowed with dirty clothes, that she was almost out of towels, but she was too tired to care.

It was only June and already stinkin' hot. The night shift at the diner had been brutal. As soon as she walked in the door at eleven o'clock and put on her apron, a whole gang of noisy kids strolled in with their smart mouths and small change. They were followed by bowling teams from the late leagues and couples from the late shows at the movie theater. At two o'clock, a busload of weary gamblers from Atlantic City pulled in. In between, she had the drunks trying to sober up before hitting the Garden State Parkway and the geezers from the retirement village who couldn't sleep nights anymore, and finally Babs and Bernadette from the strip joint down on the Boulevard showed up for their usual order of strawberry waffles. They paid their check with rumpled one-dollar bills.

The sky was turning gray when the regulars started drifting in: cops, nurses, deliverymen, bus drivers, fishing crews. When the morning shift came in, Lorraine had been on her feet for eight hours straight.

She sighed, crushed out her cigarette, and took a sip of the steaming hot coffee. Winters were the best, she mused. Good times started when the cold weather came in and the goddamn Bennies blew out. She could shoot the breeze with the other waitresses, joke around with the regulars, and even sit in a back booth with a newspaper and her own cup of hot coffee.

She'd been at Rosie's for fifteen years now, trying to raise a son on her own. She'd been an only child, and when her parents died and her weasel of a husband left, all in the same year, she'd had to suck it up and do the best she could.

But she had Edsell, and that was enough.

He'd been real sweet when he was a kid, but now that he was a teenager, it was one damn scrape after another. Notes from the principal, letters from the truant officer, visits by social workers at the Division of Youth and Family Services, for crissakes. Worst of all, Edsell's new ratty-looking friends started hanging out at her house while she was at work.

And then the shoplifting thing last month. Shit. The little bugger had snatched an eighty-dollar Polo golf shirt from Macy's at the Ocean County Mall and got nabbed as he was leaving the store. What the hell was Edsell going to do with a golf shirt? Wear it to the fucking country club?

Dumb. Dumb. Dumb.

Well, he'd been dumbstruck when the cops took him off to the jailhouse and called her at work. Because he had no priors, they released him to her.

That night, she tore up one side of him and down the other. Told him he was on the road to being a piece of shit like his father, told him to get the hell out of her house if he was going to embarrass her in front of her customers at the diner. She said if the cops ever came to her door again, she'd tell them to keep him.

For the first time ever, Edsell shouted back at her, said he was tired of her drinking, sick of cleaning up the house, told her he wanted a real mom, not one who was sleeping, working, or drunk twenty-four hours a day.

They'd stayed up the rest of the night. They'd yelled at each other, and then, finally, they'd talked—and then talked some more. She'd cried, and he'd cried, and when they were through, they hugged.

Edsell promised he'd straighten up.

Lorraine promised to cut back on the booze.

There had been other scenes, other promises before, but that night was different. Something had clicked. She hadn't realized how much she needed her vodka to get through each day. Now she was going to AA meetings, and while she hadn't stopped completely, she'd cut back, taking a nip only when she knew Edsell would be gone a few hours.

And Edsell? He'd been around more since then, helping around the house without whining, taking out the trash, cleaning up his room. Last week he'd even cut the lawn with the old rotary mower.

Best of all, Edsell had gotten himself a girlfriend over in Seaside. Missy was her name. She was small and quiet, no weird hair, no hoops in her eyebrows, no studs in her tongue, just a few tattoos on her arms and one small snake chain around her neck. Since he'd been seeing her, Edsell had started talking about getting a job, about getting enough money for a car of his own. It was almost too good to be true.

Yeah, things were getting better. Maybe someday soon she could throw the bottle out the window for good.

Lorraine yawned, put her empty coffee cup into the sink, and picked up her purse, heavy with dollar bills and assorted change. She'd count it later. Right now she needed some sleep.

As she walked into the tiny hall between the two bedrooms, she suddenly noticed how strangely quiet the house was. Lorraine felt a sudden chill despite the heat. Edsell usually slept with the radio on.

She yanked open his door.

The bed was empty.

CHAPTER 4

Mark Germano heard the telephone on its sixth ring. He threw his arm out from under the sheet and fumbled for it.

"Hello," he croaked.

Mark's eyes searched for the alarm clock: 7:38 a.m. Shit. School had been over for two weeks, and his parents and two little brothers had left Saturday for their annual two-week vacation in Myrtle Beach. He could have slept until 8:15. Who was calling him this early?

"Mark? Is that you, Mark?" The unfamiliar voice was raspy, muffled, and female.

"Yeah. This is Mark. Who's this?"

"You might not remember me, Mark. My name's Lorraine Jones. I'm Edsell's ma."

Images floated through Mark's head. Lorraine Jones. Frizzy blonde hair and a cigarette voice. Worked the late shift at Rosie's Diner out on Route 70. Her son, Edsell, had been his best friend in elementary school. They'd been Cub Scouts together, had played on the same Little League team, spent nights at each other's houses.

"Yeah, I remember you, Mrs. Jones. What's up?"

"Edsell's gone."

"Gone? What do you mean, gone?"

"I came home from work this morning, and he wasn't here." Mark heard a choked-off sob. "He's never been away all night. Something's happened. I know something bad's happened …"

Real sobs now, and Mark knew they came from a tiny, paint-peeling house near the water tower. Mark had hung out there a lot, years ago. He and Borderline and Edsell had been best pals back then, riding their bikes to the beach where they body-surfed and dunked each other in the waves. They'd fished off the piers on the bay side in the evenings and then watched forbidden R-rated movies at Edsell's house while Mrs. Jones worked. They were inseparable then.

Now Mark was a three-star athlete, and Edsell … well, Edsell was a burnout who hung around with the other potheads and freaks. Whenever Mark passed him in the crowded hallways of the school, Edsell ducked his head. That forlorn gesture always made Mark feel sad, but he didn't know what to do about it. There was no way he could invite Edsell to sit with him and the other football players and the cheerleaders.

The voice on the line was talking. He snapped back and listened. "… and I checked with my neighbors, even called some of them bums he hangs out with, but no one knows nothin'. They're such shits, they're prob'ly lying to me. I don't trust 'em. I called his girlfriend in Seaside, thinkin' he was there, but she said he left right after midnight. She's all cryin' now and hysterical. That doesn't help me at all. Something happened on the way home from Missy's. I know it."

"Did you call the police?"

"Mark, the police don't want to know nothing either."

"They don't want to know? Come on, Mrs. Jones, they're the police; they're supposed to check out stuff like missing kids."

"Listen, Mark. You probably don't know it, but Edsell's been picked up a couple of times. Last January, the cops raided a party and brought him back to me, stoned. Last month, he got caught shoplifting. They think my son's a dirtbag, so they don't care what happens to him. They tell me he's just hanging out somewheres, that he'll be home soon …" More sobs, and then Mark heard an anguished wail. "Edsell's never been gone all night. Something's wrong. I know it."

The crying slowly subsided. Mark could almost see Mrs. Jones's face contracting, pulling itself back into control. Lorraine Jones had a habit of running her hands through her wild hair, and he imagined her doing that now.

"I don't have anyone else to call, and I remembered how you and Edsell was such good friends back then. How you used to play over here all the time." She paused and drew a deep, hissing breath. "Listen, Mark, I know you're a hot-shot football star. I seen your pictures in the papers. I thought … maybe you could do something …"

"What do you want me to do, Mrs. Jones?"

"Ask the kids, the ones that hang out with Edsell. Call me if you hear anything, anything at all."

"Okay, Mrs. Jones. Today's the first day of summer school. I'll ask around when I get to South, find out if anyone's seen him."

"Promise you'll call me. Promise."

"I will. Don't worry, Mrs. Jones. I'm sure Edsell will turn up soon."

CHAPTER 5

"Jeez, I'm going to be late," Mark muttered as he ran out of the house, pulling a clean T-shirt over his still-dripping hair. He hopped over the door of his ancient Jeep Wrangler, rammed it backward out of the driveway, and turned toward Toms River South High School. At the first intersection, he rummaged around the glove compartment for a comb, pulled down the mirror, and savagely brushed at his thick, brown hair. No time for a shave today. The parking lot was nearly full when Mark drove up to the school. He jumped out and sprinted to the main entrance. When he was halfway through the parking lot, he heard a low rumble behind him. A shiny, orange 1970 Dodge Challenger slipped diagonally into two spaces on the far side of the lot.

There was only one car like it in Toms River. Borderline Fenton climbed out, saw Mark, and hurried over.

"Hey, buddy. What're you doing here?" Mark called out.

"Taking Algebra II."

"You're joking."

"Nope. I messed around, and Old Lady Smythe threatened to fail me if I kept it up. I did. She did. End of story." Borderline pulled at the gold stud in his ear. "What are *you* doing here?"

Mark grinned. "Taking Algebra II."

"No way."

"I got a C from Smythe, and a C is not acceptable to my father or to Princeton University. He's making me take it over."

A long, shrill whistle sounded from inside the massive school.

"Awww fuck. Symthe's gonna fail us both."

Borderline and Mark started running for the big front doors of the school.

"I gotta talk to you," Mark panted as they rounded a corner in the hallway. "Edsell Jones is gone. His mother called me this morning."

"No shit. The twerp. Where's he gone?"

"I don't know, but I promised Mrs. Jones I'd ask around. Have you seen him recently?"

"Nah. Not since he started hanging out with C.M. and his crowd. I'm not getting into trouble."

"Listen, I promised I'd help. She's a nice lady, and she was frantic, said he'd never been gone all night before. She's got no one to turn to, so do me a favor and ask around today. Come over after school. We'll compare notes."

"I can't. I'm working at the garage till five. Fererici's got a couple of guys on vacation right now, and they need me."

"Okay then, come over tonight. I'll call Stacey and ask her to come too. Oh shit, the door's closing. Hurry!"

CHAPTER 6

Edsell sensed he was in a strange place before he even opened his eyes. The smells were antiseptic, like the Clorox his mother used to clean the bathroom at home. There were no traffic noises from the Garden State Parkway. He couldn't hear the hum of their window air conditioner or the beat of the music he usually slept to.

His nose itched, but when Edsell tried to scratch it, he couldn't move his hands. He strained to put his hand up to his face but couldn't move his arm.

What the fuck? His eyes flew open. White ceiling, white walls, and directly in front of him, a window with beams of sunlight surrounding an opaque shade.

Edsell's eyeballs swung wildly. He was tied to a bed—not just a bed, but a hospital bed. His mouth was taped shut, and there were tubes running into both of his arms.

Edsell couldn't move. He couldn't yell or scream for help.

He looked to the left and saw another bed with a ghostly, white-draped figure, also hooked to tubes, which led to bottles suspended on chrome stands behind the bed. The figure's mouth was not taped, but a cloth gag was tied across his mouth. The kid's eyes were closed. He looked so pale and still that Edsell wondered if he was dead.

Edsell began to panic. *Where the hell am I? Did I have an accident on the way home from Missy's? Did I get hit by a truck? Is this a hospital?*

He struggled against his bounds. Sweat broke out on his forehead, and his pits got damp. He rattled the bed with his struggles.

The boy next to him opened his eyes and then turned and looked directly at Edsell. His eyes were remote and sad but tearless. He slowly shook his head and then turned away and closed his eyes.

CHAPTER 7

H eading to his construction site near Whiting, Joshua was a little later than usual, but it wasn't a problem. His men were busy sheetrocking the house on Elm Court. He knew they'd be working just as hard without him there as they did when the boss was on site. The house would be finished soon, and he had a second one under contract. Business was growing in the senior communities like Whiting as more people retired to Ocean County from the overpopulated areas in North Jersey.

Joshua swung his truck around a corner and passed a series of old cranberry bogs. He smiled as he remembered this morning's adventure: a huge deer so close he could count its eyelashes.

Deer are territorial animals. Old Mitch would walk the same game trials, browse identical meadows, drink from selected streams, bed down in familiar thickets.

The big deer would be back to that meadow, and so would he.

At the Watson place, Joshua cut a wide detour through the woods. No sense in asking for trouble; everyone in the pine woods knew the Watson place was bad news.

Two years ago, he and Tony had been the first to see the strangers.

The big farm house had stood empty for years after Old Man Watson died without a will or any living relatives. When it was put up for sale by the county for back taxes, Joshua looked at it himself, but he had second thoughts when he discovered how much work was needed just to make it habitable. It was easier to stay on in his parents' old cabin and fix it up.

When the Pinelands Commission told him the fifty acres of creeks, abandoned cranberry bogs, and pinewoods couldn't be subdivided, it put an end to any thoughts he had of buying it or developing the property.

On the morning he first saw the strangers, he and Tony had been scouting for deer, as they often did in the summer months. Carrying bows and practice arrows, the two boyhood friends had been popping at stumps, saving a few broadheads for small game. As they looked for deer tracks, neither spoke much, just a few words here and there, mostly about the next deer season.

At the unexpected sound of hammering in the stillness of the pines, Joshua and Tony exchanged curious glances and silently moved in for a closer look.

From the tree line, they watched several men unload paneling, electrical equipment, pipe, and acoustical tiles from a flatbed truck. Joshua couldn't remember that any jobs had been offered to local builders. Who were these guys?

A few days later, Joshua learned that the work crews came from out of state, and all the vehicles carried Maryland plates.

As the weeks went by, the renovations continued at a steady pace. The few Pineys who lived nearby silently watched and speculated. The stories that circulated were varied and imaginative. Some said the new owner was a retired businessman who planned to raise purebred Arabian horses there. Someone heard that the new owner was a mobster hiding from the FBI. Still others thought the new owner was a double agent who was being given a new identity by the CIA.

Old Ben Sampson, whose tiny woodlands cottage lay a half mile from the Watson place, told him the strangest story about the old Watson place over beers one night.

"Didn't like what was happening out there," Ben said in a gravelly drawl. "Strangers coming here, not talkin' to anybody, not even buying a burger or a beer in Chatsworth. Shades in all the windows, pulled down night and day. So I decided to find out for myself just what was going on, but I did it slowly, a little at a time.

"Each time I took my hounds out for a run, I just happened to go by," he said and added another plug to the chaw already in his cheek. "Soon as they finished fixin' up the house, they took down all the trees around. Wasted all that pinewood. Just trucked it away like it was worthless. The house stood in the middle of a two-acre clearing when they were done. No grass, no shrubs, just pure sand and dirt and the stumps of the cut-down pines.

"I'll never forget the last day I went over there, Joshua. Scared me half to death. I was just standing with my hound, looking at the house, when this big galoot walked up to me holding an ax. I could see the blade was sharp and shiny. Then this other guy walked up with a sputtering chain saw and held it out in front of him.

"They just stared me down, Josh. My hound started to whimper, and as I shushed her, the big guy said to move on, that they didn't want anyone hanging around their property. The other guy revved up the chain saw just then, and I skedaddled.

"Son, I served in Korea, and I was never scared there like I was that day, right here, less than a mile from my very own house. I don't know who those people are, but I don't want anything to do with them. I told everyone to stay away."

Joshua knew that once the locals had heard Ben's story, they cautioned their kids to stay away from the Watson place whenever they roamed the Barrens on their dirt bikes and all-terrain vehicles. Soon everyone gave the old cranberry farm a wide berth. Whoever lived there obviously did not want company, and in the live-and-let-live code of the Barrens, that unspoken request was honored.

After a while, most people lost interest.

CHAPTER 8

A s Joshua drove into the tiny village of Chatsworth, he mused on its long and checkered history. The town was located in the heart of the Pine Barrens. One hundred years ago, the town had been a crossroads town and an important stop on the railroad that ran through the center of New Jersey. The railroad was long gone, and the factories that had fueled the stores and shops had closed decades ago, but for the local Pineys, hikers, and hunters, Chatsworth remained an important village, a place to meet and greet, trade stories, and fuel both their trucks and their bellies.

What drew most people to Chatsworth these days was Buzby's, the old country store in the center of the village. It had a penny-candy counter, Coke and birch beer in glass bottles, and oversized sandwiches. Like him, truckers and builders, hunters, and cranberry growers drove miles out of their way to sit at the scratched and wobbly, linoleum-covered tables while they wolfed down Buzby specials and traded stories. The corners of the ceiling were dusted with cobwebs. The walls were decorated with raggedy old Christmas wreaths and outdated flyers for yard sales and turkey shoots.

Joshua pushed open the red-framed glass door, squeezed over to the counter, and ordered a tuna sub with lettuce, tomato, onions, and roasted peppers. As he pulled two birch beers from the top-lift case, he noticed the only available seat was at a table occupied by a woman he had never seen before. She sat, oblivious to the noise around her, scribbling in a spiral notebook.

Joshua collected his sub, greeted some truckers he knew, and walked over to her table. He waited until she looked up and noticed him.

Her long, dark hair was brushed carelessly into a loose swirl on top of her head with small, loose wisps on either side of her face. She pushed the wayward strands back with both hands, looked up at him, and smiled. He was charmed, not because her smile was wide and generous and revealed white, even teeth, but because her gray-green eyes looked directly at him.

Strange, he thought; most women did not look right into a man's eyes at first. Some never learned to do it. Even after becoming lovers and exchanging the most intimate bodily secrets, some women held back a part of themselves.

And now, in the middle of the lunch crowd at Buzby's, a woman with wild, unruly hair looked into his eyes and smiled.

"Can I join you?" he asked. "I'm Joshua Reed."

"Sure," she said, and pointed to the empty chair. No useless posturing or flirting, just a simple affirmative.

He put his plate and the birch beers on the table and eased into the scarred and sturdy captain's chair. She extended a firm hand and said, "I'm Theodora Constantinos, Teddy for short."

She's obviously not a Piney with that name and that city accent, thought Joshua. He said, "Well, Teddy-for-short, you're eating one of the best sandwiches in town. Actually, they're the only sandwiches in town." He bit into his sub.

"I know. I've been here two weeks, and I've already sampled most of their soups and sandwiches." She closed her notebook and poked the pencil behind her ear.

He took a second bite of his sandwich and chewed for a few moments. "Did you move here?" he asked.

"No, I'm working in the Pine Barrens doing research on my doctoral thesis. I rented a house for six months, and even though it has a kitchen, I'm not much of a cook."

"Thesis? Christ, you mean you came here from a college to study us backward Pineys?" Joshua looked around and whispered dramatically, "For God's sake, don't tell anyone, because if we find out what you're doing, we won't talk to you, or if we do, we won't tell the truth. You've got to be born and bred here for three or four generations before you even begin to belong. Pineys never tell anyone, especially outsiders, what we really think."

She laughed, a big generous laugh.

"Don't worry, Joshua. I'm not here to study the strange and mysterious Pineys with their legends and their lost towns and their devils."

"Then what are you studying?"

"Boykin's Lobelia."

Joshua arched his eyebrows. "Boykin's what?"

"Boykin's Lobelia, or Lobelia Boykinii in scientific terms, is an endangered plant that's found in the Barrens' swamps. I'm a botanist, and that's what my thesis is on."

"Yeah? What's it look like?" Joshua asked.

"It's an herb that grows up to three feet tall. It has a hollow stem and few branches, with blue to white flowers. I'm hoping to find enough of them to take some cuttings back to the lab at Rutgers. I'm going to take photos and map out their locations here in this part of the Barrens. I have permission from the Pinelands Commission to do my research here."

Joshua swallowed a gulp of birch beer, leaned back in his chair, and considered her.

"You don't look like a college professor."

"Now that is a sexist remark." Teddy laughed. She balled up her wax paper and napkin and stuffed it into her empty coffee cup. "Okay, what do you do?"

"I'm a carpenter." Joshua reached into his pocket, pulled out a business card, and handed it to her.

Teddy read the card. "Reed Construction. New Homes and Renovations." She smiled that gorgeous smile again. "You don't look like a carpenter to me."

He laughed and thought of asking her out right then and there. No ring on her finger, but she probably had a boyfriend parked in her rented house, some college wuss who was writing a goddamn thesis on butterflies or frogs. Joshua wiped his mouth and watched her as she bit into a deli pickle. Nice lips, full and soft. A good appetite and great hair.

Maybe. Maybe worth a try. After all, he had his own business, one that grew bigger each year. He was as good a man as any, college or not, and probably pulled in more dollars a year than a college professor.

"Teddy, I have a question for you."

"Okay, what is it?"

"How about dinner over in Toms River tonight? I know of a couple places with great food." He paused and looked at her intently. She wasn't smiling. "That is, if you're free," he added in what he hoped was a casual tone.

"I have a question for you too, Joshua."

"Yeah? What?"

"Are you free?" Teddy asked. "Is there a Mrs. Joshua somewhere? I don't do research on property that's already taken, if you get my drift. Scientific integrity, you know."

Joshua smiled broadly. "No, there's no Mrs. Joshua, and no girlfriend either."

"Then we're on. Pick me up at six thirty. I'm in the little, blue house on the end of Peacock Street. Do you know it?"

"Yep. See you then."

CHAPTER 9

That evening, when Joshua pulled up in front of the small, blue house on Peacock Street, Teddy was waiting on the front porch. She wore simple, brown slacks, a sleeveless, white shirt, and tan sandals. Her dark brown hair flowed freely over her shoulders, and as he helped her into his truck, he caught the fresh, clean smell of soap.

They drove to Toms River on back roads. The evening sun was warm, and Joshua kept the windows of his truck open.

Joshua didn't talk much. He was content to watch the beauty of the pine forest, the small boggy areas, and the hawks flying overhead. Teddy seemed lost in thought too, as if she were sharing his inner musings.

Finally, when they came to the suburbs of Toms River, Joshua drove past box stores, gas stations, and fast-food restaurants.

When they walked into the restaurant just off Route 37, Enzio himself greeted Joshua and asked who the beautiful lady was. Joshua introduced Teddy and grinned to himself as Enzio led them to the best table by a large window that overlooked a small, lighted courtyard ablaze with flowers.

"You must come here a lot," Teddy remarked.

"No, not really. Enzio's son Tony and I grew up together, and we don't see each other much anymore because we're both tied up with our businesses. In the fall, we always take time off to hunt together."

Teddy nodded, and Joshua continued. "Enzio's brother owns two big cranberry farms just south of Chatsworth. About ten years ago, he financed this place for Enzio, and it's been a moneymaker ever since."

"Cranberries are big business in the Barrens," said Teddy. She picked up the menu and scanned it. "Looks like real Italian food is served here. I can't wait to order. In Philadelphia, we had several wonderful, old family restaurants, both Greek and Italian." She scanned the menu for a few moments and then asked, "What's good?"

They ordered antipasto for two and then Agnello Imbottito for her and Risotto alla Fiorentina for him. Joshua usually ordered scampi but decided that a dish heavily laced with garlic was not a good idea on a first date.

While they waited for their order, Enzio brought over a bottle of Chianti.

"For you, Joshua, and for your lovely friend, Teddy. Why have you stayed away so long? We never see you anymore."

"Just busy with the business and wandering the pinewoods when I find time."

Enzio snorted. "Aaaah. You and Tony, still sneaking around with your bows and arrows. Like kids playing. Did you know Tony's running the whole operation at Shamong for my brother now? He was here last Sunday with his wife and kids." Enzio put his hands over his belly and laughed. "Life is good, Joshua. You need to settle down like Tony. Ahhh. Here's the antipasto. Enjoy!"

Enzio winked and disappeared into the kitchen.

Joshua had flinched at Enzio's remark about settling down, hoping that Teddy wouldn't take him for some desperate bachelor trying to find a wife. It was, quite frankly, the farthest thing from his mind. A nice girlfriend, a cordial and loving relationship, perhaps, but that was all he wanted right now.

They ate slowly while trading stories about their lives. Teddy had grown up in Philadelphia and then attended LaSalle University where she majored in botany. She had a master's degree in Earth Science and was working toward her PhD at Rutgers.

"My father is Greek, mother's Italian," Teddy said. "They started with nothing and worked incredibly hard to put me through school. They owned a small janitorial service. When my sister and I weren't in school, we worked with them, waxing floors, washing windows, cleaning bathrooms. I worked nights while my friends partied. I studied in the afternoons when they went to the mall. When I dreamed, I dreamed of trees and blue skies, of flowers and endless fields of green grass. Of places without cars and noise ..."

"So now you're a plant expert."

"That's right. The trees I saw as a kid were the ones in the park. The animals I knew were behind bars at the zoo. In my freshman year at LaSalle, I looked through a microscope, saw living plant cells, and was hooked. Now I teach undergraduate courses at Rutgers, and in the summer I get paid to spend my days in forests and fields doing research on rare species. I couldn't be happier."

"I know how you feel," Joshua said. "I grew up here. In the service, I hated being crowded in with all the guys. When they sent me to the Philippines, I stayed on the base for as long as I could stand it. Then I'd rent a car and drive up into the foothills outside Manila."

"Now you're back in the Barrens."

"Yeah. I started a carpentry business few years ago, just fixing up old houses, adding porches, that kind of thing. Now I'm building new ones over near Whiting in some of the areas you can still build on. I have enough work to keep me busy most of the year. In the fall and winter, I take time off to hunt."

Oh-oh, here it comes, thought Joshua, *the anti-hunter thing*. He instantly regretted mentioning his favorite pastime. He was surprised when she asked, "What do you hunt?"

"Deer mostly, but also rabbits, squirrels, ducks, raccoon." Joshua hesitated. "With a bow. I'm a bow hunter."

Her eyes widened. "You're joking. Like Robin Hood?" she grinned.

"Bow hunting is real hunting, old-fashioned hunting like humans have done for thousands of years. Bow hunters are quiet. We know the woods, and we track our prey. We're not shooting from three hundred yards away with an electronic sight." Joshua paused and looked at Teddy. She didn't seem to be repelled by his admission to bow hunting. "What? You kill Bambi?" That was what most outsiders said, sneering with self-righteous contempt. Surprisingly, Teddy just looked curious.

"Tell me about it," she said.

And he did. Slowly and hesitantly at first, but then as the main course was served, expansively, savoring the telling. Years of his boyhood when he hunted with his dad, his love of the Pinelands, and the peace he found when he roamed its forgotten trails.

Teddy sat and listened and asked questions, sipping her wine and nodding as he explained. Then in the middle of a sentence, Joshua stopped and asked, "How come you're not all fluttery and upset about my hunting?"

"Have you ever hunted endangered animals? Bald eagles? Cougars? Wolves?"

"No. Never."

"Then there's no problem with what you do. Deer are plentiful. They have no natural enemies left to thin the herds. If we didn't have hunters, we'd have zillions of deer eating up crops, getting hit by cars, trampling our children. I did a study once of a large suburban park where no hunting was allowed. They called it a game preserve, and everyone assumed it would be a deer paradise, but the deer were pitiful. Diseased, starving, sores on their bodies, swollen bellies, their fawns were weak and crippled. That's what happens when there's no population control. Hunting is fine, as long as you know what you're doing."

"The Reeds have always hunted," Joshua said. "More wine?"

"Why not? This stuffed lamb is fantastic, tender with just the right amount of seasonings. I'd like to come here again," she said.

Joshua smiled as he poured more wine. *Why not, indeed,* he thought.

CHAPTER 10

Even though Mark asked around after class, no one knew where Edsell was. He grilled the few jocks who were in summer school, but most of them wouldn't even admit to knowing Edsell. A couple of the girls said they had seen him in Seaside within the last couple of days.

That figures, thought Mark. *He's got a girlfriend there.*

Lorraine Jones called while he was at school and left a message telling him that the police had to wait forty-eight hours before filing a missing person's report. Her voice sounded frail and desperate, and as he hung up the phone, Mark wondered what it would be like to have only one relative when he had so many.

He had a mother and father and two little brothers, Sal and Ricky. Nonna Adelina lived in a tiny house on the back of their big corner lot just off Hooper Avenue. Years ago, when Pappa Salvatore died, his grandmother gave her house to Mark's father, and he, in turn, converted the detached garage into a tiny house for her.

Nonna Adelina had always been part of their lives, advising Mark in her Italian-laced English, cooking big dinners for the family on Sunday afternoons, and babysitting for his little brothers. Heck, the only reason he had been allowed to stay in Toms River while his family went on vacation was because he was under the watchful eyes of his Nonna.

There were Germano aunts, uncles, and cousins all over New Jersey from Secaucus to Cherry Hill. They came in assorted ages, shapes, and sizes, and the older members of the family often conversed in Italian.

Each Labor Day, everyone came to his house for the annual reunion. It was a feast of lasagna, tortellini, sausages and peppers, braciole, polenta, and his favorite eggplant Parmigiana made by Nonna Adelina. Aunt Rose always made anise cookies shaped into little bows. Uncle Tony always brought the big espresso maker from his restaurant. At the end of the evening, the older men and women men sat under the big oak tree in the backyard and drank tiny cups of dark coffee laced with Sambuca.

The men played bocce and horseshoes. The women told stories and rocked the babies. Boyfriends and girlfriends were brought to these gatherings for inspection. The Germano family was loud, intrusive, and annoying, yet unabashedly loving and supportive.

He couldn't imagine what it would be like if it was just him and his mother.

At precisely 5:30, he heard a knock on the back door, and there stood Nonna with a tray of food.

"Here, Markus. You eat my lasagna. You growing boy, you need food."

"It smells great," he said as he put the tray in the kitchen. "Do you want to eat with me?"

The tiny woman shook her head.

"No, bambino. I go to see Salvatore now and bring him flowers."

She stood on her tiptoes to give Mark a quick kiss and then turned and walked back down the path to her tiny cottage.

Adelina walked to St. Joseph's Cemetery every day. The Germano gravesite was adorned with a cross, an eternal flame, and, during most of the year, fresh flowers in a cement vase.

The tombstone was a double one in the shape of two hearts. Salvatore and Adelina Germano's names and birthdates were engraved on it. Salvatore's date of death was on the shiny, black marble heart, but there was a blank space after Adelina's date of birth.

"I sleep with Salvatore someday," she often said with a grin. "I've gotten so old and fat, I hope he know me when I come."

Mark peeled back the aluminum foil from a small casserole of steaming hot lasagna and dumped some on a plate. Another bowl held a salad with oil and vinegar dressing. Two pieces of roasted garlic bread were carefully wrapped in crisp, white paper.

As Mark slowly ate his dinner, he thought about Edsell and Borderline. The three of them used to be so close, almost like family. Spending nights at each other's houses, going to the arcade in Seaside. They'd even camped in his uncle Gino's backyard in Belmar, making s'mores and telling ghost stories late into the night.

He was still good friends with Borderline, but neither of them hung out with Edsell much anymore. Their old friend had gradually taken up with a risky crowd. Mark knew the omnipresent Germano family would have had a fit if they saw their precious son hanging out with kids who were tattooed and pierced and wearing chains. Besides, he found there was not much to talk about with Edsell anymore. He wasn't into sports or books, movies or TV, or clothes or much of anything. It was hard to imagine what Edsell did in his spare time.

High school was tough. Everything depended on who you hung out with, what kind of clothes you wore, the clubs you joined, the sports you played, the music you listened to. Certain tables in the lunch room belonged to prescribed groups, so did certain bathrooms. Even outside the school, there were trees, bushes, worn spots in the grass, even cracks in the parking lot that were staked out.

The entire school was a minefield, and you had to be cool to survive. You had to know what to wear, who to talk to, where to sit, and even where to piss.

Mark's friends were the jocks and the cheerleaders, and the rest of the school looked up to them, and that felt good most of the time.

Edsell was in with the funky kids who were pierced and tattooed and dyed their hair pink or orange or green. Some even shaved it off completely. They listened to Metallica, Slayer, and Iron Maiden.

There were other groups at South. The brainiacs, the nerds, the sluts, the drama-geeks, and smaller sub-groups of those.

Borderline, on the other hand, did not hang out with any set group. He was smart, but his grades were average. He was on the shit list at the principal's office because Dr. Wilkins did not appreciate stink bombs in the locker pit or nude centerfolds that mysteriously appeared on the walls of the boys' bathroom. Likewise, the athletic director was not amused by scoreboards that went berserk and spelled out obscenities in the middle of closely-contested football games.

By his junior year, when anything strange or perverse happened at South, Borderline was called in for questioning.

Borderline walked the minefields at South without a map. He wasn't a jock, but he led whole sections of the stands in rousing cheers at football games. He escorted the head cheerleader to the junior prom last year. The brainiacs secretly admired his daring pranks and tried to imitate him in small, furtive ways. Borderline had friends among the burnouts; he was a hero to the marching band.

He'll probably wind up as a politician, Mark thought. *Shit, he'll probably wind up as president.*

As Mark scraped his plate clean with a slab of garlic bread, he heard a low rapping on the sliding glass door next to him. He pulled the vertical blind aside.

From the other side of the glass, two impish, brown eyes looked at him. Below the eyes, two dimples danced on either side of a wide smile.

"Stacey? You said you couldn't come," Mark said as he slipped the door open. "Hurry, come on in. Nonna went to the cemetery, but if she comes back and sees you here, she'll be over with a plate of cookies. How'd you get away?"

"I told my mom I was going to the mall with my cousin Millie," Stacey said. "She'll cover for me. What's up?"

"I'll tell you both what's up when Borderline gets here." Mark pointed to the remains of the lasagna. "Want some?"

Stacey shook her head. Mark took a second helping.

He glanced at Stacey as he ate. Short shorts, long, tan legs thrust into white sandals, last weekend's sunburn just starting to peel across the bridge of her freckled nose. Gorgeous enough to be a cheerleader, but Stacey wanted no part of it.

Stacey was captain of the swim team and pitcher for the varsity softball team. She didn't lead the cheering; her fans cheered for her.

She and Mark had been together for six months despite all the stupid rules that Stacey's parents laid down. Stacey could see him only three times a week, and some of those nights had to be spent with the family. He'd been at the Greenes' last night playing Monopoly with Stacey's two younger brothers. What a pain in the butt that was.

The doorbell rang, and Stacey stood up. "I'll get it."

Mark finished his lasagna as Borderline walked into the kitchen. "What's up?" asked Borderline.

"Sit down, and I'll fill you in."

In a few short sentences, Mark outlined his phone conversation with Lorraine Jones and how he'd asked around school to see if anyone had seen or heard from Edsell.

Most of the kids didn't know he was gone; everyone agreed that he'd be back soon.

"So what do you think?" Mark asked. "His mother says he's never been gone all night before."

"How does she know?" Borderline answered. "She doesn't get home until after seven in the morning."

"Edsell was in my class in grade school," Stacey said. "I always thought he was cute, but most of his friends are weird. Maybe he went somewhere with them. We can all ask around, and that's fine, but I don't understand why you two are all worried about him. He's not in our crowd or anything."

Mark stared across the room and then frowned at Stacey.

"You're right, Stacey. He's not in our crowd now, but he used to be my best friend. We hung out together, and he was different then. Funny, smart … he always beat me in any stupid game we played. But now I can't hang out with him anymore because my 'cool' friends wouldn't approve." Mark paused. "Maybe if I hadn't cared so much about being cool, Edsell would still be my friend, and he wouldn't have hung out with those creeps."

"Shit, it's not your fault he's in a weird crowd now," said Borderline. "You didn't do anything."

"That's the point," Mark spat. "I didn't do anything."

There was long pause while Borderline and Stacey looked at each other, and Mark stared down at the floor.

Finally, Borderline spoke. "I've got an idea. I'll stop by the diner tonight and talk to Mrs. Jones. I've seen her a few times at Rosie's, and she knows me. I'm thinking that she might not be telling us everything. They could have had a fight, and she doesn't want to admit it. There's got to be a reason he's gone."

"Good idea," Stacey said. "In the meantime, Mark and I will ask around. In fact, I'll try and locate Missy. Do you think Mrs. Jones has her number?"

"She said she called her right away when she found Edsell hadn't come home. I'll call you with her number," said Mark. "Let's meet at the beach tomorrow afternoon and compare notes. Can you get off from work, Borderline?"

"Probably. The boss owes me a favor."

"Great. I don't have to be at McDonald's until the dinner shift. I'll pick you both up at twelve thirty. I've got extra beach badges. I'll bring them."

CHAPTER 11

As Joshua drove back to Chatsworth through a darkness that was pure, Teddy pointed at the side of the road and asked, "Where do all those little dirt roads go? Most of them aren't even mentioned on my maps."

"Some of them are old developments that were planned and never happened. Others go to towns that don't exist anymore. Because everything grows so slowly in the Barrens, they don't get overgrown, even after a couple of decades."

"I know. That's part of the charm here. Things don't change or they change slowly, at least in the plant world."

Joshua turned to Teddy and gave her a long look. "I want you to be careful when you're out here by yourself." He waved at the vast darkness outside their window.

"Why?"

"Because if you get lost, there's no way to get your bearings because there aren't any big hills or other landmarks. The land is flat, so the creeks and streams twist and turn and head north and south and every which way, and there's peat bogs and cedar swamps scattered around. I fell into a bog two years ago, and suddenly I was up to my chest in thick, gooey mud. Lucky for me, Tony heard me hollering and pulled me out."

"You make it sound like the Pine Barrens is the most dangerous place in the world. I can tell you've never seen South Philly." She looked at him speculatively. "Are you trying to scare me?"

"Nope, just want you to be careful. Some strange folks live in the Barrens, folks that don't want to be seen or known."

"Come on, Joshua. You can't frighten me with those old legends of lunacy and inbreeding and Jersey Devils. I've been out here two weeks, and all I've seen are a few hikers on the Batona Trail."

"Most people out here are harmless, but there are a few you might not want to run into." He paused as though deciding whether he should continue, then sighed and shrugged his shoulders. "Just south of here by a couple of miles lives a Vietnam vet. He saw some bad stuff over there, got shot in a couple places that counted. When the VA released him, he found his wife had run off and took his only daughter with her. The guy went nuts. They put him back into a psychiatric hospital for a while, then released him. He's built a shack way back in the pines, and he pretty much lives off the land. I've seen him and talked to him, but he's not someone you want to run across unexpectedly. In a city, he'd be one of those street people who walk around mumbling to themselves. Folks leave him alone because he doesn't bother anybody; he just wants to be by himself."

The cool air blowing into the truck window made Joshua happy. It would be cooler on the job tomorrow. As they drove into Chatsworth, he saw a few scattered windows glowing dimly, but most of the town was dark.

When the oversized tires of Joshua's truck crunched on the gravel driveway in front of the tiny house on Peacock Street, he turned to her.

"One more thing. Stay away from the Watson place on Dukes Bridge Road. You've probably seen it if you have an aerial map. It's a big, old house in the middle of fifty acres of pinewoods and old cranberry bogs."

"I saw it last week, but it looked like the people were away. The shades were all pulled down."

"They keep them that way. They've made it plain to everyone around that they don't want to be bothered."

"Well, trust me, I won't bother them. I'm studying plants, not people." She cocked her head and peered at him in the dim light of the panel lights. "You got any more advice?"

He pointed to the tiny, white sports car parked on the grass next to the house. "Trade in that little tin can and get something with four-wheel drive. You'll get stuck in the sugar sand in that thing."

"I've got a leased Bronco with four-wheel drive in the garage. That's what I take into the Barrens." She grinned at him in the half light. "Come on, Joshua, I'm a big girl. I've done field research in remote areas all over the world. I've even been to the Amazon. I carry a compass, a can of mace, a knife, and a snake bite kit."

"Okay, okay. I was only trying to help." He paused. "There's one more thing."

"What?" Her eyes were dark and shadowed now.

She faced him now in the half light. With one big hand, he gently felt the soft tangles of her hair at the back of her neck and was instantly aware that he hadn't been with a woman for a long time. He wanted her, with her mane of dark hair and her direct eyes, but when he put gentle pressure on the back of her neck, she stiffened.

He released her with a pent-up sigh.

"Look," he said. "I'm not going to push it. I won't take it farther unless you want me to."

A light, warm breeze drifted into the open window of the truck. A light went out across the street as Teddy reached for the door handle.

"Just be my friend for now?" she asked.

"Glad to. If you need help or someone to talk to, call me. You've got my card. I only live a couple miles from here."

"I'll call you soon, Joshua." She opened the door and climbed out. "Thanks for dinner. My treat next time."

Teddy walked to the front door, fumbled with a key, opened the door, and slipped inside with a quick wave. He heard the click of the lock in the still night air.

He eased the truck onto the deserted street.

She'd have to be the one to call.

CHAPTER 12

A mile east of the Garden State Parkway on Route 70, Rosie's big neon sign glowed red and yellow in the heavy night air. In the wee hours of a Tuesday evening, the twenty-four-hour eatery was drowsing with only a few cars in the lot. When Borderline walked in, two tables were occupied.

Borderline sat down in a corner booth. When a young waitress with black braided hair approached, Borderline ordered a Coke and then asked if Lorraine Jones was working tonight.

"Yeah, she's here. Why?"

"Tell her I'm a friend of Edsell's."

Within seconds, Lorraine Jones strode out of the kitchen. Her rumpled uniform sported a large ketchup stain on the breast pocket. Her eyes were rimmed with dark circles; she looked like she was staring out of a pit.

"Howie?" she said. "Howie Fenton?"

Borderline nodded. "Yeah, it's me, only everyone calls me Borderline now."

"Oh, my God. I remember you from the old days when you was at my house all the time. I've seen you here, but you were always with a crowd of kids, and I didn't want to butt in and ask how you were." She looked at him curiously. "They call you Borderline now?"

"Yes, ma'am. I'm helping Mark look for Edsell."

Mrs. Jones flung herself down on the other side of the greasy table and wiped away tears that suddenly sprang from her eyes.

It was hard to begin the conversation. He didn't want her to start crying or pitch some kind of hysterical fit. How would he feel if someone close to him suddenly disappeared? As if she had read his mind, Mrs. Jones continued. "Howie, I don't understand it. Why would Edsell just go away? How can this happen?"

"I don't know, Mrs. Jones. Has Edsell ever gone on a trip before? I mean, do you have relatives out of town? Or maybe ..." Borderline didn't quite know how to say this. He took a deep breath and plunged. "Did you perhaps have a fight?"

Lorraine Jones drew in a deep breath, pulled her shoulders back, and said, "Sunday night, we ate dinner, and he said he was going over to Seaside to see his girlfriend. I left the house at ten thirty to come here. When I got home the next morning, he wasn't there. His room was a mess as usual, but I could tell his bed was never slept in."

Borderline's Coke arrived. Lorraine touched the arm of the waitress.

"Lena? Cover for me. Okay?"

The dark-haired waitress nodded and disappeared through a set of swinging doors.

"Did you call the police?"

"Yeah. Big deal. Toms River is part of Dover Township, and this time of year, with all the beach people, the cops don't have time for nothing. They asked me a bunch of questions, made me fill out some forms and bring in a picture of my boy. They told me to come back Wednesday if he didn't come home. Wednesday, for chrissakes."

"Why Wednesday?" asked Borderline.

"That's when the forty-eight hours is over and the police can officially say he's a missing person. Shit. Edsell's never been gone all night since he went to a sleepover at Mark's house back in sixth grade. Where would he go?"

"Maybe he's staying with friends for a couple of days."

"Without calling? No way. Listen, Borderline, my son may be a little messed up, but he wouldn't just disappear. He wouldn't do that to me."

"Did you talk to his girlfriend?"

"Yeah, Missy's all upset too. She told me they watched some old movies on TV. Edsell left around one o'clock, told her he was going home. She hasn't seen him since. No phone calls. Nothing. It's like he disappeared into the air," she said.

The rest of the conversation produced little that was helpful. As Borderline left Rosie's, he promised to call Mrs. Jones if he heard anything at all about her son.

This rots, he thought as he walked home through the quiet streets of Toms River. *I snuck out of my house to come here at two o'clock in the morning, and I didn't find out anything that I didn't already know.* He kicked an old discarded Coke can down the sidewalk. *But I'm still with Mark all the way. We're going to find out what happened to Edsell. We're going to do whatever it takes. His whacked-out friends aren't going to do anything to help, but we will, by God.*

Maybe Stacey had learned something from Missy.

CHAPTER 13

Edsell was awake, wide awake with an awareness he'd never had before. Every cell in his body was a receiver; every ounce of his body listened, felt, smelled, saw, and tasted.

He lay in a bed, clad only in a pale blue hospital gown. In the long hours since he woke up strapped to a bed in this white room, he had listened intently to the sounds around him, trying to piece together just where he was and why.

A big, ugly dude in a black jumpsuit came in every so many hours and adjusted the tubes and vials that were hooked up to him and the other kid, checked some machines next to each bed that were bleep-bleeping and graphing some kind of information. The same man took each of them one at a time, unstrapped their arms and legs and unhooked the tubes and took them across the hall to a bathroom. After that, they were each made to walk up and down the hallway.

A thin man in a white shirt and tie came in periodically to look at the dials and machines and drip lines in his arms. He never spoke. Only the guy in the black jumpsuit ever said anything, and it wasn't much.

"Exercise," he said to Edsell the first time he got him out of bed. He pointed down the hallway, and Edsell dutifully walked down and back.

"More," said the man. "Keep walking."

Edsell counted two doors on each side of the hallway with a larger door on the end. A staircase at the other end led downstairs, but what was there? More rooms with beds? A kitchen? He'd heard dishes clank and smelled coffee. What was this place?

The tape was kept over his mouth and only removed for feeding purposes.

"Listen, kid," said the man and leaned over Edsell. He spoke in a whisper. "We'll keep the tape on for now. If you behave and do as you're told, I might take the tape off tomorrow and give you the cloth gag like Bradley over there." He smiled a terrible smile. "It's much more comfortable. But I must warn you, if you try anything, the food and water will go away for ..." He hesitated. "A few hours ... maybe even a day or two. You'll get thirsty and hungry while you lay in your own piss and shit. Get my point?"

Lunch was chicken soup and some kind of protein shake. For dinner, they ate a ham sandwich with mac and cheese. Not bad tasting, but not good either. He sensed that nourishment was first and foremost in the minds of his keepers, not taste or enjoyment.

Edsell did as he was told. His mouth was dry, his throat hurt, and he was enormously hungry. His lips and cheeks were raw where the adhesive tape was put on and ripped off every few hours. He wanted to shout and scream every time they took off the tape, but he knew that he needed food and water to survive, and he certainly did not want to be tied to the bed indefinitely.

Whenever he looked at Bradley in the next bed, all he got was a blank stare. There was something going on behind those blue eyes, but it was veiled and frightened.

There were others in the building, he knew. He heard beds creak, heard people shuffling up and down the hallway. There were moans and muffled cries.

Other patients? Other kids tied to beds like him? Why?

He got to know White Shirt's walk because his feet were clad in leather-soled shoes that clicked on the floor in measured steps. Ugly Dude wore black running shoes and moved almost noiselessly around the building.

Periodically, he heard music, piano or violin music from far away. A radio? A record or tape player?

Edsell thought there were pine trees around, because he could smell them and hear the soft swish of wind blowing through pine needles in the distance.

He was somewhere in the Pine Barrens, far from traffic, houses, and people. Occasionally, he heard an airplane, but it was high and far away, just a vapor trail in the sky.

He'd been awake most of the day, and now it was dark outside, had been for several hours.

On Sunday, he'd been running the vacuum cleaner while his mother washed clothes. That night, he'd gone to Missy's house in Seaside. She was a year older than him, lived in a tiny walk-up with a sister named Megan. They both lived in Medford but had summer jobs at the arcade.

He and Megan and Missy had passed around a toke, and then they did a few shots while watching *Beverly Hills Cop* on TV. They'd been so mellow, laughing at the fight scenes, giggling at the crazy antics of Eddie Murphy.

Later, as he stumbled home, that guy from South offered him a ride, and that was the last he remembered until this morning. He must have passed out in the van because everything was blank until he woke up in this bed. He thought he had only been out for a few hours, but who could tell? Maybe it was longer …

His mother must be frantic. His friends would think he'd gone off somewhere for a few days. Missy would worry, but what could she do?

Why were they keeping him here? Would he be here until his eyes went dead like the kid next to him? How long would that take?

Edsell pushed his head back into the pillow and stared at the ceiling. He knew he couldn't cry because his nose would fill up and he'd have trouble breathing.

He urged himself to take deep breaths. *Relax. Breathe. Relax* …
Edsell slept.

CHAPTER 14

Lorraine Jones strode into the Dover Township Police Station wearing her newest uniform. She had starched her apron, polished her white shoes, and her hair was slicked back with bobby pins and hairspray. Her makeup was brief—a little foundation, some blush, and a hint of orange lip gloss. She didn't want to look like some whore.

At the desk, she asked to speak to the person in charge of missing persons.

"That would be Sergeant Robert Polanski," said the desk clerk and reached for a phone. "Let me see if he's available."

"Bob? There's a woman here to see you." Pause. "Okay, I'll ask." The desk clerk turned to Lorraine. "What's the nature of your business?"

"My son. My son, Edsell Jones, is missing for a day and a half, and nothing's being done about it!" She tried to contain herself, but despite her best efforts, she heard her voice rising in both pitch and volume. "I need to know what's being done! I need to know right now!"

The desk clerk turned back to the phone. "Bob? Did you hear that?" She paused. "Okay. I'll send her back."

She pointed down a hallway and said, "Third door on the right."

Lorraine smoothed her hair nervously and walked down the hall. The door was open, and a burly sergeant in a blue uniform sat behind a large, littered desk.

"What's the problem, ma'am?" he asked. "Weren't you in here yesterday? We filed the report and took down the information. I believe I told you we have to wait forty-eight hours before we can put out anything."

"Yes, but I can't wait. There's nothing on TV about Edsell, no flyers or posters around town. You've got to help me find my son."

Lorraine finished her speech with her hands on the sergeant's desk and her face as close to his as she could manage over the piles of books and folders.

The sergeant's small mouth curled down. "Calm down, Mrs. Jones. Like I told you yesterday, by law we must wait forty-eight hours before we file a missing person's report. Do you know why?" He half-stood and leaned forward until his ruddy face was inches from Lorraine's.

"Why?" she asked, trying to control the anger in her voice.

"Because, Mrs. Jones, these kids are not lost. They're at a friend's house, or they went to visit their daddy in Trenton. They hitchhiked to New York for a rock concert." The sergeant paused, pushed his face forward, and raised his eyebrows. "How do you know he's not just hanging out somewhere with his buddies?"

Tears bubbled up in Lorraine's eyes. "Because he's very responsible. He's never done this before," she finished in a whisper.

"Yeah? Responsible?" said the sergeant, picking up a file. "I have it on record that he was picked up at a pot party eight months ago, and then, let's see … in March we found him drinking beer out on one of the docks with a gang of kids. He's how old?"

"Seventeen," said Lorraine.

"And then there was the incident about a stolen item at Macy's Department Store in Ocean County Mall … Need I go on?" The sergeant folded his arms across his wide chest and spoke clearly and firmly.

"Your son is probably just partying somewhere with his friends," he said. "I'm sure he'll be back soon. I'll file the missing person's report first thing tomorrow morning. In the meantime, please let me know if, ahhhh …" He looked down at the folder. "Edsell shows up.

Now, if you'll excuse me, I have work to do. Thank you very much, Mrs. Jones. We'll be in touch."

The sergeant picked up a file folder and opened it. He glanced up and saw Lorraine still standing there.

"Good-bye, Mrs. Jones," he said firmly.

CHAPTER 15

The next morning, Mark got up early. The parking lot was nearly empty when he pulled up to the school and parked under a large oak tree that framed the entrance.

As long as Mark could remember, Edsell had always walked to school. Edsell's house, on the edge of the school district, was a twenty-minute walk away. Mrs. Jones couldn't drive him because she was usually working or sleeping. There was only one car in the Jones family, a beat-up, old, red Pinto with rust spots on the bottom panels. He'd never seen Edsell drive it.

For a change, Edsell had passed all his classes this past semester and was not in summer school.

Mark had seen Edsell walking into the north entrance to the high school dozens of times. He always wore jeans, a rumpled T-shirt, worn sneakers, and his Pittsburgh Steeler cap. Back in the old days, Edsell had been shy and a follower more than a leader of their little gang. Now most kids in the school thought he was a clueless dweeb, a poser who was quiet, smoked an occasional joint, and didn't make any trouble. The burnouts and the deadheads let him hang out with them because he was harmless.

Toms River South was massive. It had an old section with brick walls, high ceilings, and tiny windowpanes. Mark's father had been a student there twenty-five years ago. Since then, a new gym had been added and then a wing of classrooms with an auditorium. Five years ago, more additions were made: classrooms, offices, and a second gym. Toms River South now sprawled over several acres that also contained a football stadium, baseball diamonds, soccer fields, and a track.

As Mark looked at the school, he saw a round figure scurry into a side door near the gym. As far back as he could remember, Mr. Nerf had been a fixture at South. He was always cleaning, mopping, and hovering in the background. Mark wasn't sure he or anyone else knew the janitor's real name anymore, not since someone had laughingly referred to him as Mr. Nerf. The name had stuck.

The lot was filling up now, and a steady stream of students was filing into the front entrance. Time to go.

As he climbed out of the Jeep, he looked up at the bright blue sky. Jeez, it was hot. He couldn't remember the last time it had rained. The drought was impacting his neighborhood lawn-cutting business in a big way. The only ones he still cut had automatic sprinkler systems.

A bell shrilled inside the school. Mark sighed as he braced himself for another morning of algebra.

CHAPTER 16

That afternoon, Mark stood with his feet embedded in wet sand and watched as a ship disappeared over the horizon. The sky was still cloudless. The low rushing sound of the waves and the beat of an old Aerosmith tape mingled pleasantly with the whoops of children playing at the edge of the surf.

Mark inhaled deeply of salt air laced with suntan lotion, pizza, fries, and cotton candy from the boardwalk behind him. He'd been coming to Seaside since he was a little boy. Back then, his mother dragged Edsell and Borderline with them, and he could remember the three of them digging a huge hole, deep enough to stand in, until the lifeguard came over and made them fill it up.

Now he was here with Borderline and Stacey, but where was Edsell?

Mark picked up a broken shell, skipped it into the water, and walked back to the blanket. Since last night, he and Borderline had questioned most of their friends, but no one had any idea of what might have happened to Edsell. Stacey had called Missy, introducing herself as a friend who was trying to find Edsell. The girl had sounded upset and weepy over his disappearance. Missy said they had watched TV, partied a bit, and then Edsell had left to walk home. Another dead end.

Stacey was asleep now, sprawled out on her stomach across half the blanket. Borderline sat on his beach towel watching a large woman chase a shrieking toddler up the beach. Mark whisked sand off the blanket and sat down.

"I'll never get old, I'll never have kids," Borderline said. "Imagine crawling into bed with that heifer." Borderline inclined his head toward the heavyset woman who was now holding the screaming, kicking, little boy in her arms. "You know, Mark, you'll pork out someday like everyone else. All those beautiful muscles that you work so hard to maintain will slowly turn to flab. You'll marry some totally awesome chick who'll have a couple of your kids, and then she'll turn into that."

"No way, jerk," said Mark.

Mark and Borderline kept their voices low while Stacey slept. They talked about classes and teachers and school gossip and their coming senior year. Miss Goldstein was smokin' hot. Mrs. Kraus was nasty. Mr. Betts was a good guy, even though he was a chemistry teacher. Mr. Harrison was a world-class loser.

"The guy is such a poser." Borderline laughed. "It's the freakin' last day of school, and I'm in the back of the class talking to Brenda, and he says, 'If you two don't take a chill pill, I'm going to wig out!' Can you believe it? A chill pill? Wig out? Here's a forty-year-old guy with a receding hairline and fat, round belly trying to sound like one of us."

"Just your basic, generic loser," Mark said. "What's in the cooler? I'm getting thirsty."

Borderline rummaged around in the cooler and found two cans of Coke. He handed one to Mark. "You know who's the strangest one in the whole school?" he asked.

"Dr. Wilkins?"

"Nope. He's just a tight-ass principal, happy to be in his office and not in the trenches, teaching the likes of us. Not Wilkins."

"Mrs. Johnson, the music teacher?" Mark asked in a high, sing-song voice.

"No, not a teacher."

"Not a teacher? ... I know! Mr. Nerf! What's his name, the janitor."

"You got it," Borderline said. "The guy's been at South so long that no one remembers his real name anymore."

"I can't stand the guy, and here's why. When I was a little kid, my mom brought me and two of my younger cousins to the high school for a play, one of those children's theater things," he said. "In the middle of it, I had to take a leak. My mom couldn't leave my cousins alone, so she sent me off by myself."

"So what happened?"

"I got lost. Some lady took me to the bathroom, but when I came out, she was gone. There was no one around, and I was in a hallway that looked like it was two miles long. The classrooms were dark, and I imagined there were blood-sucking monsters behind those black, empty windows in each door. I walked down the exact center of the hall, my new shoes making this awful clacking sound. Then, all at once, this big shadow fell across the floor in front of me, and a high-pitched, whispery voice said, 'Are you lost, young man?'"

"Nerf?"

"Yeah. He was standing over me with his moon face and those beady, black eyes. I should have been glad to see him, but when I looked up into those dark marbles, I was more scared of him than of all the three-toed, hunch-backed, drooling ghouls hiding in the empty classrooms."

"What'd you do?"

"I yelled and ran back down the hall as fast as I could," Mark said. "When I got to the end, I saw lights and people. The play was just letting out. My mom was pissed because she thought I'd been messing around somewhere."

"But Nerf didn't do anything. What made you so scared?"

"He laughed."

"He laughed? That freaked you out?"

"Yeah. Because when I started crying, he started laughing, and that soft, wheezy laughter followed me all the way down the hall. I knew in a heartbeat that this guy would tear the wings off butterflies or stomp a baby mouse for the fun of it."

Mark sipped his Coke. "Why made you mention Nerf?"

"I heard him say something strange today, and I didn't want to mention it while Stacey was awake."

"What'd he say?" Mark asked.

"I walked past Nerf's office this morning just as the phone rang, so I stopped and listened." Borderline lowered his voice. "Nerf said something about a kid who would never be missed."

Mark sat up and stared at Borderline.

"C'mon, is this one of your tricks? Like the bucket of caterpillars in the girls' locker room? Like the Party Naked on the scoreboard at homecoming last year? Like—"

"No, absolutely not," Borderline interrupted. "It was real strange. Nerf said, 'Summer school's full of them now. We've got losers here from all over the county. Trust me. I was very careful to out check this kid. No one's going to miss him.' Those were his exact words. I swear it."

Mark sat quietly and looked at the surf. The tide was coming in. The waves were getting higher and closer. They'd have to move their blanket soon. He turned and squinted at Borderline.

"What do you think we should do?" he asked.

"I don't know." Borderline slowly crushed the empty Coke can. "But it gave me the creeps, and it made me think of Edsell and the other messed-up kids at school, guys like CM and Wooley and the rest. If one of them disappeared, who would notice? Who would care? Most of them are fighting with their parents, they're suspended from school half the time, smoking, drinking, doing other stuff. What if one of them disappeared?"

Borderline leaned forward, picked up a shell from the sand, and threw it into the waves. He looked at Mark and continued.

"Their families would make some noise, but you and I know that you can't really find a kid if he wants to get lost, not here on the Jersey Shore. Maybe the parents are tired and bummed out. They could even be on drugs or booze too. They might be glad the kid's gone. No more money disappearing from the old man's wallet, no more midnight calls from the cops, no more visits to the principal's office ..." Borderline sat up and leaned toward Mark. His voice was barely audible over the increasing roar of the surf. "What if a burnout disappeared, and instead of him running away like everybody thinks, someone takes him?"

A cold splatter of spray hit Mark in the face. "But why would anyone take a kid? Why would anyone want Edsell, for God's sake?"

"I don't know," Borderline said, "but I got a bad feeling when I listened to Nerf today."

"We can't do anything." Mark ran his hand through his hair. "I mean, like what could we do? You heard half a phone conversation from a guy who's been working at the school for years."

"Well, I'm going to keep an eye on old Nerfie." Borderline looked out to sea. "I'm going out to Frenchy's Bar to talk to CM and his crew."

"Why?"

"Listen, we've talked to everyone we know, and we got nothing. You and I talked to Edsell's friends, Stacey talked with Missy—nothing. I know CM pretty well. He's probably Edsell's closest friend these days. He comes over to Federici's once in a while and talks to me about cars and stuff. I'm going over to Seaside to talk to him and his buddies. Maybe they know something we don't."

CHAPTER 17

The rising tide was nearly up to their blanket. Mark looked at the water level, turned to glance at Stacey, and then winked at Borderline.

"Uh-huh." Borderline responded, grinning back wolfishly, the golf stud in his ear gleaming in the sunlight. Mark got up quietly and began to gather their towels and beach bags, moving them back toward the boardwalk.

Mark noticed that most of the other sun worshippers had moved their blankets, umbrellas, beach chairs, and coolers out of the way of the rising tide. Only the blue blanket with the long, lithe body in the tiny, white bikini remained, a peninsula of humanity jutting out into the churning sea on a slightly higher sandbar.

Several people were watching.

"You're not going to leave her there, are you?" asked a woman who was holding a baby.

"Yep," he said to the woman. He turned to Borderline and whispered, "She'll get us, but it'll be worth it."

"God, will she get us," Borderline moaned.

Seconds later, a wave began to form several hundred yards out to sea. It rose and then fell, gathering speed but still not breaking. Smaller shoreline swells retreated to join the big mother that was gathering for an assault on the beach. A hundred yards away, it began to crest and murmur. White foam formed at the cascading top of the giant wave as it raced toward them. The crowd stepped back quickly, gathering small children in their arms.

Suddenly a woman screamed, "Look out! The wave!"

Stacey lifted her head. Even from a distance, Mark could see the sleep lines on the side of her face and the bewildered look in her eyes as she tried to figure out where she was, who was yelling, and why.

In the next instant, she knew.

The wave crashed in on Stacey, covering both her and the blanket. For a moment, all that Mark could see was a bikini-covered butt.

When the wave finally receded, Stacey was several yards down the beach, covered with sand and bits of seaweed. From under her wet, snarled hair, two eyes blazed.

"I'll kill you both. You dipsticks. You turds!"

Stacey started toward Mark with a measured pace. He backed up, hands in front of him, palms upward.

"Now, Stacey, it was just a joke."

Stacey circled silently, never taking her eyes from his face. Out of the corner of his eye, Mark was aware of Borderline, gliding away to a safe distance.

The crowd that had watched the wave inundate Stacey now began to encourage her.

"Yeah, Stacey. Get him!" someone in the crowd shouted.

"C'mon, doll. You can do it!" someone else yelled. As Stacey and Mark circled each other, there was a subtle movement toward the water. Stacey pushed that way, and the crowd moved with her.

They were almost at the water's edge, Mark within Stacey's reach.

The heavyset woman with the toddler had followed the crowd. She stood near the edge of the water, a small smile twitching the corners of her mouth. As Mark stepped by, the woman thrust out her foot, and he went down in a heap, rolling down the sandy slope toward the crashing waves.

In an instant, Stacey was on him, pulling and rolling him farther into the surf. Another huge wave crashed, and the two disappeared.

Mark knew he was lost. Stacey was a strong swimmer, and furthermore, Mark didn't want to hurt her. He could tell that Stacey, on the other hand, wanted desperately to maim him in any way possible. It was an uneven fight from the start, and Mark knew it as she held him under the waves.

He came up gagging and coughing.

"Up, up! I give up!"

She pushed him under one more time and then turned and started back to shore. As Stacey emerged from the waves and walked up to dry sand, the crowd roared its approval.

She grabbed her wet blanket and beach bag and then marched off, casting a catlike grin at Borderline. As she disappeared down the boardwalk, Mark realized they had all come in Stacey's car.

Their wallets, clothes, and shoes were locked in the trunk.

CHAPTER 18

H e sat alone at his desk, a man no one would notice in a crowd because he was, thankfully, short, round, and nondescript. A blessing in his present situation.

His name was Wilbur Nelson, but he knew the kids called him Mr. Nerf. He knew the students at South thought he was a loser and a jerk and a nerd, and that did not bother him one teensy little bit.

He'd heard it all and seen it all in twenty-two years of sweeping hallways, emptying waste baskets, and cleaning up vomit. He had done his job so well, so unobtrusively, and for so long that he had become one with the walls, the doors, and the paint on the ceiling.

He was the invisible man.

And oh, the invisible man was everywhere. He listened and watched. He knew when the pretty, blonde cheerleader got knocked up and her boyfriend hustled his friends for the money to take care of it. He knew that the center on the basketball team had lured a little freshman girl under the bleachers in the football stadium one night last fall. He heard his teammates talking about it in the locker room, and later, he found the exact spot, the grass all mashed down and bloody.

At night, the invisible man opened lockers and explored all the secret stashes: vodka, cigarettes and joints, condoms, pills, powders, and magazines that were sold behind the counters of convenience stores.

Nerf scratched himself and stretched out his legs. The shitola would sure hit the fan if he told what he knew.

Oh, the kids were young and smart-alecky and tough. They thought they owned the world, but the invisible man knew better.

Nerf opened the top drawer of his desk and took out a small mirror. He held it to his face and scrutinized the small lines around his eyes. They *were* getting smaller, less noticeable.

In the back of his mind had always lurked the terrible question, the question every man asked as he passed the big five-o. What if he got old before he really had a chance to enjoy himself?

The ugliness and inevitability of aging frightened him: losing things, losing control of his bodily functions, losing control of his mind. He didn't want to forget what day it was, where his reading glasses were, what his prick was for. He didn't want old, droopy-breasted, slack-jawed Mother Nature to force him into a hideous, foul-smelling corner. He didn't want her to grab him by the throat and slowly suck out his life.

Nerf picked at a hangnail and grunted with satisfaction. Things had surely changed in his life in the last two years.

The speaker on his desk clicked and then hummed. Mrs. Epstein's high-shrill voice came on.

"Sorry to bother you, Mr. Nelson, but one of the students just upchucked in the hall outside the cafeteria."

"I'll be right there, Mrs. Epstein."

Invisible man rides again, Nerf thought as he opened the closet door and took out a mop and bucket. Only a few more years, and he'd fly this cement block chicken coop. He'd lie on a pink coral beach somewhere in the Caribbean with a cold margarita in one hand and the sweet tit of a willing native girl in the other.

In that warm tropical sunshine, old Nerfie would remember this day and drink a toast to all the losers, geeks, and nerds of the world.

CHAPTER 19

The third day of his captivity passed slowly for Edsell. He'd been up twice to walk the hallway, to eat nondescript food, and to drink water. His arms were beginning to chafe at the insides of his elbows where the IVs ran into both arms. The tape had been replaced by a cloth gag, but his mouth still hurt. Even worse, his legs were more wobbly each time Ugly Guy got him out of the bed. Could he even run if he had the chance?

Because of his mother's work and sleep schedule, he had always walked everywhere. No family station wagon or sedan dropped him off at school. Edsell Jones walked to school, to the stores, to his friends' houses. His legs were strong, but now they were beginning to fail him.

More worrisome was the kid in the bed next to him. He'd obviously been here a long time and could barely walk anymore. Ugly Guy half-pulled, half-pushed him back and forth, threatening him with no food or water in a low voice. The kid's face was pale, and his big eyes were moist and sad, beyond hope.

Every command, every statement made by Ugly Dude was spoken in a barely audible whisper. This morning, when he was eating his oatmeal, Edsell had started to say something out loud and was immediately tied down flat in the bed, hooked up to the tubes. He was left hungry and thirsty and needing to piss for a very long time.

He had learned not to say anything in the first day of his captivity, but this morning, he couldn't help himself, and now he was sorry he'd lost his cool.

Jagged thoughts blew through his mind. Did anyone besides his mother know he was gone? Did anyone care? Had she called the police? His mother was probably hysterical, but no one would listen to her, especially after that incident at Macy's. And besides his mother, who gave a shit? He had no brothers or sisters, no father.

Would the dirtbags he hung around with notice that he was gone? And if they did, what could they do? They probably thought he had hitchhiked to Atlantic City. He had talked about doing it a couple of times.

Missy was worried, he was sure of that, but what could she do? She couldn't miss work. Her parents lived in Medford ... He shouldn't have done those shots. That's what messed him up.

There was no one to help, no one to save him.

Why was he being kept in this bed? What were the tubes in his arms? Something was being put into his system, and that totally grossed him out. What was it? He kept thinking that they needed him for something. He was being kept alive for some reason because if they wanted to kill him, they would already have done it.

No matter what happened, he wasn't going to lose hope like the kid next to him. He would listen and observe everything around him.

Maybe he could find a way out.

CHAPTER 20

After a long, hot shower, Teddy stood in front of her mirror and drew a deep, cleansing breath. She wore a white cotton bra and white cotton panties, and she liked what she saw: a woman who was fit, tanned, and attractive.

Last winter, before she received notification that her grant for the Pine Barrens Study had been approved, she'd been strangely depressed and restless. After years of classes and lab work sandwiched around a heavy teaching schedule, she was finally a thesis away from becoming Dr. Theodora Constantinos, Professor of Botany at Rutgers University. It was a dream she had had for most of her life, but now that the precious doctorate was within her grasp, the excitement was gone.

One night, she and her sister, Angela, went out to dinner. Feeling oddly vulnerable, she mentioned her strange malaise to Angela. Her sister shook her head and said, "You don't know why you feel crummy? Teddy, you sacrificed everything for this day. You did without fun and friends and men for years to get your PhD."

"But ..." Teddy protested.

"Yeah, yeah, I know it was what you wanted, but you gave up so much to get it." Angela smiled. "Speaking of men, when was the last time you had a serious relationship with a male human being?"

"Last year," Teddy said defensively. "With Ken."

"Get real," Angela said. "You dated him for two months and were bored to tears. You ditched him like a plate of fuzzy leftovers from the back of your refrigerator."

Teddy giggled. "You're right, Angela. I guess it's time for me to relax and have some fun. I promise that if I get the grant, I'll spend time at the beach and come to Philly to visit you. Hey, maybe we can both take a weekend off and drive up to New York, see a play …"

"Meet some men," Angela said. "Count me in."

Teddy's somber mood faded on her first day of field work when she stood in a tiny, sun-streaked clearing and felt the silent pine forest around her. She was technically curious then and eager to explore the strange, pristine wilderness of the Pine Barrens. She'd worry about meeting a man later. Right now, the forest called her.

During the first few weeks, Teddy roamed the Pinelands. She took notes, observed the flora and fauna, visited state parks and historic villages, and walked the old trails. In the evenings, she studied maps, technical books, and journals and then peppered her reading with old diaries, collections of folktales, and legends. She reread John McFee's classic, *The Pine Barrens*, for the third time.

Her joys were simple: watching deer graze along the old, abandoned Tuckerton Railroad, seeing a fox and her kit run across a narrow, sandy trial. On one special afternoon, Teddy sat on the bank of a clear Barrens lake while four white tundra swans floated like mirrored clouds upon the still water.

Teddy sighed contentedly at the memory and looked closely at her reflected face in the mirror. The tenseness around her mouth was gone. Her complexion was clear and tanned. Her brown eyes looked back with a steady, peaceful gaze.

She pulled the towel off her head and vigorously pummeled her long, thick hair and then ran a wide-bristled brush through it. When it was pulled and twisted into a loose knot on top of her head, she put on clean blue jeans and gathered a pale yellow, sleeveless cotton shirt in a loose knot at her waist.

It felt wonderful to be rid of the day's sweat and grime. The plants she catalogued today had been in a difficult location, and she had spent hours crawling through thick underbrush that was swarming with green flies. As she slipped on her sandals, Teddy decided to drive to Barnegat for an early dinner. Afterward she would walk on the sand at the edge of the sea and watch gulls cross the twilight sky.

As she opened the front door, she almost fell into the waiting arms of Joshua Reed, who was just extending his hand to knock on the door.

"Joshua. How nice to see you!" Teddy exclaimed.

"I want to apologize," Joshua said, rubbing the back of his neck. His shirt was wet with streaks of sweat, and the stubble on his face held particles of sawdust. He smelled of sweat and freshly cut wood.

Not an entirely bad scent, Teddy thought. "Apologize? For what?" she asked.

"I've been meaning to call you but wanted to wait until we finally finished the house. The owner wanted some changes at the last minute and promised me a bonus if I got it done in time, so it's taking longer than expected."

"You don't have to apologize, Joshua. I've been trekking all over the Barrens, cataloging plants, taking slides, and gathering live specimens for the lab. I've been gone from dawn to dusk too."

"Do you ever take a break?" Joshua asked.

"Not right now. I'm in the middle of some very important work. In fact, I'm going to be out in the Barrens all weekend. Why?"

"We're filing for the CO on Friday. There's some landscaping to finish up—sprinklers, mulch, shrubs, sidewalks. We should be done soon, and I'll be ready to celebrate. How about coming over to my place for dinner Friday night?" He hesitated and then forged ahead. "Come on, Teddy. I'll pick up some steaks, and we can just kick back and relax for a few hours. I'll even cook the dinner."

He assumed I'd be available, Teddy thought, flushed with annoyance. Then, as she looked into the clear, guileless, blue eyes of Joshua Reed, the tiny spark of anger faded. *That's just the way he is, spontaneous and ready for fun.*

What the heck, she thought. *So am I.*

"I'd like that," she said. "Unless you're cooking hog jowls or tripe or some other Pine Barrens specialty."

"I'll get two T-bones and some baking potatoes." He glanced at his watch. "I've got to go meet one of my guys at the irrigation place in twenty minutes. Six thirty on Friday. Does that work?"

"I'll be there. But wait, where do you live?" Teddy called.

Now it was Joshua's turn to flush. "Go out Route 72 and turn onto Old Mill Road. Look for a sign that says Reed about a mile in and take the left-hand fork. It's straight ahead about a mile from there."

"Got it. I'll be there. Can I bring anything?"

"No, just yourself."

CHAPTER 21

For two days, Borderline kept an eye on Nerf's office. He passed by as often as he could and hoped no one would notice.

Nerf arrived each morning at eight thirty and went directly to his tiny office near the gym. Borderline caught glimpses of him writing at his desk and talking on the phone. Later in the morning, Nerf patrolled the corridors and classrooms of the massive school and mopped up spills, emptied wastebaskets, and dusted windowsills. As head of maintenance at South, he performed only light daytime work and handled administrative details. The rest of his crew came in late in the afternoon when the kids were gone. They waxed floors, scrubbed bathrooms, and performed minor repairs that were best done when the school was empty of students.

At noon, Nerf locked his office, climbed into his blue van, and drove away. There was nothing unusual in his behavior.

Borderline worked late on Thursday night, detailing a car for a new customer who needed it in the morning. When he was done, he drove to Seaside. He knew that CM's group was probably drinking at Frenchy's, cruising the boardwalk, or smoking out on the dark, misty beach.

The wild crowd was the most democratic clique at the school, Borderline mused as he locked the Challenger. No one cared what your daddy did for a living or where you lived. You only needed attitude, in-your-face attitude, and a willingness to try risky things.

Borderline thought of Reggie and CM, of Charles and T. Rex and the girls that hung out with them. They scorned honors assemblies, team sports, student government, and school-sponsored clubs. They loathed Top 40 pop and disco, Gap and J. Crew clothes, and all other school cliques. Some kids were pierced, others were tattooed. They had long hair, short hair, orange and pink hair, beards, crew cuts, and shaved heads. Everyone's style was his own. Drugs and booze were a big part of it, but there were posers in the group who didn't party at all, and that was acceptable too, as long as they kept their mouths shut about everyone else.

When Borderline reached the boardwalk, he scanned the crowd that eddied around him. Nine o'clock was cruising time at the Jersey Shore. The senior citizens had eaten their early-bird specials hours ago and retreated to their age-specific ghettos. The kiddie rides were mostly dark. The long stretch of sandy beach rustled with black water and low, white, lacey breakers.

It was time for the young and the wannabe young.

Lights from the rides flashed in the night mist. Screams emanated regularly from the Swiss Bob, the Pirate Ship, and the Enterprise. The tiny cars of the haunted house clanked their passengers past graveyards and ghosts even as the target range exploded in a war between paying customers and moving, two-dimensional jungle beasts.

Hawkers called out on every side.

"Come here and spin the wheel, kid. Try your luck and win a stuffed animal, a beach towel, a carton of smokes. Come on, kid, you got a buck, don't cha?"

Borderline shook his head and walked on through the crush of people until he heard a heavy rock beat. He stepped into Frenchy's and waited a few moments for his eyes to catch up with the rest of his senses. When he could see, he pushed through the crowd until he found Wooley and Alex, two of CM's friends, in a booth near the back door.

"Where's CM?" he shouted above the music.

"Dunno," Wooley said, speaking in a lisp because of a new stud at the end of his tongue.

"Was he here?"

"He's out looking for someone. Can't remember … aw … yeah … the kid with the funny name. Eddie, no … Edsell. The jerk's been gone for days, and his crazy mother's blaming us. She's calling CM's house all day long. His dad got so pissed off he turned off the phone." Wooley shrugged his shoulders. "We don't know where the little fuck is, so everyone needs to bug off and leave us alone."

"Thanks, man," said Borderline. He turned and walked out the back door. The damp sea air hit him in the face with a cold slap as he slipped around a dumpster and down the back alley to his car.

Four days had passed, and still there was no sign of Edsell. Where was the little goober? Staying with friends? Partying and losing his sense of time? Had he taken too much of something? Was he still alive?

Borderline shivered as he remembered Nerf's raspy voice saying, "Trust me, no one's going to care about this one."

Borderline turned the ignition key. The 383 hemi-engine roared to life.

CHAPTER 22

orraine Jones sat on a worn plaid couch in the living room and stared at the television. Afternoon sunlight poured through the filmy picture window and across an ashtray on the coffee table that was filled with half-smoked butts. Next to it, the remains of an Italian sub lay on its greasy wrapper and leached the scent of salami and onions into the air.

On the TV screen, a beautiful blonde woman in a sleek, red dress slowly and deliberately put her arms around the neck of a dark-haired, handsome man. She smiled up at him with her perfect teeth and nipped at his ear.

After weeks of suspense-filled maneuvering and intrigue on her favorite soap, Randy and Serena were finally getting together, and Lorraine didn't give a shit.

She flicked off the television, got up, and walked into the kitchen. She opened the door of the cabinet over the sink and stared at the bottle for several minutes. Her trembling hands clenched into hard fists, and her arms stiffened at her side.

"No, I can't," she whispered and pushed the door shut.

There was no way she could take a drink now. What if the police called with information about her son? What if Edsell showed up on her doorstep or called from some nearby town asking her to pick him up? She could not be out of it for even one minute.

She'd told Lena about Edsell disappearing on the first day he was gone, and now, each time she showed up at Rosie's, her old friend grabbed her arm and whispered, "Any news yet?" Each time Lorraine saw Lena's worried face, it increased her own anxiety, so she was never away from the situation. She should have kept it all to herself. What was Lena going to do? The woman had four kids of her own and a disabled husband to care for.

Lorraine walked back into the living room. There were perspiration marks on the couch where she had been sitting. No surprise there. She'd been having hot flashes for the past three days. Menopause? Lack of booze? Nerves? Something was making her sweat like a pig.

She picked up a pink and white crocheted blanket from the recliner, placed it across the couch, sat down, and lit another cigarette. The flame of the lighter danced in her hand, and she peered at it as if it could answer her questions.

Edsell had been gone for five days now. She'd been at work each day. The police and the kids knew she could be reached at Rosie's, so she felt safe when she was at work. She had to keep busy, to go through her normal routine while inside, her life fell apart. As long as she was taking orders and hurrying from table to table in her soft, laced-up white shoes, she wasn't shaking.

Thank God it was summer, and the diner was hopping.

She hadn't even picked up groceries, just a carton of cigarettes from ShopRite. The milk in the refrigerator was curdled, she was out of bread and cereal, but she couldn't bring herself to go to the grocery store for fear she'd miss a phone call.

Dozens of scenes played through her mind. Edsell walking on one of the piers, stumbling, and falling into the bay. Edsell swimming in the ocean at night, a sudden sucking riptide, a white arm flailing above the waves. Edsell walking home, an eighteen-wheeler approaching, the sound of screeching tires.

Edsell's body in a ditch.

His body drifting across the cold ocean floor.

Tears welled again in Lorraine's eyes. *Bring him back, sweet Jesus. He's all I got. I'll never drink again. I'll be good, I promise.*

I'll go to church every Sunday, never lie, never have sex again, pay my bills on time. I'll work in the fuckin' soup kitchen, take in stray cats and dogs, whatever it takes ...

She sat and rocked back and forth, humming a tune she remembered from Sunday school a hundred years ago.

"Jesus loves me, this I know ..."

CHAPTER 23

M ark was pulling on a clean pair of khakis for dinner at Nonna's house when the phone rang. On the third ring, he grabbed the receiver.

"Yeah?" he snapped.

"I got an idea, Mark," Borderline said. "There's something we can do about Edsell."

"What?"

"Come over now. My parents went out for dinner. We can talk."

Mark looked at the clock on the nightstand: 4:55. He couldn't bag dinner with Nonna. She had probably cooked all day, and she would surely be suspicious if he didn't show up. Nonna was smart, and if she thought something suspicious was going on, she might even call his father in Myrtle Beach.

That would not be good.

"Come on, Mark. We need to talk," Borderline pleaded. "I think we should follow Nerf."

"What? You're out of your gourd." Mark paused. "Look, I need to have dinner with Nonna Adelina. Gimme an hour."

He'd make up something about having to help his friend with summer school homework. If there was anything that Nonna and the older Germanos prized, it was education. School and grades were important.

"You good boy, you go helpa your friend," Nonna said and pinched his cheek when he told her he had to leave to help a friend with his homework. "God bless you, Markus. That's how you move up in this world."

CHAPTER 24

At 6:20 p.m. Teddy got into her white Bronco and drove out of Chatsworth. The directions were easy, and she quickly found the small wooden sign. An arrow at the bottom of the old painted board pointed down a winding, narrow dirt road that curved into pines and scrub oaks.

Pinus Rigida and Quercus Ilicifolia, Teddy thought, cataloging plants automatically as she drove.

Soon she saw black water on her right. Probably the site of an abandoned mill or cranberry farm, she mused as she drove carefully on the narrow road. She knew that despite a natural appearance, many Pinelands lakes were flat on one end where earthen dams had been built by early settlers.

Clumps of red chokeberry bushes with clusters of tiny, green berries that would turn bright red in the fall dotted the swamp with color. A sweet pepperbush with dark green, pointed leaves grew next to a large swamp azalea that was covered with fragrant pink blossoms. In the late afternoon sun, dozens of honeybees buzzed around it in a halo of moving light.

A spotted turtle ambled across the rutted road. Teddy gently braked to a stop and waited. *This is a Barrens traffic jam*, she thought. *Not like Philly at this time on a Friday night, that's for sure.*

Life was all around her, small, quiet, and tenacious. The plants and animals here in the Barrens had all adapted perfectly to poor soil, black bogs, and acidic, iron-rich water.

She put the truck into first gear and glanced at her watch. Almost six thirty. Teddy wondered what the evening would bring. After their initial dinner, she had seen Joshua's truck a couple of times around town.

On Thursday morning, she had asked Alice Marshall, her neighbor, about Joshua. Alice was a small, bird-like woman, a real Piney who had lived in Chatsworth her entire life, married a local, raised a bunch of kids, and now was living out her years as a well-respected widow who loved both coffee and gossip. Teddy had indulged her passion several times and had been impressed with the woman's down-home intellect and knowledge. She knew everyone in that section of the Barrens.

"Joshua Reed? Nice young man," Alice said. "Got a good business. Surprised he ain't found someone yet, but then he's particular. He was dating a pretty girl from Jackson Mills for a while, but nothing came of it. Like I said, Joshua's real picky." Alice paused and narrowed her eyes. "Why do you ask?"

Teddy shrugged. "Just wondering. He's seems really nice."

"Well, he's a stubborn, old Piney, born and raised in the Barrens. His daddy and his granddaddy lived in that cabin of his. Great-granddaddy, too. His ma raised them kids all by herself when Josh's pa died. A couple of years ago, his ma sold the cabin to Joshua and moved on over to Waretown to be near the grandkids. Joshua's sister lives there, has two of the sweetest little girls you ever saw."

Alice peered at Teddy. "I hear Joshua's fixed up the cabin right nice. Added a room or two, put in new plumbing. Real shame he don't have a wife and kids."

As the sandy track curled upward into a low hill, Teddy saw the house. It belonged in the pinewoods. Grey cedar shakes blended into and became part of the surrounding pine forest. The front was nearly all windows with a small porch at one end and a big stone chimney at the other. No lawn and no plantings or flower beds, just white sand and clumps of sedge grass and switch grass and mats of pine needles.

Joshua's big, black truck was parked in front.

As she climbed out of the Bronco, the front door opened, and Joshua walked out in his bare feet.

"Right on time again. I do so admire punctual women."

"Nice place," Teddy said.

Joshua smiled and gestured around him. "I grew up here. Matter of fact, I was born in the same bed I sleep in today."

"This was your parents' house?"

"Yep, and my grandpa's before him."

"My, you do have Piney roots, Joshua."

"Proud of it," Joshua said with a shrug. "Come on in. I'll show you around."

Teddy noticed the doorway was high and Joshua did not have to duck to enter. Perhaps all the Reeds were tall.

The room she walked into was unlike any she had seen before. The ceiling was high with heavy beams and two large, brass ceiling fans. The top half of the front wall was mostly windows, as was the back of the room. The bottom half was paneled in knotty pine. On one side sat a large trestle table with two long benches and two captain's chairs. To the rear was a kitchen area with cabinets of the same knotty pine. At the other end, a deep, overstuffed, burgundy couch and a heavy oak rocker faced a massive stone fireplace.

The late-afternoon sunlight made everything golden. Shafts of sunlight fell on a large deer head that hung over the fireplace. Teddy walked over and counted fourteen points.

"Yours?"

"My dad's. He shot that buck with a recurve bow. Dropped him at fifty paces." Joshua shrugged. "My dad died when I was just a kid."

"I'm sorry."

"Me too, but he lived long enough to teach me to love the woods. We'd go out at night before he got sick just to see how quietly we could move through the trees. It's good practice."

"Why?"

"A bow's not like a rifle or even a shotgun. A bow hunter's got to get close in ..." Joshua paused. "Hey, I'm not talking about hunting anymore today. You were kind enough to listen to my stories at Enzio's. Tonight is going to be different."

The air between them suddenly filled with silence. Teddy turned and walked slowly around the room. Joshua's cabin was all-purpose, plain, and utilitarian, yet it was rich and harmonious with its wood grains and deep green and red plaid cushions.

"Your home is beautiful," Teddy said.

"Thanks. It's comfortable. The house stays cool because the west wind flows across the room. With the windows open on three sides, all I need are ceiling fans; I hardly ever use the air. When it gets really hot, I sleep right there on the couch under the fan. It's the coolest spot in the house."

Teddy interrupted her inspection of the cabin to stop at a stained, yellow shirt and equally discolored yellow helmet that hung on a large hook near the kitchen door. She touched the sleeve. The fabric was heavy and course. She leaned forward and sniffed.

"Fire retardant?"

Joshua nodded.

Teddy turned the shirt and saw an insignia on the right sleeve. It was a yellow shield ringed in green with a green tree in the middle. Division of Parks and Forestry.

"You're a firefighter? For the Forestry Service?"

"It's called the Forest Fire Service. I'm way down the list to be called right now because most of my construction jobs are too far away. I can't get back here in time. They don't call me unless it's a really big one."

"Why do you do it? Isn't it dangerous?"

He shrugged. "Fires are part of the Barrens, Teddy. You know that from your research. Wildfire is in the Piney blood. My dad was a firefighter. He was made section warden the year before he died. My friend Tony is a district fire warden now. He's got his own brush truck. If there's a fire and I can get to it, I ride with Tony."

"Good Lord, Joshua. You are a multitalented man. Next you're going to tell me that you run marathons and play the violin."

Joshua burst out laughing. "No, but I'm a helluva good cook, as you're about to discover." Joshua looked at her intently. "If I don't start soon, you'll never know how really good I am."

Teddy broke his gaze and turned to the kitchen area. Joshua had already prepared most of the simple dinner. Two well-trimmed steaks waited on a white platter. A wooden bowl held a green salad, and biscuits peeked out from a cloth-covered basket. Teddy touched the biscuits. They were still warm.

"You made these?"

"Dill biscuits. Old family recipe."

"Can I help with anything?"

"I'm just about finished except for grilling the steaks and the onions." Joshua opened the refrigerator. "Would you like a glass of wine or a beer? I've got iced tea also."

"A cold beer would be wonderful," Teddy said. "Here, let me set the table. It's the least I can do."

An hour later, Teddy and Joshua were settled comfortably into the overstuffed couch. They had devoured the steaks and salad and buttery dill biscuits while they talked and laughed and traded stories of their childhoods. The tales were different yet linked with common threads of family and friends.

Teddy told Joshua about the night she ran away from home. She'd had a huge argument with her mom and snuck down the fire escape to her Uncle Joe's deli two streets over. He made her a pastrami on rye, and while she ate it, he listened to her tale of parental oppression. When the sandwich was finished, he respectfully talked her into going back home.

Later, when her mother came in to kiss her goodnight, the pastrami on her breath was a dead giveaway.

Joshua countered with stories of how he and his friends had ridden wildly through abandoned sand and gravel pits on their mini-bikes, raising trails of dust as they performed daredevil tricks on a track they had made of mounds of sand and old wooden doors and planks.

"We all wanted to be Hollywood stunt men when we grew up. When I think of some of the stuff we pulled, it's a miracle any of us survived in one piece."

They sat peacefully on the couch, each lost in thought. The light from the setting sun streamed horizontally across the room and made everything golden. From outside came a patter of strange "pa-tunk" noises.

"What's that noise?" asked Teddy. "It sounds like someone hitting a nail."

"That's a carpenter frog," said Joshua. "My dad used to tell me they made furniture for the elves and the fairies that live in the swamp. I believed him."

Joshua turned to face Teddy. His strong face was half-shadowed in the late evening sunlight, his eyes hidden under heavy brows. Teddy suddenly felt a need to touch him to see if he was real. She wanted to see how he felt under her hands. He was different from other men she had dated. Taller, stronger, tougher.

In silence, Teddy slowly reached forward with both hands until the tips of her fingers rested lightly against the sides of Joshua's face. He twitched as her hands touched him.

Teddy turned his head to the light until she could see his eyes. The pupils were large and surrounded by irises of brown flecked with gold. His lashes were long and dark.

They looked at each other for a long time until Joshua cleared his throat and spoke in a soft, husky whisper.

"I told you before that I won't do anything you don't want me to, and I still mean it."

Teddy dropped her hands and grinned at him, the small crinkles around her eyes illuminating and magnifying her smile.

The silence stretched out again, and she inhaled slowly. *I've got to make the first move*, she thought. *It's going to be my choice as to how far this will go.*

Teddy exhaled and then slowly leaned toward Joshua. A hint of a smile crossed his face, and the last thing she saw as their lips came together was the outline of pine trees against the darkening sky.

CHAPTER 25

Edsell's eyes snapped open. Footsteps in the hall. It was dark in the room with only the faint outline of moonlight at the rim of the window shade.

The door opened silently, and two dark figures entered, visible by the light from the hallway. Edsell closed his eyes, pretending to be asleep. They walked over to Brandon. He heard rustles and the clink of metal.

"This one's ready," someone whispered. "It's been two weeks."

Edsell slitted his eyes and peered through the darkness. He could see the bulk of Ugly Guy and a smaller, thinner figure wearing pale blue surgical drapes. The smaller figure disconnected the IVs. Ugly Guy removed the cloth ties that held the boy to the bed. The blip-blip of the machines on that side of the room suddenly stopped.

What was going on? Was the kid being released? Had they been treating him for some illness or an addiction? Was Brandon going home?

They raised the boy up onto his feet between them, and then the three figures shuffled out the door, closing it with a solid click behind them.

Their footsteps receded down the hall. Edsell heard thumps at the far end as they went down the stairs. A door closed downstairs, and then silence.

What was that all about? What did they mean when they said the kid was ready? That it had been two weeks?

Hours or minutes later, a door slammed, and an engine roared to life. Probably the same blue van that had brought him here. He'd heard it before in the past several days.

Were they taking the kid somewhere?

In all the silent hours that Edsell had been hostage in the same room, he had never been able to get a response, not even a facial twitch from Brandon. Just the same blank, sad stare.

And now Brandon was gone, and all he'd ever known was his name. Edsell stared at the outline of the empty bed next to him.

Edsell could no longer remember just how long he had been lying there. The days blended together into one awful haze of helplessness.

But why was he here? He didn't have any noticeable injuries, no places that hurt except where the IVs were.

It was all so troubling, so weird. Now his roommate was gone.

Where had they taken him?

CHAPTER 26

The weekend passed quickly. Mark knew that Borderline had to work at Federici's on Saturday. On Sunday morning, his friend usually went to church with his parents. This Sunday, the family was driving up to Middletown to take Borderline's Aunt Emily out for her seventieth birthday.

Mark worked out at the gym on Saturday morning and cut lawns on Saturday afternoon. One of his customers asked if he could trim the hedges too, so he didn't get home until late. On Sunday, he took Nonna to Mass at St. Joseph's and then drove her to the ShopRite for groceries and to Bruno's Deli for fresh mozzarella cheese, olives, and bread. He cut the family lawn. When he was finished, he used the leaf blower on the sidewalks and porches of both his house and Nonna's.

Stacey wasn't around because she had to work at McDonald's both Saturday and Sunday. They had managed some make-out time in Mark's car on Saturday night, but he didn't get very far because Stacey was tired, in a bad mood, and still in a snit about getting dunked by a wave at the beach because of him. All she wanted to do was talk about what was going to happen on Monday.

But Mark was okay with that. He was strangely happy because now they were a group, a posse with a plan.

Thirty minutes before class on Monday morning, Mark pulled up in front of the Fenton's immaculately-kept brick colonial in the heart of the tree-lined, old section of Toms River.

How the Fentons had produced a son like Borderline was a complete and unexplained mystery, Mark thought. Perhaps he was a changeling, the son of a NASCAR driver switched at birth with a pale computer-geek baby.

Borderline's parents were older, graying, tweedy-looking people. His father, a laser scientist at Bell Labs in Holmdel, was a multiple-doctored, introspective man who published articles in scientific journals and watched the History Channel.

Mrs. Fenton was a thin, fluttery woman who played bridge and spent much of her time ministering to an extensive rose garden in the sunny backyard of their two-story home.

As Mark honked, Borderline came sprinting out of the house, followed by his mother waving a brown paper bag.

"Your lunch, Howie," she called. "You forgot your lunch."

"Save it, Mom. I'll eat it later. I promise." He jumped into the Jeep. "Move it, Mark."

Borderline blew her a kiss as Mark pulled down the street.

"Oh, Jeez, she's into health foods now," Borderline groaned. "Sprouts, that's what she made me. A cucumber and sprout sandwich on pita bread with yogurt dressing. Can you see the guys at Federici's Auto Body if I pull a sissy sprout sandwich out of my lunch bag?" He groaned. "Why can't I have a ham and cheese on rye or a simple baloney on white?"

"What?" Mark laughed. "All those nitrates? Jumping in there and attacking your body like little Pacmen? Crunch, crunch ... there goes your stomach, your eyeballs, your pecker! Forget it, pal, you'll be eating sprout sandwiches forever."

"Okay, okay," Borderline said as they neared the school. "Let's get serious. We're almost there."

"I'm ready. I even topped off the gas tank last night. But what if Nerf just goes home after school? Then what?"

Borderline punched his fist on the dash and said, "Then we keep following him. Today, we'll use your Jeep. Tomorrow I'll get a car from Federici's. If we use different cars each day, he won't suspect he's being followed. I called Mrs. Jones this morning. Edsell's still missing. The cops have filed all the reports, but there's nothing coming in."

"Did you hear from CM, Alex, or Wooley?"

"Nope, not a word from anyone. I saw Missy at the arcade at Seaside, and she told me the same thing she told Stacey, that Edsell was at her place until sometime after one that morning. Seems like she and her sister were the last persons to see him."

"Is she upset?"

"Yeah. They all smoked a little weed and did some shots while they watched a movie. She's bummed for letting him leave when he was messed up. She thinks Edsell fell off the causeway bridge or tripped into a canal somewhere."

"Shit. That's got to feel bad. What's she like?"

"A little loopy but okay. I think she might be pretty, but it's hard to tell because her face is red and puffy from crying all the time. Missy swears he didn't just run off, and if you think about it, why would he? Missy told me that Edsell's mom is a drinker, but she's cut back on the booze, and she and Edsell are actually getting along for a change. He and Missy are crazy about each other ..." Borderline paused. "Things are going good for Edsell for the first time in years, and he runs off? No way. Something happened, I just feel it. Something bad."

Mark pulled into a space near Nerf's van. It was going to be hard to concentrate on algebra today.

CHAPTER 27

At noon, Mark had his head tucked under the hood of his Jeep when Nerf came out of the school. Borderline slouched inside on the passenger seat, his forehead just visible over the dash.

They waited until the van was halfway down the street and then followed it. Nerf drove through Toms River on Route 530, passed under the Garden State Parkway, and headed due west. Soon the small homes, real estate offices, and convenience stores on the outskirts of the town gave way to pine forest. As the traffic became sparse, Mark hung back, grateful that his Jeep was a dark color.

When Nerf got to the junction of 618, he turned right. Mark kept a careful five hundred yards between them and followed suit.

He noticed that the woods on either side of the road had burned sometime in the past. The tops of the trees were green, but the trunks were blackened, and most of the middle and upper branches were broken off. Between the charcoaled, dusty, gray underbrush, patches of white sand glimmered in the sun. The burn lasted for several hundred yards, and then the forest turned green again.

As they approached an intersection, they passed a small green and white sign that said Bamber Lake. Beyond the crossroads, small houses were tucked among the trees.

The brake lights came on as the blue van stopped at the red light. Mark slowed to a crawl. When the light turned green, Nerf drove straight through the intersection and onto a smaller road.

"I can't follow him in there," Mark said as he applied the brakes and pulled to the side of the road. "I've been on his tail all the way from town. He'll know he's being followed."

Nerf's van disappeared around a bend. Mark waited as the green light turned yellow and then red. He drummed his fingers on the steering wheel until the light turned green and then gunned the Jeep across the intersection.

They quickly passed the lake and its few scattered house and then plunged into the pine woods once more. The cracked macadam surface ended, and the road under the Jeep became white sand. A second dirt road went off to the right, and few yards farther, another branched right.

"What if Nerf took one of these side roads?" Mark asked.

"I don't know. Just keep going."

Next to him, Borderline leaned forward, his face nearly touching the windshield. The road circled to the left, then to the right. Other roads joined in a seemingly random pattern.

"This looks like a development that never happened," Borderline said. "Someone built these roads a long time ago. Look at the ruts and washouts. This stuff's been here a long time."

Shimmers of pale, silvery dust hung in the air around them. Was it theirs? Or Nerf's?

Mark stopped the Jeep and turned to Borderline. "I don't know about you, but I'm getting the creeps. If we go much farther, we won't be able to find our way back."

"Turn off the engine," Borderline said and stood up on the front seat of the Jeep. He grasped the windshield and leaned forward. "Maybe we can hear something."

A hot, dusty quiet fell around them. Far above, a lone hawk circled in the clear blue sky.

"I think we should get out of here," Mark whispered. "If Nerf comes back along one of these roads, he'll recognize us in a heartbeat. How would we explain what we're doing out here in the middle of the Barrens? Besides, we don't know who or what else is around us. We're in the middle of fucking nowhere."

"Shit, I know that creep's up to something," Borderline said. "I hate to give up."

"I still think we should blow this place." Mark started the Jeep. "Let's go back to town. Maybe Edsell's home, and we can forget all about this."

But Edsell didn't come home.

CHAPTER 28

As the first weak light of dawn filtered through the window shade, Edsell looked across the room and tried to see the other bed.

Edsell had been by himself in the room for hours yesterday, which was worse somehow than having the silent, sad-eyed Brandon in the next bed. At least there had been a human being nearby.

He'd heard them during the night, hauling a limp body into the room, placing it on the bed, hooking it up to the tubes and bottles that had been brought in the previous afternoon. They'd had to turn on a light to insert the needles and tubes. Basically, they were doing the same stuff to the kid that they had done to him a week ago. IVs in both arms, adhesive tape on the mouth, legs and arms tied to the hospital bed. The kid appeared unconscious, had never moved or uttered a sound.

Now, in the gray light, Edsell looked him over carefully. He was young, black, thin, and tall. His hair was in dreadlocks, and he was dressed in the identical blue gown that Edsell was wearing. His mouth was taped shut, and his arms were tied to the bedrails with white strips of cloth.

Edsell could hear the kid breathing and listened for a while until suddenly, the kid's breathing became uneven. His eyes flew open, and he looked wildly around the room. It was the same drill that Edsell had done just days ago, and it was uncanny to watch, like seeing himself all over again.

He saw the surprise, the fear, the agony, the terror. He heard the struggle, the quick, watery nasal breaths, the gagging against the cruel tape.

But Edsell was not Brandon. He might not be able to speak because of the gag, but he could communicate. He could help the new kid in some small way.

When the kid's eyes finished spinning around the room and came to rest on him, Edsell raised his eyebrows, widened his eyes, and then gave the kid a slow wink.

I'm here, and I know what you're going through, he said with every facial expression he could command.

The kid frowned, made an ummmm sound, looked at his bound hands and feet, and then focused on Edsell's face once more. The terror was still there but had lessened.

The kid raised his eyebrows in one huge questioning look.

Edsell nodded slowly and then winked again.

He would be there for the kid, he silently vowed, until they both got out.

CHAPTER 29

The Tuesday before the July Fourth weekend dawned with more hot, cloudless skies. The weather had been unusually warm and dry on the Jersey Shore throughout the spring and early summer, and the local merchants were jubilant. Sunny spelled money for everyone who owned a business at the beach.

Shopkeepers tuned in the weather channel each morning and then smiled broadly at the long-range forecast of hot and dry. Each day, more people migrated to the crowded coastal towns. Renters illegally sublet their extra space. Occupancy was actually well over 100 percent as more and more tourists crowded the beach towns to escape the heat wave.

The police were extraordinarily busy. Cars overheated, and traffic backed up on the narrow roads that ran north and south on the barrier islands. Many smaller, cheaper rentals had no air-conditioning, and as the temperature soared, tempers flared, and arguments escalated between family members and neighbors. Someone threw a beer bottle over a fence. Smoke from a grill blew into someone's bedroom. A house full of fraternity brothers threw a party for three hundred of their closest friends. In the bars, fights started over televised ball games, women, and the ownership of the stools closest to the big-screen TV.

The police were working overtime all up and down the Jersey Shore. One missing teenager was not a huge priority. The kid probably went off with his friends and forgot to tell the old lady he was going. Hell, every cop on the shore was working overtime just to keep the tourists in line.

At eleven forty-five in the morning, Mark and Borderline sat in an old, green Dodge coupe across the parking lot from Nerf's blue van.

Mark saw the fat janitor walk out of the school and climb into his van. Borderline turned the ignition and followed at a distance.

Nerf drove to a supermarket and came out with several bags of groceries. From there, Nerf drove to Toms River East, one of the other three regional high schools.

Summer school was not held at East, so the parking lot was deserted. Borderline drove by slowly, and they watched as Nerf unlocked a side door and disappeared inside. Borderline circled the block and then parked in front of a small, white house that had a full view of the school. Forty-five minutes later, Nerf came out with several yellow sheets of paper, which he folded and tucked into his pocket. He bought gas and then drove through Toms River and under the Garden State Parkway onto Route 530.

"All right." Borderline smiled. "He's going to the Barrens again."

Nerf took the same route he had taken on the previous day, past the burn, then Route 530 to 618, then onto Route 614. When they neared Bamber Lake, not a car was in sight except for the blue van ahead of them. Again, Nerf pulled across the intersection and disappeared into the pine forest.

"Shit, he's going in there again, and there's no point in us trying to follow him through that maze of roads." Borderline thumped his fist on the steering wheel.

"Kind of makes me wonder what he's doing in there," Mark said slowly. "What's in those woods?"

"We've got some time; let's hang out here for a while and see if he comes out. I'll park over behind those trees."

Borderline pulled the old Dodge under the pines. The small, scrubby oaks and wild blueberry bushes that grew along the road partially concealed their car. Through the branches, they had a direct view of the road into Bamber Lake.

"What do we know about this place?" Borderline asked. "I think we're in the middle of the Pine Barrens here."

"We studied the Pine Barrens in eighth grade, remember?" Mark said. "I wish I could remember more about what we learned. The whole area is really weird. The ground is white sand, the trees are mostly pines, and something about strange plants and animals. I remember our teacher had a small carnivorous plant on her desk that she said came from the Barrens. I think the whole place is some kind of protected environmental zone."

"Wonder what that means."

"It means you can't build anything new unless you get permission from the government. It's mostly state forests and preserves now."

"Maybe we should get some books or maps," Borderline said. "Something that'll tell us what's out here, where the roads go. I'll run over to the library tonight and see what I can find."

For forty-five minutes, Mark and Borderline waited in the dry heat. The radio played softly as they leaned their heads back and watched the road ahead of them.

"Hey, I've got an idea." Mark sat up and stared at the small road that disappeared into the trees. "What if you get those maps, and we come out here tomorrow morning while Nerf's in school?"

"What? The Princeton applicant wants to cut class to play detective? Your old man would have a cow."

"How's he going to find out? C'mon, let's do it. Nothing else we've done has helped. Edsell is still missing, and I have a bad feeling about Nerf. If we scope out the place and find nothing, maybe you'll shut up about it, and we can get back to a normal summer. You remember? Parties and surfing and babes? All that stuff we haven't been doing."

"Okay, okay, but let's take your Jeep. We might need four-wheel drive in there."

Borderline turned the ignition key, and the old car started with a metallic groan.

CHAPTER 30

L ater, at Borderline's house, Mark sat at the kitchen table with Borderline, a plate of homemade oatmeal cookies, and two tall glasses of milk in front of them. Mr. Fenton was still at work, and Mrs. Fenton was in the backyard spraying her roses.

"What do you think, Borderline?" Mark asked as he reached for a cookie. "Are we on some bogus detective trip? Are we letting our imaginations run away with us while we do our imitation of a Dirty Harry stakeout?"

"I don't know." Borderline sighed. "Nerf's got a pass key to East, but I don't think that's unusual for a head janitor in the same school district. I just don't understand why he would go there now. East's not even open because summer school's at South this year. I wonder what was written on those yellow sheets of paper."

"Who knows? A list of supplies?" Mark asked. "What I'm wondering is why Nerf goes out to the Barrens every day. And why does he take groceries with him? Does he live out there? Hey, I've got an idea. Let's look him up in the phone book. Where is it?"

Borderline went over to a small desk in an alcove near the back door. He thumbed through he pages of the Ocean County telephone directory.

"Right here. Wilbur Nelson on Mayfield Avenue. That's right off Route 37. He lives here in Toms River."

"So why is he going out to the Barrens every day?" asked Mark.

"I don't know, but we're about to find out. I'm getting a creepy feeling about this whole thing."

Borderline sighed again and leaned forward. He broke up his cookie, lined the pieces up in a straight line, and thought back to grade school. Mark remembered him doing the same thing in the cafeteria in grade school. Funny how some things never change.

Mark also thought about Edsell Jones and how he been a regular kid back then, popular and well-liked. But adolescence had not been kind to Edsell. He grew tall and thin and clumsy; the kids called him "stick" and "beanpole." They tripped him in the hallways and knocked the books out of his hands on the bus.

To make things worse, whenever Edsell became upset, his oversized hands assumed a life of their own, cracking knuckles, picking at hangnails, scratching, pulling tiny pieces of lint off his clothing. So the kids teased him even more, calling him "octopus" and "hands" and worse.

During this time, Edsell's dearest possession was a Pittsburgh Steelers cap with a Super Bowl pin on it. Left behind by his wandering father, Edsell found it in the back of a closet in his mother's unkempt house. The cap went on his head and stayed there except when a teacher made him take it off. The hat got scruffy and worn, and the proud black and gold degenerated into shabby gray and yellow, but it was part of Edsell, his statement to the world that his dad had been a Steeler fan during the glory days.

Mark took a gulp of milk and then said, "Sometimes I think we're wasting our time following that creepzoid Nerf around. What could we find out here? We live in Toms River, New Jersey. What's the worst possible thing that could happen around here? A traffic jam on Route 35? Bad pizza at Joey's?"

Borderline shrugged, and both of them looked out the big bay window next to the kitchen table. In the backyard, dozens of rose bushes danced with color in the warm breeze. Mark knew that Borderline's mother spent hours lovingly watering, pruning, weeding, and spraying her roses.

But who cared for Edsell? Who had nurtured him?

"The worst possible thing?" Borderline tuned to Mark. "I don't know. Maybe Nerf is a weirdo who likes young guys. Maybe he's some kind of killer. I don't know."

"Okay, okay. I hear you," Mark said. "But think about this: what if Edsell went to stay with his Aunt Tillie in Trenton, or a cousin in Staten Island? He could be anywhere. We know that Mrs. Jones has had some drinking issues. It's possible she doesn't remember him leaving, and this is all a bunch of nothing."

Borderline looked annoyed. "First of all, my friend, there is no other family. And secondly, I've seen Lorraine Jones's face. You've seen it too. We're doing this for her. And for Edsell."

Mark stood up and shrugged. He took a handful of cookies from the platter and wrapped them in a paper napkin.

"My fee, buddy, for this detective caper. We go to the Barrens tomorrow."

CHAPTER 31

Wednesday morning brought continuing hot, dry, clear weather. A fog bank that perched over the coast on Sunday night tiptoed out to sea, and a huge high-pressure system that enveloped everything from Kansas to the Atlantic Ocean settled in.

At eight forty-five, Mark pulled into the school parking lot with Borderline and looked to see if Nerf's van was there.

It was.

As they drove out of Toms River, Mark reached into a paper bag and pulled out something wrapped in white paper. He held it out to Borderline.

"Here's the payoff for your mom's cookies. I ate them all last night."

Borderline sniffed loudly. "Jeez, only a true friend would do this. My favorite: garlic bagel with scallion cream cheese. No sprout sandwich today!" He unwrapped the soft bagel and bit into it. "Mmm-mm-mm. If you're eating one of these, Mark, you'd better not go near Stacey today. That is, unless she likes dragon breath."

Mark laughed as he bit into his bagel. "After one of these, I'm dead in the water. Nothing works—not gum, breath mints, sprays, or mouthwash."

Borderline took a huge bite and said to Mark. "You know, these bagels are a great idea for our detective work today."

"How's that?"

Borderline snorted. "Look. We're on our way to the strange and mysterious Pine Barrens. If we get into trouble, we can breathe on the bad guys, and their guns will melt."

"Guns? Get real. That weasely dweeb Nerf with a gun? Never. In fact, the more I think about it, the more I'm sure we're doing this to get out of summer school for the day."

Borderline sighed and popped the last chunk of chewy bagel into his mouth.

"Okay, jock. Here's the plan." Borderline pulled several folded sheets of paper from the pocket of his jeans. The wind ruffled them, but Borderline quickly rolled up his window to cut down on the air streaking through the topless Jeep.

"I looked through a lot of old books and maps at the library last night. It's really strange out here, Mark. That whole section behind Bamber Lake is nothing but a blank, white space on the maps. We lost Nerf in the middle of nowhere."

"But what about all those old roads? Don't they go anywhere?"

"Not anymore. Remember how the roads ran every which way? That's an old development that was started back in 1972. The builder went bust after he put up those few houses by the lake."

"Those roads are that old? How come they're not all overgrown?"

"Everything grows slowly in the Barrens."

"Why?" asked Mark.

"The soil. There's no real dirt, just pure white sand. Some of the trails in the Barrens are really old, like maybe a hundred years or more. The stuff I read was interesting. The Barrens used to be a happening place. They made bog iron. There were a bunch of furnaces where they made cannon balls and stuff. There were glass factories and all kinds of mills. They even built sailboats on some of the rivers. A lot of people lived out here then."

Mark looked at the pinewoods on either side of the road. "So what happened? Where'd they go?" he asked.

"Someone invented a cheaper way to make iron out in Pennsylvania, so the iron mills closed down. The rest of the factories went under, and people moved on. Some of the roads connect towns that aren't there anymore."

"Ghost towns, come on. Ghost towns?" Mark said.

"Not real towns anymore, most of the buildings have fallen down over the years. Maybe there's only one house left with an old geezer living in it way out in the middle of nowhere. Sometimes there's nothing left but mounds of dirt and a couple of old foundations. A couple of books talked about fires, big ones that burned up a lot of the Barrens years ago. A lot of the old houses were lost in those wildfires."

Mark was getting a little impatient with Borderline's long lecture on the Pine Barrens. "This is great stuff you're telling me, buddy. What's it got to do with Nerf? Why is he out here?"

"That, my man, is the big question," said Borderline. "One of my maps shows an old road called Dukes Bridge on the other side of the maze. Something might be out there."

"Maybe Nerf's got family or friends in the Barrens."

"Maybe," Borderline said. "That's what we're going to find out."

Mark slowed at the Bamber Lake intersection and then shot across the road when the light turned green. Moments later, they were on a narrow dirt road. Mark drove slowly, switching to four-wheel drive when the sand deepened. Soon they were in the maze.

"Check out the tire tracks and follow the roads with the most tire tracks," Borderline said.

Mark maneuvered around several corners, following the most traveled ruts until he came to a fork.

"Which way?" he asked.

"Turn right. If it dead ends, we'll come back and start again from here."

Borderline watched the speedometer and wrote notes on the back of one of the maps.

"What are you writing?" Mark asked.

"I'm keeping track of what turns we're making and how far we go on each road. That way we won't get lost if we need to come back this way."

"You're some kind of genius. You should be the one applying to Princeton, not me," Mark said with a laugh.

They continued through the pines. Gradually the other trails became fewer until they were driving on a single, narrow strip. Crooked branches laden with dark cones reached toward them from either side of the trail. Mark ducked to avoid an overhanging branch and then stopped the Jeep and turned off the engine.

"What're you doing?" Borderline asked.

"Taking a leak."

Mark opened the door and dropped softly down onto the powdery soil. He walked a few feet away to a small oak. As he unzipped his jeans, the quiet closed around him. Nothing moved. Nothing stirred. Not a sound could be heard except his pissing, and even that was hushed by the sand as it quickly soaked up the yellow stream.

It was spooky out here, Mark thought. No birds, no crickets, no frogs, no wind. Everything was dry and dusty and deadly quiet as if someone had turned off his ears. On the way back to the car, a twig snapped loudly under his foot.

The past few months had been unusually dry and hot. He couldn't remember the last time it had rained. Mark reached out to move aside a branch near his face, and it broke off in his hand. How would they ever stop a fire out here? There were no fire hydrants; that was for sure.

A fine line of sweat had formed on Mark's upper lip by the time he climbed back into the Jeep. The sound of the door shutting was like a clap of thunder in the still air.

"I got to tell you, Borderline, this place is weird. It's too darn quiet. And dry. I keep thinking, what if there was a fire out here?"

"Yeah I know what you mean," Borderline said as he looked down at the map. "But we're not turning back now. If this is Dukes Bridge Road, we'll eventually come out on Route 539. I can get us home from there on paved roads."

The dark green Jeep continued slowly down the narrow, rutted road. Mark glanced at his watch. Only ten thirty and hot as hell. He wished he had a can of Coke in his hands right now.

CHAPTER 32

As the Jeep rounded another narrow bend in the road, Mark saw an old house just ahead of them.

He eased his foot off the accelerator and bumped the Jeep back into first gear. They rolled to a soft stop and sat for a moment looking at the house.

It squatted in the middle of a large clearing, a dark and forbidding presence. It was old and big, two stories with a porch across the front. An attached garage gleamed new and coppery next to the dark cedar of the main house.

A black Suburban was parked in front of the garage. Dozens of low stumps protruded like worn molars through the sand and pale wild grass that surrounded the old house. The soft dead suede of fallen pine needles carpeted the edges of the forest that circled the old building.

"Hello, what have we got here?" Mark asked.

"A house we're about to check out," Borderline said quietly. "Someone lives here. Someone who can afford a brand-new customized Suburban that I know sells for twenty grand or more. This is not the home of a poor, old Piney hermit-geezer."

Mark pointed at the house. "Look. Every window has a shade on it. Why? Who's going to look in? There's not another house for miles."

"Maybe this is where Nerf comes."

Borderline and Mark stepped out of the Jeep and slowly walked toward the house.

"What if somebody comes out and they want to know what we're doing here?" Mark asked.

"We tell them we were driving around and got lost. We need directions."

The big house loomed above them.

"I'll go to the front door," Borderline whispered. "You move around to the side and stay back a little."

Mark watched as Borderline took a few strides forward. As his foot hit the bottom step of the porch, a shade rattled up, and a window flew open on the second floor. Mark heard a crashing sound, and then a loud, harsh scream split the air, lifting and rising up and up until it hung in the air like a decibeled question mark.

Borderline was on the porch, so he leaped backward until he could see above the roofline. Mark ran around the corner of the house. They both saw a face in an open window, a distorted, young, pale face with its mouth open, its eyes bulging, a scream emanating from its mouth. Suddenly the face disappeared, quickly jerked out of the window like a *Sesame Street* Muppet. Exit stage right.

Borderline ran up the low porch stairs calling, "Hold on, I'm coming. I'm coming."

Then, as suddenly as it had started, the screaming ended in a gasp. Another figure appeared in the window. An older adult face with glasses peered down. Beneath the face was a white shirt and tie.

Borderline pounded on the door. "Open the door! Open the fucking door!"

Thirty seconds later, Mark heard a loud click. The door swung back, and he saw a man dressed in black coveralls standing in the frame. He was tall and very thin, with a face from a horror flick. A large, hooked nose took up most of his face. His eyes pitched downward at the outer corners. Long, hollow cheeks ran slackly down on either side of a mouth filled with sharp, yellow teeth.

The mouth opened and spoke in a deep voice.

"This is private property. Please leave."

As the repulsive man started to close the door, Borderline lunged forward and put his foot on the doorsill.

"Look, mister. Someone in this house just screamed his head off. What's going on?"

The ugly man's eyes turned into slits. The loose skin along his jawline tightened. "It's none of your business. Please leave."

Borderline turned to Mark and shrugged. "Fine with me. This road is called Dukes Crossing, isn't it, Mark? I just want to make sure I have the right location when we call the police about the screams we just heard. Come on."

As Borderline and Mark started to turn away, a second man in dark slacks, white shirt, and blue paisley tie materialized in the doorway. It was the man they had seen in the upstairs window.

"Wait, boys," he called. "I really don't think you should do that."

They hesitated.

"I'm Dr. Anton Vogel, and this place is special, very special," the man said in a deep, cultured voice. "You're going to make a lot of very important people unhappy if you go running to the police."

Dr. Vogel was about forty years old with a strong, handsome, chiseled face and close-cropped brown hair. A pair of half-glasses hung on a gold chain around his neck.

Mark stood there unable to think of anything to say, but Borderline shrugged and rocked back on his heels with his hands in his pockets. "Unhappy? Someone's going to get unhappy?" he drawled. "That dude upstairs sounds about as unhappy as anybody I've ever heard. Isn't that right, Mark? There was a lot of world-class unhappiness in that scream a minute ago."

Dr. Vogel stepped out onto the porch. He closed the door behind him, and his thin lips formed into a tight smile.

"Listen, boys. I'm not supposed to tell anyone what we're doing here, but it looks like I'm going to have to share my secret with you. Can I trust you?"

"Maybe," Mark said. "Why?"

Dr. Vogel sat down on the porch steps and motioned for Mark and Borderline to sit next to him.

"It's really quite simple, boys. This is a private drug-treatment center, and that young man upstairs is one of my patients."

"A rehab?" Mark asked.

"Yes. I take only a few young clients who have already been to other clinics and hospitals, but to no avail. Their families have spent thousands of dollars on treatments, and nothing has worked. They are brokenhearted, desperate people." Vogel sighed and shook his head. "I accept only six patients at a time and then put them through a lengthy, very specialized course of treatment. It's arduous, but it works. My clinic currently has an 80 percent success rate, even with the most difficult, long-term addictions."

"But why keep it a secret?" Mark asked.

"That's a good question, son. You're a smart fellow, I can see," Vogel said with a smile. "There are several reasons. First, the treatment itself is still in the experimental stage."

Dr. Vogel paused, and three horizontal lines in his forehead deepened as he continued. "Second, you have no idea how selfishly the average citizen reacts when he finds out a drug rehabilitation center is going to be built near them. Petitions, pickets, endless protests, even lawsuits. Without any real facts and with pure emotionalism, they mistakenly assume some drug-crazed brute will escape, rape their wives, abuse their children, and steal their cars." He shook his head and sighed. "Sometimes their biggest fear is that their property values will go down."

Vogel stood up and looked around at the ring of silent, gnarled pine trees.

"I built this center here in these beautiful pine woods because I thought my patients would be safe here, far from the temptations of the city." He extended his hands with the palms up. "I was hoping and praying that I would not be disturbed until my research was finished and my treatment announced to the world." He lowered his voice. "My entire life has been devoted to helping these unfortunate young people. I'm asking—no, I'm begging you to keep my secret. Please, boys, you cannot tell anyone about my project here. Not even your parents or your friends."

Mark looked at Borderline. He nodded.

"Sounds okay," Mark said to Vogel. "But I don't understand why that kid was screaming like that."

"Try to understand that my job is a difficult one. Sometimes my patients wake up from their rest periods and have residual drug-induced hallucinations. That's simply what you saw and heard." Vogel shook his head and looked up at the second-floor window. "Poor Kenneth, he's having a horrendous time during his second week of therapy. It is a very critical period now. However, I can guarantee that when he leaves here, he'll be in an entirely new state of mind."

Vogel extended his hand to Mark and then to Borderline.

"Good to meet you, boys. You look like such fine, clean-cut, young men. I know you'll keep our little secret and not make any trouble for the poor souls that I'm trying so desperately to heal. Now, if you will excuse me, I need to get back to my patients. Remember, boys, not a word to anyone."

CHAPTER 33

Vogel strode back into the old farmhouse, pausing at the door to wave at them. As the Jeep disappeared down the road in a cloud of white dust, he closed the heavy door, locked it, and leaned against it. He was furious.

"Chee-rist almighty," he whispered. "Why did that kid get loose just as those teenagers pulled in? Damn, damn, damn."

He turned and lifted the corner of the window shade. The Jeep was gone, leaving behind a silvery cloud of dust. The rage of Vogel's face slowly turned to concentration.

"Jack," he called softly.

The tall man's head appeared in a doorway.

"Yeah?"

"How did that happen? How did Kenneth get loose? You incompetent idiot!" He stamped his foot.

The man in black started to stammer. "I was just getting him out of bed for his walk. He must have heard the car pull up."

"Never mind, we'll talk later. Right now, I want you to follow that Jeep, but don't let them see you. Get the license number."

Vogel heard the Suburban start as he walked up the stairs.

From now on, he would be more diligent with the restraints. It was a problem he wrestled with constantly. Such a difficult thing to accomplish, keeping these young men alive while all the indulgent, modern poisons they had inhaled, ingested, or injected were flushed from their systems. Sometimes he lost them as they screamed into their gags and twitched against their bindings. If their central nervous systems convulsed too badly, they were useless to him.

Vogel turned down the hall and opened a door.

Two narrow beams of light spilled through the sides of the opaque window shade and fell on several stainless steel racks that held bottles of various sizes and shapes clustered at the head of each of the two hospital beds. Long tubing led to the still forms. Vogel leaned forward and adjusted the drip on a bottle of pale white, viscous liquid. Next to him, two machines pulsed bright green and red dots across black monitors.

This one will be ready soon, he thought.

The eyes on the bed followed him around the room as he made small adjustments to the bottles and checked several dials on the machines at the other bed.

"You'll be ready soon, Edsell. That's your name, isn't it? Edsell. Like the old Ford car that didn't sell."

Vogel laughed quietly as the eyes followed him.

"Well, Edsell, my little waste bucket, I think we'll be able to use you after all. It's been a long fight, but the worst is over now. Your useless life is about to become important, even after everything you've done to destroy it."

He reached a long, tapered finger toward the silent figure and touched him on the forehead.

"Soon, Edsell. Soon."

CHAPTER 34

For several minutes, the Jeep bumped down Dukes Bridge Road. Borderline and Mark stared ahead at the winding dirt road. Neither said a word.

Finally Borderline broke the silence. "What do you think? Is that guy on the level?"

"I don't know. His story makes sense, I guess, but I hated that screaming. God, it was the worst. Tore right through me." Mark shivered.

Borderline nodded. "Me, too. That kid sure sounded like a hurting unit. I wonder what they did to shut him up."

"This whole setup makes me wonder if that old house is where Nerf goes. And why?" Mark asked. "Is this so-called rehab connected to Edsell?"

"The guy who came to the door first, was he a freak or what?"

"He was big and gnarly," Mark answered. "What was really weird was, as soon as you said the word police, Dr. Vogel practically catapulted out onto the porch. He was falling all over himself to tell us about his secret little drug rehab place. Maybe we *should* call the police."

Borderline pulled on his ear and frowned.

"I don't think so. What could we say? Some kid in a rehab is screaming? The guy's a doctor, remember? We'll look like fools and maybe spoil it for the people he's trying to help. Besides, what police?

I mean, there isn't a real town around here. The state police probably take care of stuff in the Barrens, and for sure I'm not calling them. They're not like the wussie cops at the boardwalk, strolling around fondling their guns while they check out the string bikinis.

"So what should we do? Forget about it?" Mark asked.

"No, we can't do that either. Something's going on, something strange. Think about it. I hear Nerf talking on the phone about a kid who won't be missed, and this is a couple of days after Edsell disappears. We know Nerf comes out here to the Barrens and brings bags of groceries. We find an old house in the middle of nowhere and hear a kid screaming his head off. Some guy in a white jacket says it's a drug rehab. Maybe it is and maybe it isn't."

"Do you think Edsell's in here?"

Borderline narrowed his eyes and stared ahead at the winding dirt road that led through the pine forest. "I don't know. The guy said rich kids. Edsell's got no money. But I keep wondering, where are the nurses or other staff? There was only one car parked outside. Vogel said *we* several times. Who's *we?* Vogel and that ugly guy? Maybe it's Vogel and the ugly guy, plus Nerf."

They drove slowly through the Barrens. The pale green of the forest was close on both sides of the Jeep. For several minutes, neither spoke a word. Finally Borderline turned to Mark.

"I've got it. A way to find out if Nerf is connected with that place."

"Yeah? How?"

"Tomorrow morning we'll leave a note on Nerf's desk telling him to call Vogel. No number, just *Call Vogel.* If he calls someone, we'll know he's connected to this thing, whatever it is."

"How are we going to be able to watch him? We just cut class today. If he sees us hanging around his office, he'll be onto us in a minute."

"Not us."

"What do you mean, not us?"

"Someone not in summer school. Someone we know and trust. Someone who can keep both a secret and a straight face."

"Like who?"

"Stacey."

"Shit on that! Stacey? No way. We're not getting her into this," Mark said. "You don't know how overprotective and old fashioned her parents are. I'm the football player who's applying to Princeton, and they're not crazy about me. If they ever found out what we were doing, they would go screaming to the police."

"C'mon," Borderline protested. "It's no big deal. They'll never find out. Besides, she knows most of it, and she won't really be involved. All she's going to do is check out Nerf's reaction when he finds the note tomorrow morning."

"I don't like it. And you know why? Because we're going to have to tell her everything."

"Big deal. Stacey'll keep it quiet."

"Okay, okay," Mark mumbled. "I'll call her tonight and work out the details."

CHAPTER 35

I t was twenty minutes after noon, and the old farmhouse was silent except for the distant low hum of the oversized four-zone air-conditioning system that kept the temperature inside at an even seventy-two degrees.

Dr. Anton Vogel walked into his small bedroom, carefully pulled back the white bedspread, and then lay down on the cool, pima cotton sheets. He had monitored the patients, finished lunch, and now it was time for his afternoon rest period. He crossed his hands upon his chest and closed his eyes.

Images of the unexpected visit from those hideous boys flashed through his head. He forced himself to relax by alternately tensing and releasing each arm and leg in turn. As he did this, he repeated the same message to himself over and over. Nothing would happen, the boys believed his story. He was safe. Nothing would happen. They believed his story. He was safe.

He had to keep moving forward. Nothing could get in the way of his grand plan.

As he looked back over the years, Vogel was pleased with what he saw. His was a comfortable solitary existence, uncluttered by family or friends. He had nothing to distract him from his work, his mission.

In his undergraduate days, while his classmates eagerly explored the bodies of their girlfriends in the damp backseats of beat-up old Fords, he was at the library and in the laboratory. In truth, after a few clumsy experiments fostered more by curiosity than need, young Anton Vogel decided that the achievement of sexual gratification through the cooperation of another human being was horribly complicated and not worth the effort. Little had happened since then to change his mind.

Instead, he found cerebral and visceral pleasure in his work, in classical music, and in the writings of the great poets and philosophers. Vogel considered himself a Renaissance man who explored the limits of the mind and pleasured himself with the chaste, sensuous bliss of Mozart, Shakespeare, and Kant.

In the evenings, a glass of fine old Port after a Spartan meal brought relaxation and restful sleep. On certain rare celebratory occasions, Vogel gave himself over to his one vice, a single Havana cigar.

There was much to celebrate of late, and at times Vogel wanted to run into the Pinelands sunlight crying, "Eureka! I've found it!" like Archimedes of old, but he restrained himself and kept his secret to himself—the brave and extraordinary secret of extending human life.

In other moments, he felt a warm glow as he anticipated a future that recognized Anton Vogel as one of the great scientific minds of the millennium. A smile crossed his thin, precise face as he visualized his name in every science textbook, shoulder to shoulder with Copernicus, Pasteur, and Einstein.

CHAPTER 36

Chicago, 1954–1980

H e had his mother to thank for everything. She had been his guide and inspiration, his mentor and his soul mate. His fondest memories were of sitting with her at the kitchen table in their tiny Chicago apartment. As the rosy evening faded outside the single narrow window, the shabby, worn room became important and bright. His mother would kick off her white crepe-soled shoes, carefully unpin her tiny, starched nurse's cap, and pour herself a cup of Earl Grey tea.

Too exhausted to sleep, Estelle Vogel decompressed each evening by telling her son details of that day's surgeries. For eight, twelve, sometimes fourteen hours a day, Estelle was scrub nurse to the brilliant Dr. Emory Wakefield as he mapped the human brain at Chicago General. Shoulder to shoulder with the famous surgeon, she clicked the tiny neurosurgical instruments into his hand as he pressed and probed.

Other lesser attendees came and went with instruments, bandages, sutures, and gauze. Other lesser attendants monitored IV drips, respiration, and heartbeat. The lowest echelon held cups of orange juice to the parched lips of Dr. Wakefield and his head nurse, Estelle Vogel.

His mother was his world during those years. His father never existed, not even in words from his mother's lips. When he thought about his biological father, he imagined a nebulous being whose only known function had been to ignite the small spark of life that became Anton Vogel. As a boy, Vogel liked to pretend that he came into existence through some chromosomatic cataclysm because, quite frankly, the image of his bright, beautiful mother yielding beneath a man was obscene.

His mother had conceived and delivered an illegitimate son during a time when that term was actively and hatefully employed. Anton Vogel loved her with a simple, pure flame because he believed, with a child's unconditional confidence, that she had born him to share her life.

Anton listened and asked questions. By the time he was ten, he knew the human brain as a wondrously capable, wet, glistening, gray mass bathed in spinal fluid. Estelle told him that when a certain area was stimulated, the patient's right hand came up. When another was probed, the patient uttered garbled speech. Each area of the brain controlled specific motor responses—the heartbeat, touch, memory functions, reflexes, and rational thought.

During his adolescent years, Anton inhaled medical books and journals. He learned the names of surgical instruments; he knew blood types and body types and what a periosteum layer was. He understood the difference between the cerebrum and the cerebellum. In his eighth grade art class, he drew graphic pictures of the visual cortex and the basal ganglia, to the consternation of the teacher and the delighted squeals of his fellow students.

Anton was a quiet, gifted student, and in his senior year of high school, he applied for, and received, a full academic scholarship to Northwestern. Four years later, he was accepted into medical school at the University of Chicago. An internship at Cook County Hospital followed and then a residency at Chicago General. Vogel specialized in his heart's desire, and by the age of thirty-two, the Estelle Vogel's curious son had been transformed into Dr. Anton Vogel, neurosurgeon.

As the years passed, he and his mother reversed roles. At the end of each day, it was Anton who hurried home to their townhouse. He and Estelle sat together at a glass table in the breakfast nook and shared a pot of Earl Grey tea while he recounted his adventures within the human brain.

She loved hearing of tumors and blood clots, or strange exotic growths of blood and tissue, or missing parts, or colors and smells within the cranium. Estelle alone understood the beauty and complexity of his work. She gloried in his triumph when, in a dangerous eight-hour procedure, he successfully excised a large encapsulated glioma from the parietal-occipital fissure of a young father. She shared his frustration when, despite the best efforts of her brilliant son, a beautiful five-year-old girl succumbed to a rapidly growing medulloblastoma.

Just as Vogel was obtaining eminence as a gifted neurosurgeon, the singular tragedy of his life occurred.

On a rainy Thursday night, a car full of teenagers high on marijuana and beer ran a stop sign. Six adolescents died in a crunch of metal and glass as their car collided with Estelle's station wagon. Vogel felt nothing for them, not one shred of pity, for in that horrifying instant, Vogel lost the woman who was his mother, his mentor, and his only friend.

The depression that followed was relentless, a dark stalker that followed him day and night. Vogel mourned his mother's vitality and intellect. He painfully missed their conversations over tea, her understanding of his work. He suffered migraine headaches and developed disc problems in his lower back. For weeks he toyed with the concept of suicide.

During this black period, he continued to work; more surgeries, more time in the lab, more reading of obscure journals and ancient books. Work was the only link with his beloved Estelle.

But then, like a gift from his mother in her far-off cosmos, Vogel discovered something that had the potential to lift his deep darkness and make him whole again. His discovery was so strange and promising that it changed the whole thrust of his career. It started one morning as he was removing a benign growth from the left hemisphere of the brain in a forty-four-year-old male. The tumor was small and encapsulated; it should have been a routine procedure. Vogel had injected a new, experimental, neurologically-sensitive radioactive isotope into the bloodstream of his patient. The isotope outlined the lobes of the brain and showed a vivid three-dimensional image on a monitor that hung above the patient.

Two hours into the surgery, the patient unexpectedly suffered a severe myocardial infarction, or heart attack. As the operating room team jumped into Code Blue, Vogel happened to glance up at the monitor and was astonished to see a strange new flare of color in the patient's brain. It radiated out from under the pineal gland, glowed in the inner forebrain, and pulsed around the longitudinal fissure.

Despite their best efforts, the patient's vital signs slowed and stopped, and he passed into clinical death. As the cardiac monitor went flat, Vogel saw the unearthly glow disappear from the overhead screen.

That evening, Vogel sipped a glass of wine and pondered the light. The burst of color had come from a region in the very center of the brain. Had the new experimental isotope illuminated an activity or enzyme in that site that was unknown to present-day neurology? Vogel knew that the functions of many areas of the brain were still not understood.

The next day, he called in a technician and asked her to test the scanner to make sure the glow was not the result of malfunction of the scanner.

"Don't know why you called me in, Doctor," said the tall brunette that afternoon as she packed her tools away. "This machine's brand-new, but just in case, I ran every conceivable test, and it's right on target." From that moment, Vogel hungered for other patients, for more surgeries where he could use the same tracer. He never saw the strange glow again, but then he never lost another patient during surgery. He actually hoped that another patient would die during surgery so he could see if the greenish light came again, but weeks might pass before that happened. Oh, he was perfectly willing to arrange such an event, but he held back. What if someone in the OR saw a sudden lethal slip of the scalpel? What if someone else noticed the green light?

Then, on a cold blustery morning, as he sat in the cafeteria with three other doctors, he heard that a surgical position had opened up at Helmsford State Hospital for Chronic Diseases in Pennsylvania.

Vogel applied for the job and was immediately accepted.

CHAPTER 37

Pennsylvania, 1981–1982

Helmsford was perfect. Located north of Pittsburgh, the large, old, public chronic diseases hospital consisted of several red brick buildings grouped around a small lake. Ancient oaks and beeches overhung cracked cement walkways and patchy lawns. The venerable old hospital had the look of a neglected university campus.

Helmsford housed a variety of diseases and disorders. There were disastrously malformed adult infants in oversized cribs, middle-aged women with advanced multiple sclerosis, young adults in the final stages of muscular dystrophy, children with severe cerebral palsy, elderly stroke victims, dozens of men and women with Alzheimer's, and a whole building of tubercular patients in various stages of contagion.

Most of the patients were poor, and many were wards of the state. Almost everyone was covered by Medicaid or Medicare. Many patients had outlived family connections and interest, and only a few had regular visitors. People were admitted to Helmsford Hospital, but most never came out again unless it was in a body sack or box.

It was an ideal place for Vogel's research: a state-run warehouse for the diseased, the damaged, and the dying. Helmsford was a bureaucratic maze of triplicate forms and computer authorizations. The administrator had stayed in command for twenty-two years by running a quiet, status-quo, money-making operation for the state.

As head of neurology, Vogel knew he would have carte blanche in determining which surgeries were performed and on whom. But he was also a prudent man and moved ever so slowly with his plan.

For several months, he did patient evaluations and performed several uneventful surgical procedures. He quickly discovered that requests for surgeries were easily approved.

He knew the administrator was thrilled to have him on staff, especially if he could extend the lives of the chronically ill. The venerable hospital thrived on life-saving procedures—intravenous feedings, catheters, heart monitors, pacemakers, and dialysis machines. Helmsford was in the business of providing essential care for several hundred patients who were tapped into the vast system of government and private insurance company reimbursements.

Finally, Vogel was ready to begin. He would operate on an elderly man with a brain embolism. The requisite forms were sent through channels and approved. He would use PET F-19 to outline the brain. If the man just happened to die, maybe he would see the green glow again.

Early one morning, he explained the procedure to the surgical team. He would remove all or part of an embolism that had put the sixty-four-year-old patient in a perpetual semiconscious state. Removing the clot from the artery could allow fresh blood to circulate in that area of the brain and would likely restore some brain and body functions.

At the conclusion of his little speech, Dr. Bernard Williams said, "Yeah, let's do it."

Vogel knew the anesthesiologist had an affinity for various prescription drugs and had been quietly released from two large Cleveland hospitals. Bernard was overqualified and bored at Helmsford, but the job paid reasonably well and provided access to an extensive pharmacological storeroom. Bernard would make no noise about surgical inconsistencies.

Vogel's scrub nurse was Linda, an army retiree who was used to a rigorous chain of command. She was unquestionably loyal to superiors, and that was perfect for what he wanted to do.

The circulating nurse was Roland Muhammed. Unlike many of the state employees at Helmsford, he was an eager and ambitious man from the inner city who had just missed getting into medical school. Instead, he had gone on to become a very competent and skilled trauma and operating room nurse. Vogel knew Muhammed was knowledgeable, and that was good. On the other hand, his ambition made him dangerous.

The ancient operating room with its marble floor and its high rotunda ceiling was a far step from the gleaming, white, state-of-the-art facility at Chicago General, but it would do.

As soon as the patient was seated in the surgical chair and properly sedated, Vogel cut through the periosteum and lifted the white and pink flap of skin to expose the skull. As he cut the first hole into the pale, boney tissue, the tiny power saw made a tinny, high-pitched whine.

After drilling four small holes, Vogel asked for the giggly saw. Just before insertion, he glanced at his staff to see how they were doing. Linda's heavily made-up eyes were large, round, and focused. Bernard looked bored, but Roland leaned forward. The dark planes of his face were taut. His eyes were bright and observant.

Vogel felt a pinch of apprehension.

Vogel erased the worry from his mind and threaded the diamond-edged saw into one small hole and out the other. Two quick pulls of the blade, and the skull was split. He quickly repeated the procedure at each of the other points and then gingerly lifted up a section of skull to expose the bluish-gray, gelatinous brain.

Neurosurgery was the most refined, most delicate kind of surgery. There were few blood vessels in the brain, so there was little bleeding. After being up to his armpits in blood and chaos at several emergency rooms during his internship and residency, Vogel savored the restrained quiet of neurosurgery.

The scanner showed the entire brain outlined in various blue tints ranging from cobalt to azure. In the left hemisphere, near the area of the speech cortex, were the dark outlines of the blood clot that had caused the man to lose his speech and most of his motor functions.

Vogel had carefully checked the hospital records and learned that his patient's wife had died several years ago. The man had no children, no siblings, no living parents, and no estate. Not one visitor or telephone call had been logged in over six years. The man was a living, breathing Social Security number, kept alive by the hospital for government funds.

Death would release this man from his half-world of intravenous drips and feeding tubes and catheters. Arranging for that death would be an act of kindness.

It would also allow him to see if the green light came again.

Vogel moved his scalpel over the surface of the brain and plunged it through the dark mass until it was near the stellate ganglion. The slow steady blip-blip of the heart function changed into an irregular pattern.

"Hang in there, Mr. Smithfield. I'm trying to remove some dead tissue to allow more circulation in the area," he said urbanely, as if teaching a class at the university.

He pressed down again through the soft gelatinous mass and watched the monitor.

"I hope the blood clot is not too close to the ..."

As he spoke, Vogel thrust his scalpel forward under the clot and quickly severed most of the left side of the brain stem. The patient gave an involuntary lurch. Vogel forced his eyes to stay down and away from the monitor.

"Oh, dear," said Vogel and straightened up.

As Vogel had anticipated, the surgical crew stood back as the heart rhythms became erratic, the rate of respiration slowed, and the blood pressure dropped. The room was quiet, except for the blip of the heart monitor and the delicate hiss of oxygen. No one moved into the frenzy of a Code Blue because Mr. Smithfield was a *Do Not Resuscitate* patient.

Vogel glanced at the monitor. An intense green light radiated from below the pineal gland near the center of the brain. It lasted a few seconds and then faded away.

Linda and Bernard stared at the dying man, but Vogel stared at the monitor. With a quickening heart, he saw the green glow in the elderly man's brain and the soft fade as the heartbeat slowed and stopped. He looked over at Muhammed, and the cheeky bastard was staring up the screen too. Damn.

Vogel flipped off the screen. "That's it, folks. Sorry we lost him. It would have been nice to see Mr. Smithfield functioning at a higher level, but the clot was too large, too well established." Vogel sighed heavily. "Linda, call the morgue. I'm going to my office to fill out the report."

CHAPTER 38

For two years, Vogel quietly continued his surgeries at Helmsford. He performed several remarkable procedures in which patients were brought back from the brink of death to new life. Because of his skill, he was able, on occasion, to literally make the blind to see and the deaf to hear.

During this time, Vogel wrote substantive articles for several medical journals but never mentioned his adventures with the dying. He refused offers of employment from three prestigious teaching hospitals, offers that would have quadrupled his salary and put him in charge of whole departments. He needed to be at Helmsford.

The risks of brain surgery were great under the best of circumstances. At a chronic- diseases hospital, mortality rates were predictably high because of a compromised and elderly population. Vogel knew that at Helmsford, no one would question him about the fact that an extraordinary number of patients died on his operating table within an eighteen-month period.

Linda assisted often, and that was good. She was efficient and useful in the operating theater. Another retired army nurse named Dee was an occasional substitute. Vogel suspected that she and Linda were lovers, but those things mattered little to him.

Everything was coming together in his notes, his reading, his laboratory observations, and his surgeries. His discoveries were immense, profound, almost beyond belief. He had found a living enzyme that burned in a greenish glow during the very moment of death. The chemical seemed to be the life force, the driving mechanism of the entire body.

The radioactive isotope used when he first saw the glow at Chicago General had been experimental then. Other, better isotopes for imaging had been discovered last year, but as far as he knew, PET F-19 was the only isotope that showed the green glow. When PET F-19 was discontinued from mass production, Vogel was still able to special order it from Chalk River Laboratories in Ontario at hideous expense. He couldn't hide the bills from the bureaucrats that oversaw the finances of Helmsford, so he paid most of the cost himself through a direct check to the lab and then had them send a reduced bill to the hospital.

His 401-K plan had been decimated, but Vogel didn't care. It would all be worth it in the long term.

He had only one problem: Roland. The young black man was smart and eager, always volunteering to assist, asking questions, standing too near in the operating room. Vogel suspected that he ferreted out the dates and times of Vogel's surgeries so he could be available. He even volunteered to be scrub nurse when Linda and Dee went on a Caribbean cruise together.

Roland's questions were incisive and erudite and annoying. He probed Vogel's diagnosis and questioned the medications he prescribed. He chatted about mortality rates and casually mentioned patients who died in surgery. Whenever Roland was near, Vogel was apprehensive and annoyed.

Then, in June of Vogel's second year at Helmsford, Roland approached him one evening and asked if they could have a cup of coffee together. Vogel thought longingly of his quiet, immaculate apartment and his new CD of the Berlin Symphony but forced himself to be gracious.

"Certainly, Roland," he answered. "In fact, it will be my treat."

"Why thank you, sir," Roland said and led the way into the small coffee shop in the reception building.

They sat at a small booth next to an open window that streamed fresh cool air into the musty, old building. Vogel's mind raced underneath his calm exterior. What did Roland want? The young man had been stirring his coffee for over a minute now. The spoon clicked, clicked as it circled in the gray liquid.

Vogel looked out the window. Near the lake, swimming ducks formed overlapping Vs in the still water.

Roland finally placed the spoon on the saucer and looked up. "I don't know quite how to put this, but I've noticed something about your surgeries."

"Yes?" Vogel asked softly. "Go on."

Roland shrugged, and his eyes were luminous in the reflected light of the setting sun. "I got my nursing degree at Pitt and did my practical at Saint Christopher's, but I never saw anyone use scanners and radioactive isotopes as much as you, especially PET F-19. No one uses that anymore, but it sure makes everything show up real good on the monitor."

"That particular dye helps me to be more precise in my surgery."

"That green glow is something, isn't it?" Roland persisted. "The way it only happens when we lose one."

"Really?" Vogel looked out the window again. The ducks were gone, and the still water now reflected the massive shape of Building III.

Roland leaned forward and, with unwelcome familiarity, placed his long, bony fingers on Vogel's forearm.

"Yeah, the way I figure it," he whispered, "you've found something, something important. That's why you're here at this dump. I checked up on you; you're pretty high up in medical circles. You write articles for the *Journal of Medicine*, for *Lancet*. Why, you're even listed in Who's Who of Medicine. I started wondering why a rich, famous doctor would take a job at a run-down state hospital in a Pennsylvania hick town, a job that pays peanuts.

Vogel withdrew his arm. His face remained blank.

"I don't know why I'd do that, Roland. Do you?" he asked softly.

In the long silence that followed, the spoon again circled the white ceramic cup. Click. Click. Click.

"Because at Helmsford, you have all the patients you need," Roland said. "An endless supply of human guinea pigs, thanks to good old Uncle Sam and the bureaucratic maze of a state-run hospital."

"You have a very active imagination, Roland," Vogel whispered. He leaned forward until their noses were a foot apart. "Just where is this bizarre theory taking you?"

"The green light. That's what's happening." Roland smiled widely. "The rest of the biopsies and tumors and strokes, all the other surgeries you perform, they're just window dressing for the ones that die. The ones that make the glow ..." He hesitated. "Sometimes you even help them along."

"That's preposterous. You are obviously sneaking drugs out of pharmacology."

"No way. I'm too smart for any of that stuff. Saw too much of it in my old neighborhood."

As Vogel watched, Roland took a long drink of his lukewarm coffee and then carefully placed the cup on the saucer. He leaned back against the hard, gray, plastic booth. His dark eyes never left Vogel's face.

Vogel felt a sudden chill and looked around the coffee shop to see who else might be listening. Two nurses at the far side of the room were talking softly. He could hear voices back in the kitchen. The coffee shop closed at nine o'clock each night. It was now eight forty-five.

Roland continued in a soft, secret voice. "After you discovered the glow in the brains of the old patients, you wanted to check out the younger ones. Like that kid last week. Remember? The vegetable from Building III? Drooling in his crib for years, but all of a sudden he needs brain surgery for a suspected tumor of the pituitary. His pretty green light lasted a long time. Whatever that stuff is, it's stronger in the younger ones, isn't it?"

Vogel again struggled to maintain his outward composure. He had to remain calm until he found out what Roland wanted. There was a quid pro quo somewhere that was quietly edging toward him.

"You are right, Roland. I have found something, something, ah ... interesting."

Vogel watched as the studied, casual grin on Roland's face mutated into a wide, triumphant smile.

"I knew it. I knew you had something!" he said. "What a setup. No witnesses, no family members to question procedures, and a fat, happy administrator who will agree to anything as long as it brings in the cash from Medicare and Medicaid."

Vogel waited for Roland to continue. Could he have misinterpreted Roland's motives? Perhaps the young man was, after all, captivated by the science and wonder of his miraculous discovery. Perhaps he, Vogel, could become a mentor for the young lad. He missed the camaraderie of his early days in medicine. He still missed his mother.

But without a single question concerning Vogel's discovery, without even a small, curious question regarding the green light, the quid pro quo dropped onto the table, and Vogel simultaneously felt a great sadness and an inexorable rage.

"Yes, sir, the way I figure it, you're going to help me get into medical school. Oh, I passed the exams, but barely, and barely just isn't good enough. I need a sponsor to write recommendations, maybe even make a few telephone calls. Stuff like that. Once I get accepted, I'll be off to doctor school with my big black lips sealed forever."

Vogel felt a tiny stab of pain in his right temple. His blood pressure must be elevated. Roland had no questions or interest in his fabulous work; instead he made a veiled threat to expose Vogel if he did not help him get into med school.

He must be very, very careful. Allow nothing to get in his way.

Vogel kept his voice calm and even. "I'd be delighted to help you, Roland. Why don't you come over to my office tomorrow night and bring the forms. I'll need to get some background information so I can correctly answer any questions about you."

"That would be great, Dr. Vogel. What time?"

"Is eight o'clock good for you?"

"I'll be there."

CHAPTER 39

At precisely eight o'clock the next evening, Vogel was sitting at his desk reading when he heard a rap at his front door. Roland's familiar figure was silhouetted against the long glass pane that bordered the side of the door.

The book in Vogel's hands was a technical treatise called *Neuroglobin D and the Regeneration Issue*, written by a colleague, Dr. Wilton Abraham. It explained the latest research into the area of the brain near the pineal gland and theorized that this spot might be a control center of the regenerative processes for the entire human body. More research was needed, the author explained, but this area seemed to regulate and direct the process of cell renewal that produced new blood cells from bone marrow, new skin cells from the endodermis, and new hair from hair follicles until the entire body recreated itself over a period of approximately seven years.

"Come in, son. Come in," Vogel called.

Roland was dressed in a cream-colored, button-down shirt and sharply-creased khaki pants. A yellow and green paisley tie and brown loafers finished the studied, casual look. He carried a large manila envelope.

Vogel smiled and adjusted his own tie. The boy was obviously trying to mimic him. Too bad he hadn't learned to mind his own business.

"Let's take a look at what you've got, Roland. Here, have a seat. But first, how about a cup of coffee? You'll find that mine is superior to that swill in the coffee shop. This is Hawaiian Kona; I think you'll like it."

"I could use some coffee," Roland said. "I was up late last night getting all this information together for you."

Vogel took two delicate English bone china cups from a cabinet and poured coffee into both.

"Cream? Sugar?" he asked.

"Just cream. Thanks, Dr. Vogel."

Roland sipped his coffee and then opened the envelope.

"I've applied to Chicago General, to Northside in Pittsburgh, and to the University of Illinois. Are there others I should consider?"

"Perhaps Michigan. I know the dean quite well."

Roland stifled a yawn. "I sure am sleepy tonight. Sorry."

"That's okay, Roland. You just need some more coffee. Here, give me your cup."

Precisely five minutes later, in the middle of filling out the requisite questionnaire from Michigan, Roland's eyes started to droop. Vogel watched carefully as his head lolled and his mouth went slack.

Suddenly Roland's eyes opened and then widened in horror. His words were slurred as he croaked, "You put something … in the … coffee … Dokerrr Vogllll … Wha's goin on? … Wha …"

Silence. And then Vogel heard the satisfying sound of Roland's limp body tumbling off the chair.

CHAPTER 40

R oland woke to find he was sitting upright in a chair with tape across his mouth. His head was immobilized with steel clamps. His arms and legs were restrained with straps. The inside of his right elbow hurt, and when he looked down, he saw an intravenous drip inserted into a vein. White tape secured it.

Vogel's face popped out from behind the chair. He smiled warmly.

"Roland, I am delighted to have you here with me. You have no idea how much I need you. You will have vast importance in my work; I am ready for the next step."

Roland could not move. Only his eyes rotated back and forth in his dark face, flashing white as they followed Vogel's progress around the room.

"Have you ever seen a bone marrow harvest, Roland? It's a fairly routine procedure wherein a long needle is inserted into the hip bone of the healthy patient to withdraw marrow. That marrow is later inserted into a cancer patient of similar blood type. Within days, the cancer victim begins manufacturing new healthy blood cells and bone marrow. The results are often quite miraculous, I assure you."

Vogel stood in front of Roland, and his voice became softer. The smile faded.

"My theory, dear Roland, is that we can do the same thing, yet faster, with a direct extraction from the regenerative center of the brain. I have a patient in Building III, a Mr. Weikert. He is eighty-one years old and suffers from several medical conditions brought on by his advanced age. He has moderate dementia caused by the clogging of the carotid arteries, irregular heartbeat, arthritis, calcification of the lungs. His blood type matches yours exactly."

Vogel picked up a long, thin needle from a silver tray and disappeared behind Roland.

"I wonder what will happen to Mr. Weikert if he receives an injection of that green glow you're so curious about? Perhaps between us, we can perform a little experiment."

Roland felt a sharp, painful thrust at the back of his head, at the very top of the spinal column where it joined with the skull. His body tensed. This could not be happening to him. The future was bright; he would be a doctor someday. A rich black doctor with a Mercedes in the driveway of his grand, brick suburban home …

Early the next morning, Nurse Sally Larson hurried into Room 641 in Building III. She was late, and it was past time to dispense medication, to check temperatures and blood pressures, to change diapers and sheets.

Suddenly a voice range out, "Hi, cutie. Can you rustle me up some breakfast? I'm starved. Been waiting all morning for you."

Nurse Larson started and quickly turned. She clutched the crisp white linens to her chest and stared open-mouthed at the bed nearest the window.

Mr. Weikert was sitting up in bed.

"Whadaya say, honey. Get some grub and put down this damn bed rail. I gotta take a leak."

The nurse dropped the sheets on the floor and ran down the hall. Without waiting for the elevator, she sprinted down two flights of stairs and knocked on the door of the attending physician.

"Doctor, come quickly. Something's wrong with Mr. Weikert."

CHAPTER 41

Now, five years later, in the heart of the New Jersey Pine Barrens, Phase Two of Vogel's project was moving along splendidly. He was extracting regularly, thanks to the discreet and inventive Wilbur Nelson, who was able to supply young men in sufficient numbers.

Early on, he'd been able to garner the enthusiastic support of General Morris and the Foundation for the American Way. They had come up with a plan where the foundation would fund his "clinic" in the Barrens and his "research," thereby having exclusive access to the distribution of his magic elixir. It was all part of a grand master plan, a way to influence and control the correct people in the ever-shrinking global community.

Because of space limitations in the old farmhouse, a special miniaturized version of the scanner had been built for him at enormous expense. The walls surrounding the tiny operating room had been modified with lead shields, but from the outside, it remained the old Watson place, with only a new attached garage as a reminder that the old farm had changed hands.

The garage was essential because the van could pull in, the automatic doors would shut, and no curious passerby would see what was being taken from it: food, medical supplies, equipment, or unconscious young men.

General Morris himself had flown in last November to witness a procedure. He was most impressed, praised Vogel, and promised his and the foundation's full continuing support.

Most importantly, a colleague was even now secretly conducting crucial chemical and biological analyses of his newly-discovered enzyme at an off-campus laboratory associated with MIT. If the enzyme's peculiar properties could be duplicated and produced in quantity, Vogel's gift of life would become enormously important to the entire world.

He dreamed of that world often. The magical enzyme, code-named Zelon, would be readily available to the right people. His colleague in Boston had estimated another two to three years before he could isolate Zelon, and then another, perhaps shorter period of time before they could duplicate it in the laboratory.

In the meantime, he, General Morris, and the foundation had collaborated on a small select list of persons who were already receiving injections of Zelon. Others were on a waiting list. The aging king of an oil-rich Middle-Eastern country was a candidate, as was the failing CEO of an American company that developed and manufactured computer chips for the military. The short list included an Asian prime minister, a senator, two congressmen, and a governor who was a potential presidential candidate. At his request, they had added a composer and the recipient of a Nobel Prize in literature.

All were certified to be in a state of compromised health. All were told that Zelon was a new experimental vitamin, available only through the foundation. It was fascinating, intoxicating work.

From the time of his discovery, to the development of his plan, to the recruitment of Morris and the foundation, the entire operation had been virtually flawless. Flawless, until a couple of wandering adolescents showed up at his door this morning.

Vogel turned sideways in his bed and brought his knees up to his chest to ease a cramp in his lower back.

He could see them clearly. The tall, brown-haired, muscular one looked like a football player, one of those young men undoubtedly called a jock. The other was a short, tough guy with a small swagger.

That one was definitely dangerous with his cheeky threat of calling the police.

Vogel sighed and then buried his head into the down pillow. He was sure he had convinced them with his story of a rehabilitation center. He'd gotten the plate number of the Jeep from Jack, and now he would ask Wilbur Nelson to find out who the owner was.

He had to be careful. There was too much at stake now.

CHAPTER 42

Later that afternoon, Edsell was tied back in his bed after a short, rushed walk up and down the hallway and a quick dinner of cut-up chicken and rice and applesauce. Ugly Dude had been brusque and quick and strangely distracted.

Edsell was in a hopeful mood for the first time since he was brought to the old house.

He knew the guy in the next bed was named Jared because he'd overheard a conversation yesterday between Ugly Dude and the White Shirt Guy when they were adjusting some dials on the machines that monitored the bed next to him.

"Jared's pretty clean," said White Shirt. "We don't need two weeks for him."

"Good. These two will both be ready by the first of next week," said Ugly Dude.

"Scott's almost ready. We can do him on Saturday night, then these two on Monday," said White Shirt.

Something was going to happen to him and Jared on Monday. What? Were they sending him home? To another place like this? It was all so confusing.

Then around noon today, there had been a commotion inside and outside.

A car had pulled up near the building. He'd heard voices outside, and then suddenly something down the hall crashed or fell, a window flew up, and a voice started screaming.

He heard a hard pounding on the outside door, voices yelling from outside, and then the screaming stopped abruptly.

Doors slammed inside, and there was a murmur of voices below their window. A few minutes later, a car pulled away, and a few minutes after that, Edsell heard the familiar sound of a larger vehicle pulling away in the same direction.

During the whole noisy scene, he and Jared had grinned under their gags and eyeballed each other. Help might be coming, coming soon. Someone knew about this building, knew they were here. Who had screamed? Another kid who got loose?

Would the strangers call the police? Of course they would. Weren't screams something the police would investigate?

He and Jared lay in their beds and winked and blinked at each other.

CHAPTER 43

The next morning during Algebra, Borderline asked to be excused to go to the bathroom. He hurried down the hall to the john and flung open the door. Empty. He looked under the stalls. No feet.

Borderline grabbed handfuls of coarse brown paper towels, crumpled them into balls, and dropped them into a toilet. When the bowl was filled with soggy paper, he pushed the flush lever.

The toilet made a gurgling sound. The pulpy mass started to go down, but then the weight of the paper clogged the sewer line. The water kept running, and within a few seconds, a cascade of water was pouring onto the gray tile floor.

Just then, a dark-haired kid that Borderline remembered from his gym class opened the door.

"Jeez, Bill," Borderline said. "I don't know what happened here. It looks like a freakin' flood. Can you run and get Nerf? I'm late for my class."

As Bill scampered off toward Nerf's office, Borderline quickly turned and sprinted down the hall in the opposite direction. Two turns later at the backside of the gym, he peered around a corner and watched Bill pound on the janitor's door. Nerf came out, listened to Bill for a few moments, and then pulled a bucket and a mop from the closet and disappeared around the far corner.

Pulling a folded piece of pink paper from his pocket, Borderline opened Nerf's door. The room was small, with pale yellow, cement block walls. A gray metal desk, a gray metal chair, and a three-drawer filing cabinet almost filled the room. He placed the folded paper on the desk and then quickly tried the drawers of the file cabinet. The first one slid open easily, revealing hanging file folders with various labels listing cleaning supplies, work schedules, electrical schematics, and names of plumbing supply houses.

The next drawer opened also. More files. As Borderline pulled the hanging folders toward him, he noticed something black and yellow in the back of the drawer behind the files. He reached in and pulled out a worn and shabby Pittsburgh Steelers cap. A gold and black Super Bowl pin glinted on it.

"Oh shit," he whispered as he shoved it back behind the folders.

The third drawer was locked.

Borderline ran into the hallway and glanced through the large glass doors that led outside. As planned, Stacey was there, leaning against a wide-spreading maple tree. He gave her the thumbs up sign and raced back to class.

"Did you get lost, Mr. Fenton?" asked Mrs. Smythe as he slid into his desk at the back of the room.

"No, ma'am. Just stomach cramps. Must have been that broccoli casserole my mother made me eat last night. I feel so sick."

The class tittered as Borderline put his head down on the desk.

"That's quite enough, young man. All right, class. Who can tell me the function of Y in this equation? Mark?"

Stacey stood in the shade of the old maple and looked at her watch. Only forty-five minutes until her shift at Mickey D's. Nerf had better show up soon. Thank God she was already wearing her aqua and pink uniform.

Five minutes later, Stacey saw Nerf approaching with a mop and bucket. Without looking in her direction, he put the cleaning tools in the closet and disappeared into his office.

Stacey quickly opened the heavy outside door and tiptoed across the hallway, her white sneakers noiseless on the glossy floor. The Venetian blind on Nerf's office door was open. She saw him glance at his desk and then pick up the pink piece of paper. As he read it, a look of fear came over his face, and then one of puzzlement.

He reached for the phone and dialed quickly. Stacey heard him talking, but the words were muffled by the heavy door. He seemed agitated, drumming his fingers on the desk, shifting his weight from one foot to the other.

All at once, he turned unexpectedly and saw her at the window. Stacey quickly knocked and put on her best dimpled smile.

Nerf said something on the phone and then laid it on the desk. Stacey opened the door, poked her head in, and said, "Mr. Ner ... I mean, Mr. Nelson?"

"What?" he snapped.

"Yesterday I went to the library to see Mrs. O'Shea about my college recommendation, and I think I left my pocketbook there. She's not here this morning, and I've got to find my purse. I need to get to my job, and I drove over here without my driver's license ... and I don't want to get stopped."

Stacey fidgeted under Nerf's stare. What was he thinking behind those small, dark eyes?

"Nothing's been turned in," he said brusquely. "You must have lost it somewhere else. I have an important phone call. If you'll excuse me ..."

"Can you call me if you find it?"

"Yes, yes. I'll call you. Good-bye."

"But you don't know my name or my phone number."

"Okay, okay. What's your name and number?"

"Stacey Green. Number 555-1276."

Nerf grabbed a stubby pencil and wrote the number down on a pad.

"Good-bye, Miss. I'll call you."

"But, but you don't know what it looks like," Stacey protested. "I mean, it's a cool bag my grandmother gave me for my last birthday, and it looks fabulous with my new white shorts and red print top. It's from a fancy store in Palm Beach, and my granny would be so upset if she knew I lost it. She lives in this condo in a senior citizens' place, and she's the sweetest old—"

"Stop! Stop!" Nerf barked and picked up the phone. "Hello, hello. I'll call you right back. What? No, I'll call you right back."

Nerf slammed the phone back into its cradle, closed his eyes, and shuddered. He took a notebook and a pen from his desk. His lips were tight, and his forehead gleamed with moisture.

"Your purse?" he asked softly. "What does it look like?"

"Red … yeah, it was red. With a navy drawstring and navy pocket … and some white stripes on the back."

"Red and navy with white stripes. I'll check the library and our Lost and Found drawer. If it turns up, I'll call you."

"Gee, thanks, Mr. Nelson. You're a doll, a real nice man. So helpful." She smiled and widened her eyes. "Thanks a bunch. Granny's coming for a visit next month, and if I don't have the purse, well, you know how grannies are." Stacey smiled again. "Thank you."

Nerf wiped his hand over his face. "Good-bye, Miss."

He opened the door, and Stacey stepped through it into the empty corridor. She heard Nerf close and lock the door behind her. Halfway down the hallway, she glanced back and saw the blinds were closed.

CHAPTER 44

===

ate that evening, Mark sat in a corner booth at Nick's with Stacey and Borderline. The old pizzeria had served three generations of Toms River residents, and it was obvious that Nick's customers did not come for the ambiance. The windows were foggy with grit, the salmon pink walls had not been painted in years, and the scarred tabletops exhibited a gallery of graffiti and old cigarette burns. Cracked gray floor tiles held the shadows of old grease marks.

A huge pizza steamed on the table before them. Pepperoni, sausage, onions, mushrooms, and sprinkles of sliced garlic peeked through the mozzarella and provolone cheese. Mark leaned forward and separated a slice from the Nick's Special and then slid the hot savory wedge onto his plate. Borderline and Stacey did the same.

For several minutes, the three friends were silent as they divided and devoured the warm, spicy pizza. A pitcher of iced tea washed it down. Finally, Mark sat back with a sigh as he licked his fingers.

"Best pie in town," he said as he wiped a spot of sauce from the table with a crumpled napkin.

"Time to talk," Borderline said, "but keep it down. We don't want the whole town to know what we're doing." He turned to Mark. "What do you think?"

Mark spoke in a low voice. "Until today, I kept telling myself that there was nothing going on, that there was a logical reason for Edsell being gone, that he'd be back with some wild story about hitching a ride to New York or Philadelphia." He picked up a leftover crust of the pie and munched it absently. "Even when we heard that kid screaming out at that house, I *wanted* to buy the story of the clinic for rich kids. In fact, when this thing started, it was almost fun. Like we were kids again, playing detective, making up stuff, pretending it was real."

"And now?" Borderline asked.

"There *is* something happening," Mark said. "The Steelers cap in Nerf's office puts a lock on it. That cap could only be Edsell's."

"Do you think Edsell's out there in the Barrens?" Borderline asked.

"Maybe they're torturing him or something," Stacey whispered. "Remember the kid that screamed when you found that old house? There really *are* insane creeps in this world, like that Ted Bundy guy. Remember? How many people did he kill before he got caught?" She shivered and drew her arms across her chest. "I don't even want to think about it. Edsell was such a nerdy, cute kind of guy. He had a great smile."

"Stop saying *was*," Mark hissed. "You make it sound like he's dead already."

"We gotta *do* something, but what?" Borderline said. "Nerf knows someone's on to him because of the note we left."

"There's a scary thought." Stacey shivered again.

"Okay, okay. Let's chill out, think this through," Borderline said. "We know that Nerf's mixed up with Vogel. Stacey saw him call someone as soon as he found the note."

"And he didn't even look up the number," Stacey added. "He looked worried while he was talking on the phone and then nearly jumped out of his skin when he saw me. He was real fidgety while I was telling him the lost pocketbook story."

"I repeat the same question, guys. What do we do?" Borderline asked. "Go to the police?"

"What if we're wrong?" Mark said. "What if one of the other janitors found the cap somewhere and turned it in? Maybe Nerf is just saving it for Edsell. If we go running to the cops with our story, we'll look like jerks."

Borderline leaned back, put his hands behind his head, and gazed at the ceiling fan that rotated slowly above them. He brought his eyes down to Mark.

"All right. Forget the cops. What about our parents? Mark, your family's down in the Carolinas for two weeks. Can you call your dad and tell him everything?"

There was a long silence.

"No, I don't think so," Mark said. "My dad's already pissed because I'm here in summer school and not on the annual family vacation. He'd get all excited, hop a plane, and come home. I wouldn't want to be near him if it turned out to be nothing ..."

Stacey nodded. "Mark's dad can be kind of tough." She looked at Borderline. "What about your parents?"

"Get real. They live in another world. My mother spends her time going to Garden Club meetings and reading cookbooks that feature a hundred ways to cook tofu. My dad does the exact same thing each day at the exact same time. Goes to work, comes home, pours himself a glass of wine, then reads the *New York Times* until dinner, which is precisely at six o'clock. My dad listens to NPR, for God's sake. Do you think he's going to believe this shit? No way."

Mark and Borderline turned to Stacey.

"My parents? Not in a million years. In the first place, they're not real thrilled with me seeing Mark. And you, Borderline, they think you're some kind of juvenile delinquent. They'd be wild if they thought I was involved with anything like this."

"The problem is that we keep talking about this, but we're not doing anything," Borderline said.

"But what can we do?" Stacey asked vehemently.

"Not *we*, Stacey," Mark said. "You're not doing anything; that's for sure."

"And why not? You guys are up to your butts in this stuff. You tell me all about it, I help you, and now you say I'm not involved. That rots, Mark. I *am* involved."

Mark glared at Stacey while she looked to Borderline for support.

"Back off, Mark," Borderline said. "We have to leave Stacey in. We need her for a backup."

"A backup?"

"For when we go back to the Barrens."

"What?" Mark said in a loud voice. "No way."

"Shh-hh-hh, keep it down," Borderline whispered as he glanced around the room. The battered, old wall clock said 9:50, and only two tables still had customers. "I was thinking that we should go back to that house on Dukes Bridge Road and check things out for ourselves before we involve anyone else."

"Yeah? How's that going to work? That doctor guy will come out and tell us the same story, or if we really irritate him, he'll call the cops on us, and then what will we say?"

"We go at night."

Mark leaned back in his chair and frowned. "You're kidding. Tell me you're kidding."

Borderline leaned forward and spoke in a low voice. "Listen, with a full moon, we can find our way back to that house without using headlights. Remember how the roads out there are white sand? They'll show up in the moonlight. I took notes on the turns we made and the mileage when we drove out there. I think I can find my way back."

"Jesus, Borderline. Do you hear yourself? Back to the Barrens at night? That place gives me the creeps during the day."

"It won't be so bad; no one will know we're there. We drive with our lights out and park near the house. I'll work my way up close and listen. If I hear anything that tells me it's not a real clinic, we'll get out of there and then go right to the police."

Mark and Stacey stared at Borderline across the debris-littered table. They jumped as a huge shape suddenly appeared next to them.

"You kids want anything else, or can I close up and go home now?" asked Nick.

They looked around. The other tables had their chairs stacked on top. Nick's wife was sweeping the floor near the front entrance. She glanced at them as she flipped over the Closed sign.

"Sorry, Nick. We didn't know it was so late," Borderline said. "What do we owe you?"

A few minutes later, Mark, Stacey, and Borderline stood in a circle under the pale yellow glow of a streetlight. The rest of the stores around them were dark; only the lights of a convenience story shone a half block down the street.

"I'm not sure about this plan, Borderline." Mark leaned against the lamp post and shook his head. "The whole thing sounds incredibly dangerous."

"Not really, if you think about it," Borderline said. "We'll be in a dark-colored Jeep with four-wheel drive. Anyone else driving in that area will have their lights on. If someone comes along, we'll just drive off the road for a few minutes and let them go by. They'll never even know we're there."

Maybe ... maybe it will work," Mark said.

"It will work," Borderline said. "Stacey's the backup. If she doesn't hear from us by nine o'clock the next morning, she'll call the police and tell them everything."

Mark crossed his arms on his chest.

"Let me tell you something, Borderline. That place out there scares me, and it's not just the house. Those pine woods are too quiet for me. It's like something out there is waiting to happen. I felt it the last time we were there."

"That's because you're a city boy, Mark. You're used to streetlights and traffic. I'll bet the people who live in the Barrens love all that peace and quiet."

"People? What people?"

"Look," Stacey interrupted, "on the other side of that building. Over there." She pointed. "That's a full moon."

Mark and Borderline moved several paces to the right and looked. A full moon glowed silver against the black summer sky.

"Okay, that's it. We'll do it tomorrow night," Borderline said.

"But what if it's cloudy? What if it rains?" Mark asked.

"Rain? It hasn't rained in months," Borderline answered. "Come on, it's the beginning of the Fourth of July weekend. Tomorrow night, everyone will be busy with parties and cookouts; no one will notice what we're doing. I'll tell my parents I'm spending the night at your house."

CHAPTER 45

The next morning, Mark woke up at six o'clock. He lay in bed and worried about their plan to drive to the Barrens tonight. So many things could go wrong. Was there anything they could learn before they went? What missing pieces of the puzzle could they find?

Mark tried to remember details about the house in the Barrens. It was old, two stories with a big wraparound porch. It sat in the middle of a small clearing with no landscaping or shrubs to soften its bulk. There were no fences around it and no signs to indicate that it was a rehabilitation center.

The tall, homely man who had answered the door wore black coveralls. Who was he and what was his job there? He looked more like a bodyguard than a doctor or nurse.

Vogel, on the other hand, did seem like a real doctor with his long words and concerned face, his white shirt and paisley tie. He said he was treating six patients. Six important, young patients. Was he?

And what about that awful screaming? If the old farmhouse was not a clinic, what was it? And who was that kid?

Mark worried and finally got up. He called Borderline, knowing that he was probably waking up the Fentons. To his relief, Borderline answered the phone.

"You're not able to sleep either, are you?" Mark said.

"No, buddy. I'm really bummed out about this whole thing."

"Me too. But I was just thinking about something. Last year, a kid named Lester was suddenly gone from my shop class. I heard he went to live with his dad in Pennsylvania, but no one ever knew for sure."

"What's your point?" asked Borderline.

"Just this: what if other kids have disappeared? What if Edsell isn't the only one? Most of the high schools around here have hundreds of students. We've got South, East, and North. Outside of Toms River, there are big regional schools like Lacey, Jackson, and Point Pleasant. Families move in and move out, people get transferred or divorced. Some lose their jobs and move to smaller houses, others get promoted and buy bigger ones. On top of that, there are poor families that live in the beach rentals during the winter months and then move elsewhere when the rents go up in the summer. Their kids are always coming and going."

"I see what you mean. I wonder if there's a way we can find out if there are other missing kids," Borderline said.

"The police must have reports … wait, I've got it," Mark said. "Stacey's got a cousin who works down at the police station. Maybe she can get some information for us about missing kids. I'll call Stacey. She doesn't go to work until later today, so she can probably go over to police headquarters this morning. I know it's the weekend, but maybe her cousin is working today. They never shut down the police stations."

"Tell her not to let anyone know the real reason she's asking," Borderline cautioned.

"No problem. Stacey's cool. She'll make up something."

CHAPTER 46

On Friday morning, Teddy parked the Bronco next to dark water that mirrored clumps of false asphodel, millet grass, and pickerelweed. She unloaded her equipment and then stood at the edge of the bog and inhaled the warm, pungent smells.

The cedar swamp stretched out in front of her, dark and mysterious. The black still water was lit by thin beams of sunlight that filtered through a high, dense canopy formed by the ancient trees. In only a few weeks, Teddy had grown to love the Pine Barrens. It was a fragile, haunting place, unlike any other in the world. The life forms around her were strange, tenacious, and adaptive. The many rare and endangered species within its boundaries made it a botanist's dream. Curley Grass Fern, Crested Yellow Orchis, Arethusa, False Asphodel, Red Wilkweed, and, her special favorite, Boykin's Lobilia.

The ancient cedar swamp was a perfect habitat for Boykin's Lobilia. She had mapped several locations of the herb in the past few weeks and was hoping to find enough of the elusive plant to bring live specimens back to the lab and the water gardens at Rutgers.

Boykin's Lobilia was a tall, spindly plant, with delicate pale blue or white or purplish flowers. It was blooming now in the Barrens.

On Teddy's left, an old dike stretched out into the swamp. The old earthen structure was too narrow for her truck but fine for walking. She didn't want to slosh through black water and climb over slimy, old, submerged logs unless she had to.

Teddy pushed damp strands of hair away from her face. It was hot again today. The air was still and dry.

The faint odor of smoke hung in the air like a silent, gray bystander. Joshua had warned her about wildfires, but Teddy already had textbook knowledge of them. She knew that when the Barrens were dry, the vegetation burned hotter and faster than California chaparral.

Perhaps she should buy a scanner and carry it with her, tuned to the Forest Fire Service. A major fire had burned part of Wharton State Forest in the southern part of the Barrens just days ago, and she didn't want to get caught in something like that. She was alone each day in the Barrens, and no one knew just where she was. Right now, there was no way anyone could warn her about a dangerous fire.

A burst of pain in her upper arm reminded her that she had not put on her insect repellant this morning. Teddy swatted at the green fly in irritation as two more buzzed around her face. She quickly put the backpack down, rummaged inside for the small bottle of evil-smelling lotion, and applied it liberally to her arms, face, and neck. She'd have to take a long, hot shower before she saw Joshua again tonight.

It was good to be in a relationship again. She had almost forgotten how truly pleasurable a man's body was. Who would have thought she would fall for a man who hunted and fished, who knew how to grill steak and to pot roast venison?

Joshua Reed was an incredibly soothing, considerate man who understood her love of wild growing things. She was content as never before, and she wondered what had ever attracted her to Ken last year and why she had been depressed after the breakup.

Teddy compared his thin runner's body with Joshua's powerful frame. She recalled a tedious afternoon of grocery shopping with the unfortunate Ken. He had meticulously examined the labels on every single can and package, checking for fat, carbohydrates, sodium, calories, and additives before each purchase. Her sister was right. Ken had been boring, incredibly boring.

Not so with Joshua. Teddy chuckled as she remembered the thick steaks he had grilled last Friday night. When the T-bones were seared black on the outside and rosy on the inside, Joshua expertly carved the smoky meat into thin diagonal slices. The grilled Vidalia onions had been sweet and glossy. The salad was a simple mix of leaf lettuce and tangy radishes sprinkled with olive oil and Balsamic vinegar. The homemade dill biscuits were hot and light, and she devoured three of them without thinking of calories.

Their dinner plates had been old and chipped, and her fork had a bent tine, yet it was a most satisfying meal.

Teddy flushed as she recalled the rest of the evening. They had spent a long time just talking and then more time comfortably touching and exploring each other in every possible way ...

She would have liked to spend the whole weekend with him, but her work in the Barrens was too pressing, and she had to continue. They had seen each other for a few hours on Saturday night. Her place, this time, but she had driven into Medford and picked up Chinese food. There was no way she wanted to try out any ill-advised, poorly-executed recipes on Joshua at this stage of their relationship. Plus, she didn't even own a cookbook.

She'd set the table and put the food into glass serving dishes. All in all, it was a fine meal. Afterward had been fine too.

Better pay attention, she told herself, *and stop daydreaming.*

She took her binoculars from the backpack and scanned the still water and the small islands of vegetation that dotted its surface. She needed to find a large stand of Boykin's Lobilia so she could get cuttings and live specimens for the lab. Because the weather was unusually hot and dry, the blooming season would come early and be over quickly.

Suddenly, she saw a flash of color ahead and to the right. Along the edge of the bog, she saw tall, spindly plants with sky-blue flowers on top. The color was the most intense Teddy had ever seen on any Boykin's Lobilia, and she was thrilled.

Teddy dropped her pack on the sandy dike and took out her camera and tripod. After checking the film, she added the close-up lens to her Nikon and then stepped off the sandy dike and into the dark, wet coolness of the swamp. With the sun at her back, the best place for photographs was from the bog side toward the bank. With her feet on the slippery bottom and the water at knee level, she slowly waded an uneven twenty yards to the blue flowers.

Dozens of Boykin's Lobelia. She grinned. Enough for cuttings, pictures, enough to take live specimens back to Rutgers. Teddy knew that it was not just about finding and cultivating rare species of plants. It was about preserving the varieties of nature while it was still possible. Many rare plants had been discovered to have beneficial properties.

Some of the carnivorous plants she had studied might provide a new way of controlling mosquitoes in areas of the world that had high rates of malaria or West Nile disease. Several recently harvested rare plants had proved beneficial in cancer treatments.

The setting was exquisite. Green moss glowed on the massive trunks of the old cedars, and luminous water danced with thin rays of sunshine. With any luck at all, the photographs would be magnificent.

CHAPTER 47

On Saturday afternoon of July Fourth weekend, Dr. Anton Vogel walked down the narrow upstairs hallway of his clinic. His crepe-soled shoes made a soft hiss on the polished oak floor. Despite the searing heat outside, the inside of the renovated farmhouse registered a cool seventy-two degrees.

He resisted the urge to check on his patients one more time and opened the door of his office. He stood for a moment savoring the large room's simple harmony. Books, scientific journals, and notebooks were precisely arranged on a wall of dark oak shelving. A Bang and Olufsen sound system glowed with discreet red, green, and white lights. To the right, a long, narrow table held a computer, modem, printer, and fax machine. On the left, polished oak filing cabinets held all his research.

Vogel sat down at his cherry wood desk and ran his fingers over the smooth surface. The desk had an intriguing history. In the roaring twenties, it had belonged to a Wall Street broker. When the market crashed and the poor man discovered that his ruin was complete and irretrievable, he opened a window and jumped fifteen stories to the pavement below.

When Vogel heard the story from the antique dealer and saw the faded sepia news photos that confirmed it, he wrote out a check for the full asking price.

Only four items sat on Vogel's desk: a telephone, a Stiffel lamp, a yellow legal pad, and the remote control to the sound system. He pushed a button on the remote, and the room filled with the lush primal tones of Beethoven's Fifth Symphony.

When they were first renovating the old cranberry farm, General Morris had balked at the expense of Vogel's private suite. He refused to authorize the installation of the sound system until Vogel gently reminded him that complete isolation in the Pine Barrens was dreadful for a man of culture, and perhaps there were others who might be interested in his unique product, others who would be happy to indulge a few simple requests.

And so the sound system was quickly installed. It made Vogel's life not just palatable, but pleasurable.

Vogel leaned back in his chair and let the music soothe him as the crescendo at the end of the first movement filled the room. He always felt sad when he considered the great musical geniuses of the past. So many had died prematurely. What fabulous works were lost because the advance of age robbed Beethoven of his hearing and ultimately his life? What wonderful works might Mozart have written if he had been blessed with even a few more productive years? Mozart had been only thirty-five years old when he met his end.

Everything worthy and beautiful took time to develop, and thus, time became the enemy. Scientific advance was measured in years as thousands of minds probed and pushed the limits of knowledge ever farther. Each inventor built upon the foundations and discoveries of those who had gone before.

But now, *in one monumental leap,* a golden age was about to dawn.

It had not been easy, and he had been compelled to do a few unsavory things, but other great men in human history had endured problems too. Even now there was a glitch, a minor one to be sure, but still a glitch.

Vogel opened the top right-hand drawer of the desk and withdrew several pieces of fax paper. He placed them carefully on his desk and stared at Wilbur Nelson's crabbed and heavy handwriting.

*Mark Germano, 863 Pelican Rd., Toms River. Senior
at Toms River South. Age 17.*

*Howard Patrick Fenton, 34 Robin Ct., Toms River.
Senior at Toms River South. Age 18.*

*Stacey Greene, 10 Wicks Mill Rd., Toms River. Senior
at Toms River South. Age 17.*

Attached to the list were three pages copied from last year's yearbook. On each, a face had been circled with a red marker. Vogel recognized the young men as the two who had been at his front door on Monday. The girl had an unfamiliar face, but if Nelson was right, she was part of the small glitch that might grow into a major upset unless steps were taken immediately.

His work was at a critical stage now. His operation could not and would not be moved. The location was perfect; the nearest house was over a mile away, and all the local hicks thankfully ignored him. Oh, they had brought hideously sweet and unhealthy pies and cranberry muffins to his door when he first arrived, but he gently turned them down, alluding to a health problem and a need for isolation. They had not returned.

The only real center of human habitation in this part of the Pine Barrens was the town of Chatsworth, a two-bit miserable collection of small houses, trailers, and body shops where the riffraff spent their time changing the oil in their trucks, admiring each other's tattoos, and listening to the decidedly boorish plinkety-plink of hillbilly music.

The thousands of empty acres around him would stay vacant because they were protected by the strict environmental laws that guarded the Pinelands National Reserve, better known as the Pine Barrens. Here, in the middle of the pine forest, without fencing and guards and surveillance systems, his project was safer than Fort Knox.

Safe, that is, until two teenage punks stumbled onto Dukes Bridge Road just when a patient slipped his restraints and started shrieking. He had been sure his cover story of a drug rehabilitation center had worked. He had foolishly believed that the boys would honor his appeal for secrecy.

He had been wrong.

Something had to be done immediately. Some way had to be found to silence the two young men. An accident, perhaps. A weak bridge rail over a tidal basin. A car flipped over with scattered, empty beer cans. Better yet, thought Vogel, drugs injected into the boys while they were still alive, and then drug paraphernalia scattered about. With careful planning, the problem would be eliminated.

His dear, chubby friend would help. Wilbur Nelson was the best part of the entire operation. He was a most willing worker, a fat ferret who would do anything, anything at all for a small injection of his magic potion. Nelson was a local with local knowledge and a ring of passkeys that gave him access to the confidential records of every school and administrative office in Ocean County.

It was Nelson who found the boys. With consummate skill, he cunningly searched out the lonely, rejected misfits with thick file folders, probation officers, and Department of Youth and Family Service workers. Thus far, Nelson had been able to deliver an ample supply, but if the current arrangement ceased to work, there were other sources. Camden, Newark, Philadelphia, and New York stood ready to cough up their flotsam and jetsam.

Vogel picked up the phone and pressed a button. He heard the automatic dial kick in.

"Yes?" The thin, hissed question floated back to him over the miles of telephone wire from Toms River.

"It's Vogel. We're doing a procedure tonight. Jack and I should be finished by eleven. Can you come then?"

"I'll be there."

"Good. We also need to discuss our little problem. Maybe you'll have some ideas tonight on how to eliminate it. We'll talk after the procedure."

CHAPTER 48

On Saturday afternoon, Stacey Greene walked into the Toms River Police Station, smiled at the officer behind the desk, and asked, "Is Millie Greene in?"

The young rookie looked her over.

"Maybe," he said with a slow smile. "Who shall I say is here?"

"I'm her cousin Stacey."

"Be right back, Cousin Stacey."

He opened an opaque glass door behind the main desk. Stacey heard the clack-clack of a copy machine rhythmically spewing paper. A phone on the young officer's desk rang with a tremulous chime.

He hurried back in, grabbed the phone, and pointed to the side office.

"Go on in," he said, pointing down the hallway, his hand over the receiver.

Stacey entered a long, narrow, crowded room. She knew Millie was working today because she had called her aunt this morning. File cabinets lined one wall, and a copier and a fax machine sat on a long, rectangular table. There were three desks piled high with papers, folders, plastic-bound reports, and large manila envelopes. Each desk held a computer and a keyboard. Because it was Saturday, only one computer screen was lit; only one desk was occupied.

Millie Greene jumped up as soon as she saw her cousin and walked quickly across the room to embrace her.

"Stacey, what's happening? Is everything okay?"

Stacey hugged her cousin. "I'm fine." She smiled.

"How's Mark?"

"Good. He's in summer school. Would you believe it?"

"Mark? I thought he was a stud *and* a brain."

"He got a C in algebra, so his father made him stay home from their annual family trip and retake the course in summer school. He needs to bring up his grade-point average for Princeton. Unbelievable, but of course I'm happy he's home."

Millie nodded. "I've met his father, a hard ass, Mr. Perfect." She looked at Stacey with a quizzical look on her face. "I know you didn't come here to catch up on the family news. What's up?"

"I'm ... I'm doing research," Stacey blurted.

"For what?" Millie raised one eyebrow.

"It's kind of an over-the-summer project for my sociology class next fall. On missing kids."

"Mr. Dauber's having his class do a research project on missing kids? You're kidding."

"Not the whole class," Stacey stammered. "Just me. For extra credit. I'm ... I'm thinking of majoring in law enforcement when I go to college. Honestly, it sounds like such an exciting field."

Millie shrugged. "I guess it's okay. You should talk to Captain Miller first, but he's away for the weekend." She hesitated. "I don't think he'll mind if I check some files for you."

Stacey breathed a small sigh of relief. "I need information on the numbers of missing kids reported in Toms River. Older ones, like high school, maybe junior high."

Millie opened a file cabinet and thumbed through some files. "You mean like that Jones kid that disappeared last week?" she asked.

"Yeah. Is he the only one? Are there others?"

Millie turned to Stacey with her fingers separating the files. "I'm just a secretary around here, so this isn't official or anything, but yeah, there's always missing kids. They get put on the NCIC forty-eight hours after they're reported missing."

"What's NCIC?"

"The National Crime Information Computer. It sends out information to police stations all over the country, listing the kid's height, weight, eye color, the clothes he was wearing when he disappeared, plus a picture."

Stacey nodded and looked at her watch. It was late, and the cabinet looked like it held a lot of files. Worst of all, Millie had warmed to the subject.

"It's a zoo around here when a kid is missing. The parents run in, all crazed and crying and yelling about how their child is gone. They make all sorts of noise, but when our guys check it out, the kid is usually spending the night at a friend's house two doors up the street." Millie paused. "But sometimes, the kid is really gone. Gone for good."

"How many kids are missing right now?" asked Stacey.

"Let me see." Millie thumbed through more files. "We keep the central files from some of the smaller police departments here, so actually we've got more cases than our township. You know, a lot of these disappearances involve child custody battles. The mother moves and takes the kid with her and doesn't tell the father, stuff like that. Some of the kids already have a record with us. Drugs, shoplifting, DWI ..."

"What do the numbers look like for the last few years?"

Millie leafed through the files and counted names. "Got a pencil?" she asked. "Write this down. There were two unsolved cases five years go. Four years ago, there were none." She stopped suddenly. "Wow, look at this. Two years ago it jumped to six."

Millie rifled through more files. "Last year I remember typing a lot of reports. One, two, here's the Conner boy. What a hard life he had. His father used to beat him black and blue; his mother would never file charges against the old man. We figured he'd run off to his sister's place in upstate New York, but we never really knew. Six, eight, nine. Good grief. We had nine last year. I didn't realize we had so many."

Stacey held her breath. "How many this year?"

Millie closed the heavy drawer with a sharp thud and then opened the top drawer of a cabinet near the door. Seconds later, she turned to Stacey.

"Five already this year."

"Jeez, Millie. Twenty kids disappear in two years, and nobody notices? Isn't that scary? Aren't the police suspicious?"

"I don't know. I just type the reports and keep my mouth shut." Millie looked over her shoulder at the doorway. "I probably shouldn't be telling you all this stuff. You need to talk to Captain Miller."

Stacey peered at her watch. "Maybe I will, but right now I need to get to work."

"Wait. I'll write his number down for you. He'll be in Monday. Call him. And good luck with the paper. Say hello to your mom and dad."

Stacey hurried past the appreciative eyes of the young policeman. *Twenty missing kids*, she thought as she hurried down the street to her car. Edsell was only one of many who had disappeared over the last three years. Maybe the guys shouldn't go to the Barrens tonight. She spotted a telephone booth across the street in a gas station and jogged over to it. God, it was hot, she thought as she wiped her forehead.

She threw in some change and punched Mark's number. Busy. What was Borderline's number? She rarely called him and couldn't remember it. Same exchange as Mark's, but was it 3249 or 4932? Shit, she was late for work now, and the guys weren't leaving until after nine o'clock tonight. She'd have plenty of time to call after she got to work.

At six o'clock, Stacey tried to call Mark from work, but the line was busy again. She looked up Borderline's number in her manager's phone book. It rang three times, and then Mrs. Fenton's soft recorded voice came on. "You have reached the Fenton residence. Please leave a message, and we'll get back to you as soon as possible."

Her manager was frowning at her over his glasses. Behind him, she could see customers lined up ten deep at each of the registers.

Stacey spoke quickly. "Borderline, it's Stacey. Call me at work. I've got some news."

She dialed Mark's number. Still busy.

The manager's arms were folded across his chest, and he was tapping his foot.

Shit. She hurried back to the counter and said, "Welcome to McDonald's. Can I take your order, please?"

Behind her, french fries sizzled. Despite the air-conditioning, the interior of the fast-food restaurant was hot, and tempers were high. McDonald's was swamped all night. To add to the mayhem, two people on the evening shift never showed.

She couldn't get away to call again until after eight o'clock, but no one was home then at either house. As she took orders and filled cups with soda, she told herself that Mark and Borderline were only going to the Barrens to look around. But what if something went wrong? And what about all those missing kids? She knew that a few went missing each year, but the numbers in the last three years were way too high.

CHAPTER 49

When Teddy drove into Chatsworth, the sun was low on the horizon, and she was exhausted. All her specimens had been safely transplanted into the boggy terrarium at Rutgers. Rolls of film had been dropped off at the custom photo studio.

When she pulled into her driveway, Joshua's truck was parked across the street. He was sitting on her front steps.

"Where were you?" he asked as she jumped out of the Bronco. "When I kept getting your answering machine, I got worried."

"You're sweet, Joshua, but I've been in the swamps all day." Terry smiled excitedly. "I found a huge patch of Boykin's Lobilia just a few miles from here in the cedar swamp along Webbs Mill Creek. I've been waist-deep in bog water for hours, taking slides, then cuttings, then live specimens. I even climbed an old pine tree to get an overhead shot."

Suddenly, she noticed that Joshua was drawing back with a strange look on his face.

"What's wrong?" she asked.

Joshua held out his hands as if to keep her away. He sniffed loudly.

Teddy sniffed too and realized that she smelled like bog water, mud, sweat, and insect repellant.

"I know you've been in the bogs." Joshua smiled. "You don't need to get any closer."

She laughed and held out her arms.

"Come on, Joshua. Give me a big ole kiss."

Joshua backed away. "Um, how about a rain check?" Joshua looked at his watch and took one more step backward. "We're starting a new project next week. I've got to pick up supplies this weekend, and then I'll be busy the rest of the week. Why don't you come over for dinner tonight? I'll pull some venison stew from the freezer and slice a few tomatoes. If you come over, I promise to listen to every tiny detail about the swamps and your Boykin-plant watchamacallit."

A quiet evening, some homemade stew, Joshua's big comfortable couch …

"That's a deal." Teddy scratched a bug bite on her cheek. "I've got to get inside and shower. I can't stand myself right now."

"I could give you a hand with that."

"I'm afraid you'd give me more than a hand. Go on, get out of here." She laughed. "I'll see you later."

CHAPTER 50

While Stacey worked and worried, Mark walked through the hot horizontal light of what should have been a pleasant July evening. As the concrete pavement passed beneath his shoes, Mark's lips twitched in silent dialogue, and dark inkblots of sweat patterned his pale yellow T-shirt.

He'd stayed at the gym for an extra hour, lifting, working the machines hard, working out the tension. Finally, the loud clangs of the universal machine sent the manager over to ask him if there was a problem and to please tone it down for the sake of the other people in the gym.

Good thing he came over, thought Mark. *I could have pulled a major muscle with that kind of stuff. Out of control is not good when you're lifting.*

On his left, a long line of cars ground eastward through Toms River to the causeway and the barrier island towns of Seaside, Ortley Beach, and Lavallette. Exhaust fumes mixed with the scent of new blacktop patches. Horns blared, and suddenly under his feet Mark felt the irritating thump of an overly-loud sound system.

He stopped, turned, and leaned into the open window of a red Pontiac. "C'mon, buddy, give us all a break and turn it down."

The large-faced man in the passenger seat smiled with wide, beige-colored teeth, passed him a single digit curse, and then flipped the volume all the way up.

Mark turned away and started jogging.

Why had he popped off at that stranger? The guy was big and nasty-looking and could easily have climbed out of his car and thrown a punch. A police record for street fighting would not look good on his Princeton application.

Shit, he couldn't ever remember feeling this jumpy. Everything was close and getting closer. For two weeks, he had been wrapping himself in a comfortable cocoon by saying, *There's nothing to worry about. Edsell will be back any day now, and next week we'll all be laughing about his mysterious disappearance.*

But Edsell hadn't come back, and with each passing day, that illusion was unraveling.

Mark turned onto Parkwood Avenue, glad to be out of the sight and sound of the cars crawling their way to the beaches for a long July Fourth weekend. Two blocks later, he was on his own street of modest clapboard and brick homes. It was good to be home, good to have some time to veg out before they left for the Barrens.

Suddenly, as Mark stepped onto the curved flagstone walk that led to his house, he heard footsteps pattering up behind him. A small hand grabbed his elbow, and he turned and looked down into Mrs. Jones's bloodshot eyes. Her frizzy blonde hair was a fierce halo, and the smell of cigarettes and sweat hung over her like a cape.

"Mrs. Jones," Mark said.

"You promised me you'd try to find Edsell. Remember?" She thrust out her chin. "I ain't heard from you."

Mark nodded carefully. "I've been asking around, Mrs. Jones, but no one's seen him."

The woman shook her head back and forth slowly, as if it hurt her to move. "You used to be his friend, you and Howie ..." Mark raised his eyebrows, and Lorraine said, "I mean Borderline." Her eyes bore up into his. "You said you'd help."

"Look, I haven't seen him." Mark backed away. "But if I hear anything, I'll call you. I promise."

Tears welled up in Lorraine's swollen eyes. Her shoulders slumped, curved inward, and then moved in a series of long, trembling sobs.

"Oh shit," Mark whispered and touched her shoulder with his open palm. She turned into him and leaned her head into the middle of his chest like a small child. He held her awkwardly.

"He's all I got, Mark," she wailed. "I don't know what I'll do if he doesn't come back."

Finally, her sobs abated, and the tiny woman stepped away, pulled a rumpled tissue from her small shoulder bag, and blew her nose into it. She placed a cigarette between her thin lips, flicked a yellow plastic lighter with shaky hands, and inhaled deeply. The smoke circulated a second time out her mouth and up into her flared nostrils.

"You was always a good boy, Mark," she said. "I wish to God Edsell had turned out like you."

"Don't worry, Mrs. Jones. He'll be back," Mark said.

But Edsell's mother shook her head, exhaled a long white ribbon of smoke, and walked away into the dusky shadows of the large, old maple trees that lined the street.

Damn, the last thing he wanted was to run into Mrs. Jones right now. There was no way he could tell her anything yet. She'd go nuts if she thought Edsell was in the Barrens. She'd go screaming to the police and everyone else, and if the whole thing was nothing, they'd look like fools. Worse, Dr. Vogel might press charges; the parents of the kids in the clinic might even get involved. They were rich, weren't they? Maybe even lawyers' kids. Powerful families might be involved. Who knew? His parents would get called and have to come home early. Stacey would be in deep shit, and so would Borderline.

If his dad found out he had skipped summer school yesterday and was wandering around the Pine Barrens at night, he'd be grounded for months.

As Mark unlocked the front door, he heard the phone. Maybe it was Stacey, letting him know what she had found at the police station. He ran for the kitchen and picked up the phone.

"Hello, Mark. How are you, son?"

"Fine, Dad. Listen, could I call you back?"

"Not really, son, unless there's some emergency going on there that I should know about. Is there?"

Only a missing friend, a weird house in the woods where people scream, a janitor who might be a kidnapper, Dr. Strange Vogel. Plus, your son and his best friend are going to the Barrens tonight to investigate.

"No, Dad. Everything's fine."

"Your voice sounds funny. You sure everything's okay."

"Everything's fine, Dad. I was just ... just waking up from a nap."

"That's nice, son. Hot out there, cutting all those lawns, isn't it? Well, we just thought we'd call and let you know that we're leaving in a few minutes to drive up to Stone Mountain for the weekend. We managed to get a campsite at the last minute. It's a place your mom's always wanted to visit. Magnificent scenery. Sorry you can't be with us, Mark."

"Yeah, me too. I'd sure like to be there. How are Timmy and Dan?"

"Here, let me put your mother on for a minute. She'll tell you all about the fishing trip today and the show we saw last night at Carolina Opry. Did you cut our lawn?"

"Yes. I did it on the weekend."

"Great. Well your mom wants to talk to you for a while. This is the first time we've gone on vacation without you, and I know she misses you. Hold on. I'll get her."

Twenty minutes later, Mark finally hung up the phone. There were no lights blinking on the message machine, so he guessed that Stacey had not made any drastic discoveries at the police station.

Time to relax. Mark pulled a Rolling Stones CD out of the case, put it in the stereo, and turned it on. One of the joys of having his parents gone for two weeks was the chance to play any music he wanted, at any decibel he wanted. Mark lay down on the old brown leather couch and closed his eyes.

It was hard to believe that two weeks ago he'd been like the rest of the seniors at South, his mind focused on babes, cars, surfing, and where the next party was. The Barrens was just some deserted land west of town.

The music vibrated around him. The dishes in the china cabinet rattled gently. The last rays of sunshine filtered weakly across the room.

He'd listen to one more song and then shower and get dressed.

CHAPTER 51

That same evening, Borderline's mother unlocked her front door at seven thirty. She carried a package of powered insecticide, a red spray duster, and a surgical mask in a large, white plastic bag. Japanese beetles were attacking her roses, and she was going to get rid of them right now.

She quickly changed into old, tan khakis, a long-sleeved checkered shirt, a straw hat, and cotton gloves.

Her husband was away at a dinner meeting, so she sprayed, weeded, and watered her precious roses until it grew too dark to see. At nine thirty, she put away her gardening tools and walked upstairs to draw a long, soothing, warm bath.

When Mr. Fenton came home at eleven thirty, he noticed the blinking light, listened to the messages, and wrote several notes onto a clipboard that hung next to the phone.

He found his wife asleep in bed with a new gardening catalogue in her work-worn hands. He shook her gently and asked, "Where's Howard?"

Mrs. Fenton squinted up at him.

"Where's Howard?" he repeated. "There are several messages for him on the answering machine."

"I ... I ... let me think. Oh, yes. Howard was going to Seaside with Mark, and then he was going to spend the night at the Germanos'.

With Mark's family away, I thought it nice of Howie to go over and keep him company."

"Stacey sounds upset. She says it's important that he call her."

"Oh, you know how teenagers are, dear. Everything is a crisis to them. She's probably wondering what time they're meeting at the beach tomorrow."

CHAPTER 52

The darkness crept from east to west over the Barrens until only a few pinpoints of light glowed in the vast pine forest. Chatsworth was a cluster of light, as were the tiny towns of Speedwell, Jenkins, and Bamber Lake. At far distant intervals, the lights from a few individual homes in over a million acres of Pinelands were hardly noticeable.

Borderline and Mark were silent as the dark green Jeep cut through the night. The top was off, and a hot wind whipped across their faces. According to plan, they both wore dark shirts, pants, and shoes.

Mark peered into the blackness beyond the headlights. The moon wasn't up yet, so here, away from Toms River, the night seemed more intense, more focused. A single car approached and cast a halo of light that bravely advanced and then quickly fled behind them. After that, the darkness gathered even closer.

While Mark kept his eyes on the road ahead, Borderline studied the white sand on the shoulders of the paved road. It gleamed in the glare of the headlights, but would it be bright for them to drive on when the moon rose?

"My parents called tonight." Mark spoke into the hot wind.

"Yeah? What did they want?"

"Nothing, just the usual stuff. Did I cut the lawn? Am I eating well? How's Nonna Adelina?" Mark sighed. "They're all going camping this weekend at Stone Mountain. They're calling me on Monday when they get back."

"Okay, Mark, what's up?" Borderline asked. "Something's wrong. I can tell by the way you're talking."

"To tell the truth, I felt strange talking to them. You know, pretending everything's fine when it's not. My mouth was talking about the weather while my brain was jumping around thinking about tonight."

"I know what you mean, Mark. I had to stay busy every minute today. My boss asked me to stay late and detail a car, and it was weird because I was glad to have something to do. I never worked so hard on a car before! When I left Federici's tonight, that Lexus looked brand-new!"

"You told your mom you were sleeping over at my house tonight?" Mark asked.

"Yeah. She thinks it's just wonderful that I'm keeping you company now that your family's away." Borderline spoke in a perfect imitation of his mother's high, sing-song voice.

Mark reached forward and turned the radio off. They were almost to Bamber Lake now. No sense in attracting attention.

"Something weird happened to me this afternoon," Mark said.

"What?"

"Edsell's mother came up to me right outside my house, just when I was getting back from the gym."

"Oh, God. You didn't need that!"

"She looked awful, like she hadn't slept in days. She kept crying and grabbing my arm and begging me to find her son. I didn't know what to say." Mark paused. "I felt like shit, but I couldn't tell her about any of this stuff."

"You did the right thing." Borderline looked out at the lonely road and the blackness around it. "We can't say anything to anybody yet, but there's no way in hell we're turning back now. We're not ignoring what we know. Sometimes people know something bad is going down and ignore it because they don't want to be involved. Well, I'm scared shitless, but I'm not turning back."

"I'm with you, pal," Mark said. "But remember, we're only checking things out. If we hear or see anything, anything at all that sounds dangerous, we're sneaking out of there and calling the cops."

"Speaking of cops," Borderline said. "Wasn't Stacey supposed to go over to the police station and talk to her cousin?"

"Yeah, but I guess she didn't find anything or she would have called us this afternoon."

A few minutes later, they reached Bamber Lake. As soon as they were past the houses, Mark stopped the Jeep and turned off the headlights. Blackness enveloped them, but gradually the dark shapes of trees and bushes came into focus. The dim outline of the road was barely visible in front of them.

"There's no way I can drive around without turning on the headlights," Mark said.

"So we'll wait." Borderline squinted at his watch. "The moon should rise in a few minutes. When that happens, I'll bet you can see to drive."

As Mark turned off the engine, a vast silence drew itself around them. The only sounds were some small rustles in the brush and the sighing of the wind through the pine needles. An owl hooted in the distance.

Then slowly, a glow appeared on the horizon. It became brighter and brighter until the top edge of the moon popped up above the branches of the scraggly pines. They waited until the soft yellow turned into a cold, hard white and the forest was illuminated with a pale radiance. The sandy road gleamed before them.

"Here we go," Mark said and turned the key.

The sudden roar of the engine caused a furtive scurrying in the bushes on their left. Mark shifted into first gear and put the Jeep into four-wheel drive. He automatically reached for the headlights and then willed himself not to touch the switch.

As they moved forward, Borderline turned on a penlight and started reading directions to Mark.

"Two-tenths of a mile forward, then a right."

He shone the penlight onto the speedometer for moment and then flicked it off.

"About three hundred yards, then hang a left."

The Jeep crawled slowly and steadily through the twists and turns of the old Bamber Lake Development. Then, all at once, the pine woods went pitch black around them.

Mark jammed on the brakes.

"Just a cloud." Borderline looked up at the sky. "Wait a minute or so. It doesn't look like it'll happen again. Look, there's only two more clouds up there, and they're moving away. There, that's the last one. Go ahead."

After more twists and turns and whispered directions, they reached the end of the maze.

Dukes Bridge Road stretched ahead. The moonlight cast shadows through the wispy, bent trees. Once more, they heard the echoing hoot of a hunting owl.

While Mark followed the glow of the white road, Borderline scanned the dark woods in front of the Jeep. Mark glanced up now and again to see if more clouds were coming, but the sky remained clear.

After forty-five minutes of creeping down the sandy road in low gear, they saw a light ahead of them through the trees.

"We're getting close, Mark. Let's stop here," Borderline said.

Mark took his foot off the gas and shifted into neutral. The Jeep coasted for a few yards, and then the deep sand of the road brought it to a silent stop.

CHAPTER 53

Through the trees, they saw the dark shape of the house. One window glowed at the far end.

"Now what?" whispered Mark.

"You wait here while I go up to the house and listen. Maybe I can see in that window. Keep the engine running and your foot off the brake. We don't want anyone to see red brake lights."

Borderline climbed over the side and dropped noiselessly onto the soft, white sand.

"Be careful," Mark whispered as he took off his seatbelt and leaned back against the door.

Borderline walked forward cautiously in the shadows of the moonlit trees. A twig snapped loudly under his left foot. He stopped and waited and listened but heard nothing.

Soon the bulk of the old house blotted the moonlit sky. Borderline moved slowly forward into the darkness, holding his hands straight out in front of him. He remembered that there were no shrubs around the house, no little picket fences, just soft sand. When he touched the rough cedar shakes, he silently moved down the wall to the left until he was next to the lighted window.

He heard muffled voices on the other side of the glass. A narrow strip of light beamed between the blind and the window molding. Borderline closed one eye, leaned forward, and peered in.

Directly in front of him was a strange, upright white and chrome chair that looked like something a dentist would use. It had a triangular metal frame on the top where the headrest would normally be. White cloths covered the seat and armrests.

"Okay, Jack. Put him into the chair."

The voice was familiar. Was it Dr. Vogel?

Two forms in loose green garments with green masks covering the lower part of their faces appeared from the left. They carried a limp figure dressed in white. As they approached the chair, the figure suddenly lurched.

"Watch out, Jack. Hold him tight. Get his legs."

The voice was Vogel's.

Within a few seconds, the two men had overpowered the smaller figure and placed him into the chair where he faced the window, no more than ten feet from where Borderline stood in the dark. The kid was young, his head was completely shaved, and his mouth was taped over. As the men in green fitted his legs into a large metal clamp in the footrest, the boy's eyes became wide, and tears welled in them. He struggled as the men placed a strap around his waist and fitted his hands into small clamps in the armrests.

"Good work, Jack. Now position the head."

The voice was Vogel's. What the hell was going on, Borderline wondered. Was this the secret drug therapy?

Jack placed the metal frame around the boy's head and then turned some knobs until it fitted tightly against the bare scalp.

"Jack, those head clamps are not tight enough." Vogel spoke in a tense, angry voice. "The head cannot move."

The man named Jack leaned down and adjusted several more knobs.

"Is that better?"

The voice of taller one belonged to the guy in the black jumpsuit who had first opened the door of the old house.

"That's excellent," Vogel said. "I'm ready to proceed. Turn on the monitor."

Jack disappeared. A long metal cylinder with thick glass on the end emerged from the left and advanced toward the head of the restrained boy.

Vogel spoke with a new intensity. "Focus it. Closer, closer. Ah, there we are. Lock it in."

Vogel moved around to the back of the chair and sat down. Only part of his head and one green shoulder was visible from behind the bound figure. The chest of the boy rose and fell rapidly. The terrified eyes seemed to look right through the window at Borderline.

After a few seconds, a humming sound began. Vogel spoke again. "I'm ready. Give me the aspirator." After some movement behind the chair, all was still again in the room. "Here we go."

Suddenly the restrained white figure grew rigid. The fingers clutched the armrests; the knuckles turned white.

"Steady, steady, my friend. It will soon be over." Vogel spoke in a low, excited voice. "Jack, keep checking the monitor. Am I on course?"

"Yes. Keep going … just a little more … There, you're home."

Immediately the young man's eyes widened, and his chest rose in a sustained, muffled moan that faded slowly into nothingness. As Borderline watched, the terror-stricken eyes gradually lost their fear, lost their meaning, lost their focus. They became as empty as the glass eyes on a Teddy Bear.

Borderline's stomach convulsed. There was no visible movement from the young man in the chair. He was as still as stone, concrete, or steel.

He was as still as a corpse.

Borderline desperately stifled the urge to vomit. Sweat dripped down the side of his face. Through a daze, he dimly heard Vogel speaking.

"That was quicker than usual. General Morris will be pleased. Here, pack this into the cylinder and take it up to McGuire. The jet should be waiting."

"What about him?" Jack asked.

Borderline breathed deeply and desperately, trying with every muscle in his throat not to vomit. He needed to hear what was being said.

"Take the vial to McGuire. I'll get the body into the bog while you're gone. Nelson should be here any minute. He'll give me a hand."

Nelson? Nelson? Who was Nelson?

With a sinking feeling, Borderline remembered Nerf's real name. Wilbur Nelson. *Shit. If he's coming here, he'll drive up right behind the Jeep.*

Borderline quickly turned away from the window and sprinted toward Mark as distant headlights shone through the trees beyond the Jeep. He ran quickly and quietly, all the while locking his teeth to keep himself from yelling to Mark. Maybe they could get out before anyone saw them.

Borderline reached the Jeep and cleared the side in a one-handed leap. Mark jumped in alarm, the whites of his eyes gleaming in the moonlight.

"Out. We gotta get out," Borderline hissed. "That's Nerf coming in behind us."

Mark turned. The headlights were coming up the road. Fast.

"He's speeding up," Mark cried. "Oh, God. My foot's on the brake. He's seen the brake lights."

The blue van speeded up and caught them it its headlights. The horn sounded a series of long, insistent blasts.

"Come on, come on," Borderline said. "Move it!"

Mark flipped on the headlights, shifted into first, and stomped on the accelerator. The wheels spun in the sand and then dug deep and caught. They moved forward.

The front door of the house flew open. Someone ran to the Suburban and pulled it quickly out of the driveway. Mark's Jeep was caught in the headlights of the two vehicles. Each one blocked their escape.

"Go! Go!" Borderline yelled.

"Where?"

"Into the woods. We can get away through the woods. Hurry."

Mark gunned the engine and cut the wheel to the left. The Jeep flew into the pine forest. The Suburban and the van followed.

Mark wheeled the Jeep right and left, around shadowy, twisted pine trees and clumps of small, thick oaks. Branches tore at the sides of the Jeep, and the underbrush made a loud scraping noise underneath. Borderline hung onto his seat, and as they bounced through the forest, he alternately prayed and swore.

The lights from the Suburban loomed closer.

"Faster!" Borderline yelled. "Faster!"

Mark crushed the accelerator down to the floor and spun the wheel to avoid a tree on the left. Another twisted pine loomed on the right.

Suddenly Borderline cried, "Look out!"

A large fallen tree lay in their path. As Mark put his foot on the brake, they hit it at full speed. The Jeep sailed into the air, its headlights knifing the hot summer night. With a loud crunch, it settled upside down into the soft Barrens sand with all four wheels spinning in the air.

The force of the Jeep hitting the log catapulted Borderline and Mark into the air, and they crashed headlong through branches and brush. Mark flew off to the left and, after a free fall of thirty feet, connected with a midsize cedar. His head hit a glancing blow on the rough bark, and with a soft whimper he crumpled into the fetal position at the base of the tree.

As the Jeep flipped over, its wheels still spinning and its headlights pointing through the underbrush and sand, Borderline dropped from the sky feet-first into the black waters of a bog. As he struggled to rise, the soft ooze sucked him deeper.

CHAPTER 54

M ark's one good eye opened with a flutter. He was in a small room with closed windows. Through the half-open blinds, he saw the tops of pine trees. The sky behind them was a pale, luminous gray. Where was he? Was it early morning or late in the evening?

When he tried to move, he found he was strapped to a bed. When he tried to speak, he discovered a large wad of gauze in his mouth that was held in place by adhesive tape. He couldn't see out of one eye, and his head hurt on that side with a throbbing, piercing pain.

As Mark became conscious of his total and complete helplessness, a terrible claustrophobia overwhelmed him, and for the first time since he was a small boy, he lost inhibition and control. He strained and writhed until he was soaked with sweat. He cried and made animal noises into the gag, and when it was wet with his sputum, he started to gag.

Then in a flash from somewhere in the depths of his panic-stricken brain shot the crystal clear knowledge that if he gagged, he would choke on his own vomit. With a mighty effort, Mark drew in a deep, shuddering breath through his nose, and then another and another. He continued to inhale and exhale for several minutes until his breathing slowed and his heart stopped racing.

Mark was barely on the edge of control when the door opened and three men came into the room. He recognized Vogel, Nerf, and the tall man in black who had answered the door on the first day they saw the house. The trio stood near the door and watched dispassionately while Mark regained control and his harsh breathing subsided. Finally, Vogel stepped to the side of the bed.

"What a surprise, Mr. Germano. It seems that you ignored my advice and became curious about my laboratory," he said. Vogel was impeccably dressed in a white shirt, blue paisley tie, and navy slacks. "You came here last night looking for your little friend Edsell, didn't you?"

Mark stared at Vogel. He tried not to move, not to struggle.

"Allow me to answer the questions I see in your eyes, Mark. Yes, Edsell Jones is here with me, and he is now almost completely free of chemical additives." Vogel smiled thinly. "We have flushed all the poisons out of his system. His eyes are clear, and I dare say his young mind is clear too, probably for the first time in months. So you see, in our own little way, we *are* a drug treatment center."

Dr. Vogel rubbed his long, tapered hands together. The pale light from the windows fell across his lean face and emphasized his deep-set eyes and high cheekbones.

"Too bad poor Edsell will never enjoy the fruits of his long and arduous fight." Vogel shrugged his shoulders. "I see more questions lurking in your eyes, Mark, so let me explain. Your friend is about to be sacrificed for a noble cause. I'm sure you are aware that Edsell Jones is a good-for-nothing, useless piece of human flesh. In other words, a parasite on society."

In the coolness of the small room, Mark could feel sweat running down from his temples into his ears. What was this wacko talking about? What sacrifice? What higher cause?

"You are still young, Mark. You have not yet learned that the world is divided into two groups: the givers and the takers. Those who contribute and those who drain. Each year, the ranks of the takers grow larger as we're forced to deal with the chronically unemployed, the career criminals, the addicts, and the just plain lazy."

Dr. Vogel moved forward until he was next to the bed and then leaned down until he was inches from Mark's face. There was a strong smell of mint on his breath, and through crossed eyes, Mark saw a half-dissolved white Life Saver floating around in the pink mouth.

"These misanthropes all had a chance to lead productive lives. They threw that chance away," Vogel said. "They, by their own actions, have condemned themselves."

Mark struggled against the restraints and emitted a smothered groan. Vogel straightened, placed his hands behind his back, and moved a few paces away from the bed.

"Balanced against the derelicts, we find the positive people of the world. These are the givers, the credits to society. Blessed with intellect and talent and leadership, they enrich us all." Vogel's voice trembled with intensity. "Why shouldn't these blessed ones be given long and productive lives?"

He extended his hands out to the side, palms up, like a priest giving the benediction.

"And thanks to me, they shall," he said and then turned and strode out of the room.

Nerf stepped forward. His soft face creased into a fake benevolent smile as he slowly shook his head. The small, close-set eyes gleamed.

"Hey, Mark, remember me? I used to watch you at school. Big jock, big football hero. Sitting with the other jocks in the cafeteria with all the pretty girls hanging around. I'll bet you'd like to know where your pal is. What's his name? Oh, yeah. I remember now. They called him Borderline."

Borderline. Oh God. Where was Borderline? Tied to another bed somewhere?

"Drowned in the swamp," Nerf said flatly. "Too bad. I kinda liked his style." Nerf turned to the tall man behind him. "C'mon, Jack. Let's go downstairs and get a cup of coffee."

"I could use a cup," Jack said as he followed Nerf out of the room. "That was a rough night."

Mark listened to their footsteps fade away from his door and then down a flight of stairs.

No, cried Mark silently. Borderline couldn't be dead. He tried to remember what happened during the chase through the pine trees.

The Jeep had hit something and then flipped over. He could remember flying through the air and landing against something hard. After that, nothing. He seemed to remember a distant splash right before the darkness covered him.

An enormous sadness swept over him, and he closed his eyes. His best friend was dead.

Pictures rushed through his head of all the great and wild times they'd had, the pranks they had pulled off, their first beers, a trial smoke behind Federici's Auto Body in the seventh grade. Girlfriends, football games, proms, pool-hopping in the ritzy town of Mantoloking the summer of their freshman year ...

Borderline couldn't be dead. Nerf was making it up, trying to mess up his head, and yet, not one of them looked worried or concerned. Vogel was totally calm and cool. If Borderline had gotten away, wouldn't Vogel be jittery or nervous?

So it was probably true, Mark thought, and an infinite sadness overwhelmed him. His situation was totally hopeless. His family was away, not just in North Carolina at a resort hotel, but camping in the mountains. No one would know he was missing until Monday night when his mother called and got no answer. Even then, they wouldn't be alarmed because they would think he'd gone out with Stacey or was spending the night at Borderline's house. It would be a couple of days before anyone even got worried. A couple of days. Shit.

Stacey. Stacey would know something had happened when she couldn't reach them. She'd tell her parents, and they'd call the cops. But would that be soon enough? Vogel sounded like a nutcase with an agenda. God only knew what he might do. Mark's mind reeled with a million questions. What had Borderline seen through the window? What had frightened him so terribly?

Aw, shit ... Borderline. Mark felt tears sting his eyes. Any help that might come, if it ever did, would be too late for Borderline.

CHAPTER 55

T he light outside the widows of the large oak-beamed room was predawn pewter. A small lamp glowed warm and steady among the indistinct black bulks of furniture. A brass ceiling fan blew tepid air across the flushed face of the young man on the couch.

"He's been out of it for hours. Do you think he'll be okay?" asked Joshua as he leaned against the stone fireplace and sipped a mug of coffee.

"He's breathing normally now," answered Teddy from a rocking chair near the fireplace.

"He didn't look too good last night when I pulled him out of that bog, all covered with muck, barely breathing. It scared the hell out of me." Joshua threw his coffee into the sink. "He looks better now with the mud washed off and your jeans and shirt on him."

The wan figure on the couch groaned once. His hands came up in a weak, defensive gesture and then dropped to his sides.

"Police, get the police," he mumbled with his eyes shut.

Joshua moved to a stool next to the boy and gently placed a big palm on his forehead.

Borderline's eyes opened. He looked up at the dark rafters and then around at the large room. He was lying on an overstuffed couch with a blanket over him. A huge fireplace and a mounted deer head above it filled one wall of the room. Where was he?

Borderline focused on the huge man sitting next to him. He had several days' growth of beard, bushy eyebrows and deepset brown eyes. Beyond the man, on the far side of the room, a slim, pretty woman sat in a rocking chair near the fireplace. She was wearing jeans, a sleeveless plaid shirt, and boots.

She caught his eye, smiled, and moved next to him, sitting on a stool next to the bed. She spoke in a warm, friendly voice. "Hi. I'm Teddy Constantinos, and this is Joshua Reed. Welcome back to the real world. We were beginning to wonder if you'd ever wake up."

Joshua asked, "How're you feeling, son? Can you talk?"

It all came back in a rush. The chase, the sudden stop, the head-over-heels flight through tearing branches into a black, slimy swamp. The last thing he remembered was thick, choking mud in his mouth as he tried to scream.

"Police, got to get the police," Borderline croaked as he tried to sit up. "Mark's back there … Edsell …"

As Borderline raised himself up on his elbows, the room lurched around him and then settled back into place.

"Take it easy. You're with friends," Joshua said. "Suppose you tell us what happened last night. Then we can all decide what to do next."

"Where am I? How did I get here?" Borderline asked.

"You're in my cabin. I brought you here last night. I was out roaming the Barrens, night stalking some critters when I heard a commotion start up—a van and a Suburban chasing a Jeep every which way through the pines. The Suburban was gaining when the Jeep hit an old cedar log and flipped over. I heard branches shaking, something flying through the air, and next thing I know there's a splash in the bog right by where I was standing. I grabbed a tree branch with one hand and pulled you out with the other. Boy, you were a mess."

Teddy continued. "Joshua carried you here. We cleaned you up and put you to bed on the couch."

"But Mark. Where's Mark?"

"Who's Mark? The other kid in the Jeep?"

Borderline nodded.

Joshua shook his head. "I don't know, son. As I pulled you out of the mud, someone jumped out of a van and started coming toward us shouting and yelling. I didn't waste any time, just picked you up and skedaddled out of there." He paused and then looked intently at Borderline. "What in hell's going on over at the Watson place?"

"Watson place?"

"Yeah. That old farmhouse near the swamp where I found you. Something strange is going on over there. What happened last night?"

Before Borderline could speak, Teddy rose from her chair.

"Hold on, Joshua. Another couple of minutes aren't going to make any difference. Let me get some broth into him before you ask any more questions. Look at him. His eyes are big as saucers, and his face is white as a sheet. He looks like he might pass out again."

"But Teddy …" Joshua protested.

Teddy silenced him with a glance and then walked to the couch where she knelt down next to Borderline. She felt his forehead and then picked up his wrist and pushed down gently with her index and middle finger, feeling his pulse. She cupped his face in her hands and looked into his eyes.

"You're going to be fine, kid, as soon as you get water and a little food in you. What's your name?"

"Howard Patrick Fenton," he answered. "But everyone calls me Borderline."

"Where do you live, Borderline?" she asked gently.

"Toms River, ma'am. I'll be a senior at Toms River South next fall."

Teddy got up and went to the stove, lifted the lid off a simmering cast-iron pot, and ladled out some deep brown liquid.

Teddy set a steaming bowl of broth on the stool, lifted Borderline into a sitting position as easily as if he were a child, and then plumped up some pillows behind him. She handed him the soup and said, "Here, eat first. Then we'll talk."

Borderline took a sip. The soup tasted strong and salty with a wonderful, strange aroma. Was it beef?

"This is great," he said. "What is it?"

"Venison broth. Joshua makes it and keeps a stock of it in the freezer." She nodded toward Joshua and winked. "He's not a bad cook."

As Borderline ate the soup, the dark chase and the suffocating mud seemed like a bad dream.

He looked at the man who had saved his life. Joshua was sitting in a big armchair now, gazing out the window at the forest outside. He looked relaxed yet powerful. A faded blue denim shirt spanned his massive chest. Worn blue jeans, a Western belt, and soft brown moccasins finished his simple attire.

Who were these people? Joshua had a soft, slow twang when he talked. Teddy spoke in the brisk, clipped voice of the city. Who would ever want to live out here in the middle of nowhere? Where did they work? Or did they just hunt and fish? The cabin was too nice for that kind of life. Someone had paid for the plaid chairs and the brass fireplace accessories, the braided rugs, the paintings on the walls.

When he finished the last spoonful of soup, Borderline lay back with a contented sigh. Teddy looked at him expectantly and said, "Go on, tell us what happened."

CHAPTER 56

Borderline started at the beginning, sparing nothing, letting the words tumble out. He told about Edsell Jones disappearing, about Nerf, about Stacey and Mark and how they found the old house in the Barrens. About Vogel and the pink note and the Steelers cap in the back of the filing cabinet. When he got to the moonlit drive to the old house, Borderline's words slowed. When he described what he had seen through the window, his voice dropped to a whisper.

"Then … then I saw the kid's face change. It kind of relaxed, like maybe fell asleep, but not asleep because his eyes stayed open. Not blinking, not looking at anything at all …"

Teddy came to his side and held his hand as he described Nerf's unexpected appearance, the chase through the pine woods, the shock of hitting the log, and then the horrifying fall into the bog.

Joshua sat quietly during the long recitation, his eyes riveted on Borderline. As the story progressed, his thick eyebrows came together, and his lips drew together in a tight line. When Borderline finished, Joshua leaned forward and looked directly into Borderline's eyes.

"Son, I know this is hard for you, but I want to go over every word that you heard at that place. Tell me every little thing you can remember. I need to hear it again and in as much detail as you can remember, because I'm taking notes now."

So Borderline described the whole scene again. Joshua interrupted him frequently, asking detailed questions about what he had seen and overheard. When he got to the part where Vogel told Jack to take the vial to McGuire, Joshua interrupted.

"You're sure he said McGuire?"

"Positive. I remember thinking that I had been to an air show at McGuire when I was just a little kid. Mark and I went with his dad and uncle and a bunch of cousins."

"McGuire Air Force Base," Joshua said slowly as he rose and paced around the room. The huge base sat on the northwestern edge of the Barrens. It was no more than twenty minutes from the old Watson place. He turned back to Borderline.

"Anything else? Try and remember."

"Yeah, something about a general. Vogel said some general would be pleased. I can't remember the name. It was Marsh or Morse. It started with an M. Morris?"

"A general? You're sure he said general?"

"Yeah. Vogel said General Morse, or Morris, would be pleased. He said a jet was waiting to pick up the vial at McGuire. The guy Jack was to take it there."

Joshua stood and rocked back on his heels with a puzzled look on his face. The old Watson place had been the subject of Pinelands gossip for a couple of years now. Unknown strangers bought it, fixed it up, trucked in computers and other equipment. Could it be a secret military operation?

Joshua shook his head. Impossible.

Yet the men who had renovated it had Maryland plates on their trucks. They had never spoken conversationally to anyone, never went to town for lunch or supplies, never bought gas at any of the local stations. And of course, there had been some deliberate attempts to scare people away, especially hunters and kids on their ATVs, and old Ben Sampson.

Joshua looked out of the window at the pitch pines and scrubby oaks, the wild blueberry bushes and sheep laurel that ringed his cabin. A red-headed woodpecker flew by and landed near the top of a pine tree. The staccato drill of the bird searching for insects punctuated his thoughts.

The Barrens were vast and vacant, mused Joshua, a million acres of pine trees and scrub oak, all protected by federal and state environmental laws. There were only two other houses in the five square miles around his property. One was the Watson place. The other was the tiny shack where old Ben Sampson lived with his hounds.

If someone wanted to set up a secret operation here, our way of life would play right into their hands. Everyone out here is a stubborn, independent cuss. Our ancestors stayed when the mills and factories closed while softer men moved on. We don't need the police, we don't trust the government. Except for the environmental stuff and the restrictions on new construction, there aren't any rules out here. We mind our own business and take care of our own. Someone from the outside could use that to their advantage.

Joshua turned back to Borderline. "How do you feel now?" he asked.

"Better, but I'm worried about Mark. What if Vogel has him? What if he's …"

"Hold on, son. We'll find out soon. I'm going to the Watson place and have a look see. If you're strong enough, you can come along and identify the people out there."

Borderline's face brightened.

"Stand up and see how you feel," Teddy said.

Borderline threw off the blanket, rolled off the couch, and stood shakily. He looked down at the jeans and red shirt and then raised his eyes to Teddy. "Mine," Teddy said. "You would look like a clown in Josh's big clothes. Go on, walk around some more."

Borderline walked to the kitchen and back several times. Joshua knew the kid was okay because with each step he stood straighter and looked more in control.

"I'm okay. Nothing hurts," Borderline said.

"The mud probably saved you from breaking any bones when you fell," Joshua said. "Here's your sneakers. They're still damp, but the muck's gone."

As Borderline laced up his sneakers, Teddy and Joshua stood near the fireplace and talked softly.

"Why don't you call the police and let them take care of this?" Teddy asked.

"We can't, Teddy. We've already used up too much time. If this kid's story is true, there's something big and ugly going on at the Watson place, but I'm not calling anybody until I check it out for myself."

Teddy frowned. "There's no way this kid could have made up all that stuff, and you know it."

"Okay, okay. But how do I explain it over the phone to a desk sergeant? And even if he believes me, the police will need a search warrant from a judge before they can send a patrol car to the Watson place. That doctor won't let anyone inside without a warrant; you can bet on that. Shoot, the whole dang thing will take a day and a half, and I'm not waiting that long."

"But, Joshua—"

"Don't worry. We'll cut through the woods. They won't even know we're coming. I'll get into the house one way or the other and find out if this kid's telling the truth."

Joshua strapped a leather holder onto his belt.

Teddy's eyes widened.

"Just my hunting knife," he whispered. "I'll leave the bow here. I'm a hunter, remember? If you hadn't fallen asleep right after dinner, and if I hadn't gone out night stalking, who knows what would have happened to that boy? I *know* what I'm doing."

CHAPTER 57

The pale gray of the dawn sky had changed into an oppressive hot blue by the time Joshua and Borderline left the cabin. A crow cawed in the distance with a raspy, lonesome croak that reminded Joshua of dead things and black night.

As they crossed the clearing and entered the warm, dry shadows of the pine woods, Joshua paused and leaned close to Borderline.

"Voices carry out here, Borderline," he said softly. "If you need to say anything, whisper. And watch where you plant your feet. The sand will muffle our footsteps, but if we aren't careful, the snaps and crackles of the dry branches and twigs might tell them we're coming."

For twenty minutes, Joshua kept an even pace. In silence, they followed narrow game trails that skirted streams and swamps and small forest meadows. Borderline followed closely behind Joshua.

"Quiet," hissed Joshua. "Watch where you plant your feet; you're making a helluva racket back there."

At Borderline's crestfallen face, Joshua realized that most kids who were raised in the Barrens hunted the Pinelands and knew how to walk softly among the twigs and dry branches. This kid was born and raised in a city. He was a noisy explosion of rustling branches, crunching leaves, and snapping twigs. Plus, he was breathing heavily. *Maybe I should have come alone*, thought Joshua.

Joshua stopped suddenly, and Borderline nearly ran into him.

"What's wrong? Are we there yet?" Borderline asked in a low, breathy voice.

Joshua leaned aside and pointed to a low bush with a pink ribbon tied to it.

"No, I stopped because that pink ribbon means there's a rattlesnake nearby," he said.

"A rattlesnake? Here? No way. They're out west, like in Arizona or Texas."

"We've got lots of rattlers around here. There's a guy, a herpetologist or some such thing, who catches snakes and puts itty-bitty monitors on them. Whenever he finds a nest of rattlesnakes, he ties a pink ribbon on a bush."

Joshua stepped around the bush. Borderline followed and eyed each piece of ground that passed under his feet. The hot morning sun shed bright rays through the sparse overhead vegetation and illuminated the dry sand and bristly patches of old, gray pine needles under his feet.

Joshua walked slowly, Borderline following close at his heels. Ten minutes later, the old house was visible through the trees. They approached cautiously and then stood silently behind a cluster of small oak trees.

"Whose trucks are those?" Joshua asked.

"The Suburban is Vogel's. The blue van belongs to Nerf."

Joshua waited for several minutes, his eyes scanning the surrounding woods.

Borderline fidgeted and sighed and then tugged at Joshua's arm. "Come on," he said. "We can't just stand here all day."

"Hold on, son. There's at least three of them and only two of us. Your friend Mark may be inside. There might be other kids, and who knows what else in there. We can't go rushing in. Let's ease up closer."

As Borderline and Joshua slowly moved toward the house, the back door opened, and Nerf's soft, round figure emerged carrying a dark green, plastic garbage bag. Joshua looked at Borderline with a question on his face.

"Nerf," Borderline mouthed.

Fifty feet from the house was a small wood frame that held two black garbage cans. As Nerf approached the cans, Joshua circled quickly and noiselessly behind him. When Nerf opened the lid and dropped in the green plastic bag, Joshua sprang upon him, covered his mouth with a great hand, and wrenched him backward through the woods. Nerf's doughy cheeks quivered when he saw Joshua's hunting knife, and when Borderline stepped out from behind a scrub oak, the quiver deepened into a twitch.

Joshua spoke softly into the man's small ear. "Howdy, little round man. Do you know this kid?"

Nerf nodded, his close-set eyes blinking rapidly.

"That's good. Real good," said Joshua. "Maybe you'd like to tell me what the hell's going on around here."

Joshua pushed the point of his knife into the fat man's neck with gentle increasing pressure. As the pale skin yielded a small trickle of blood, Nerf gasped. "Don't hurt me. Don't hurt me," he wheezed. "I'll tell you everything."

CHAPTER 58

Once more, Borderline followed Joshua through the woods to the old house. They had tied Nerf to a tree using a torn and twisted piece of his own shirt. A second piece was stuffed into his mouth.

Borderline's stomach felt ragged, like he'd eaten something that had been kept in the refrigerator too long. Nerf's story was horrible. Guys his age, some younger, had been stalked and brought to the old house, then tied to beds, hooked up to tubes, and kept alive to be killed. The worst part was that the dreadful scene he witnessed through the window last night was not a single event, but a procedure that had been repeated over and over again. Probes inserted into living brains, liquid sucked out as their eyes turned glassy. Bodies dumped into a bog.

Mark was in that house. What if he …

Sweat spread over Borderline's body. It trickled down his temples, ran past his ears and down the sides of his neck. He could hear his breath, involuntarily loud and heavy in the still, dry air.

Borderline tripped on a root and almost fell to the ground.

Joshua stopped and turned.

"You okay? You don't look so good."

"I'm all right. We've got to get there now. We've got to find Mark."

"Calm down, son. They're down to our size now, and I do remember some of what I learned in the military. We'll be in the house before that fat fool is missed."

CHAPTER 59

Anton Vogel paced up and down the glossy oak floors of the upstairs hallway of the old farmhouse. Each time he passed the window at the end of the hall, a floorboard squeaked noisily. The sound added an unwelcome punctuation point to his darting thoughts.

Something had to be done. There had to be a way out of this mess. He would not pack up and move. He had worked too hard and too long. Plus, the location was perfect.

Because his precious product was only viable for six hours, he had to be near an airport that could access Washington quickly. That airport needed to be a military one where no one would question the arrivals and departures of flights authorized by a retired two-star general. The staff at McGuire probably thought the old man had a girlfriend stashed away in the New Jersey Pine Barrens. In true military fashion, they did not ask questions.

The delicate nature of the harvesting procedure required absolute secrecy.

Vogel was immensely proud of the fact that with only two helpers he had been able to deliver shipments to General Morris for twenty-four months without a hitch. They were a superb team.

Jack, while not evidencing great mental acumen, was sober and tight-lipped and surprisingly strong.

Nelson was delightfully clever. He got himself into schools and administrative offices like a veritable cat burglar. He checked computer files and medical records and found the leads that brought in the right boys. When anything unexpected occurred, Nelson displayed a cold proficiency. In another time and place, he would have been the Inquisitor, the Hangman, the one who torched the pyre.

Vogel ground his teeth. He'd never find another setup like his one. Even if such a place could be found, it would take months to purchase it, and more months to convert it and install the equipment. There was too much at stake now. The foundation had important clients who were desperate for the product and willing to do anything—make critical donations, vote for a certain bill, manufacture a specific product, funnel funds to the right accounts, speak the right words at United Nations meetings ...

Vogel halted outside his office door and then slowly raised and lowered his shoulders while he dangled his arms and hands loosely at his side. He flexed his fingers. *Relax, Anton. Get hold of yourself. Nothing has been lost. You can work it out.*

But the relaxation exercises did not stop his mind from skittering around the events of the past twenty-four hours. One kid was at the bottom of the bog with a sunken Jeep on top of him. His friend was tied to a bed in Room D. Perhaps that was a mistake, but at the time, it seemed foolish to waste an unexpected source of clean product.

But what if the boys had friends who knew they were coming to the Barrens last night?

What about the girl, Stacey? Was she part of it? Where was she now?

Vogel rubbed his temple gently with his index finger. What he needed now was seclusion, music, and cup of hot tea.

"Jack," he called.

Jack's long, bony face poked out of Room A.

"Yeah?"

"I am terribly stressed right now, and I need a few moments by myself. Please make a pot of tea and bring it up to my office. Use the Earl Grey."

Vogel closed the door and immediately turned on Chopin's Concerto No. 1 in E Minor. He leaned back in his chair and crossed his arms over his chest.

After several minutes of deep breathing, Vogel's mind cleared. He would send Nelson home this morning and tell him to stay there until he, Vogel, contacted him personally. He would extract the new boy after he had his tea and ship the product right away. Morris would be pleased because he'd be one extraction ahead of schedule.

Just in case anyone came around asking questions, he'd wear his white doctor's coat for the next few days and dangle a stethoscope around his neck. Jack would wear his whites and carry a clipboard. He'd keep the kids heavily sedated. If anyone came and looked around the lab, they would see a small, private rehabilitation center with several very ill patients.

The other kid was dead in the bog, and the Jeep had been pulled over and sank on top of him. Branches from a fallen pine tree obscured everything. He was safe, very safe.

Vogel put his hands behind his neck, kicked off his shoes, and a trace of a smile flitted over his thin face. It would all work out just fine. Destiny had brought him this far. Destiny would not let him down.

CHAPTER 60

Steam rose from the stainless steel kettle in an irritating whistle. Jack turned off the burner with a hard twist of the knob, and immediately the urgent shriek dropped in pitch and degenerated into a neutral hiss. Where the hell was Nelson? The fat creep was probably catching up on his sleep somewhere.

What a night they had had. Every muscle in Jack's body ached. They had used winches off the Suburban to right the Jeep. Then they pulled it over to the deepest bog and pushed it in right over the spot where the kid had dropped in. Because the water was so clear, they cut down small trees and built a layer of branches over it. Working in the dark and using only their flashlights, it had been a bitch of a job. And hot. Christ, he couldn't remember a night like that.

Then, after two hours of sleep, Vogel woke him up and insisted that all the normal morning routines be continued. So faithful Jack-the-chump had washed and bathed the boys, emptied their urinals and bedpans, adjusted their IVs, and then fed and exercised them. Jack worked while Vogel took a long shower; Jack worked while Vogel fluttered up and down the hall. And now, Jack was still working while Vogel sat on his fine, thin ass and listened to that God-awful, sissified, candy-ass music.

And Wilbur Nelson, the fat frump, had watched the morning news and fixed himself breakfast. Bacon and eggs, no less. Oh, he offered some to Jack, but it was a laugh. When did Jack have the time to sit and eat?

Jack carefully poured hot water into Vogel's china teapot. The boss wanted certain teas, certain cups, a paper-thin glass goblet for his after-dinner nip each evening. That was okay; for what he was paid, Jack would make all the prissy little cups of tea the boss wanted. Being here in the Barrens in this old farmhouse was his assignment, and he would fulfill it to the best of his ability.

But Nelson pissed him off.

"Nelson," he called. "Get your fat, lazy ass in here."

Jack put the teapot and a matching cup and saucer on a silver tray. Then he carefully placed a bowl of colored sugar crystals and a tiny platter of thin-sliced lemon next to it. He threaded a white linen napkin through a silver napkin ring and looked at his watch. Another two minutes, and the tea would be steeped.

Still no sign of Nelson. Damn if he'd let him nap all morning. Jack strode down the hall and yanked open the door to a tiny, poorly-lit lounge.

The television was tuned to a well-muscled blonde in skimpy tights who was exhorting viewers to kick left, reach, kick right, in a high-pitched bubbly voice. The room was empty and smelled faintly of old farts.

Where the hell was Nelson? He couldn't be upstairs because Jack would have heard him on the stairs. Maybe he was snoozing out on the back porch.

Jack stalked through the kitchen and flung open the door.

"Nelson?" he called, stepping out on the porch. "Where the hell are you?"

Suddenly a large hand snaked around the corner and grabbed his neck. Jack's deep, sunken eyes widened and bulged as Joshua's finger tightened on a certain pressure point near the spine. For several seconds, Jack's toed-in size 13 black Reeboks did a pitiful dance above the floorboards. Then his long bony body sagged and softened, and he soundlessly slipped to the floor.

CHAPTER 61

Joshua motioned for Borderline to follow him into the house. The first room was a kitchen, new and efficient with bleached oak cabinets, a white tile floor, and countertops. A tray with a teapot and one cup sat on the counter. Joshua felt the pot. It was hot.

He heard music. Was someone playing a piano?

He walked through the kitchen door and into a large formal living room and dining room in the front of the old house. In the hallway beyond, a set of stairs led up to the second floor. The music seemed to come from above.

Borderline started up the stairs, but Joshua grabbed his arm.

"Wait," he whispered. "We'd better check out the rest of this level before we go up."

They tiptoed to the rear of the house. They found a bathroom, a tiny bedroom with a single rumpled bed and a dresser, and then a small dark lounge with leather chairs and a small television tuned to an exercise program.

One more door. It was closed.

Joshua leaned forward and placed his ear against the door. Silence. He slowly turned the knob and pushed.

"It's the room," Borderline hissed. "The one I saw through the window."

Joshua's eyes raked over the small, white room. He saw a gurney, a white dentist's chair with an attached head frame, bottles and tubes, some black cases with numerous dials and controls, and an overhead monitor. Oh, God. It was all true; every last awful word of the kid's story was true. *There must be more kids in here, held hostage.*

He had to get them out, but where was the doctor, the monster who was in charge of all this?

"Upstairs," he whispered. "Stay with me."

CHAPTER 62

Vogel was annoyed. Where was his pot of tea? Where was Jack? What in God's name was he doing all this time?

He heard a creak on the stairs. *Aha. Here comes the tea.*

A lengthy silence. Then another creak on the stairs. Jack didn't need to sneak up the stairs, and Wilbur was as heavy footed as an ox. It was someone else. Who?

Vogel sprang up, raced soundlessly to the door in his stocking feet, and quickly turned the lock. As he stood and watched, the knob slowly turned and then stopped with a muffled click. Another long silence. He heard voices on the other side of the door, and then someone pounded on it.

"Open up, Vogel." It was a stranger's deep voice. "You're finished, pal. We know what's going on here."

Who was it? Who knew his name?

The pounding continued as Vogel ran to the window and looked out. No police cars, no strange vehicles. Whoever was pounding on the door had come through the woods.

Where was Nelson? Where was Jack?

Vogel seized the jade lighter on his desk and flicked it open under the drapes. A tiny pink flame flickered as he touched the ivory-colored cotton. A spark glowed for a moment, and then flames began climbing the sides of the window.

"Just a moment," Vogel called. "I'll be right there."

Vogel leaped from curtain to curtain, touching them with the lighter. The old house and everything inside would burn in minutes, he thought. There were no fire departments nearby, no hydrants, nothing to stop the fire. By the time the ashes cooled, he would be several states away.

The pounding on the door increased in fury. The door rattled on its hinges. Vogel quickly opened the polished wood filing cabinets and scattered papers on the floor. A thick layer of smoke gathered above his head like a dropped ceiling in the tightly-sealed room.

Vogel ran to the window and opened it. Instantly the flames roared and crackled as fresh air rushed into the room. Vogel brushed aside the flaming curtains and flung himself out on the porch roof. He scuttled over the edge and dropped to the ground below.

CHAPTER 63

Joshua smelled smoke, looked down, and saw thin finger of smoke curling out from under the door. What the hell? He quickly braced his massive shoulder against the door, took three steps backward, and charged.

The door burst open, and he hurtled into the midst of a fire. The blast of heat punched him like a giant fist, searing his lungs, choking him. Joshua scrambled backward out of the room on his hands and knees, pulled the door shut, and leaned his back against it.

Borderline had dropped to the floor in the hallway as the superheated air hit him. They lay next to each other, coughing and gagging.

"Vogel's gone out the window," Joshua gasped. He pulled a small table over to the door and propped it under the doorknob. "We don't have a lot of time. If there's anyone up here, we've got to get them out now."

He yanked open the first door in the hallway and saw a young man lying on a hospital bed with tubing hooked to his left arm and a square of adhesive tape over his mouth. His left eye was bruised almost shut, and there was a large bandage on his forehead. The right eye looked past Joshua and widened in recognition. His bound arms bumped up and down on both sides of the bed in mute staccato.

"Jesus. It's Mark." Borderline rushed to the bed. "Don't worry, buddy, we're getting you out of here."

He tore the adhesive off Mark's mouth as smoke began to filter into the room.

"They said you were dead," Mark croaked.

"Get him loose, Borderline. I'll check the other rooms," Joshua called as he disappeared into the smoke-filled hall.

Borderline unbuckled the restraints and Mark lurched off the bed. His well-tanned, muscular legs and arms protruded from the flimsy, blue hospital gown.

"Wait," Borderline cried, pointing to the IV hooked up to Mark's arm.

"No problem," Mark rasped as he ripped out the needle and threw the bottle and stand across the room with a crash.

In the hallway, the smoke turned darker. The door frame of Vogel's office was outlined in a red glow. With each second, the noise of the fire increased as individual crackling sounds swelled into a single bellow.

Two white-clad figures staggered toward them from the other end of the hallway, coughing and rubbing their eyes. One was tall, thin, and black with his hair in dreadlocks, and the other white kid was short and white and looked strangely familiar.

"Edsell!" Borderline yelled. "You're alive!"

Edsell peered at them. "Borderline? Mark?" His voice was a shaky croak.

"Don't talk. Get out *now!*" Joshua bellowed from within the smoke. "All of you. Get out *now.*"

Borderline pointed toward the stairwell. "Mark, take Edsell and this other kid down those stairs and outside. I'm going to help Joshua."

Edsell and Mark stumbled down the stairs as Borderline ran down the smoky hallway. Suddenly the door to the office burst open behind him, and he felt a rush of pain as flames scorched his back, sucking at him.

Where was Joshua? He opened the door. Two empty beds. Another door and another empty bed. He could hardly see through the smoke. He found the last door with his hands, fumbled with the knob, and then flung it open.

"Get in and shut the door," Joshua roared from the window. "Damn it, I thought I told you to get out. Never mind. Get over here and give me a hand."

Smoke filled the room like a thick, white fog. Joshua was leaning out the window with his big hands around a pair of thin, pale arms. Two more white-clad boys were on the floor. One lay still with his mouth open. His chest heaved, and his eyes stared straight up at the ceiling. The other boy crawled on the floor, his body racked by coughs and wrenching gags.

"Let yourself fall," Joshua called to the hands that held desperately to his own. The fingers suddenly released and disappeared. "Now move away," he called out the window. "Oh, shit. That kid isn't moving, and I can't drop the next one on top of him. Borderline, climb out the window and drag that kid away. Hurry, before the whole building goes."

Borderline climbed backward out the window, hung by the frame, and then dropped as far to the left as he could. A short kid with big eyes and a smudged face lay on the ground directly under the window. He was hacking and crying and shaking. Borderline took his elbow and pulled him upright.

"It's okay now," he said. "You're safe. C'mon, we've got to get out of here."

Borderline pulled him away from the house, sat him down a few yards away, and then ran back. Two bare feet pierced the smoke that now poured from the window. The feet moved lower until a limp shape dangled above him. Borderline grabbed the ankles, and a kid fell into his arms.

"Drag him away," Joshua called as he pushed another pair of legs out the window.

The next boy fell in a heap before Borderline could catch him. Right behind him came Joshua, headfirst with a tongue of flame in pursuit.

As they pulled the last boy away from the house, Mark staggered around the corner with his left arm supporting Edsell.

"Hey," he called. "When I came out, the tall, ugly guy was on the porch, but he saw me and ran into the woods."

"Good. Let him run like a dog. Let him get out of my sight before I kill him with my bare hands. Let's get out of here."

CHAPTER 64

The group ran, stumbled, and carried each other into the woods. Behind the line of trees, they paused and looked back. Black, oily smoke poured from the house. Windows popped and crackled while flames roared up between the cedar shakes of the roof.

Vogel's Suburban was gone, but Nerf's van was parked next to the house. As they watched, the pale blue surface turned black on the side nearest the heat. Next, a glow appeared underneath as the gasoline tank ruptured. Seconds later, bright orange flames and roiling dark smoke engulfed the van.

Joshua looked at the trees on the far side of the house.

"The fire's spreading. Luckily, the wind is flowing northeast, away from my cabin. Can any of you guys walk? I mean a mile or more."

Edsell stood up on unsteady feet. "I can."

Jared stood next to him. "Me too," he said.

The chubby boy staggered to his feet. "I'll try."

The last two lay on the ground, moaning and rubbing their eyes. Joshua took the larger boy and heaved him on his shoulders.

"Can you take the other one?" he asked Borderline.

Borderline pulled the boy upright, stooped, and put him over his shoulder.

When they were several hundred yards into the pines, they heard a series of muffled crashes and crunches behind them.

"Just the roof caving in," Joshua said, not looking back. "Keep going."

Borderline stopped. "Wait," he said. "We left Nerf back there, tied to a tree."

Joshua's face turned to stone, and he kept walking.

"But he's tied to a tree," Borderline cried, "and the fire's spreading that way."

Joshua stopped and slowly turned around with the boy in his arms. His eyes blazed in his blackened face.

Suddenly, a long, fearful cry stretched over the rumbling of the fire. Half-human, half-beast, it rang through the pinewoods for long moments and then died in an echoing snarl.

"The fire is too close," Joshua said softly. "No need to go back to my cabin now. Move on."

Joshua had seen many house fires in his day, and as he hurried through the woods with the boy on this shoulder, he imagined what was happening right now at the old Watson place. The old cedar roof of the house would burn like tissue paper ignited with a blow torch. The ancient oak beams would last longer and then drop their dark remnants onto the floors below. They would fall randomly and indiscriminately on computers, books, kitchen pots and pans, hospital beds, and fine English china.

Minutes later, he heard the walls of the old house caving inward, screeching down chimneys and fireplaces until the burning mass plunged into the crawlspace below where spiders fried and millipedes burrowed deep into the sand.

The frightening result was that, with each crash and crumble, thousands of bright sparks were flying high into the air to be carried to the northeast by the wind. Those bits of hot light would flutter onto dry needles and oak leaves. They would dance into parched Pineland grasses and settle comfortably among the rushes and reeds of the cedar swamp.

Fed by the forest and fanned by the wind, a wildfire began.

CHAPTER 65

The big, black Suburban lurched over the old macadam road. Dr. Anton Vogel clenched the steering wheel like a life preserver on a stormy sea. His face was streaked with black, and his usually immaculate white shirt was stained with perspiration and soot. Vertical black and copper-colored streaks on the front of his clothing marked where he had slid down the cedar shakes of the porch roof, scrambled over the gutter, and dropped to the ground. Blood oozed from a gash on his shoeless right foot.

A singular thought thumped rhythmically in his mind as he kept his throbbing foot pressed firmly on the accelerator: *I'm alive. I'm alive. I'm alive.*

It had been close, so very close. The horrible pounding on the door. The loud, deep voice shouting his name. The curtains billowing with flames. The choking smoke.

Who had pounded on his office door? How did that person know his name?

He'd been so careful, so discreet. No one in this whole region even knew his name. More disturbing than the pounding was the question of Jack and Nelson. Where were they? Vogel clenched his teeth and fervently prayed that his two worthless assistants had been reduced to deaf, dumb, and blind ashes.

Exposure was an unthinkable nightmare. He would be handed over to the howling ignorant masses, and they would have no vision or appreciation for his work. There would be an indictment, arrest, prosecution, a trial. He would be convicted and sent to jail to mingle with the very dregs of society.

His story would be revealed by the press. Vultures, all of them, feasting on him, plastering his face on the cover of every two-bit supermarket tabloid.

Vogel shuddered, and an involuntary groan rattled his chest. As soon as he got to a main road, he'd find a phone and call General Morris. He was too upset to think clearly now. Morris would tell him what to do.

The Suburban scrambled around a tight turn in the road, and suddenly flashing lights appeared at the end of a long straightaway. Vogel braked and wheeled the Suburban into a small side road. When he was hidden among the trees, he watched the rearview mirror. A few seconds later, a small, red fire truck whizzed by.

Damn. Someone had already reported the fire. More and more trucks would be coming, perhaps even ambulances and police. He might get stopped and questioned.

It would be best to stay in the woods and wait until the main road was clear.

Vogel looked down at the tatters of paisley silk hanging around his neck. He undid his tie and flung it out the window. He took his white handkerchief from his pants pocket, and when he wiped it across his face, Vogel was dismayed to see black stains on the soft linen. He wiped and wiped, folding and refolding the handkerchief.

Finally he adjusted the rearview mirror and looked at himself. One tiny smudge remained below his right eye. He rubbed it away.

Vogel turned the air conditioner on high and adjusted the vents to blow on him. As his heartbeat slowed and his body cooled, he kept his eye on the mirror. Two more fire trucks went by and then a white pickup with a flashing yellow light on the cab.

Perhaps it would be wise to stay off the main roads, he thought. On this narrow lane, he might not run into anyone else. The fire surely had spread to the woods, and all the locals would be busy either fighting it or scrambling to get out of its way. No one would notice a dusty vehicle slowly driving away on the back roads. He released the brake.

After ten minutes of careful driving, another larger dirt road joined Vogel's, and the narrow avenue widened. No problem now. He'd be on a paved road soon, and then he'd look for Garden State Parkway signs.

But suddenly the road branched and bisected with two other roads and narrowed again. Vogel was afraid to turn because the side roads looked worse than the one he was on. They were narrow and deeply rutted. Dangerous.

At the top of a low grade, the road turned sharply left and then twisted down a long sloping hill. It turned left again and for a while ran next to a small creek with tea-colored water. The vegetation was lush near the creek bed. Tall, unfamiliar grasses and wide-leafed shrubs threatened to enclose the narrow road. Vogel accelerated, and the Suburban clawed through the boggy glen and up another low hill.

At the top he stopped. There was nothing ahead but small, twisted pine trees and the usual scrubby underbrush. *What a godforsaken place*, thought Vogel. *The absolute end of the earth.*

A subtle dry haze lay over everything, and for a moment, Vogel wondered if he was driving in circles and crossing his own dust trail. He moved forward again slowly and then realized he smelled smoke.

Vogel abruptly stopped the Suburban and lowered the window. The smoke was there, all right, a grim reminder of the burned-out lab and his losses. He scanned the road ahead. There were no tire tracks in the rutted sand. Perhaps he should turn back after all.

What was his relationship to the sun? The shadows of the trees in front of him fell across the road from the left. Did that mean he was traveling west? Away from the Parkway, back toward the fire?

Suddenly, Vogel heard the distinct clatter of a helicopter off to this left. Through the tops of the pines, a red and white helicopter cruised above the trees.

Vogel closed his window. *Damn.* He did not want a police or news helicopter following him. He needed to get out now, but there were no road signs in this hellish place.

He put the Suburban in first gear and inched forward on the rutted road. His vehicle was dark, thank god, and would not be very noticeable in the pine forest.

As he slowly drove down the road, a small lake appeared on his left, and then he saw it, his temporary salvation: an old hulk of a building with one side open. An old abandoned factory? The wheels of the truck struck the remains of a paved road.

If he could pull under that roof and stay hidden for an hour or two, the fire fighters would do their job and leave. The fire would be out, and he could find his way out of the hideous, infernal, never-ending pine forest.

Vogel carefully pulled the Suburban into the old building, turned off the engine, and leaned back in his seat.

He was very, very tired. He couldn't risk driving right now. He had to wait until the fire trucks and the helicopters were gone.

Vogel leaned his head back on the leather seat and closed his eyes.

CHAPTER 66

eddy heard Joshua and the survivors long before she saw them as they rustled and crackled their way through the dry oak leaves and pine needles.

As soon as she saw their soot-stained faces, Teddy ran to them. Dressed in dirty, blue hospital gowns, the boys looked like angels who had been dragged through hell.

"What happened?" she cried.

Joshua quickly handed over the boy he carried and sprinted for the house. "The Watson place is on fire," he said. "I'm calling it in."

"Vogel set it himself," Borderline panted. "We barely got out in time. This is Mark." He pointed to a tall, muscular kid with a huge bruise over one eye.

"Joshua dropped the kids out a window to Borderline," Mark said. "The fire was all around us, but we got everyone out."

Like the others, Mark's face was streaked with black soot and sweat. With his right arm, he supported a thin boy.

"This is Edsell. We were looking for him. That's how we found the house and … and …" Mark couldn't speak anymore. He jaw worked, but no more words came out.

Two more kids, dressed in blackened hospital gowns, staggered up behind Mark.

So Borderline's terrible story had been true after all, Teddy thought as she led them all into the cabin. Thank God Joshua went right over. Thank God he hadn't listened to her and waited to call the police.

She carried the smallest boy into the main room and gently laid him on the big couch. He looked to be twelve or thirteen years old and had a string of bruises along the inside of this arms and small wounds in the delicate, pale skin of his inner elbows. Dried streaks of blood made irregular patterns down his arms. Short, spiky, brown hair framed the boy's face; it looked as if it had been cut with pair of blunt scissors.

Teddy knelt on the floor next to the kid.

"You're safe," she said softly as she took his small, cold hand into her strong, warm one.

"I think his name's Michael," Mark volunteered. He told me in the woods on the way here.

"Michael?" Teddy asked. "Is that your name?"

The boy nodded, and his eyes roved around the room. They passed Borderline, Mark, Edsell, and the others and settled finally on Joshua, who had finished his call to the Forest Fire Service. The boy's small, thin mouth twitched and then moved as a series of low, croaking noises burst out of his throat. Joshua's eyes fastened on Michael. The struggle continued for several seconds while Teddy sat and softly squeezed his hand.

Finally the croaks became intelligible words.

"T-t-t-thank y-y-you."

Teddy's eyes filled with tears. She pulled the frail boy to her as his small shoulders rocked with sobs.

Joshua moved closer until he stood next to Michael.

"Son, I promise that if I ever get a hold of that sonofabitch, he'll never hurt another human being again." He motioned Teddy to the kitchen area. "I've got to get to the fire," he said.

"No, Joshua," Teddy said. "You can't leave now."

"I've got to. The Watson place was an inferno, and sparks are flying out all over the woods. The fire's heading away from us, north up toward Bamber Lake, thank God. You know how dry it's been. This is going to be a major fire, a dangerous one, and the chief will need everyone on it. You'll be safe here with the boys. Stay here with them until I get back."

She nodded, "Yes, but ..."

"Come on, Teddy. Just feed them, clean them up, and let them sleep. Let 'em watch TV."

"Shouldn't we call the police? Or a doctor?" she whispered. "And what about their parents?"

"Teddy, I heard stories on the way back here today that would make you sick, give you nightmares for years. These kids were tied to their beds and hooked up to IVs. It was like they were being kept alive for something. There's other people involved, too, maybe military types, and I don't know who else. Let's not do anything right now."

"But their families will be frantic."

"Mark's folks are gone on vacation, and Borderline's parents think he's at Mark's house. We've got maybe a day before they're missed."

"What about the other boys?"

Joshua leaned forward until his mouth was close to her ear. "Hard luck stories, Teddy. Some of them are runaways; they've all been missing for a while." His thick brows drew together. "No one knew they were at the Watson place, and no one needs to know they're here for a few more hours. As soon as we get this fire under control, I'll talk to the chief."

"Who's the chief?"

"Bill Hayes, the chief fire warden for the whole state. He's good friends with Sean Casey, the head of the New Jersey State Police. Casey will know what to do, who to call. Maybe we need the FBI. I just don't know. In the meantime, the kids stay here. Don't let anyone make any calls until I get back."

Teddy's mouth opened with a question, but Joshua pulled her closer.

"Trust me. These kids have been through enough stuff. Let them rest. I'll be back soon."

He held her at arm's length and looked into her eyes. As she nodded in silent agreement, it suddenly occurred to him that he loved her very, very much.

Teddy read something on his face and drew him close for a moment. "Take care of yourself, Joshua."

He reluctantly pulled away from her and went into the bedroom. He returned moments later with an armload of jeans, T-shirts, socks, and underwear. He threw everything on the braided rug near the fireplace.

"Okay, guys. Here's some clothes. They might not exactly fit, but they're a damn sight better than those granny gowns you're wearing. You can get washed up now, and while you do, Teddy will fix up something to eat. I've got to get out to the fire, but I'll be back as soon as I can."

Mark spoke up. "Why do you have to go? Why can't you stay here with us?"

"I'd like to, but I can't. I'm one of the guys who trained to work these big fires. They need me there until they can pull some more crews in from the other divisions around the state."

Joshua turned on a scanner on the kitchen counter. The room filled with an assortment of static and several different alternating voices.

"This is a receiver. You can hear what's going on, but you can't talk to anyone from this set. I keep the two-way in my pickup."

Joshua leaned over and listened for a few minutes.

"Just as I thought. The fire's spreading up toward Bamber Lake. Everyone's meeting at the command post. I gotta change. If I show up like this, they'll know I was in a fire today, and I don't want to answer any questions yet."

"Let me go with you," Borderline said. "I can help, I know I can. Please, Joshua."

Joshua shook his head and went into the bedroom. He quickly changed into fresh jeans. Seconds later, he was leaning bare-chested over the stainless steel kitchen sink, splashing water over his face. Soap suds clung to the thick hair at his temples. When he stood up and wiped his face and neck with a towel, he saw Borderline standing next to him.

"Listen, kid, I'd like to take you, but I can't. Everyone out there is a trained professional, even the part-timers like me. Most of us have been fighting fires since we were kids like you."

"Kids like me. You just said it. *Kids like me.*"

"Yeah, but you didn't grow up in the woods, and you don't know anything about a Barrens fire. You're not a Piney."

With an exasperated groan, Borderline turned away and looked longingly out the window.

Joshua rummaged in a large chest of drawers until he found a dark green T-shirt and then pulled it over his head. Fresh socks and logger's boots completed his attire.

The scanner on the counter squawked static and voices. Michael had fallen asleep on the couch. Teddy was busy dishing up soup and sandwiches for the others. With clean clothes and the prospect of real food, the boys were animated as they told their stories to Teddy and to each other, letting the horror flow out and dissipate in the large sunlit room.

These kids are fine here for now, Joshua thought as he eavesdropped. *If I call the police, they'll haul them to the station and badger them with a million questions. There will be reporters and photographers, TV cameras, social workers, and a whole bunch of shit. The kids might even get hauled off to foster care.*

Shoot, let them rest for a couple of hours. What harm could that do?

Sometimes, the best response to a problem was no response, he mused. Later, if anyone asked why he waited to call the authorities, he could say he didn't want to cause a stir that would bring a horde of people out to the Barrens in a dangerous fire situation. All things considered, that was part of the truth.

"Come on, Joshua." Borderline interrupted his thoughts. "I know my way around the Barrens. I studied all kinds of maps when we started tracking Nerf."

Joshua took a large bottle of water from the refrigerator and an apple from a bowl on the kitchen counter. As he walked out the back door, he grabbed a yellow shirt from a nook on the wall, wrapped it around a yellow helmet, and tucked everything under his arm.

Borderline followed him outside, silently dogging his heels. At the door of his truck, Joshua hesitated. This was a good kid, and he hated to say no, but it was against the rules. Years ago, when they needed men, the fire wardens grabbed whoever was around, put them on trucks, and sent them into the woods to fight fires. Most of the time the system worked, but occasionally the fire played unpredictable, deadly tricks. Today there were all kinds of restrictions about bringing civilians to a fire.

"I'm sorry, Borderline, but you don't know what you're asking. It all sounds exciting to you, but a Barrens wildfire is a living, breathing monster looking for something to eat. She'll cook you and blister you. She'll pour smoke all over you and then rip the breath right out of your lungs. Your throat will get scorched so bad you won't be able to talk. That thing is no neat, little suburban house fire. She's a bitch that walks and talks and roars, and when she gets rolling, you can't outrun her."

Borderline ducked his head and looked at his feet, obviously disappointed. Suddenly, Joshua had an idea. Maybe the kid *could* help by driving the truck back to his cabin after he hooked up with the other firefighters at the command center.

"Wait a minute," Joshua said, and ran back to the cabin.

He opened the door and called to Teddy. "Borderline's coming with me so he can drive the pickup back here. I don't want my brand-new truck near the fire."

CHAPTER 67

O range and white and a hundred feet tall, Cedar Bridge Fire Tower stood guard over the east-central section of the Pine Barrens. To the south and west and north, six other towers rose above the pine forest.

When drought came, and fire stalked the Barrens, the tower men's eyes grew keen. Books were unopened, tape players were silent, and sandwiches grew soggy in Coleman coolers. In the fire season, which stretched from April to October, each tower was manned from 10:00 a.m. to 6:00 p.m. The only days off were the rainy ones.

Those who worked in the small, sweltering cubicles were most often young men on their way into the Forest Fire Service, or old men on their way out.

Patrick McMurphy was twenty years old and in his first summer as tower man of Cedar Bridge Fire Tower.

On this Saturday of July Fourth weekend, his shirt was soaked with sweat by the time he climbed the last narrow steps, unlocked the padlock, and lifted up the trap door. He checked his watch. Only nine forty-five, and the air inside the tiny glass-walled room was already suffocating.

It was the hottest, driest spring and summer on record. Since April, McMurphy had spent five days a week perched 102 feet above the forest in a ten-by-ten foot glass box. He was beginning to question the wisdom of taking an entry-level job in the Division of Parks and Forestry.

McMurphy stowed his small cooler under the square table that took up most of the room. Next he turned on three small fans and started peeling off his clothes. Within minutes, the young man was in his jockey shorts with his tan Forest Fire Service uniform carefully folded under the table.

The top of the table held the circular frame of the Osborne Fire Finder, a simple sighting tool that allowed him to pinpoint the exact location of any fire within his district. A map of the New Jersey Pine Barrens hung on the wall. Each tower on the map was a red dot in a small circle marked with degrees. A piece of string hung from the center of each circle. By talking to the other towers on their radios, and by using a thumbtack and string, a tower man could accurately find the location of any fire within his area.

McMurphy turned on the radio and scanned the horizon with his binoculars. He then began his morning routine of recording and calling in the weather, temperature, and humidity.

The report had not varied for several days. Clear skies with thin, high clouds, temperature over ninety degrees, humidity under 20 percent. Because high temperature and low humidity brought fire to the Barrens, McMurphy would be busy again today. The summer had already seen dozens of fires in the Barrens. Most of them had been small ones, but a few went major. These fires were most often set by kids playing with matches, by campers, smokers, and the occasional arsonist.

McMurphy knew that below him, on the back roads and trails of the Barrens, many of the local fire wardens were already patrolling in their fully-loaded brush trucks, ready to jump on the smallest puff of smoke. When it was this dry and this hot, seconds counted.

There had been a major burn last week in the southern part of the Barrens, near Wharton State Forest. Over a hundred acres had burned, and for a while the old historic village was threatened, but finally a backfire along the old Batona Trail held the advancing fire. By midnight, the fire was *contained*. After several days of saturating the burned-out area, piggy-backing hoses from truck to truck, the fire was designated *under control*, and then finally *out*.

As he called in the last of his reports, McMurphy heard a truck door slam and then felt a sudden pounding below him. Someone was running up the steps of his tower, and judging by the shaking of the spindly old structure, it was someone large.

McMurphy grabbed his green slacks and hopped into them. As the footsteps neared the top, he knelt by the trap door, pulled it up by the handle, and looked down into the red, perspiring face of the chief.

The last person the young tower man expected to see in his sweltering roost was Bill Hayes, the state forest fire warden. The big boss.

"Chief! Here, give me your hand."

With a poorly suppressed grumble in the back of his throat, the chief accepted a hoist up into the tiny, glass-walled room. Without a word, he elbowed past McMurphy and raised his binoculars to the west where the muted greens and grays of the pine forest stretched to the horizon. McMurphy quickly raised his own binoculars, and the horizon sprang into the round sights. He panned the miles of forest until he saw it: a thin column of black smoke rising into the sky.

"Damn," the chief exclaimed. "Joshua's right. The Watson place is burning. Son, get me those coordinates while I ring up Apple Pie Hill Tower."

The chief picked up the handheld microphone and punched in the distant tower. No answer. He punched more numbers.

A voice came over instantly. "Ned Rouselle."

"This here's the chief. Where are you?"

"In my truck right under the tower, chief. I was just sitting here reading the newspaper, getting ready to go up. What's happening?"

"I'm up here in Cedar Bridge Tower looking at a *God blessit house fire,* and you're sitting in your truck waiting for ten o'clock to come! Get your ass up there right now." The chief peered through the binoculars once more. "Oh Christ, I'm looking at white smoke now. Damn fire's already jumped to the trees. Get up there and call us with those numbers."

For the next several minutes, the two radios crackled and hummed, and the phone rang several times. McMurphy danced between the table and the map while the chief spoke with Red Potter, the section fire warden. Within minutes, two Forest Fire Service brush trucks were racing to the fire.

The chief muttered, "Look at that. The smoke's growing, turning black already. Goddamn."

McMurphy raised his binoculars but watched Bill Hayes out of the corner of his eye. The chief was a legend in firefighting circles—respected, admired, and brilliant. He had come up through the ranks starting as a teen firefighter in the old days when kids were pulled out of school, loaded on fire trucks, and sent into the woods to fight forest fires.

Fire was the chief's mortal enemy, and he maintained a hands-on leadership in the battle by personally overseeing every major fire.

McMurphy had heard the chief talk about killer fires, like the one in 1963 that burned up most of the Barrens in three wrenching days of flame, smoke, and death. Each time they stopped a major fire, the chief said, "That wasn't the *big one* yet. We got her in time. But when the big one comes, watch out."

Was this the start of the *big one*?

Thick, gray smoke now mixed with the black roils of the house fire. McMurphy knew that Red Potter, the fire warden of Section B-5, would be out there soon. He'd drive his brush truck right through the woods, knocking down trees, circling the fire, spraying his 250 gallons of water on its base. Thick clouds of steam would rise into the air. The fire would hiss and crackle as other trucks joined the circle, always moving to the right, circling, circling until the fire was dead or dying.

The first fifteen minutes were critical. After that, the fire got dangerous, and the fight to kill it got complicated. More men, more equipment, bulldozers, planes, helicopters, a command center, maps, strategy meetings. In a drought like this, a skirmish could quickly grow into a full-scale battle between a runaway chemical reaction and the Forest Fire Service firefighters.

As McMurphy watched, the smoke rose ever higher. It changed color and became darker and thicker. Bright red and orange flashes glowed along the distant tree line.

The chief dropped his binoculars and looked intently at the young tower man.

"McMurphy, right? I met you at the training session."

"Yes, sir," McMurphy said, barely restraining a salute.

"Hot up here."

"Yes, sir."

"I was a tower man myself, a long time ago. Same uniform, only I usually left off the pants." A small smile danced around the thin lips of the chief, and then his face grew grim. "Feel that wind, McMurphy. It's kicking around, blowing here, blowing there, just like it did in '63." He turned toward the fire. "Nasty over there. They haven't let us in to do any controlled burns. Lots of understory built up. Leaves, pine needles, scrub brush, cones, all piled deep."

The chief opened the trap door and lowered his bulky frame onto the narrow stairs.

"The west, McMurphy. Look to the west. That's where the big ones come from."

The chief climbed into his white, unmarked cruiser and slammed the door. He turned the ignition key, and the truck roared into life. The five-year-old Ford needed a new muffler and had a pronounced tic in the engine, but there was no time to get it into the shop. The chief pulled onto the cracked macadam road, sighed heavily, and wished heartily for a three-day soaking rain. He needed a rest.

The million acres of the Pine Barrens was his responsibility, his one great love and his constant abiding fear. The small ancient pitch pines around him glowed a pale gray-green. Their flammable resins glistened in the sun as they hunkered down against the dry, hot air. They were old and tough and smart, turning inward, growing twisted with thick layers of insulating bark, keeping their precious seed cones tightly closed.

If there was a fire, the pitch pines would survive. Their thick, black bark would keep the precious, green, inner layer protected until new shoots could push out and turn into branches. Even if a fire was hot enough to destroy the old trees, new life would emerge from their tightly clenched oval cones, cones that only opened only after exposure to extreme heat. The pine forest had survived great fires for thousands of years. It would survive again.

The problem was not the forest; it was the people.

Despite restrictions on new construction, certain areas had been developed. Small groups of homes were scattered throughout the Barrens, and those homes were built right into the forest. Highly flammable trees overhanging wooden houses were a nightmare to any firefighter.

The chief dropped the cruiser into third gear and pounded down the old road. Deep lines crisscrossed his forehead, and he shrugged his shoulder against an ache in the back of his neck.

Despite his protests, funding for the Forest Fire Service had been cut, and cut again, in the past few years. The weather had cooperated, his men were well trained, and there had been no disastrous forest fires, so of course his annual budget was fair game for every cost-cutting politician in the State House. So now he was faced with a drought-stricken, tinder-dry forest, old worn-out trucks and equipment, and a reduced staff. For chrissakes, his men were even buying their own replacement rakes and shovels.

The chief turned on his flashers and stepped on the gas. Telephone poles whipped by, and the cracks in the pavement transferred into a jarring vibration in the steering wheel. He glanced at his watch and picked up the phone. He'd be at Coyle Field in five minutes.

"Johnny?"

"Yeah." It was the voice of Johnny Reb, chief pilot of the small Forest Fire Service air force.

"You heard what's going on?"

"I've been listening. Your chopper's ready to go."

CHAPTER 68

J oshua's truck trailed a huge cloud of dust as it hurtled down the unmarked dirt road. Borderline hung on to the door handle with one hand and kept his other braced on the seat of the flying vehicle. A small, black radio was fastened to the dashboard. A continuous hubbub of noise emanated from it.

"Can you drive a shift?" Joshua yelled over the din.

"Hey, I work at a garage. I know carburetors, transmissions, fuel injectors, brakes, and ball joints."

"Great, but can you drive a shift?"

Borderline laughed. "Yeah, I can."

"Kid, you did some good work back there at the Watson place. Your instincts were right on the money about Edsell and that creep Vogel."

"Thanks."

"Got a girlfriend?"

"Got a bunch of them," Borderline said.

Joshua laughed. He'd been the same way in high school. Girls had gravitated to him, and he'd enjoyed every minute of it.

The acrid smell of wood smoke increased as they traveled north and east. Joshua turned up the radio another notch.

"Listen, that's Red Potter," he said. "Red's the fire warden for this section."

A series of squawks and seemingly unintelligible voices came out of the radio.

"Red's out at the fire with his brush truck. He's got three other crews with him."

"What's a brush truck?"

"A special built fire truck for work in the pine Barrens. They buy Dodges, Fords, and GMCs and then convert them at a shop in New Lisbon. They add roll bars, heavy grills, a 250-gallon water tank, hoses, and pumps, plus double sets of tires in the back."

"I'd like to see the shop."

"I'll take you there someday." Joshua leaned forward to listen to the scanner. "I was right; the fire's moving northeast, up toward Bamber Lake."

"Bamber Lake?" Borderline said. "We went right by it a couple of times on the way to Vogel's house. Two groups of homes on either side of a small lake."

Joshua nodded. "That's it."

There was a burst of static, and then a deep, gravelly voice asked about present conditions.

"That's the chief, Bill Hayes," Joshua said. "Listen closely. Red's giving him a report now."

A slow, calm drawl came over the scanner. "Chief, she's up, and she's walking the dog," it said.

"Oh, Christ," Joshua exclaimed.

"What's wrong?" Borderline asked.

"That means the fire's crowned, jumped to the tops of the trees, traveling fast now. You can tell it's bad when Red starts talking in that slow drawl. The slower he talks, the worse it is."

"Why didn't he just say that?"

"A lot of people out here have scanners, so we talk in codes to keep from upsetting everyone. We've got nicknames or numbers for almost everything. A 1029 means a body on the ground, a 1015 is an injury." Joshua picked up the mike. "J.R. here. I'm on my way."

Ten minutes later, Joshua's pickup bumped into a clearing in the pines and lurched to a stop in a cloud of white dust. Joshua pointed to a white camper with a Forest Fire Service logo on it. "That's the mobile command post."

The camper was parked next to a small, white shingled house. Two men were stringing wires through an open window.

"They're hooking up the electric now. We've got aerial maps and phones and radios inside the trailer. The whole operation will be controlled from here. If the fire gets too close, they'll move the trailer."

Joshua hopped out, and Borderline slid across the seat to the driver's side. "Can I stay and watch?" he asked through the open window.

"You can stick around for a few minutes, but move my truck over there by that black Chevy. The chief will be landing soon, and it'd be better if he didn't see you."

"Thanks, Joshua."

"You've got fifteen minutes, and then I want you on your way. Do you remember how to go back to the cabin?"

"Straight out for a mile, then a left by the little pond. That will put me on Dukes Bridge Road. Stay on that for about two miles, then south by the big dead tree."

"You've got it."

"Good luck, Joshua."

"You take care of Teddy and the boys. I'll be back as soon as I can."

More men and women arrived. Private trucks and cars and forestry service vehicles were scattered around the edges of the yard, looking as if they had been discarded by a giant child playing with Matchbox toys. A radio squawked from inside the open door of the command post.

A group of men stood near the trailer. As Borderline watched, a short, bald man in a red shirt said something to Joshua and then pointed west. The rest of the men looked sober as they nodded in agreement. One man spit into the dirt at his feet. Another cupped his hands around a match and lit up a cigarette.

Borderline turned off the engine and climbed out of the truck. He looked and listened. This was definitely not Toms River or Seaside.

A fine, chalky mist hung over the clearing and reached into the trees massed around him. Acres and acres of trees, ominous trees. Until this moment, Borderline had thought of trees as friendly beings that belonged to the plant world. Trees held swings aloft and provided secret hiding places for little boys within their leafy branches. They gave shade in the summer, color in the fall, and Christmas trees in the winter.

But here in the Barrens, in the presence of thousands upon thousands of trees, the kindness disappeared. Here, on a hot dry day, the trees whispered danger.

Borderline heard a crashing in the woods to his left. The noise came closer and closer, and then a red Dodge brush truck emerged from the forest. It came on inexorably, crunching down small and medium trees in its path, steering around the larger ones.

The truck was equipped with roll bars and a massive grill on the front and sides. There was deep well behind the cab, and behind that, a square water tank and a hose wound up on a cylinder.

The wide double sets of tires on the rear axle churned to a rumbling stop in the deep, sandy soil just short of the men. Joshua detached himself from the group and called to the driver.

"Hey, Tony. Joy riding that truck again, are you?"

Tony smiled as he hopped down onto the sand. "Just taking a shortcut, Joshua. Getting here as fast as I can."

"Loaded and ready to go?"

"Yeah. You'll be with me. Luke and Burley are right behind me with more guys. What's up?"

"It looks bad. Red got right on the fire with two other trucks. He backfired along Red Toad Road, but it's so dry out there, the bitch jumped right over it. The chief's up in the chopper now, checking it out."

"Where'd it start?"

"The old Watson place. Started about eight this morning."

"How'd that happen? I thought the ..." Tony stopped talking and sniffed. He moved closer to Joshua. "How come you smell like smoke? You ain't even been on the fire yet."

"A long story, Tony. I'll tell you about it later."

Tony fixed him with a steady gaze, and Joshua returned the look without blinking. After a few seconds, Tony shrugged and looked away.

A muffled rumble sounded in the distance and then grew quickly into a roar. Borderline looked up. A sleek, red helicopter hurtled over the tops of the trees and then landed in a stinging swirl of sand. A crew-cut, burly man in tan shirt and slacks jumped out, ducked under the still rotating blades, and sprinted to the command post.

That must be Bill Hayes, the big boss of the fire fighters, thought Borderline.

Hayes was followed by another man wearing jeans, a stained yellow shirt, and a helmet. When the second man pulled off his helmet, Borderline saw that his hair was a bright coppery color. It had to be "Red" Potter.

Borderline edged closer, careful to stay hidden behind the parked vehicles.

The helicopter blades slowed to a leisurely rotation, and as the engine idled, a third man climbed down.

"How's it going, Johnny?" someone called.

"Wind's picking up. We had some bumps up there. Red got sick. I guess the smoke he ate this morning didn't agree with his stomach."

"Red puked?" A short man chuckled. "Hell, he's never sick. Boys, we're going to have to give Red a new name. Let's see. How does Chuck sound to you?"

"Pretty good, but I like Ralph," Joshua snorted.

"Or Cookie," another man said with a wide grin.

As the men laughed and exchanged stories about the times they'd been sick on a fire, two more brush trucks arrived and then a pickup truck. Soon fourteen men and two women stood under the trees. They wore an assortment of clothing—jeans, T-shirts, khakis, and shirts with the Forest Fire Service logo on them. Most wore helmets. The helmets were as varied as the clothing. Red, bright yellow, black, and one bright blue helmet with an Oregon sticker on the front. Bright yellow shirts were scattered throughout the group, and more yellow shirts rested on the grills and fenders of the trucks. Borderline assumed they were made of some fire-resistant material.

The expressions and postures of the fire fighters were as studiously casual as their clothing, but under the spoofing and the jibes, there was a tension, a simmering anticipation of their upcoming battle with the fire.

The door of the trailer opened with a loud creak, and three men hurried out. Borderline huddled behind an old brown station wagon and listened carefully as the chief addressed the group.

"This here's a big one, boys. She's growing and dangerous, heading north toward Bamber Lake at about four miles an hour. Red and some of the boys tried to stop her at Red Toad Road, but she jumped right over them. Right now she's tossing out spot fires. We can't get them all because it's too damn dry out there."

The faces of the men changed from serious to grim as the chief continued.

"We're going to try to hold her at Bamber by backfiring along Dover Road and up the old trail to Bull's Gut. You men know the area. I think we can save the houses. The choppers will lift water from the lake, and the local boys will spray the roofs. We'll start a backfire along the east side of the lake. I'll try and get us some Ag-cats to drop extra water."

The chief paused and looked around the group, his eyes frosty in the warm haze.

"Most of you weren't around when we had the big one back in '63. I was just a boy, but I remember it like yesterday. That fire burned up half the Barrens in less than three days." He cleared his throat. "We lost some good men."

"My pa fought that fire," Joshua said.

"So did mine," said another man on his right.

The chief continued. "You're all trained firefighters, but a lot of you have never seen a fire like this, not in drought conditions like we've got today. Be careful and keep those radios on."

The chief turned unexpectedly before Borderline had time to duck behind the wagon.

"Who the hell is that?" the chief roared.

Borderline stepped forward. Joshua jumped to his side.

"Chief, this is Borderline Fenton. He was at the Watson place when it went up. He's been a real help to me today."

"What's he doing here? You know better than to bring a civilian to a fire."

"He's driving my truck back, Chief. He asked to come, and I didn't see any harm. I'll get a ride home with Tony."

The chief stared at Borderline. "Boy, you know how to get back to Joshua's place?"

"Yes, sir. I studied maps. I know the roads, even the little dirt ones."

"It's a long story, Chief," Joshua interrupted. "I'll tell you all about it later."

"See that you do. In the meantime … ah … Borderline …" He turned to Joshua. "That's his name?"

Joshua nodded.

"Borderline, we've got a nasty fire waiting for us. You take that truck back to Joshua's cabin. *Now!*"

The chief and Red went back to the command post. The others left, three men in each brush truck, the rest in two pickups. Borderline followed their dust trail to Dukes Bridge Road. Then the firefighters turned right, and he turned left.

Darn it. He wanted to go out to the fire and watch. If he could somehow get out there, maybe he could help. A real forest fire was raging just a few miles away, and he had to go back to the dumb cabin and babysit.

Shit.

CHAPTER 69

The firefighters were halfway to Bamber Lake when the chief came back out of the command post. He saw Johnny Reb half asleep in an old aluminum lawn chair. The Jet Ranger was rumbling in the center of the yard, its blades slowly spinning.

As soon as he saw the boss, Johnny stood up.

"What's wrong, Chief? You look worried."

"I just talked to Mount Holly. National Weather Service says there's a cold front coming in from the northwest."

"But that's good news. We'll get some rain."

"Not this time, Johnny. The front's a dry one with only a few widely scattered showers. Oh, we might get lucky and catch a few drops, but ..." The chief looked up at the cloudless sky and rubbed his hands together.

"But what?"

"If that front comes in with a high northwest wind ..."

He paused and pulled a package of Rolaids from his shirt pocket and dumped three in his palm. *Thank God for antacid pills. I've got three more rolls in my jacket. Hope it's enough.*

"We'll get a sudden wind shift," he continued. "The fire will turn, and when it does, the whole right flank, two or three miles of it, will become one big, long head fire. The bitch will take off fast in front of that wind."

"Jesus."

The chief shook his head. "Wentworth said they're expecting wind gusts up to sixty miles per hour."

The chief flung the antacids into his mouth and chewed them savagely as he sat down on the cracked leather seat of the helicopter. Johnny Reb climbed in after him. The propeller spun faster and faster, and in a great cloud of dust, the chopper rose into the air.

Three minutes later, they were a thousand feet over the Barrens. Far to the southeast lay Barnegat Bay, and beyond it, the distant misty outlines of the barrier islands that held the shore towns of Loveladies and Harvey Cedars. To the north and east were the towns of Toms River, Forked River, and Waretown and their thousands of inhabitants. He could see the tall spires of the Oyster Creek Nuclear Generating Station in Forked River. Most of the shore towns were clustered on the other side of the Garden State Parkway. The fire couldn't jump that, and anyway, the wind was blowing it north right now. Lots of time to stop it.

Beneath the Jet Ranger, the pine forest stretched to the western horizon. The chief looked down through the curved bottom windows. The fire had advanced considerably during the time he had been on the ground. The rate of spread was obviously increasing, and the head fire would reach the tiny community of Bamber Lake soon.

Directly ahead of them, tall plumes of smoke rose high into the air. Bright red flames chased them upward, undulating and twisting. Far below, he saw the red brush trucks and and flashes of yellow shirts and colored helmets as his crews worked the fire. Two bulldozers cut through the woods, their pointed prows creating a long uneven line of raw earth between the oncoming fire and the village of Bamber Lake.

Soon they would backfire along that firebreak.

Red Potter, the fire warden for Section B-5, was the official incident commander, a job that always fell to the head of the section in which the fire originated. Nevertheless, Bill Hayes, the state fire warden, would always be close, circling in the Jet Ranger, haunting the command center, advising whoever was the acting incident commander.

The chief knew the men trusted his judgment. They believed that his thirty-five years of experience gave them the edge over the fire, but sometimes the chief wondered if he was getting too old for the job, wondered if he was pushing his luck. Since he'd been appointed state forest fire warden fourteen years ago, they hadn't lost a single man. Oh, there had been blisters, broken bones, smoke inhalation, evacuations to the burn center, disability claims, but no dead firefighters.

He knew he'd been lucky.

Backfiring was the chief's art, his creative expression in the dangerous world of fighting forest fires. The burning trees created a vacuum when superheated air geysered into the sky. A properly timed backfire would ignore the prevailing wind and actually suck backward into that vacuum. When the two fires crashed into each other, trees, bushes, and grass burned with a burst of incredible energy until suddenly all the fuel was consumed. Then, with blasts of white smoke, the fire would die, and it would be over.

Over, if the bitch didn't throw off sparks that started new spot fires behind the firebreak. Over, if root fires didn't burn secretly deep underground to sneak up later in some unburned part of the forest. Over, if rabbits didn't catch fire and become living, furry fireballs, torching leaves and grass in a mad race with death.

Over, if that dry cold front didn't roar in before they got the flank under control.

The chief wiped his forehead with a patterned navy and white handkerchief and wished to God he'd been to church more often in recent years.

CHAPTER 70

Joshua stood on the running board of the brush truck and watched a big, yellow dozer grind through the trees and underbrush near the village of Bamber Lake. Under his feet, he felt the vibration of the 350-cubic-inch engine. He checked the wick on his torch and hefted the tank of mixed gasoline and diesel fuel onto his back.

Tony's face popped out of the window. "Almost time, Josh. You ready back there?"

"I'm always ready."

Tony laughed and pressed down on the accelerator. Ahead of the truck, the raw, cream-colored earth along the fire line was exposed, smeared with the deep Vs of the bulldozer's treads. Jagged points of roots and stumps jutted out of the bare soil. To his left, still untouched, a small peaceful stream trickled between banks decorated with ferns, wild grasses, and bright green pillows of moss.

Behind the truck, the roofs of the houses were barely visible in the gray, smoky air. The village of Bamber Lake waited in the path of the fire. Each house was empty of people yet filled with remnants of their lives: school pictures, wedding albums, grandma's rocking chair, old quilts, handwritten recipes, bicycles, toys, and tools.

A long, hopeful white arc of water from an eighteen-wheel tanker truck sprayed the roofs, wetting them down in advance of the fire.

An overhead roar announced the old, dark green Huey on its run from the lake to the homes. The water-filled Bambi bucket beneath the old Vietnam-era chopper grazed the treetops.

Organized pandemonium, Joshua thought as he watched the scene. Everyone knew what to do, and they were busy doing it. In the cacophony of machines and tools, human voices shouted instructions, jibes, oaths, and prayers as the smoke thickened and turned black.

Joshua coughed and spit. Tears ran down his face, and from his nose a liquid stream dripped down onto his yellow shirt. There was no time to pull out a handkerchief because suddenly the leaves on the trees turned as the wind reversed and began to blow toward the fire. He felt, rather than heard, a rumbling noise.

"Chief says it's time," Tony called.

Joshua dropped some fuel on the ground, lit a match, and threw it. Flames quickly shot up from the dry leaves and grasses. He increased the drip on the torch, and the flames brightened. The truck moved slowly forward while Joshua held the torch along the edge of the firebreak. As the liquid flames touched the dry underbrush, it flared up, leaving a ragged line of fire behind the brush truck.

The smoke grew heavy, and Tony drove faster. Joshua increased the drip, and the backfire rose high along his side of the bouncing truck.

CHAPTER 71

Far above the firebreak, the chief and Johnny Reb watched as pinpoints of light grew and joined each other along the firebreak. Soon, two long, red snakes of fire extended out from both sides of Bamber Lake.

The plumes from the backfire swirled indecisively and then abruptly turned toward the roiling black smoke and red flame of the approaching head fire. The thin line of backfire widened and stretched toward the head fire, and suddenly the two joined in a violent dance. The flames flew skyward, brighter and brighter, sending massive, thick columns of smoke soaring hundreds of feet into the blue sky.

Then slowly, almost imperceptibly, the flames began to subside. The coils of thick, black smoke gradually changed into soft, gray plumes as the two fires met and joined and then slowly died.

The chief smiled. *Perfect. I got you for now, bitch.*

Johnny Reb pulled the helicopter up and around and then circled Bamber Lake at four hundred feet.

The fire line had held. The houses were safe, although several windblown sparks had started spot fires in the woods nearby, and a small grassy field near the lake was in flames.

The chief quickly directed the brush trucks to the breakouts, and soon those smaller columns of smoke turned to white steam.

To the west, points of orange light in the ravished, black and gray landscape indicated where roots and snags continued to blaze. The two flanks still burned in meandering lines, but the quick-thrusting head fire had been stopped.

"Good work, Chief," Johnny said. "You did it again."

"She's weak, but she ain't dead yet," the chief answered dryly as he searched his pocket for the antacids.

Maybe it was time to spend his summers fishing and crabbing instead of fighting wildfires. Maybe he'd surprise his wife and buy that camper they'd looked at last year in Farmingdale. They could take off next summer and drive west to visit the Grand Canyon, Mount Rushmore, Yellowstone Park, and all those places he'd only read about. He'd fish in clear mountain streams and sleep through the night without restless, sweaty dreams of fire and smoke.

Johnny interrupted his thoughts. "You want to go back to the command post?"

"Yeah. I'll call up Mount Holly and talk to Tom. Let's pray we have enough time to nail down that right flank before the front comes through."

CHAPTER 72

T hirty miles west of Bamber Lake, a small square building sat in the middle of an industrial park. The building houses the Mount Holly Unit of the National Weather Service. Each day, Mount Holly recorded temperature, humidity, precipitation, barometric pressure, wind direction, and velocity. Then, using Doppler radar, satellite pictures, computer imagining, and human observers, the unit made guesses about weather yet to come.

In the Mount Holly Unit of the National Weather Service, Tom Wentworth stood and looked down at a huge screen. The faces of the three other men were shadowy in the dim light of the large room as a computer image of central New Jersey pulsed in bright shades of blue, green, and yellow. As viewed from the satellite high above, the natural border of the Atlantic Ocean was hung with a long, irregular necklace of barrier islands that stretched from Point Pleasant to Cape May. Towns were named in white print, and the artificial boundaries of Monmouth, Ocean, Atlantic, and Burlington Counties were edged in bright blue.

A tiny, intense spot of yellow pulsed in the heart of Ocean County.

Wentworth sat down at the console and pressed several keys. As the image moved to 6,200 feet, the yellow speck jumped into a quarter-sized anomalous blot.

More buttons and dials, and the image went down to 3,700 and then 1,700 feet. The yellow blob grew, doubled, and tripled into an ominous, irregular arrowhead stretched diagonally across the screen. The bright tip poked and prodded the white letters that spelled out Bamber Lake.

"That fire sure moved fast. Looks like they backfired along Bamber Lake," Wentworth said as he peered at the screen and gently fine-tuned the image.

Tom Wentworth was the director of the National Weather Service Station at Mount Holly. Despite the searing heat outside, he was dressed in twill pants, a knit shirt, and a cardigan sweater. The offices were always a cool sixty-eight degrees to protect the computers and satellite imagers that were banked around the room.

"Damn this drought." Wentworth sighed and turned to the man next to him. "Cody, pull up the Doppler and see where that cold front is now. Charlie, call the unit in Harrisburg, Pennsylvania."

Wentworth rubbed his open hands down the sides of his slacks. Ever since he was a small boy, his palms had sweated whenever he got excited or nervous. In Little League games, the bat had flown out of his hands several times as he swung at a pitch. As a teenager, holding hands with a girl was pure agony. Most of the old nervousness was gone now in his middle years, absorbed into the easy ebb and flow of a life with a quiet, supportive woman and three active children. Still, at odd times, the sweaty palms returned.

"Harrisburg's had winds of forty-five miles per hour with gusts over sixty-five," Charlie reported. "The temperature's dropped, gone from ninety-two to seventy-five in twenty minutes. Wait. It's down to seventy-two."

"Storms?"

"Two small cells with only a trace of rain. One's in Reading, the other's just south of Lancaster. Both are heading southeast."

Wentworth sighed. The phone had been ringing off the hook all day. The oppressive six-week heat wave was about to break, and every newspaper, television, and radio station wanted immediate updates for their evening editions. McGuire Air Force Base needed information for air traffic control, as did Philadelphia, Newark, Kennedy, LaGuardia, and every two-bit visual flight airfield in between. Wentworth had put an extra man on the shift just to handle the phones, but the room was still tense and busy.

Now, adding to the mix, there was a wildfire in the Barrens, a fire that was already large enough to be picked up on satellite.

Cody, the youngest member of the weather crew, was talking on one of the two private phones that gave the caller direct access to a human being instead of the recorded updates. He held the receiver at arm's length and waved at his boss.

"For you. The chief."

He picked up a nearby phone and pressed the flashing button. "This is Wentworth," he said.

There was a lengthy pause while a voice crackled from the phone. The men smiled as their boss protectively edged the receiver away from his ear.

"I'm looking at the updates now, Chief. The front's east of Harrisburg and moving quickly. It should get to you soon. What's that?" Wentworth shook his head. "No. It should get to you around six thirty, maybe sooner."

Another long pause while Wentworth nodded and looked down at the screen, still keeping the loud clatter away from his ear.

"I can't promise you rain, Chief," he said. "We've only seen two little cells, and they're just spitting. This front's as dry as a week-old biscuit. Temperature and humidity are dropping way down as it comes through. We've got sustained winds of forty-five miles per hour over in Pennsylvania now with gusts up to sixty-five."

A loud, sexually-explicit oath rang from the phone. The three other weather service employees were all attuned to their boss's conversation with the State Forest fire warden. As the frown on Wentworth's face deepened, they all listened closely.

After several moments, the director of Mount Holly said, "I'll do anything I can, Chief. We'll keep this line open for you. Good luck."

He placed the phone back on his desk and faced the crew.

"The chief's going to have a problem with that fire," he said.

"But why?" Cody asked. "I thought they had it stopped at Bamber Lake. We saw the flare from the backfire awhile ago."

"Yes, that worked. They saved the Bamber Lake community, but the front's going to get to him before the fire crews can get the right flank under control. When the wind shift comes, that whole flank is going to turn into a monster head fire."

A chilly silence hung in the room as a phone rang. Cody grabbed it and said, "National Weather Service. Hold, please."

Wentworth continued. "The fire will change direction and turn into a wall of flame several miles long. It will burn east-southeast fast, really fast. Just imagine, a fifty- mile-per-hour wind pushing a wildfire through a tinder-dry forest." He looked down at the screen and ran his finger from the pulsing yellow point toward the coastline. "I don't know if he can stop it, and if he doesn't, that fire could burn right through to Barnegat Bay. Fourth of July weekend, crowds everywhere. They can't go east into the ocean; they can't go west into the fire. Only a few roads run north and south: the Parkway, Route 35, Ocean Boulevard. They can't possibly evacuate all those people." Wentworth nervously tapped his pencil on the computer table in front of him. "He's got to stop that fire."

CHAPTER 73

As per the chief's orders, the command post had been hurriedly moved to a small field near the Route 532 overpass of the Garden State Parkway. The dusty, white trailer was hidden behind a veil of pines that surrounded a small field. A police car sat in the narrow entrance, its lights flashing.

In the trailer, six men huddled over a table that held several maps. Their voices were hushed and tense. They knew they had to act quickly.

Three of them had fought fires in the western states where the forest often burned for weeks. In those regions, the fire flowed through the vast woodlands like a red tidal wave, raising froths of smoke that could be seen hundreds of miles away. Distances in those regions were measured in miles, not in acres. In the western states, firefighters had time—time to set up base camps, gather equipment, call in teams of firefighters from other states. They could airlift equipment and use the huge bottom-fill CL-21S airplanes to skim water from lakes and drop it in long, wet curtains on advancing fires.

But in New Jersey, everything was faster and tougher. The million acres that made up the Pine Barrens was ringed by towns and villages, by industrial parks, farms, and camp grounds. When drought came to these forests and the flash fuels turned to tinder, wildfire was not simply a threat, it was a screamed epithet.

"That's all I've got to say," the chief said. "You boys talk it over while I get myself some coffee."

He stood up and poured a cup from the ancient percolator. As the chief sipped the bitter, black liquid, he looked out the window and watched the flashing lights of a trooper's car. A frown creased his face. This was the big one, the one he had dreaded all his life.

A fire this big was complicated. It wasn't just about stopping the fire; there were so many other things to consider, to worry about ...

Whenever there was a big fire in the Barrens, reporters from as far away as New York and Philadelphia swarmed to the area. News helicopters flew around the edges of the fire with cameras rolling. Reporters without aircraft of their own sometimes went to the small visual flight airports in the region and paid private pilots ridiculous fees to take them near the fire zone. Right now, dozens of planes circled his fire.

He'd warned them all to stay high and away, but you never knew when these news-hungry clowns would show up and endanger his men.

News media on the ground were a worry too. When they couldn't find anyone from Forestry to interview because everyone from Forestry was a mile back in the woods fighting the fire, they talked to volunteer firemen. The next day, pictures of beautiful eighteen-wheel tankers with clean-faced men in long, black coats and helmets would appear on the front pages of the newspapers and on the evening news.

He needed the volunteer firemen to protect out-buildings and homes, to bring water to crossroads where the brush trucks could reload their smaller tanks. They were good men and often worked hand-in-hand with police and EMS workers, evacuating private citizens, controlling traffic near fire areas, protecting homes that were located on paved roads.

But everyone in the Barrens knew that their big trucks were useless in the woods. They were much too heavy, carried too much water, and often sank into the sand of the dirt roads and had to be towed out. Even on the paved roads, their bodies were too long to maneuver around sharp turns and twists.

The chief sighed and took another pull of his coffee. There would be no pictures of his sweaty, soot-stained men working under the legs of the fire, puking up gray phlegm while their clothes smoldered and their eyebrows singed. There would be no pictures of his small brush trucks circling a fire, no pictures of men holding a steady stream of water on a raging fire while the paint on their trucks blistered. No pictures of torch men running through the woods, setting a backfire even as the flames nipped at their heels.

That's the way it had always been. The Forest Fire Service did its job quickly and quietly with little fanfare and few thanks from the general public.

He listened to the men behind him arguing and wrestling with his plan, testing it against other options. He could order them to do it, but he wanted them to see it his way. Red was convinced. Now the other section fire wardens were talking it over.

To his right and almost unnoticed, a woman sat at a small desk and talked on the phone to the restaurants and stores that would supply food to his men. The mop-up on a fire this big would take days. The men would rake and drench the burned-out areas, break up burning snags, and patrol the perimeter for root fires and breakthroughs. They couldn't leave the fire, so food and other supplies would be sent in.

The chief's thoughts were interrupted when Red slapped the table with his open palm and said, "I don't care what you think. We can't be emotional. We've got to let those houses burn."

The chief bit his tongue and focused on two large scratches on the Plexiglas window a foot from his nose. His plan was bold and dangerous, and the decision was difficult: all isolated homes would be abandoned and allowed to burn. A few clusters of homes located near paved roads might be salvaged by local fire departments, but all of his men would pull out to fight the main battle further east.

They would drop back immediately to the Garden State Parkway and prepare to backfire from Toms River to Waretown, a distance of nearly twelve miles. Wooded areas in the center divide of the six-lane highway would be burned in advance of the fire. To make the natural firebreak even wider, they would plow additional firebreaks on the western side and set a series of parallel backfires along them. When the killer fire approached, every firefighter, every truck would be on the eastern side of the parkway, ready to attack breakthroughs. Every crop duster, every helicopter in his small arsenal would be loaded and in the air, ready to dump water or chemicals on spot fires that jumped the parkway.

"Christ, Red, I can't believe this. My sister and her husband just finished their house." The speaker was a short man in a stained T-shirt. "They worked on that cottage for three years while they lived in a trailer so small you couldn't fart and light the stove at the same time. Now, you're telling me that we're going to let it burn?"

Another man spoke. "What about my hunting lodge near Old Baldy? My grandpa built it. Half you guys have used it one time or another."

Red brushed back his hair with a hand that was blistered and black with soot.

"You don't understand," he said. "This fire's too big, too fast. We don't have time to scatter all over the woods trying to save a single house or hunting lodge, and even if we tried, we couldn't save everything. We'll evacuate everyone, then drop back and make a stand at the parkway."

Red's eyes were rimmed with red, and his lips were swollen. "Boys, when that wind shift comes through, that wildfire's going to chug through the woods like a runaway freight train, throwing off spot fires a mile ahead of herself. We've *got* to have everybody on the parkway." He paused. "If we don't stop it there ..."

In the silence that followed, the men thought of all the towns on the other side of the big divided six-lane highway. Bayville, Lanoka Harbor, Forked River, Waretown, Barnegat. Red and the chief lived in Waretown. Johnny Reb had just bought a house in Forked River. There were families and friends all along the coastal towns.

What if the fire jumped the parkway?

It was unthinkable.

"I hate to admit it, Red, but you're right," said Wavey, the fire warden of Section B-10. He spoke in a low voice. "There's no other way."

The others nodded grimly, and the chief breathed a sigh of relief. He hadn't wanted to force a decision on them and knew in his heart that they would come up with the right answer.

The chief turned to face them. "Thanks, men. I hoped you'd see it my way."

"Someone better tell Joshua." Wavey peered at the aerial map. "From what I see here, his house will be the first to go when that cold front comes through."

"Joshua's going to have a cow," Red moaned. "He fixed up that cabin real nice. Well at least there's no one there right now."

"Wait a minute," the chief said. "There was a kid here this morning; he came with Joshua, then drove his truck back. Christ almighty, he's probably still there, right in the path of the fire." He turned to Red. "Where's Joshua now?"

"Up at Bamber Lake. With Tony."

"Get a hold of him right now. Nancy, call Joshua's cabin and see if that kid is still there. Wait. That's no good. He might try to get out, and then he'll run right into the fire. Let me talk to Joshua on the radio. I can always pull the kid out with the jet ranger."

CHAPTER 74

Pale gray smoke filtered the early afternoon sunlight and caused it to shine weakly through the dried oak leaves and needles of the Pinelands. The smoke permeated the small meadows in the central pine forest. It cast a pall upon the dried grasses and fruitless, wild blueberry bushes and made the day seem older than it was.

Deep in the heart of the Pine Barrens, on a dusty, unmarked trail, hidden under the roof of an old abandoned sawmill, Anton Vogel slept in his black Suburban. He slept while the village of Bamber Lake was saved with bulldozers, crop dusters, helicopters, brush trucks, and brave men. He slept while the chief viewed the fire, Mount Holly predicted a severe wind shift, and Forest Fire Service backed up to the parkway for a last stand to save the shore towns.

Then, as the cold front came through, and the temperature began to drop, Vogel twitched and moaned in his sleep. Finally, as the wind increased to forty-five miles per hour, and a four-foot length of pine branch crashed onto the roof of his hideaway, Vogel awakened with a start.

For several seconds, Vogel looked dazedly around him. He felt cold and clammy. A strong wind rattled whipped pine branches along the side of his vehicle. He peered around him and lowered the window. Through the open slats of the ruined building, he saw that the lake and the pine trees were obscured by fog, but as soon as he coughed, he realized it wasn't fog. It was smoke.

What time was it? He checked his watch. Four thirty. Damn, he'd been asleep for hours. The wind was blowing the smoke from the distant fire in his direction. He looked outside one more time. Nothing. Just the sullen gray air and the pine trees.

He turned the ignition key hard, and the Suburban snarled into life.

Vogel backed out of the shadows of the building and quickly drove back along the small, sandy road that had brought him to the shore of the small Pinelands lake. He tried to remember the turns he had made before. Right by the big tree, then left.

Vogel paused at a juncture of three identical dirt paths. He remembered turning right here, so now it was left, but was it the hard left or the gentle one?

Vogel coughed. He was sure the smoke was thicker now.

It was the first fork; he was sure of that now. There had been an old dead tree hunched over the road just like the one in front of him. Positive now, and believing that he would soon be on Route 563, Vogel swung the wheel left.

Within minutes, he was hopelessly lost.

In the dry, whispering haze of the approaching wildfire, Vogel drove his dusty, black Suburban ever faster over dirt roads that ended in washed-out gravel pits, swamps, or vaguely familiar unmarked crossroads. With each passing moment, the smell of smoke was more bitter, and with each errant mile, his frustration and fear increased. He was out of his element now.

Ever since he was a small boy, Vogel had distanced himself from things that were disorganized or unpredictable. He preferred air-conditioning to open windows, frozen foods to fresh, recorded symphonies to live concerts. In all the years he had lived in Chicago, he never once lit the fireplace in his townhouse. Open fires were treacherous and rife with the possibility of errant sparks.

And now, his worst nightmare was upon him. He was lost in an unkempt wilderness filled with insects and animals and birds and small, slimy things that moved under a crust of dead leaves and pine needles. Worst of all, he was near an unrestrained, monstrous forest fire.

As the smoke blew hard across the narrow, sandy road, Vogel drove with one hand and held a black, sooty handkerchief over his nose.

But then, as he swung the Suburban around a wide turn, he looked up and saw the dull, silver gleam of high tension wires soaring above the tops of the trees. Fear rapidly changed to hope as he accelerated and burst into a wide expanse of cleared land that was floored with cracked, white sand and patches of brown, dry grass.

Vogel braked to a stop and studied the situation. The fat lines high above the truck had to lead somewhere, he reasoned as he sighted along their gentle swags into the distant murk. The sun above was a tarnished silver dime, and still he hesitated with his foot on the brake, his hands loosely on the steering wheel.

On the far side of the right-of-way, he saw a cut in the trees where the narrow dirt road continued, but under the power lines the cleared land was wide and gracious. It beckoned him.

The decision was easy, well-reasoned. With a quick turn of the wheel, the Suburban swayed and lurched onto the uneven, deep sand. The comforting wires rode high above him, carried on the shoulders of giant metal warriors who marched steadily through the woods. They dwarfed Vogel and his vehicle, showing him the way out, directing him to safety.

For the first time, Vogel felt a breath of hope. He was finally traveling in a straight line. Several dirt roads bisected the right-of-way, but he rejected them as soon as he saw them. He would not get lost again.

As the black truck rolled steadily and surely under the wires, the smoke grew thicker, and a wind started blowing the sand crossways in front of him. Vogel saw a flash of light far ahead, and seconds later, he heard a boom.

A thunderstorm was coming with a welcome deluge that would put out the forest fire and ensure his safe conduct from these wretched, unending pine woods. Vogel smiled and whispered, "Come on, rain. Come on, rain." He pressed harder on the accelerator, and the Suburban's wheels ground deeper into the soft sand.

Just ahead, an old cedar stump lay half-buried in the sandy ground. As the rear left wheel spun into it, a hard sliver of wood rammed into the tire and slipped between the treads.

Vogel heard a loud pop and felt the vehicle pivot. He jammed his foot down on the accelerator and pushed it into the floorboards. The engine roared, but the back wheel dragged, and the vehicle spun to the left around the shredding tire.

He pumped the accelerator and wiped his bare hands across his forehead. The smoke was heavier now, engulfing and muting the edges of the woods on either side, closing up the distances ahead and behind. Vogel coughed violently and spat yellow phlegm onto the leather seat next to him.

With a horrific, bitter curse that would have shamed his mother, Vogel wrenched open the door and crawled out. He kept his head low in the stinging, whipping sand and ran to the rear of the truck. He peered at the rear wheel. It was embedded deeply in the sand, the tire flat and loose around the wheel.

Vogel tried to open the back door, but the automatic door locks were still on. He raced to the driver's side, pulled the door open, fumbled with the automatic door lock, and scrambled to the rear.

Judas Priest, where the hell was the jack? Was there time to fix the flat?

Under the mat, Vogel found the case, clean, unused, and untried. It looked fairly simple. He pulled it out and, kneeling, placed it under the Suburban and then inserted the handle. He pumped hard several times, but the base of the jack dug itself into the sand. The frame of the Suburban did not move, and the tire stayed wedged in the sand.

He needed something to brace it. Vogel coughed again, his eyes ran, and it was difficult to see through the tears. What could he put under the jack? He needed a flat piece of wood or metal to brace it.

Vogel ran around frantically, searching the ground and the edge of the woods for some flat, hard piece of anything. The smoke was thicker, and he heard a roaring in the distance. His red, watery eyes strained to see through the thick, black smoke. He sprinted back to the Suburban and stood for a moment in his sweaty, bloodstained socks with the wind whipping his hair.

Far above him, 230,000 volts of electrical energy from the Oyster Creek Nuclear Power Plant crackled and hummed on its way north to the Lakewood substation. The current contained in the thick wires was restless. The smoky forest fire had sent billions of swirling carbon particles into the shadowy air between it and the warm, searching earth below. A partial pathway appeared. Millions of electrons danced with blue flame and sent a tentative finger reaching downward.

Vogel leaned over and looked at the deep sand under the rear wheel. He heard a loud warning crackle overhead.

Ah, the storm has arrived, he thought. *Come on, rain.*

As Vogel straightened up, his fine, soft hair stood up straight, and a random alignment of conductive particles formed a bridge between positive and negative poles.

"Oh, no," he whispered as suddenly his factual, scientific mind realized what was happening. In that millisecond, 230,000 volts of electricity crashed to the earth by the fastest, easiest route: down through the heavy smoke and then, directly through 157 pounds of very conductive blood and tissue that composed the body known as Anton Vogel.

Several minutes later, the head fire approached the right-of-way on its journey to the east. As the heat intensified, the windows of the Suburban cracked, the leather seats melted and burned, and the tires exploded one by one. Finally the gas tank ruptured and released liquid flame that rolled down a gentle, sandy slope and pooled around Vogel's body.

By the time the head fire passed, only the larger, denser bones were left. Vogel's fingers, toes, and other softer appendages had been blown away in the fierce upward drafts of the wildfire.

CHAPTER 75

tacey groaned, turned over, and buried her head into the pillow on the couch. God, was she tired! The crowds had swarmed into McDonald's last night like they were giving away free burgers and fries.

She'd slept late this morning and then settled into the couch, trying to keep her mind off Mark and Borderline by reading the latest Ann Rice novel. Where were they? And why had no one called her?

In the distance, she heard the drone of the television set. Same old Saturday routine; her father off to the golf course, her brothers playing ball somewhere, her mother cooking in front of the kitchen TV while the washing machine chugged through a week's worth of laundry.

Strange, she thought. The voices coming from the kitchen didn't sound like the usual vintage movies her mother watched on the movie channel. They sounded more like news bulletins.

Suddenly, four words detached themselves, floated down the hallway and into her ears: *Fire in the Barrens.*

Stacey sat up, leaped from the bed, and ran into the kitchen.

The small TV on the kitchen counter showed green trees, red flames, and billowing clouds of smoke. In the foreground, the dark-haired man blinked rapidly as his mouth shaped words like *wildfire, tragedy, sheets of flame, disaster.*

"Hi, Stacey," her mother greeted her with a smile. "Finished your book?"

"What's happening?" Stacey pointed to the television screen.

"A big fire in the Barrens. It's been on TV all afternoon. CNN's covering it now. Imagine, CNN right here in Ocean County."

Without a word, Stacey snatched up the kitchen phone, punched in numbers. It rang once, twice. *Pick it up, Mark,* she silently pleaded, *please pick it up.* Ten rings, no answer.

Stacey slammed the phone down, picked it up, punched in Borderline's number, and got the answering machine.

She opened the drawer under the phone, pulled out the Ocean County phone book, and thumbed through it with trembling fingers.

The place where Borderline worked, what was it listed under? Body shop? The only body shop she found sold leotards and exercise equipment. *Wait—try car or automobile, automobile something.*

Under Automobile Repairing and Service, Stacey found Federici's Body Shop. She pressed the numbers.

"Yeah?" The voice was a growl.

"Is Borderline there?"

"Who wants to know?"

"Stacey. Stacey Greene. I'm a friend."

"Well, friend, he ain't here. Never even called. Nothing. And I'm up to my eyeballs with three cars I promised would be ready tonight. If you see that punk, tell him to get his butt in here. Pronto."

The phone went dead in her hands.

"What's wrong?" her mother asked. Her carrot scraper hesitated in midair.

Stacey shook her head. "I'm not sure." Her eyes swung back to the television screen. A bumpy aerial view panned huge columns of smoke from a line of blazing trees far below. "I think Mark and Borderline might be in the Barrens." Stacey's voice trembled. "I've got to find them."

As Stacey turned to go, her mother touched her arm. "You're not going anywhere till you tell me what's going on." Her eyes searched Stacey's face. "And you can't go to the Barrens. They've been warning people to stay away, warning everyone that they'll be arrested if they try to get near the fire. The parkway's closed, and traffic is backed up all the way to the Raritan River Bridge." She tightened her grip. "What's wrong? Why did Mark and Borderline go to the Barrens?"

Stacey wrenched her arm away, and her eyes filled with tears. On the television screen, the governor spoke in front of a bank of microphones.

"I can't explain it right now," Stacey said, sobbing, "but Mark and Borderline are in the Barrens, and I'm going to find them if I have to hitchhike or crawl on my hands and knees. Oh God, I should have called them before they left ..."

Mrs. Greene took a small step backward. "But the police say—"

"Damn the police! They can't stop me. You can't stop me."

Mrs. Greene's face flamed with anger, but as her eyes played over Stacey's stricken face, the anger faded into concern and then resolve.

"Very well. We'll go together. We'll have a better chance of getting through in my big car. The local police know us. I could make up a story about a family emergency, and maybe they'll let us through." She hesitated. "Look, Stacey, I'll help you in any way I can, but I need to know what's going on."

Stacey bit her lower lip and shook her head. "It's awful, Mom," she whispered. "I'm so scared."

"Get dressed. You can tell me all about it in the car."

CHAPTER 76

The sky was dark with moving clouds of smoke as police, firemen, and other volunteers swarmed over the eastern Pine Barrens. Using bullhorns, public service announcements on radio and television, telephone calls, and personal visits, they evacuated homes, businesses, state forests, parks, and campgrounds. The police crosschecked their maps with local postal carriers to make sure everyone in the path of the fire got out.

Old Ben Sampson heard the warning and then turned off the TV. The phone rang repeatedly, but he ignored it.

He'd seen his first forest fire when he was a boy way back in 1922. He remembered a big one in the summer of 1954 when his second son was six months old. He helped fight that fire and other big ones later in '63 and '71. But these days, Red and Chief wouldn't let him on a truck anymore. They said he'd done his stint, and it was time for the young men to have a chance. He knew they thought he was too old. Now whenever there was a fire, he could only smell the smoke and watch the flames from a distance. Ben would gladly have given five years of whatever life he had left to be in the woods on a brush truck today.

His hounds knew the fire was coming. They bayed and barked, but old Ben knew what to do. He had already wet down his roof and was carrying a can of kerosene across the field to backfire the woods when a state trooper pulled up in front of his tiny house.

The young policeman got out of his car and said, "You need to evacuate your house. Orders from the State Forest Fire Warden. Grab what you can and let's go."

"Listen, kid. I knew the State Forest Fire Warden when the State Forest Fire Warden was a draggy-pants little boy," Ben shouted. "I fought and survived a lot of fires, more than you'll ever see. So go on, sonny, and e-va-cu-ate those fools that don't know how to deal with a forest fire."

"Sir, you've got to leave. I have my orders." The trooper stood his ground.

Ben swore a mighty oath at him, stomped into his house, and came out with an old muzzle-loader. The trooper was by his car, calling in for help when Ben's cousin Alfred drove up in his pickup truck.

Ben rushed over to explain the situation.

"You're an old fool, and I don't care what you do," Alfred said when Ben finished, "but I ain't gonna let you sacrifice a perfectly good pack of hounds just 'cause you want to burn yourself up in a wildfire, you stubborn, wrinkly, old asshole."

The policeman started toward them. Alfred waved him off and continued talking to Ben. "Come on, I'll take you over to the command center. They may be able to use a stubborn old coot like you for something."

Old Ben turned on his heel and, head down, walked into his house. Alfred loaded the dogs into the back of his truck, climbed in, and kept the engine running while the trooper stood and waited.

"I'm leaving now," Alfred called through the window. "Smoke's gettin' too thick for me. Bad for the dogs, too."

He released the clutch and coasted forward a few feet. The front door of the house opened, and Ben stomped out.

He scowled at the trooper, climbed into the truck, and said, "Might not come this way after all."

"Ya never know, Ben," said Alfred. "It might not."

CHAPTER 77

Near the fork of Cave Cabin Creek and North Creek, a lean, muscular man of indiscriminate age finished putting all his belongings into a deep hole. The soft, sandy sides of the pit were shored up with cracked cinder blocks that he'd taken from the cement factory up on Route 614. The top was a round slab of concrete.

The bearded ex-marine had learned many things during his self-imposed exile, and he knew it was best to get out as quickly as possible when the pine forest was burning. He also knew that if he put on a pair of jeans and a shirt and boots, he could walk unnoticed in the midst of other men. He didn't like being around other human beings but had learned to do it when necessary.

He had moved his camp many times over the years. First when a new house went up within hailing distance of his hut, and then again when some nosey kids started coming around on their ATVs and mini-bikes.

Early one spring morning several years ago, he slept too soundly, and a wildfire nearly got him. Lost his stuff then but managed to replace most of it by scavenging. He needed so little, and most of what he had were the castoffs of people who cared about material possessions.

After that happened, he built himself a fireproof foxhole for his personal belongings.

He'd seen a nice piece of land near a boggy stream a mile or so south of the Forked River Mountains, which weren't really mountains, just low hills, but that's what everyone called them. If the fire didn't get to it, he'd set up camp there. It'd be a haul bringing his stuff there on foot, but what else did he have to do with his time?

"C'mon, Grandma. Hurry. The fire's coming," the young woman called and wrung her hands. "Come on."

"There's not much time," her boyfriend echoed as he looked out of the bow window of the small, neat living room.

"I know, I know," the old woman mumbled as she shuffled back and forth from room to room. She picked up things and then put them down again. A vase, a lamp, a small statue. "I just don't know what to take. There's too much here ..."

She finally grabbed a sepia picture of a man in a white sailor's uniform and gave it to her granddaughter.

"That's Paw." She brushed the glass with a shaking hand. "Sure was handsome then. I remember—"

"Give it to me, Grandma. I'll hold it," she said. "Hurry."

Tears began to run down the old woman's face as her eyes stalked the rooms. What to leave? What to take from a lifetime?

Finally she took a painting from the wall that showed a white clapboard farmhouse and gave it to the young man. Next she hauled a large, heavy Bible from the small bookcase under the picture window and gave it to her granddaughter. Finally, she got down on her knees and rolled up a hooked rug from the floor in front of the fireplace.

"Took me six months to make this. Fiona said I was foolish to keep it in front of the fireplace, but it's been there for twenty years without a single scorch mark. I won't leave it to burn now."

A warning wail sounded from the patrol car parked in the yard.

"Oh dear. Oh dear." She sighed.

A policeman stuck his head in the door. "Ma'am, we've got to leave *now*," he said. "The fire's almost here."

He took her by the arm and led her to the waiting police car. Her granddaughter and the boyfriend followed.

Old Mitch had smelled smoke all day, and the bitter, acrid air made him restless. By noon, he snorted a warning to his smaller companion and started moving east.

The two deer walked steadily for several hours, following the game trails that crisscrossed the Barrens. They dipped their mossy antlers now and again to browse green shoots along the creek bed. Instinct moved them toward the place where the light appeared each morning, toward the place of salt smell and mist. The heat and smoke were still far away, but the old buck's senses whispered to him, and he was old enough and wise enough to listen.

CHAPTER 78

Joshua leaned against Tony's brush truck as its pump clattered and the thick black hose sucked lake water into the 250-gallon tank. He was tired, dog tired. They'd stopped the head fire at Bamber Lake and saved the small homes clustered around it. The crisis was over, and now came the long, backbreaking job of mop-up: raking, soaking the ground, cutting down burning snags. A fire this big would keep them busy for days unless there was a major rainstorm.

It was time to tell the chief about the boys, about Borderline and Mark and the Watson place, about Vogel and his lab. The only thing he'd said to the chief was that a man named Vogel had torched the old farmhouse and then escaped in a black Suburban. He'd held back the rest of the story.

Maybe it had been a mistake to leave Teddy and the boys at his cabin, but they'd looked so worn and tired, so scared and dirty and lost, that he didn't have the heart to plunge them into another storm. When news of Dr. Anton Vogel and his so-called rehab got out, there would be pandemonium. Twenty-four hours from now, cops, lawyers, reporters, and every parent with a missing teenager would converge on the Barrens. The morbidly curious and the nut cases would come out just to look around.

As soon as Tony came back to relieve him, he'd find the chief and tell him everything. Then he'd call Teddy on one of the mobile phones to make sure everything was okay back at the cabin.

The pitch of the clattering pump changed. The tank was full. Joshua turned off the intake valve, disconnected the hose, and threw it into the back of the truck.

As he primed the pump and tested it, his thoughts wandered back to the cabin. The kids had been through a lot. A little TV, some good food, clean clothing, and a nap would sure help bring them back to the real world. Knowing Teddy, she'd have them laughing by now. She'd listen to them when they wanted to talk, hug them if they needed it, crack a few jokes if things got too heavy. He sensed that she was good with kids, and that was a real plus if the relationship developed any further.

If the scanner was on, she would know the head fire had been stopped at Bamber Lake. She'd expect him to be home soon.

Where the hell was Tony? He had to talk to the chief; he needed to call Teddy.

"Joshua!" Tony ran toward him, leaping and stumbling over roots and clumps of soil. "Joshua, the fire's going to turn," he gasped as soon as he was close enough to speak.

"What? What're you saying?"

"The chief's been trying to call you, but you couldn't hear over the noise of that damn pump. A cold front's moving in from the northwest, bringing high winds."

With a sinking feeling, Joshua realized why they had tried to reach him. As soon as the wind shifted, the long, slow-burning right flank of the fire would turn, shift into high gear, and become a long wall of flame. His cabin was in its path.

As Joshua's thoughts scrambled around, the wind picked up slightly. Blackened snags in the burned-out area glowed, and a hail of sparks flew overhead. He felt a chill and then a harder blast of cold air.

Tony was talking, and he tuned in. "... I'm sorry, Joshua, but they're going to let some of the houses burn. The chief wants us all to move back to the parkway. We've got to save the shore towns."

"What?" Joshua roared.

"I know—I know it's hard to lose your cabin after everything you've done to fix it up, but the chief says ..." Tony stopped.

Joshua's heart stopped and then started up again as the full impact of Tony's words reached deep into his mind. "Teddy's there." Joshua's voice was rough and hoarse. "She's got six kids with her. I pulled them out of the Watson place before it went up."

"Shit, Joshua. Why didn't you tell me? Shit!" Tony yanked open the door to the brush truck and grabbed the microphone. "Get me the chief."

"Hayes, here."

"Bad news. Joshua says there's six kids at his cabin, plus his girlfriend, Teddy."

For a moment, all Joshua could hear was the crackle of the radio, and he wondered if they had lost the chief. Suddenly a deep voice jumped out at them.

"Why the hell didn't he say that this morning? Goddamn. The power's going down, Coyle Field just clocked winds over forty-five miles per hour, and you're telling me that instead of one kid, one kid that I could lift out with a chopper, there's seven civilians out at Joshua's cabin?"

"Affirmative."

Another long expletive while the radio crackled and Joshua hopped from foot to foot. He was the one who had insisted that Teddy and the boys stay at his cabin. How could he have been so stupid? He'd been so sure they were safe there. Stupid, stupid, stupid.

The wind was fierce now, blowing smoke and sparks across the firebreak. He could see random puffs of smoke among the green trees now. Newborn spot fires.

Another voice came on. Calm, soft, relaxed. It was Red.

"Where are you now?" he asked.

"The south side of Bamber Lake," Tony said. "We just loaded up the brush truck."

"Is there another truck near you?"

"Burley. I can see him filling his truck up now, just up the firebreak from us. Chet's with him."

"Grab Chet and Burley and their truck. The two trucks have got about fifteen minutes before the fire hits the cabin. Joshua, call Teddy on the CB and tell them to wait for you. Make sure no one tries to drive out. The fire's moving too fast. They'll be cut off before they make it out to the main road."

CHAPTER 79

Teddy sat next to Michael and held a cold cloth to his forehead. Like the others, he had washed and gotten into Joshua's big clothes. The rest of the boys had wolfed down soup and sandwiches, but he only picked at his food.

Michael didn't talk much or respond to her questions, and by midafternoon, the small, thin boy had willingly settled into Joshua's king-size bed. Unlike the others who had been talkative, Michael was quiet and withdrawn. He seemed distant as if he were lost in another, more painful world. She left him alone, and when she looked in the door a few minutes later, he was asleep.

But shortly after noon, Michael started to moan, softly at first and then loudly, piteously. His wide frightened eyes darted around the room, and when Teddy spoke to him, he didn't seem to hear. She adjusted the cloth again as his head thrashed on the pillow.

Borderline and Mark stuck their heads in the door for the tenth time in the last hour.

"What's wrong with him?" Borderline asked.

"I don't know," Teddy said. "Michael may be going into shock, or he may have an infection of some kind. I just don't know."

Teddy frowned as she wiped his flushed face. She touched his forehead with the back of her hand. It felt hotter. Michael's eyes were dull and listless and seemed to be focused on something far away.

Teddy dipped the cloth into the ice water, squeezed it, and then placed it again on the boy's forehead. He didn't even flinch.

She stood up and rubbed her arms and then looked past Borderline and Mark into the large main room of the cabin.

"What's everyone doing out there?" she asked.

"Mac and Joey are asleep in the other bedroom," Mark said. "Edsell's on the couch watching cartoons. We've been listening to the scanner. From what we can tell, they stopped the fire at Bamber Lake."

"That means Joshua will be home soon." She glanced at Michael. His eyes were closed now, but his lids fluttered, and his face twitched in restless dreams. "I'm going to make a fresh pot of coffee. You and Mark keep listening to the scanner. Maybe you'll hear where Joshua is now."

As Teddy spooned coffee grounds into the old enamel percolator, a vague uneasiness swept over her. Was Michael's problem a physical one or just an emotional reaction to the stress of the past few weeks? Teddy knew he'd been at the lab the longest period of time, at least three weeks. Like the others, he'd been taken in the night, brought to the old farmhouse, and then tied to a bed with his mouth gagged shut except for meals. Machines and tubes flushed were connected to his veins. Did he suffer the pains of cruel, instant withdrawal? If so, from what? she wondered. Pot? Alcohol? Crack?

There was no way of knowing, and right now, Michael didn't want to talk. She sensed he was a frightened boy who had had a sad, hurtful life even before this ordeal. God only knew what the last few weeks had done to him. Maybe he had been pushed over the edge.

Should she take Michael to a doctor now? She could leave the rest of the boys with Mark and Borderline and drive into Toms River, but that was a good thirty minutes away. She probably shouldn't be gone that long.

Teddy worried about the fire too. If the wildfire had been stopped at Bamber Lake, why was the smell of smoke stronger? Bamber Lake was several miles north and east of them. Joshua had told them they'd be safe in the cabin because the fire was moving away from them.

Suddenly, with a quick flash, the light over the stove went out, and the TV popped quiet. The large room became strangely still as the ubiquitous appliance hum disappeared. The television was an empty, black rectangle. Above them, the ceiling fans rotated slower and slower and then stopped.

Borderline and Mark stood next to the mute scanner and stared at her. Edsell's head appeared over the back of the couch, his face both sleepy and scared as if he had just awakened from a nightmare. In the room behind her, Michael groaned again.

Teddy picked up the phone. It was dead.

Borderline stared at her. "Is it ..."

She nodded. "No big deal, guys. The fire up north probably burned through some wires. Joshua told me about a generator stashed in the shed out back. Borderline, see if you can find it."

Mark got up. "I'll help. I know how to set up a generator. My dad keeps one at home in case we lose our electricity."

The coffee was bubbling hard now. As Teddy turned down the gas, she heard Borderline yelling in the backyard. When she opened the kitchen door, he was holding a small, red motor in his arms and smiling.

"A brand-new Briggs and Stratton generator," he said.

Mark stood behind him with a five-gallon container of gasoline.

He filled up the generator, pushed the prime, and pulled the cord. Once, twice, and then the little red motor rattled and coughed. Four pulls later, it roared into life.

Borderline shouted over the noise. "Teddy, turn off everything you don't absolutely need while I connect this up!"

Edsell and Teddy quickly turned off all the lamps, appliances, and the TV but kept the refrigerator and the scanner on.

Teddy sat nervously at the trestle table and drank her coffee while Edsell thumbed through a stack of hunting magazines. Mark and Borderline perched on the stools next to the counter and turned up the scanner so they could hear it over the rattle of the generator.

Suddenly a gust of wind sucked at the house. Borderline looked outside. Moving clouds of pale gray billowed over the tree tops.

Between the cabin and the woods, the air had changed into a thick, murky presence. The wind rattled the cedar shakes again. Then all at once, they heard a strange, new voice on the scanner.

"Teddy," Borderline called. "Listen. There's something going on."

"Shh-hh-hh," Mark cautioned.

The voice was low and calm with a decided drawl.

"I think that's a guy named Red," Borderline whispered. "He's the fire warden for this section."

"… cold front's coming through now, boys. We're getting a quick wind shift, coming in hard from the west-northwest with gusts over fifty miles per hour." A long pause, crackles and whistles, and then the same steady voice. "All units in the field are ordered to drop back to the parkway. Chatsworth, Lacy, and Manchester Fire Companies will be working with the police to evacuate all houses between Lacey Road and Wells Mills Road. Repeat, evacuate all …"

Borderline, Mark, and Teddy looked at each other. Edsell sat up on the couch and stared.

"That's us." Borderline raised his voice over the scanner. "Lacey Road's north of us, and Wells Mills Road is south."

"Shit, the fire's coming here!" Mark cried. "We've got to get out!" He stood up.

"Wait, I just heard my name." Teddy gestured with an open palm.

Some unintelligible babble came out of the scanner, followed by several other voices, a squeak, and a whistle. Then Joshua called her name.

"Teddy? Teddy Constantinos! Paging Teddy Constantinos." Joshua's voice was ragged and harsh over the small speaker. "By God, I hope you can hear me. Teddy, the fire is coming your way, but you can't leave the cabin. Repeat, do not try to leave. We're coming to take you out with a couple of brush trucks. Wet all the blankets and wait for me …"

The scanner crackled and hummed with other voices as a gust of wind shook the cabin and rattled the windows. The smoke was inside now, permeating the cabin. In the bedroom, Michael coughed.

Teddy stood up. "You heard Joshua." She spoke in a level, even tone. "Mark, close all the windows so we can save what good air we have. Borderline, get the blankets off the beds and wet them in that tub outside by the hand pump near the back door. Edsell, wake up Mac and Joey. We'll let Michael rest until it's time to go."

Edsell shook his head and stood up. He wrapped his long, thin arms across his chest and held both elbows. "I want to leave right now," he said. "We can take the truck and get out before the fire comes."

"Rotten idea, Edsell." Mark stood by a window. "You heard Joshua. We've got to wait for him."

"But what if he doesn't come? Are we going to sit here and wait for the fire?"

Edsell's thin body trembled in Joshua's loose clothing. "Not me, I'm getting out of here."

Teddy stood between Edsell and the door. "Look, Edsell, I know how you feel. I'm scared too, but Joshua promised he'd come. Remember what Borderline told us this morning? About how those trucks go right through the woods?"

Suddenly, there was a loud noise overhead. Teddy, Mark, and Borderline ran outside, followed by Edsell. A red and white helicopter hovered over the clearing, but as they stood waving, it pulled up and away and disappeared above the tree line.

"Shit, man, don't go!" Edsell yelled. "D-don't leave us!"

"It's okay. They know we're here." Teddy grabbed his hands. "Go ahead, do what I said. Get the others up and wet the blankets. Move it."

Another gust of wind hit as they turned back to the cabin. Thick, gray smoke poured through the trees. They heard a low roaring sound, and suddenly bright orange and red flames shot high into the air above the woods behind the cabin.

Maybe we should *make a run for it*, Teddy thought as she sprinted to the cabin. Anything would be better than waiting for the fire to engulf them.

CHAPTER 80

"What's the matter, Josh?" Tony asked. "It's not like you to panic. Settle down, old buddy. We've been in tight places before."

Tony kept both hands on the steering wheel as the red brush truck swayed and lurched over the dusty road. With a full load of water, the engine protested loudly at the speed it was asked to make over the sandy ruts. Joshua stared out the window at the trees that screamed by, their branches tearing at the sides of the truck. He could not look at Tony because his friend would see tears in his eyes, tears that didn't come from the smoky air.

The sunlight was obliterated as they ripped down the twisting road toward the cabin. The color of the smoke that surrounded them changed from pale gray to dark gray, then darker still until it had an oily, black look.

When Joshua could barely see the road ahead, he closed the buttons on his yellow shirt, put on his helmet, and opened the door of the fast-moving vehicle. Ducking branches, he eased onto the running board, primed the pump one more time, and then held the hose ready. The heat was intense now as the flames got closer and closer. He looked behind him and saw the headlights of the second brush truck hugging the rear bumper of the first.

Joshua heard a helicopter clattering ahead of them. It sounded close, as if it were near the tops of the trees. Through the open window of the cab, he heard Tony speaking into the handheld microphone.

"Chief? Can you hear me?"

"Read you loud and clear. I got you in sight."

"How much farther? It's getting dark down here."

"You're near a finger of the fire right now. Stay on the road and have Josh lay down some water. Once you get by the finger, you'll have some breathing room."

The truck ground forward, slower now, through the black, soupy air. The wind was a hot roar in Joshua's face. He looked back through the thick smoke and saw the bumper of the second truck a foot or two behind theirs. He knew the indistinct yellow smudge pinned to the side of that cab was Chet, ready to hose the fire.

The roar increased, and suddenly to his right, red flames broke through the black smoke, reaching toward them like malevolent, hot hands.

Joshua turned on the hose, and then they were next to the fire. He held the wide stream of water directly on the flames, and as the water hit the fire, great clouds of steam hissed and rolled up the sides of the truck.

"Just a few feet more, Josh!" Tony yelled. "Hang on!"

CHAPTER 81

At the cabin, Borderline stood on the small front porch and watched the road, a wet kitchen towel wrapped around his mouth and nose. His eyes teared as he strained to see through the heavy smoke. The rest of the kids and Teddy were huddled inside the cabin, and he was the lone lookout.

A deep rumbling sound came from the woods behind the cabin as if all the crackles and hisses of the wildly burning forest were united into a single primeval scream. It seemed to Borderline that the whole of the forest, all the living cells within the trees and bushes and grasses, all the insects and worms and small, secret animals were dying, uniting with the air like lost souls, flying heavenward in one great, noisy blast of flame and smoke.

The wind pulled at him as he coughed and gagged, but he still watched for Joshua.

Everything around him was a thundering darkness now, punctuated by the fierce red glow in the woods behind the cabin. The heat of the fire increased, and the smoke grew still thicker and blacker. He heard a loud crash behind him, and a huge ball of fire flew over his head with a roaring crackle and exploded in the woods on the far side of the clearing. Borderline prayed silently as sweat and tears mingled on his face. *Holy Mary, Mother of God. Pray for us sinners, now and at the hour of our death. Amen. Mary, Mother of God ...*

The helicopter suddenly clattered overhead, and in the same instant, two smudgy lights on the far side of the clearing materialized into a brush truck. A second truck followed close behind.

A black-faced man stood on the running board, and as soon as the truck slowed, he jumped off. It was Joshua!

"Hurry!" he shouted. "Get everyone into the trucks! Where's Teddy?"

"Inside!" Borderline screamed. "I knew you'd get here. I knew you'd get here."

The front door burst open, and Teddy ran out with Michael in her arms. Mark followed with Edsell, and the rest tottered out, wrapped in dripping blankets with wet handkerchiefs tied across their faces.

"Get into the truck!" Joshua yelled. "Hurry, the fire's almost here."

Joshua grabbed Michael's small, trembling body and placed him next to Tony. Mac and Joey squeezed in behind him.

"The truck's only built for three," Joshua said. "You two guys lean way to the right and give Tony room to drive. Mac, you get down on the floor."

He took their wet blankets, tossed them into the back of the truck, and slammed the door. Behind him, Chet put Edsell into the second brush truck. The fire roared closer; the wind flung sparks and ashes into his face.

"Hurry! Mark, Borderline, climb in!"

They hesitated.

"What the hell's the matter?" Joshua bellowed. "Get in the damn truck."

"But there's no room for Teddy," Borderline protested.

"Get in," Teddy coughed. "I'll get behind the cab with the blankets over me. I'll be okay. Joshua will be near."

Teddy climbed onto the first brush truck and dropped into the small well behind the cab. As the truck started to move, Joshua leaped onto the running board.

"Pull the blankets over you, baby, and stay down!" he called. "Don't look up, no matter what. I'll be right here working the hose."

The wildfire rumbled angrily, ever closer, as the trucks raced out of the clearing. The wind was intense now, urgent. It whipped pine trees and scrub oaks and laurel bushes like marsh grass and turned the soft Barrens sand into stinging, airborne needles. More pine trees exploded in the woods behind them. Their tops flew over the two brush trucks and sent bright showers of sparks cascading down through the thick smoke.

Joshua looked back through the wind and smoke, blinking his tear-filled eyes. Short, blue and orange flames danced on the roof of his cabin. His house would soon be destroyed, yet all he felt as he watched his boyhood home burn was a visceral relief that Teddy and the boys were with him and not back in the roaring blaze behind them.

The woods ahead were in flames now, set by the windblown sparks and fireballs. The only way out was through the inferno.

CHAPTER 82

The jet ranger swept back and forth over the advancing fire, bobbing like a yo-yo above the burning trees. Fire licked its carriers and blistered the underside. Johnny Reb struggled with the controls as the wild winds streamed skyward from the burning forest.

Suddenly, a huge column of raw, red flame tore past the right window, and the helicopter lurched up and to the left. Johnny swore an ingenious oath that lasted the full nine seconds it took to obtain a semblance of control over the bucking helicopter.

Johnny Reb glanced at the chief. His face was tight, and his eyes were tiny, harsh pinpoints. Johnny knew the boss normally loved the pitch and yawl of the chopper in tight situations, but now the veteran of many fires clung to the cracked leather seat with white knuckles.

Johnny knew what was wrong with his boss and kept his eyes averted respectfully from the chief. Bill Hayes was like a father to everyone in the Forest Fire Service. He knew each man and woman by name. Hell, he was godfather to many of their children. Now, after serving fourteen years as the head of the New Jersey Forest Fire Service without a single casualty, the chief was very, very close to losing two trucks, four of his own men, and seven civilians.

"Get down lower. Get under the smoke. I can't see 'em," he growled.

God save us, thought Johnny as he dropped the jet ranger into the dragon jaws of the fire. *We're going to lose the trucks, men, civilians, and one beat-up, old chopper.*

"Can you see them? Are they clear yet?" Johnny asked.

"They're right below us. Keep this egg beater over their heads, Johnny. The smoke's so black down there, they might get lost in it." He snatched the microphone. "Tony? Can you hear me?"

"Yeah, yeah. I hear ya!" Tony screamed.

"How you doing?"

"Just fine, 'cept I can't see past the hood, the windows are starting to crack, and I think I'm off the road."

"I'm right over you. Turn to the right. More ... okay. Now straighten up. Burley, can you hear me? Stay close."

"I got my bumper glued to his butt, Chief!" Burley yelled.

"Just a few more yards, and you'll be through. Hold on."

The red and white helicopter wallowed in smoke and flame. The pitch of the engine changed every few seconds as the rotating blades sought air in the wild currents above the flames.

Tony's hands were so wet with sweat that the steering wheel of the lurching brush truck felt like an eel just pulled from the bay. The kid next to him was limp and falling against him with each bump in the road.

"Pull him away. Pull him away," Tony croaked. "I can't drive with him laying on me."

The others pulled Michael away until the three boys were huddled against the door with their arms around each other. Tony glanced at them. All of their mouths were open pink holes as they coughed and gagged in the thick smoke.

Tony leaned forward until his face was inches from the windshield.

On the other side of the glass, everything was a black, hot pit illuminated with streaks of red flame. The sound of the fire was a freight train rolling through his head. Perhaps he'd died already, and this was hell, where he would drive on forever with gasping, smoke-seared lungs and swollen, tear-washed eyes.

In the second brush truck, Edsell sobbed. "We're gonna die, we're gonna die," he said, over and over again until Borderline suddenly turned in the tight, smoky confines of the cab and grabbed Edsell's face with both hands.

"Shut up," he spat. "We're getting out, so shut up."

Burley drove on through the roar of the fire and prayed the spunky kid was right.

Joshua held on to the roll bar of Tony's truck and kept his head ducked down into his collar. He had abandoned the hose. In the swirling vortex of the wildfire, Joshua hunched his shoulders and tried to pretend that his whole right side was not one, huge, screaming hurt.

The boys inside the cab were hollering and crying now while Tony's lips moved in silent prayer.

Under the wet blankets, Teddy was frightened. She knew the brush truck was in the midst of the flames now because the heat was intense. It probed at her and turned the wet blankets into scalding steam. The noise was unbearable, a huge roar like a jet plane taking off at close range.

Joshua was out there, exposed to the flames. She couldn't see him or hear him now. What if he had fallen off the lurching truck and was even now being devoured by the fire? Even if he was still clinging to the truck, his clothes might be on fire ...

Joshua looked down at the wet blankets that covered Teddy. They were steaming, smoldering, catching fire. He saw a slight movement underneath. *Don't look up,* prayed Joshua. *Please, baby, don't look up ...*

But then the blankets moved, and Teddy's head came out. In that instant, a huge shower of sparks rained down, and as Joshua watched, Teddy's long, flowing hair mingled with red flames, and her mouth opened in a pitiful scream that no one could hear in the hellish roar of the fire.

Joshua leaped over the side of the brush truck and onto her. He pushed her down and covered her head and her body with his.

And then suddenly, miraculously, they were out. Out of the wildfire, out of the blistering, choking heat. The rushing, hot flames receded, and the black smoke gradually changed to lighter shades of gray. They could breathe again.

The second truck was right behind them. Its windshield was cracked, and the red paint was black and blistered.

"Don't stop, keep moving," the chief cautioned over the radio. "The fire's still on your tail. You need to get to Lacey Road before you're safe. I've got ambulances waiting there."

"Thanks, Chief," Tony said.

"I'm going back to the parkway to see how Red's doing. You're less than a half mile from Lacey Road now. Take care."

The helicopter wheeled around and climbed up higher and then disappeared into the smoky sky.

CHAPTER 83

As soon as they were out of the blistering heat, Joshua peeled back the blankets, and a sobbing Teddy emerged. Her hair was in shreds; her scalp was raw and blistered. Joshua held her gently against his chest and wept openly as the truck rolled on through the thinning smoke.

Minutes later, they popped into the middle of a small sea of flashing lights.

Joshua climbed over the side of the truck with Teddy in his arms and ran to the nearest ambulance. She was quiet now, no longer sobbing. She reached for her raw, angry scalp and touched it. A tiny, rueful smile fluttered over her lips.

Two EMS workers took her from him and placed her on a stretcher.

As they lifted her into the ambulance, Teddy looked up at him. "I love you," she whispered.

"I love you too, baby. I love you so much," Joshua said softly and then backed his large frame out of the vehicle. Mac and Joey hustled in behind her, and then the doors were pulled shut. The siren wailed as the first ambulance eased away.

The crew from the second ambulance put Michael on a stretcher. His eyes were shut as they placed an oxygen mask over his face. They slid the stretcher inside and then motioned for Edsell to climb in beside him.

"Gimme a minute," Edsell said.

The boy looked around and then saw Joshua. He rushed to the big man like a scorched, long-legged bird.

"You saved me twice, man. I'll never forget you."

Joshua opened his arms to the boy and clapped him on the back.

"Your friends were the real heroes, Edsell. They didn't give up. They were the ones who found you."

Borderline and Mark walked over and stood to one side. Edsell turned to them as the driver of the ambulance called, "C'mon, kid. We ain't got all day."

"Thanks, guys," Edsell said.

"Aw, it's nothing any other red-blooded American hero wouldn't have done," Borderline said.

"Yeah, we're a couple of Supermen." Mark grinned. "Go on, get out of here. We'll see you at the hospital."

Edsell climbed into the ambulance and waved at his friends as the door swung shut. With lights flashing, the second ambulance rolled smoothly through the smoky air.

A policeman from one of the two cruisers wandered over and asked Joshua if he wanted a ride to the hospital.

"Not me. I'm going back to the fire. We've still got a job to do. Right, Burley?"

Burley nodded.

"You guys are nuts," the trooper said. "What about those two?" He pointed at Mark and Borderline. "Should I call another ambulance?"

"They're okay," Joshua said. "I don't think they need an ambulance, but maybe one of you guys could drive them over to the ER and get them checked out."

"No problem. I'll take them. Come on, guys, get in."

As the white patrol car disappeared in the wake of the two ambulances, Joshua stood for moment in the wind-whipped air and then shook himself as if coming out of a nightmare. His face was black, and his clothes were in tatters. One side of his jeans was almost completely gone, and a trail of smoke drifted from his right boot.

Two state troopers stood next to the remaining police car. They looked at Joshua and shook their heads. Off to one side, the engines of the two blackened brush trucks still rumbled. Tony, Chet, and Burley waited nearby.

As Joshua started toward them, a news van hurtled out of the smoke and screeched to a halt. Two men leaped out. One carried a video camera on his shoulder; the other clutched a microphone.

The cameraman panned the group. Microphone man rushed to Joshua as one of the troopers called out, "Hey, you're not allowed on this road. This is a restricted area."

"Come on, buddy, give us a break. We're just doing our job." The reporter flashed a press card and then turned to Joshua. "What's happening here? We saw the ambulances. Is anyone hurt?" He waved to the cameraman. "Get a close up of this guy, Harry. He looks like burnt toast."

The cameraman moved closer.

"Sir, you are ordered to leave," the trooper said. "I repeat, this is a restricted area."

The reporter thrust the microphone in Joshua's face. The camera loomed closer.

"Tell us what it was like inside the biggest fire to ever hit the Barrens. How bad was it? Just what kind of hell did you go through in there?"

Joshua turned away.

"What's wrong, big fella? Did you lose somebody? That's it, isn't it? There's casualties. I knew it, Harry. Come on, guy, tell us."

Joshua felt his right arm, the one that was blackened and blistered by the fire, the one that had brought Michael to his cabin, the one that had carried Teddy to the ambulance, develop a mind of its own. It clenched its fist into a hammer-like, hard-knuckled ball and then drew back slowly.

"Come on, buddy," the reporter said. "You were there. We need to know ..."

Despite his best efforts to be calm, Joshua's coiled fist shot out swiftly until it collided with the clean-shaven jaw of the reporter.

It smashed the soft tissue of his left cheek into the back molars, knocking one amalgam-filled tooth completely out and loosening the other.

The troopers were on the two newsmen in seconds, shoving them into the van, throwing the equipment in behind them.

"Hey, that's expensive stuff. You can't do that."

"Yes, I can. Get out of here. If I see your face again in a restricted area, I'll arrest you, and you can tell your story to the judge tomorrow after you spend the night in jail."

The trooper slammed the van door shut.

The window rolled down and revealed the flushed and angry face of the reporter. "I'll sue. There's freedom of the press in this country ... I know my rights ... just you wait ..."

As the van rolled away, the reporter's angry words faded in the hot wind.

"Sorry about that," the trooper said.

"It's okay. Thanks." Joshua rubbed his knuckle.

"How come those kids were wearing someone else's big, old clothes? Yours?"

"Yeah. They were in the house where the fire started. Their clothes got messed up, so I gave them some of mine."

The trooper took out his pad. "What's your name?"

"Reed. Joshua Reed."

"Phone number? Sorry about this, but I'm going to have file a report."

"Look, Officer, my house just burned to the ground back there, and I haven't got a phone right now." Joshua gestured toward the woods behind them. "I'm going back out on the fire. If you need me, call Forest Fire Service. They'll know how to reach me." He sniffed the air. "Smoke's getting thicker. We'd better get out of here."

"Thanks," the trooper said. "I'll be in touch."

Joshua opened the door of the brush truck. "Come on, Tony. Let's see if this burned-out truck of yours can make it from here to the parkway. We've still got a job to do."

CHAPTER 84

Toms River Community Hospital was a rambling, right-angled explosion of brick, mortar, and glass on the eastbound side of Route 37 near the Garden State Parkway. Because Ocean County was home to many retirement communities, the emergency room at Community Hospital was busy year-round. On big holiday weekends, when thousands of tourists flooded the Jersey shore, the ER was chaotic.

The elderly were brought in with heart attacks, strokes, and heat exhaustion. Vacationers were brought in after car and boat accidents, falls, fights, alcohol and drug overdoses, near-drownings, and severe sunburns.

This July Fourth weekend was worse than usual. Because a major fire raged in the Barrens just west of the Garden State Parkway, sections of the parkway were closed and that put pressure on the secondary roads. Traffic was horrific, and the police were advising everyone east of the parkway to stay home until the fire was under control.

Extra staff had been recruited in anticipation of fire-related injuries. The hospital would treat most burn cases, but the critical ones would be sent to the Burn Center at St. Barnabas in Morris County, sixty miles due north as the medevac helicopter flies.

Near the emergency entrance, Stacey and her mother stood side by side. Some passersby recognized them, and a few stopped to talk, but the worried, nervous looks on their faces quickly dried up idle conversation. They had been there for several hours, and as each ambulance howled up to the chrome double doors and disgorged patients, Stacey and her mom moved forward as in a dance and then retreated back to the brick wall.

"Mom, where are they?" Stacey wailed. "I've called them a thousand times." She looked beyond the hospital at the gray and black smoke that boiled into the distant sky. "I know something's happened. Can't we drive out to the Barrens? Maybe there's a back road that's still open."

"I think we should stay right here, Stacey. If anything's wrong, if they've been hurt, they'll be brought here."

Stacey began to pace back and forth again. Her flip-flops made a measured slap, slap, slap on the concrete sidewalk. After several minutes, she stopped and bent her head.

"Oh, Mom, I should have warned them. I tried to call Mark from work before he left for the Barrens, but the manager was furious. We had customers all over the place, kids yelling, lines of people waiting to order. I kept running to the phone every chance I got ..."

Stacey's eyes filled with tears. Her mother reached for her and pulled her close.

At that moment, an ambulance wailed around the corner and up to the emergency entrance. A second ambulance followed close behind. Stacey dabbed at her eyes with a rumpled tissue and then edged closer.

The first vehicle backed up to the ramp, the back door flew open, and an EMS worker slid out a stretcher with a figure strapped to it. It was a woman, her face black with soot. Only a few clumps of hair were left on her head; the rest was angry, blistered skin. The woman moaned softly as the stretcher rolled through the wide entrance.

"Oh, my God," Stacey whispered and turned her eyes back to the open ambulance doors.

Two young men climbed out. The first was a tall, skinny, African American kid with dreadlocks. Behind him came a gaunt, young man. His thin face was sooty, his eyes were bloodshot, and his clothes hung on him. He stood for a moment, blinking in the hazy sunlight. He looked strangely familiar ...

"Edsell," Stacey screamed.

"Stacey?" He staggered toward her.

"Oh, I can't believe it. Edsell, it's you. Where's Mark? Where's Borderline?"

Before he had time to answer, a nurse came out of the swinging doors and seized Edsell's arm. "We need you inside, young man. You can talk to your friend later."

Edsell jerked his hand back. "Hold on. This is important." A tired smile wreathed his face. "They're okay. We're all okay, thanks to a guy named Joshua. I think Mark and Borderline are in a cop car right behind us."

The nurse firmly steered him through the door.

"Hey, get your hands off me. I can walk."

Stacey turned to her mother, grinned widely, and raised a thumbs-up sign. If what Edsell said was true, Mark and Borderline would be here soon. Her mom had been right after all; this was the place to find them.

More patients came in. A small, young man who appeared unconscious was wheeled by on a stretcher. Others emerged from the ambulance and were able to walk inside. All of the patients were young with soot-streaked arms and faces. All appeared to be dressed in oversized clothing held together with belts and safety pins.

Could these be some of the missing kids whose names she had seen at police headquarters? Where were Mark and Borderline?

Finally, a state police cruiser pulled up. The rear doors swung open, and Mark and Borderline stepped out. Their clothes were stained, and their faces were grimy.

"Oh, my God, Mark! Borderline!" Stacey screeched as she ran to them. "You're safe, you're safe." All three hung onto each other, laughing and crying in the warm summer sun.

"Watch it, Stacey, you're getting all dirty," Mark said.

"Who cares? Oh, Mark, I tried to call and warn you, but no one was there. There's dozens of missing kids ..."

Mark pointed to the emergency room door. "We know. Those are some of them."

Stacey stepped back a few paces. Her glance darted from one to the other and back again.

"Okay, you guys. What happened? You were in the fire?"

"Fire?" Borderline's face took on a look of feigned innocence. "Mark, does it look like we were in a fire?"

"We were toasting marshmallows," Mark said. "Things got out of hand."

"Get real, you bums," Stacey said. "Tell me."

"The cops want us to get checked out before we do anything else," Mark said. "Can you wait?" He noticed Stacey's mother standing by the door. "Oh hello, Mrs. Greene. Can you give us a ride home?"

"Why not? I'd like to hear the story myself."

CHAPTER 85

On the other side of town, Lorraine Jones sat at her kitchen table and stared out the window. A long cigarette rested on a yellow, plastic ashtray and curled smoke into the air, while an uneaten tuna sandwich grew soggy in a waxed paper wrapper.

Her eyes shifted to a photograph taped to the door of the tiny refrigerator. It showed a young boy with dimples and a gap-toothed grin. His arms were wrapped around the waist of a pretty woman with short, curly, blonde hair. The picture slowly blurred as tears filled her eyes.

"If only I could go back and start over," Lorraine Jones whispered softly. "I'd stay home more. I'd lay off the booze and take Edsell to Boy Scouts like he wanted. I'd buy him a puppy, go to fucking PTA meetings, and cook dinners for him instead of giving him leftovers from the diner. I'd sign up for AA and go to those god-awful meetings, spill my guts out, and get sober for good. It's been twenty-four hours now since I had a drink. By God, if I ever get him back ..."

The phone rang. She watched it ring a second time as fear and hope crossed in waves over her pinched face. On the third ring, she took a drag from her cigarette and picked up the receiver.

"Mom?" Edsell said. "Mom, is th-that you? Answer me." A pause. "Mom? Are you drinking?"

Lorraine breathed out the smoke with a rush and held on to the kitchen table for support. *Oh, God ... is it possible? Edsell? Alive?*

"Naw. I'm here, I'm here, son. I ain't drinking. Oh God, you're alive, you're alive." She sobbed. "Where are you?"

"At the hospital."

Lorraine's fingers shook, and ashes spilled onto the table. "You're hurt? Oh Jesus, you're hurt. What's wrong?"

"I'm okay. Mark and Borderline are okay. We were all in the fire."

"The fire? The Barrens fire? I'm coming. I'll be right there, Edsell. Don't go away."

She hung up the phone. *Thank you, sweet Jesus, my boy is alive, he's alive.*

The impulse came over her like a wash of heat, a tingling. Lorraine stood up slowly and opened the cabinet over the sink. Yes, the bottle of Jack Daniels was still behind the red and white economy-sized box of elbow macaroni.

She picked it up, opened the screw top, and drained it into the sink. She smiled and then picked up her pocketbook and car keys.

CHAPTER 86

Early the next morning, Joshua hurried past the hospital's reception desk and into the elevator. The right side of his face was raw, and he had burn salve and gauze bandages on the right side of his hip and leg. He wore the crisp, green and tan uniform of the Forest Fire Service, and although visiting hours didn't start until eleven o'clock, he knew if he walked with a purposeful stride, no one would stop him.

Joshua had used the same technique during the long days of his father's dying. He'd been fourteen years old then and tall for his age. With a baseball cap pulled down over his face and his father's tool belt at his waist, everyone assumed he was a young maintenance worker.

For weeks, Joshua had kept a confident mask on his face each time he walked in and out of the big hospital, but once he got to his father's room, he sat like a small, lost boy on the floor next to the bed. Because his mother was working and taking care of his little sisters, she couldn't be there all the time. But Joshua could, and he was.

The nurses saw him duck in and out of Room 412 at odd hours of the day and night, but they ignored the breach of rules and even sneaked him soda and snacks from their lounge.

Since that cold December day when his father finally gave up the fight, Joshua had not been inside a hospital. The sights and smells, the highly polished surfaces, the machines that whirred and hummed and beeped—everything there gave him the creeps. When his sister gave birth to twins, he waited to see them at home. When his mother went in for gall bladder surgery, he called her every day and sent baskets of flowers but claimed he was too busy at work to come to the hospital.

But now, Teddy was here in this sterile, hostile place, and he had to see her. He rode the elevator and strode the polished hallways with a brisk step. Under the burns, his face was pale.

He paused at the entrance to Room 339, listened, and then peeked around the corner. A white-bandaged form lay on the bed, held hostage by numerous tubes and bottles. His Teddy, always strong and capable, now seemed small and helpless in the big, high hospital bed.

A short, dark-haired nurse was adjusting the drip in one of the IV bottles. She looked up and saw him.

"You can't come in here, sir. Visiting hours are—"

"Teddy," he called softly.

"She's been sedated, sir. She probably can't hear you. You'll have to come back later."

Joshua watched in wonder as the figure on the bed moved. Her hand came up, grasping, reaching for him. "Joshua?" Teddy's voice was weak and husky. Her eyes opened and searched for him.

The nurse looked at Joshua, sighed, and motioned him into the room.

Joshua tiptoed to the side of the bed and looked down at Teddy. Her thick, beautiful hair was gone, and her scalp was red, raw, and blistered. Both eyebrows were missing, as were the eyelashes. Her whole face had a half-formed fetal look to it.

Joshua touched her hand and smiled down at her. "How are you?" he asked.

She nodded and tried to smile too, but the effort ended in a grimace of pain.

"The fire?" she whispered.

"We stopped it at the parkway late last night. The shore towns are safe, and relief crews from Division A and C are out there now, helping with the cleanup."

She blinked sleepily. "Good. The boys?"

"Borderline and Mark went home. The others are still here under observation."

"Michael?"

"I'll see him before I go."

She nodded, and her eyes slowly closed.

"Teddy?" he whispered and bent close to her ear. "I love you."

Her eyes opened slowly, focused on his, and then closed. "Me, too," she muttered softly.

Joshua stood watching for several minutes. When her breathing turned even and her face stopped its twitching, he walked softly out of the room.

He'd be back. He'd see her every day, and it would be different now. Unlike his father, Teddy would get better day by day. He didn't care if her hair never grew back, didn't care if she was as bald as an egg. Soon she'd be in his arms again, and when that happened, he'd never let her go.

CHAPTER 87

Two floors below, Joshua found the pediatric unit. When he stopped at the desk, a gray-haired nurse who was writing on a clipboard looked up. "Can I help you?"

"A kid was brought in yesterday from the fire. I think his name's Michael. Is he here?"

"Yes, down the hall in Room 224. Are you family? We've been trying to find out who he is, but he won't tell us his last name."

"No, I'm with the Forest Fire Service and helped pull him out of the fire. I wondered how he's doing."

The nurse smiled. "Much better. He's fighting a wicked infection in his arm, some kind of puncture wound. He's on an antibiotic drip now, and the last time I made the rounds, his temp was down."

"Can I see him?"

"I don't know why not. There's no restriction on visiting hours in pediatrics, but no one has been to see him. We don't even know who to call to let them know he's here. Maybe you can find out who he belongs to. He's in Room 224."

Joshua walked down the hall, checking the numbers on the rooms until he came to 224. It was a brightly colored room containing an empty crib and a small hospital bed. Michael lay in the bed with his head turned toward the single window. The Venetian blinds were partially open, and golden bands of sunlight crossed his peaceful, childlike face.

As Joshua approached the bed, the boy turned, and a great smile crossed his face and lit up his eyes.

"Joshua!"

The big man beamed down at the boy and then reached down and shook Michael's hand gently.

"How're you doing, son?

"Better. How'd I get here? They told me an ambulance brought me, but the last thing I remember is lying in a bed with Teddy stroking my forehead."

"You don't remember anything about the fire?"

The boy twisted up his face and then shook his head. "Not much, just a few quick flashes of fire and smoke, sort of like a rock video with strobe lights."

"Good. It's better that way."

"What happened? I really want to know."

"The fire got close to the cabin," Joshua said. "We had to pull you guys out with a couple of brush trucks."

"I missed all that?"

"Be glad you did, Michael. We had some pretty hairy moments getting out of there. I expect the other boys might have nightmares for a few days."

"Where's everyone?"

"Mark and Borderline are home. The rest are here in the hospital under observation for twenty-four hours. They'll probably let them go sometime today. By the way, how come you're not telling anyone your last name?"

Michael turned his face to the sunlit window again and closed his eyes. Long moments passed while Joshua waited, not wanting to speak for fear the boy would retreat inside himself again.

Finally, Michael turned his head and looked at Joshua.

"Do I have to tell?"

"Why don't you tell me your story? Then the two of us can decide if anyone else needs to know."

Another long silence, but this time the boy's eyes stayed locked on Joshua's while an inner battle raged behind them. Again Joshua waited and said nothing.

"Okay, I'll tell you, but you've got to promise not to tell anyone else," Michael finally said.

"I promise," said Joshua. "I won't tell anyone, not unless you agree."

Michael began in a small voice. "When I was a little kid, I lived in a big, white house with my Mom and Dad and my baby brother, Jeff. I went to school and played with my friends and watched TV, and everything was great until ..." Michael stopped, and his lower lip and chin began to quiver.

"Go on," Joshua prompted softly.

"I remember an afternoon. We were in the park near my house. My Mom and all the other moms were sitting at a picnic table talking. I remember she had Jeff's stroller right next to her. I got tired of playing on the swings, so I walked away. I only wanted to follow a squirrel to see where he lived ..."

"And?"

"And I remember walking around a big tree ..." He paused and drew a deep breath and then rushed on, speaking quickly and quietly. "This guy grabbed me, put his hand over my mouth, and started dragging me to his car. I remember he smelled funny ... I remember trying to call for my mom, but ..."

Michael's shoulders shook, and tears filled his eyes. Joshua sat down on the bed and put his arms around him. When the boy's sobs subsided, Joshua held him gently at arm's length.

"Michael? Is that your real name?"

"Yes."

"What's your last name, Michael?"

Another silence. Then the boy whispered, "My name is Michael Douglas Emory."

"Where do you live, Michael? Do you know the address of the big, white house?"

"My mother taught me when I went to kindergarten. Number Eight Signal Road, Newtown Square, Pennsylvania," he said slowly and carefully, then added quickly, "but you can't call my mom and dad."

"Why not? They must be so worried about you. You've been gone all this time."

The boy's tear-filled eyes widened into wells of sadness. He looked down at the white sheet and blanket that covered him. His small hands suddenly took hold of the blanket and pulled it up to his face.

"They won't want me back anymore," he whispered.

"That's not true, Michael. They're your parents. They'd want you back, no matter what."

"But, Joshua, I did some bad things. This guy kept me in his room and made me do awful stuff." Michael sobbed and drew long, shuddering breaths. Joshua took his tiny hand in his large one. Finally, Michael was able to continue. "One day he fell asleep and forgot to lock the door. I ran away, but I knew I couldn't go home anymore, so I did more bad things, disgusting things, just to stay alive. To live." Michael's voice was strong now, angry. "You know what, Joshua? I was glad when that fat guy got me into his van. I was glad when Vogel tied me to that bed because I knew he was going to kill me, and … and … I wanted him to!"

As the boy finished the last few words in a wail of despair, Joshua felt a rush of conflicting emotions. Rage at the nameless, faceless pervert who had abducted Michael. Anger at Vogel and the additional pain he had inflicted on this helpless, hurting kid. Most of all, he felt pity for Michael and for all the homeless, lost kids like him.

Joshua leaned down and cupped the boy's face in his two large hands, tilting it upward until Michael's eyes were focused on him.

"Look at me, Michael. It's not your fault. None of this is your fault. I know your mother and father will want you back. I know it as sure as I know I'm sitting in this room."

A small glimmer of hope shone on the young boy's face for a moment.

"You think so? I've been gone so long."

"They'll want you back no matter what, but right now you need to tell your story to the police. Maybe they can catch that guy and make sure this doesn't happen to some other kid. And we need to call your folks."

Michael sighed. "Not yet. Not yet. I'll think about it, Joshua. Come back tomorrow. In the meantime, you promised not to tell. Remember?"

"I won't say anything to anybody, Michael. And I'll see you tomorrow."

CHAPTER 88

Joshua rode the elevator down to the main lobby of the hospital. He was lost in thought as he walked through the two consecutive automatic doors leading out into the sunlight. The outdoor air still carried a hint of smoke.

"Joshua," a familiar voice called. Red and the chief strode toward him.

"How're you doing?" the chief asked.

"Okay."

"How's Teddy?"

"Just saw her. She's hurting, but she'll mend." Joshua's eyes narrowed. "Why are you here?"

"Red and I need your help, Joshua," the chief said.

"Aw, come on, for chrissake. I was on the fire for twenty-four hours, I got blisters and burns all over my body, I took my first shower two hours ago, and it hurt like hell. Now, you two bozos are saying you need me? Chief, I told you everything I know last night. Read my head." Joshua shook his head firmly from side to side. "The answer is no," he said over his shoulder as he walked away.

"Fire investigation," the chief called to Joshua's retreating back. "You were there when it started. We need you to come out to the Watson place with us."

Joshua turned and spread out his arms. "Come on, Chief. I was on my way to my Ma's house. That sweet woman promised to make me pancakes and eggs with bacon cooked real crisp, just the way I like. I can almost taste it now."

"We got jelly donuts in the truck. You can have some."

"Aw, shit."

The chief's white cruiser bounced down Route 618 toward Bamber Lake. The tic in the engine was still pronounced, but since most of the brush trucks were at the shop in New Lisbon, he knew he'd be waiting a long time for a much-needed engine overhaul.

On both sides of the road, the forest had been incinerated into black, sooty ash. Within the devastation, burning snags still glowed, and smoke still rose in puffs from burning embers. Without a drenching rain, it would be days before the fire was officially declared out.

Each wildfire is different, Joshua mused. Sometimes the fire burned the bottom understory of brush, grass, fallen leaves, and pine needles and left the tops of the trees intact. At other times, it raced through the tops of the trees and left the lower growth untouched. Different conditions caused different kinds of burns. Here, in this particular area, the fire had passed in a hellish fury, leaving not a single green shoot. This fire had sucked the color and the life out of everything in its path.

"One of the pilots spotted a 1024 yesterday." The chief interrupted Joshua's reverie. "A body lying next to a burned-out vehicle under the high wires."

"Yeah? What kind of car?"

"Looks like a four-by-four of some kind. Bronco, Suburban, maybe a Cherokee."

"The body probably belongs to Vogel," Joshua said.

"The doctor at the Watson place? The one you told us about that kidnapped all those kids?" Red asked.

"Yeah. He took off in a Suburban right after he torched the house. The damn fool probably tried to take a shortcut and drove himself right back into the fire." Joshua smiled. "That's good news."

"Let's talk straight, Joshua," the chief said. "So far, I've been able to keep a lid on this by keeping everyone out of the fire area. We downplayed the kids at the hospital, kept them from making calls, but the media's starting to sniff around. I want to call in the state police to investigate this so-called rehabilitation center he was running, but before I do, I want to have a quick, private look-see. We'll call it a fire investigation, but first I want your story."

As they bumped over the narrow Pinelands roads, Joshua filled in more details about Vogel and the things the boys had told him. He started with the night he pulled Borderline out of the swamp and ended by describing his visit with Michael this morning.

"I feel a bit responsible for all this." Joshua gestured at the charred forest. "If I hadn't gone rushing out to the Watson place, if I had called the police right away, maybe Vogel wouldn't have had the chance to set the house on fire. Maybe none of this would have happened. Teddy would be okay, and I'd still have my cabin."

"Yeah, and maybe that kid Mark would be dead, and some of the others." The chief rubbed the back of his neck. "As slick as this Vogel character was, he might have gotten away and set up another lab somewhere else. Think about that when you're feeling sorry about what you did."

"He had backing. That I know," Joshua said. "There were other people involved. The stuff was flown out of McGuire Air Force Base by jet. It was sent somewhere, to someone."

"I'll call Sean Casey as soon as we look around. The state police chief will know what to do with this. He's been in his job almost as long as I've been in mine."

CHAPTER 89

When they arrived at the Watson place, Joshua saw a gaping hole where the old farmhouse had collapsed into its basement. Only a few smoldering timbers and the burned-out hulk of a central air-conditioning system were left to show that two days ago, this had been a large imposing building.

"We left the one they called Nerf near a tree back behind the house." Joshua walked around the ruins and past the small square of blackened chain-link fence that had surrounded the garbage cans. "Let me see, it was back round this way."

Red and the chief followed Joshua through the burned-out forest. With each step, ashes rose up into the air. The ground was still hot underfoot.

Red leaned over and put his open palm near the earth. "Turf fires," he said.

Finally, Joshua stopped near a still-burning snag. A charred body was next to the trunk. The wind had slowed to a gentle, variable breeze that lifted the scent of burnt flesh around them. It was Nerf, but his bulk had been considerably reduced.

The chief broke the silence.

"My pa told me that after the big fire of '32, they found four victims with their arms wrapped around trees," he said quietly. "The wind gets so fierce in the middle of a wildfire that you grab onto a tree to keep from blowing away."

The chief turned and walked back to the cruiser. Joshua and Red followed without speaking.

Should he have tried to save Nerf? *No,* Joshua told himself. The kids were more important, and he had made that choice when the fire started.

Joshua's face was grim because he had seen at close range what happens when the hot, red bitch embraces a man.

In the cruiser, the chief peeled foil from a fresh cylinder of white antacid tablets and popped two into his mouth.

"We've got a job to do here, boys, so let's finish it. I need to file official reports about the origin of the fire. We have you as an eyewitness, Josh. You can attest to the fact that the fire started when Anton Vogel torched the house. Now that we have that settled, let's see what else we can find. You mentioned something about a bog, about a place where they may have dumped bodies. Where do you think that spot might be?"

"I know this part of the woods pretty well," Joshua said. "Me and Tony used to roam this whole area when we were kids. We spent hours sneaking up on rabbits and raccoons and deer and all kinds of varmints." Joshua looked around. "Things look different since the fire, but the nearest bog is over there." He pointed to the northeast.

Again the three men walked through the smoky desolation. Moments later, they stood at the edge of a flat stretch of water that was covered with a thin layer of ash.

"There's a couple more bogs down that way," Joshua said, "but this one is the oldest and deepest. It's a natural peat bog. The others were built along the creek bed by old man Watkins's father back in the days when it was a working cranberry farm."

Red peered at the old bog. Beyond it, a line of flat ponds stretched into the distance like flat, pewter plates. "This here's a big area. We won't have time to search every bog." Red spat a thin stream of tobacco juice at the base of a smoldering tree stump where it hissed and sent up a coil of white smoke.

Just then, Joshua noticed a set of parallel tracks buried in the ashes. "Maybe these will show us where to look." He followed the parallel depressions to the edge of the water and squatted down. The water was a pale gray, matte surface, streaked with clear patches of water from the freshening breeze.

All at once, a gust of wind exposed a large patch of tea-colored water. Just below the surface they could see a layer of green pine boughs.

"Damn, a tree must have come down just before the fire," the chief exclaimed.

"Wait," Joshua said. "That's not a tree. Those are cut branches. Here, grab my arm."

Red held Joshua's arm as he leaned out over the water.

"Don't let go of my arm, pal," Joshua warned. "This one is a deep sucker. Me and Tony used to try and find the bottom with sticks. We never could."

Joshua reached into the water and slowly pushed aside the branches. The bright sunlight probed downward through the clear, tea-colored water as the debris cleared, and there, several feet below the surface, he saw a dark, angular shape.

"Pull me up, Red. There's a vehicle down there. Looks like a Jeep."

Red heaved on Joshua's arm, and they scrambled up the bank. The three men stood quietly and looked down at the bog.

"If there's a Jeep in there," the chief mused, "there's bodies in there too." He wiped his face with an open palm. "Jesus, the whole damn story is true."

"The boys told me that Vogel bragged about it," Joshua said. "Bragged about how he was doing this scientific research. Bragged about how he'd be famous someday."

The acrid smell of smoke blew around them in the breeze. Red coughed. "I expect he'll be famous someday, but it ain't gonna be for scientific discoveries." He spat again.

The chief turned and sprinted for his truck. "I'm calling Sean. This is more than a fire scene. I want him here before we touch anything else."

Forty-five minutes later, two state troopers and a stern-faced man in a dark blue suit stood with Joshua, Red, and the chief. A tow truck ground its gears, and with sucking wet noises, a dark green Jeep rose slowly from the depths of the bog. As soon as it was clear, the men leaned over the black, peaty water. Black leaves and sticks and other debris eddied beneath the surface.

"Send down the hook," the chief said.

The tallest of the two troopers dropped the three-pronged hook into the water. It splashed and disappeared into the muck. The trooper stood on the bank and moved the grappling hook back and forth along the bottom until it caught.

"Here, give me a hand."

Joshua and the trooper pulled. There was something down there, something that was coming slowly up toward the glistening surface. They pulled harder, and more of the dripping, leaf-clotted rope emerged.

"Whatever it is, we've almost got it," Joshua panted.

Suddenly, a hand broke the dark, littered surface of the pond. It was followed by a body that was bloated and stained to the color of dark tea by the iron water of the Barrens. The mossy smell of the bog was quickly overlaid with the sweet stench of rotting flesh.

"Jesus H. Christ," exclaimed the chief.

Sean Casey said nothing, but his mouth tightened to a slash across his ruddy Irish face.

Joshua held the dripping rope and its hideous burden. He could feel this morning's donut crawling up his rib cage. The other men's faces were ashen. One trooper turned and ran twenty feet into the burned-out forest where he retched. The sound was strangely smothered in the warm, ash-laden air. It added an exclamation point to all their thoughts.

"Get that body up on this bank." Casey spoke in a tight, clipped voice. "Send the hook down again. I'm calling the FBI."

Joshua and the men pulled the bloated body clear of the water. It rolled onto the bank, gathering gray ashes and small sticks on the puffed surface. Everyone stepped back, holding handkerchiefs to their mouths while Joshua and the tall trooper cast the silver hook into the dark water once more.

Back and forth the rope sailed on the still surface. Seconds later it caught on something, and the two men once more pulled on the thick, slippery rope. This time, the bog yielded its burden quickly as a head rose to the surface, followed by a body. This one was darker and less bloated. The face was partially eaten away by something that lived beneath the dark water.

Casey punched numbers into his mobile phone while Joshua and the trooper pulled the second body onto the bank.

"Get me Isaac Powers at the FBI in Washington. No, I don't want the Trenton Office. I want Washington." A pause while Casey tapped his feet in the dusty ground. "This is Sean Casey, New Jersey State Police." Another pause while Casey brushed at a streak of white ash on his navy suit jacket. "I don't give a shit who he's having lunch with. Page him now."

CHAPTER 90

Late that afternoon, several cars filled with average-looking men and women dressed in nondescript clothing arrived at Toms River Community Hospital. One man walked into the administrator's office on the second floor and closed the door behind him. The rest of the men split up into small groups and proceeded directly to the rooms of the boys who had been imprisoned at the Watson place.

The doors quickly closed, and a soft murmur of voices were heard from inside. When the men left, a guard was posted at each door.

Three miles east of Community Hospital, Borderline Fenton lay half-asleep on a couch in the living room. He never thought he could be this happy to be home with his dorky parents. Right now, he loved this house with its fussy antique furniture and its rose garden. He loved it with a reverence and fervor he had never felt before. The TV was on, and even though the Mets were losing to the Pirates six to zip, he didn't care.

When he first got home that afternoon, he took a long hot shower and then pulled back the covers on his bed and buried his face in the sweet-smelling, crisp, white sheets. He pulled on his oldest, most comfortable pair of raggedy jeans and then went downstairs and dove onto the deep, soft couch in front of the TV.

From a great distance, Borderline heard a knock at the front door. The knock was repeated, louder this time, more insistent. Borderline closed his eyes tighter and burrowed his head into the soft damask pillow.

More knocking. Borderline sighed and got up. No sense in waiting for his parents to hear it in the backyard. Whatever idiot was knocking was obviously going to keep on knocking. He limped to the door, and as he opened it, two men flashed badges and pushed by him into the living room.

"My name is Rudman, FBI," the first man said. "This is Agent Smith. Are you Howard Patrick Fenton, also known as Borderline?"

Borderline nodded.

"Is anyone else at home?"

"My mom and dad are in the garden out back." He pointed to the back patio.

Smith walked through the family room and opened the french doors.

"Excuse me, folks," he called. "Would you come in, please?"

Mark and Stacey were curled up in a large double hammock next to the pool in the Greene's spacious backyard. Mark was asleep, his face sweat-sheened and peaceful in the warm July air. Stacey's head was on his shoulder as she traced circles on his chest with her index finger.

"Stacey. Stacey," her mother called in a strange, hesitant voice. "Some men are here to talk to you and Mark. Please hurry."

CHAPTER 91

That same day, the chief ordered all of the roads that led anywhere near the old Watson place to be sealed. Orange ropes and barricades went up, even on the smallest of trails. A Forest Fire Service truck or police car sat at each entrance. No one was allowed to pass without written permission from the chief.

Those who asked questions were told, "Fire scene investigation."

Ambulances came and went but without sirens or flashing light.

One Trenton reporter accidentally got through to the chief, and he had the nerve to question what was going on. Why were ambulances needed at a fire that was under control?

The chief held his temper and patiently explained that it was merely a precaution on his part in case the fire flared up again. There were still some burning snags around, and of course, they always had to watch for turf fires. His men had successfully battled the worst wildfire in the history of the Pine Barrens and saved the shore towns. His mission was to keep those men safe while they performed the hazardous job of investigating the origins of this disastrous fire.

The reporter asked if the rumors he'd heard were true, that the fire had begun in an old farmhouse and, furthermore, that the house had been deliberately torched.

The chief said they were exploring every angle. They suspected arson and were meticulously searching for clues before the rain that was due tomorrow destroyed the evidence.

He did not tell the newsman that a whole crew from the FBI was even now at the Watson place, sifting through the ruins, dredging the bog, and scouring the nearby woods. He did not tell the newsman that all telephone calls in and out of the Watson place for the past three years were being traced, or that the flight plans of all planes out of McGuire were being meticulously reviewed.

He did not mention that so far, eighteen bodies had been dredged out of the bog and sent to the regional FBI forensics lab. It appeared that all of the bodies were male. All of them were young.

CHAPTER 92

Bethesda, Maryland, USA, and around the world. July 5, 1988

The Foundation for the American Way (FAW) occupied two floors of a multiuse building in a large office complex near the Washington Beltway in Maryland. Most of FAW's neighbors were subdivisions of federal agencies and institutions. A few were private corporations connected in some way to the United States government.

Few people in official circles knew about FAW. Even fewer knew that its tenuous, secret operations reached into the White House, the Senate, the House of Representatives, and the Pentagon. Only the director of FAW and the president of the United States knew that in the last two years, this tiny foundation had had major influence on world events and major funding. With the proper care and nurturing and absolute secrecy, that influence would continue for many years.

On this very day, on several continents, FAW touched many lives.

A desert palace was hushed in the cool hours before dawn. A solitary figure padded softly through the polished marble halls. When that lone figure approached a massive, golden door, a large, uniformed man stepped out of the shadows. The guard's eyes widened in recognition; he pulled open the heavy door and stepped aside with a low bow.

A large canopied bed occupied the center of the huge, high-ceilinged room, and on that bed, a feeble old man reclined on many pillows. Only the rise and fall of his bony chest gave indication that life still existed in his wasted body.

As the visitor approached, the old man's eyes opened, and his head slowly turned. The young man saluted and then knelt on the floor beside the bed.

"Is it true?" The old man spoke in a labored whisper.

"Yes, Excellency. I have verified all of their claims."

For a long time, the only sound in the large room was the hiss of air passing through ancient lungs. Then the breathing grew heavy, and a long, bony arm reached out and grasped the shoulder of the man kneeling by the bed.

"Contact General Morris. Tell him I am coming and I agree to his terms. Order the jet."

In a small Central American country, General Rodriquez was visiting his mistress in the seaside home he had built for her. The house was luxurious, built to specifications by the premier architect of his country.

Rodriguez had personally designed many aspects of the residence. Walls of glass overlooked the sea, and each had a privacy panel that slid noiselessly into place at the touch of a button. The opulent master bedroom suite featured a vast, oval bed with a mirrored ceiling, a huge, gold and granite bath with its own small garden of white orchids, and a closet with dozens of silk lounging robes.

Two years ago, he had added a small private suite for those nights when he simply needed to rest his sixty-five-year-old body. Those solitary evenings had grown in number within the past year, and sometimes he wondered if the hour's trip to the hideaway was still worth it.

A full staff of hand-picked servants cooked and cleaned and verified the complete and utter faithfulness of young Angelique, or whoever took her place when he tired of her.

Earlier this evening, General Rodriquez had returned from a small, private hospital near Washington, DC. At the hospital, he had undergone a complete physical followed by an injection of some very special vitamins.

The mirrored ceiling reflected a rumpled bed, scattered pillows, and a rosy, languid Angelique lying across the lap of the general. He stroked her long, black hair as she murmured to him.

"You were magnificent, sir. I have not been loved like that. Ever."

Rodriguez smiled broadly, and as he bent to kiss her warm mouth, he again felt the stirrings of desire.

Angelique opened her eyes wide. "Surely not again, so soon," she said with a smile.

Rodriguez warmed to her embrace with but one thought: *May the Holy Virgin and all the saints bless my dear friend, General Morris. May the Lord himself smile upon the United States of America and its gifted scientists.*

The meeting was over. As the eighty-year-old committee chairman walked briskly away to his chambers, two junior members of Congress stood in the doorway and watched.

"You know, that old reprobate is going to last forever. He'll still be head of this committee when hell freezes over." The young congressman from California spoke softly through gritted teeth.

"Stubborn, old sonofabitch." The second congressman agreed. "I've got to tell you, Frank, I hate his elitist, reactionary point of view more and more each day."

"Did you hear him going on and on about Franklin D. Roosevelt? FDR, for God's sake. What bullshit. He sounded like my grandfather."

"I don't know how he does it. The schedule he keeps would kill a man half his age."

"Maybe it's genetic. I hear his grandfather lived to be a hundred and four."

"The way he's going, so will he."

CHAPTER 93

General Tucker Morris, the executive director of FAW, was a rotund, middle-aged man given to clearing his throat before he spoke, a practice he had deliberately adopted during his twenty-five years in the military. When Tucker Morris cleared his throat, everyone in the room listened.

After retiring from active duty, he continued the practice, much to the annoyance of both his wife and his mistress.

The hands of the antique grandfather clock in the corner of his office showed nine thirty. The magnificent view of the Capitol rotunda outside his window was obscured by a thick, gray mist. General Morris sat at his desk and leafed through a pile of clippings. Across from him, a tall, thin, homely man in a gray suit sat at attention.

Morris had just cleared his throat.

"Good work, Clarence, or should I say, Jack." The general smiled. "It was a stroke of genius to put you into the Barrens as part of Vogel's staff. He never knew you were more than a lackey."

"No, sir, I made sure of that."

"Thank you, Clarence. You have been a great help to us. We'll need your services again someday soon, I'm sure."

"Thank you, sir." The tall, thin man stood up, saluted briskly, and walked out.

General Morris leaned forward and sorted the clippings again. He selected one, put on his half-glasses, and as he read, the barest hint of a smile crossed his face.

> *The worst fire in 40 years swept through 95,000 acres of the New Jersey Pine Barrens yesterday, destroying 45 homes and businesses, killing 3 and injuring 47.*
>
> *The dead are listed as Dr. Anton Vogel of the Vogel Rehabilitation Clinic near Chatsworth, Wilbur Nelson, an employee of Toms River South High School, and Anne Blake, an elderly woman who died of a heart attack as firefighters were evacuating her from her home near Bamber Lake.*
>
> *Firefighters were hampered by fierce winds brought on by an approaching cold front ...*

Morris read each clipping slowly, savoring each word, each line. They were all similar in content.

What luck, he thought. *What colossal, unbelievable luck.* It was a miracle that Vogel had no donors at the clinic when the fire started. All his records and files had burned in the fire, and everyone who could have talked was dead. He couldn't have planned it better himself.

Morris congratulated himself. He had had an uneasy feeling in his gut for the past year about having only one clinic. A good military man never went into a campaign with one option, one plan of attack, and because he was a cautious, meticulous planner who liked to imagine every contingency, Morris had set in motion the plans for a second clinic nearly six months ago.

Now, it was nearly operational.

The new doctor, a brilliant young Pakistani with huge ambitions and larger immigration problems, had been given all the duplicate files that Jack had smuggled out of Vogel's clinic. New property had been purchased near Camp Lejeune in North Carolina. Equipment was even now being installed in an old summer home on a remote tributary near the coast.

He had followed Vogel's original plan, the one that had worked so well before: a small, discreet operation with access to a military airfield. One doctor, two assistants. If all went well in the next few weeks, there would hardly be a blip in the pipeline of those eager to receive FAW's gift.

His secretary's line buzzed discreetly. Morris picked up the phone.

"Yes?"

"General Morris, there are some men here to see you."

"Who are they? I'm not expecting anyone."

"They say they're from the FBI."

A cold hand grasped some vital organ deep within Morris's abdominal area. No, it couldn't be. Everything had been destroyed. There was no way, no reason for anyone to link him with Vogel.

Don't get excited, he admonished himself and drew a deep breath. The men were probably from the local agency headquarters here in Washington. They most likely wanted him to speak at one of their training seminars. He'd done it before. He'd do it again.

The secretary's voice came on again. "General? What should I do?"

"Why let them in, Janet," he said expansively. "I'll be happy to see them."

Exactly three seconds later, five men strode into his office. One remained by the exit door. One went to the executive bathroom, opened the door, looked inside, and then stood in front of it. The remaining three stood in a line before his desk.

"General Morris? General Tucker A. Morris?" The one in the middle addressed him in clipped tones.

"Yes." The cold hand was back in his guts.

"It is my duty to inform you that you are under arrest for capital crimes committed in conjunction with the Vogel Clinic near Chatsworth, New Jersey. You have the right to remain silent. Anything you say or do may be used against you in a court of law. You have the right to an attorney—"

"I want my attorney. Now!" barked General Morris.

CHAPTER 94

Michael sat propped up on pillows in his room in the pediatric section of Toms River Community Hospital watching a talk show. The camera centered on a fat woman in a shiny, purple dress. She was shouting at her husband, a short, dark man with big, sad eyes. The woman's teeth were bared in a snarl. Her fists were clenched, and her whole body jiggled and shook with rage.

Michael flipped off the television in disgust. His mother had been a soft-spoken, gentle woman. His favorite memory was of her making cinnamon French toast on Saturday mornings. He loved those slow, easy breakfasts. His parents talked and read the papers while he looked at cartoons.

After breakfast, they would all clean the house together. His dad ran the vacuum and washed the kitchen floor. His mother scrubbed the bathrooms. His job was to dust the tabletops with a soft rag.

Some things he remembered clearly from those days, and some things had faded, but Saturday mornings were like a video that ran over and over again in his mind.

Michael shut off those memories with an effort and wondered what would happen next. The swelling in his arm was gone, and his head wasn't so fuzzy anymore. He had told Joshua everything. This morning, two men from the FBI came in with Joshua, and he'd had to run through it again. When he started to cry in the middle of the second round of questions, Joshua stood up and asked the men to come back later.

Right now, he was tired of talking, tired of the questions, tired of the whole thing.

He closed his eyes. It was easy not to worry about anything now. Nothing could be done anyway. The adults in the world were in charge of his life now. It was better to imagine those Saturday mornings ...

"Michael?" It seemed so real. He could almost hear her voice. "Michael, wake up. It's Mom."

He opened his eyes and saw his mother standing in the light from the window. His dad stood behind her. They were older and grayer than he remembered, but they both had tears in their eyes and big smiles on their faces.

His mother spread her arms and came to the bed, gathering him to her. Her perfume was the same. Her body was still soft and gentle. He looked over her shoulder at his father.

"Son, welcome back." His father smiled, and his voice broke in the middle of the words.

His mother couldn't talk at all.

And neither could he.

EPILOGUE

One year later

Wildflowers, grasses, and ferns prospered in the revitalized, nitrogen-rich, burned-over Barrens soil. Dead snags stood like dark statues in the lush growth, but they would fall eventually and reunite with the earth. Here and there, heat-ravaged pitch pines sent fragile, green shoots out of their dark, gnarled bark.

On the floor of the forest, the thick, tight cones of the pitch pines had exploded in the heat of last summer's fires, and now hundreds of needled green puffs grew among the grasses and ferns.

Old Mitch grazed alone now. His companion, the smaller buck, had bolted back into the forest when the fire came near. The deer that had survived the great fire were fat now with the new succulent grasses. Tiny fawns followed their mothers around the Pineland meadows. Many of them carried the genetic imprint of Old Mitch.

In a small vale near the Forked River Mountains, in one of the few pockets of the Barrens that had not seen fire in a hundred years, a bearded man sat fishing with a bamboo pole. Three hundred yards behind him, a snug camp had been dug into a low hill. A tall, white oak provided cool shade, and thick laurel bushes provided a natural screen.

| 313 |

Two canoes filled with laughing teenagers floated by slowly in the calm, tea-colored water. They saw the fisherman and waved. He smiled, and just as he waved back, he felt a tug on his line.

In the vast burned-out area that encompassed the center and eastward edge of the Pine Barrens, several homes were framed out, and others were nearly finished. A few families had abandoned their gutted homes and moved on, but most of Pineys were busily rebuilding. The land was theirs, and they would live upon it as best they could for as long as they could.

Fire had come to the Pine Barrens as it had for thousands of years. Restoring, shaping, sustaining.

On a warm spring afternoon, a crowd gathered in a wide, grassy field east of the town of Chatsworth. The men were dressed casually in jeans and plaid shirts. Many wore the uniform of the Forest Fire Service. The women were colorful in bright dresses, skirts, and blouses. Some of them carried babies. Others watched as toddlers and older siblings chased each other through the meadow.

A host of tables and chairs had been set up near a green van from Enzio's Restaurant in Toms River. A twenty-foot table groaned under a load of veal Parmigianino, meatballs, sausages and peppers, fried calamari, baked ziti, and crisp, green salad. Baskets filled with torpedo rolls and garlic bread had been placed on the smaller tables along with bottles of Frascati and Chianti. Two kegs of beer were tapped and waiting in ice-filled tubs. Two large coolers held iced tea and soda.

Three young men and a young woman stood off to one side of the crowd.

"They should be here soon," Mark said.

"They say the procession will come from over there." Stacey pointed down a narrow dirt road at the far side of the meadow. "I don't know about you guys, but I can hardly wait for this."

"Another great guy bites the dust." Borderline sighed heavily as Stacey punched him in the arm.

"What an awesome day for a wedding," Edsell Jones said. "Look at that sky. Makes you glad you're alive."

The other three looked at him and grinned.

"You got *that* right," Borderline said. "How's your mom doing?"

"Most days are good. She's on the phone a lot with her friends from AA. She goes to meetings two or three times a week, but the best thing is she hasn't had a drink since the day I disappeared. Not one." Edsell smiled. "She's quieter and not as shaky, and we actually talk. You know, about my job and stuff, what I'm going to do after I finish school. It's weird sometimes; we're both different people now."

"That's cool," Mark said. "I can remember how your mother hounded us and hounded us when you disappeared. She was going to get you back, not matter what. If she hadn't convinced us that something was really wrong … Well, I can't even imagine."

"Enough said." Borderline spoke in a hoarse voice. "It's over, thank God. I hope that Dr. Vogel roasts in hell forever."

"Amen to that," Mark said.

"Listen," Stacey interrupted. "I think I hear them coming."

"There! I see them." Borderline pointed.

A line of shiny, red brush trucks and one white cruiser appeared on the far side of the field. As soon as the crowd saw them, they shifted close to a wide, wooden arch decorated with daisies and red roses.

The trucks circled the field in a slow parade with their lights flashing and then parked in a row facing the crowd.

A tall, muscular man with thick, dark hair stepped down from the first truck and walked to the flowered arch. Three other men climbed out of a second truck and joined them. They were all dressed in the crisp, green-and-tan uniform of the New Jersey Forest Fire Service.

The third truck yielded three young women in long dresses of pale blue cotton denim. Each carried a bouquet of daisies and red roses.

A hush fell on the crowd as a lone harmonica began to play "Amazing Grace."

An older man, also dressed in the uniform of the Forest Fire Service, climbed out of the driver's side of the white truck and walked around to the passenger door. When he opened it, a tall, young woman stepped down.

She was dressed in a simple, white cotton dress and carried a bouquet of red and pink roses. Her dark hair was short and fell onto her forehead in wispy bangs. Her face was reddened on one side, and part of her right eyebrow was missing.

The chief took her arm, and they moved toward the arch where Joshua stood waiting. Teddy smiled widely at him, and when he returned the grin, she walked forward with a firm step.

Stacey wiped her eyes. "Isn't she beautiful?" she whispered.

"You got that right," Borderline answered. He blinked hard and began to clap. Mark and Edsell joined in, and soon more and more people around them started clapping until the whole gathering was clapping and cheering.

ACKNOWLEDGMENTS

Many thanks to the men and women of the New Jersey Forest Fire Service for sharing their stories and their knowledge with me. These include but are not limited to: Maris Gabliks, Jeff Brower, David Harrison, Frank Scerbo, Tom Tansley, Roger (Scottie) McLachlan, Joe Hughes, Bob Stauber, Bill Edwards, Samuel Moore III, Art Bethanis, and Paul Brenner.

I would also like to thank various residents and researchers of the New Jersey Pine Barrens for helping me learn about the people and ways of that region. These include Bobby Van Pelt, Betsy Carpenter, Norma Milner, Marilyn Schmidt, and Christian M. Bethmann.

Thanks also to Tom Jardine and Jim Bemiss for flying me over the Pine Barrens out of Allaire Airport; to Don Larson who taught me about weapons, especially bow hunting; Jim Lowney of the Oyster Creek Nuclear Generating Station who taught me about power plants and how electricity moves through high-tension wires; Frank Scerbo who taught me about volunteer fire departments; and finally to Jane Bateman, former operating room nurse for brain surgery, who taught me the sights and sounds of that theater.

I had many readers who offered comments, suggestions, and corrections as I was working on this book. These included family and friends and neighbors in several states. Thank you all. I could not have done it without you.

Grateful thanks to Elizabeth Day and Claire Matze at Abbott Press for their help in editing my manuscript.

My husband and best friend, Gene Bonstein, was essential to my efforts. Thanks, honey, you are part of this book.

My dear friend Maria Medici, an avid reader and supporter of my efforts to write a novel and get it published, did not live to see my efforts come to fruition. After a long, valiant battle, she succumbed to breast cancer before my novel was published.

Thanks, Maria. This one's for you. I can see you grinning right now.

ELSA BONSTEIN BIOGRAPHY

Elsa Bonstein is a child of Finnish immigrants, Arvo and Elvi Latomaa. She grew up on a small farm in rural Maryland, five miles from the nearest town. The family's circle of friends included Swedes, Danes, and other Finns who also owned small farms in and around Cecil County. She is fluent in Finnish and has visited her parents' home country several times. Her earliest memory is sitting in her father's lap while he read *The Secret Garden* to her in Finnish.

An only child with an addiction to reading, she dreamed of becoming a writer someday and of touching others as she had been touched by her favorite authors. She attended the University of Syracuse, graduating with a BA in sociology and journalism.

She and her husband Gene raised four daughters while living in New Jersey. During this time, Elsa became a freelance writer for various magazines and newspapers in the area. She has written business, travel and feature articles, restaurant reviews, op-ed pieces, children's stories, and humor.

Today, she lives in North Carolina and writes for the *Brunswick Beacon* and other publications. Her popular column (Golf Gab) has won several awards since she started writing it eleven years ago.

An avid golfer, Elsa served for seven years as a founding board member and public relations chair of The First Tee of Brunswick County. Today, her *PR Handbook* is used by the nearly two hundred chapters of The First Tee both here and abroad.

Find Edsell! is her first novel. She writes the kind of fiction she reads, edgy thrillers with a hint (sometimes more than a hint) of romance.

elsabonstein.com